PENGUIN BOOKS

Single in the City

Michele Gorman was born and raised in the US, but did indeed know where Scousers come from when asked on the Britishness test and is now a card-carrying Brit. She lives happily today in a central London flat (with big closets).

Single in the City

MICHELE GORMAN

PENGUIN BOOKS

PENGUIN BOOKS

Published by the Penguin Group
Penguin Books Ltd, 80 Strand, London WC2R ORL, England
Penguin Group (USA) Inc., 375 Hudson Street, New York, New York 10014, USA
Penguin Group (Canada), 90 Eglinton Avenue East, Suite 700, Toronto, Ontario, Canada M4P 2Y3
(a division of Pearson Penguin Canada Inc.)
Penguin Ireland, 25 St Stephen's Green, Dublin 2, Ireland (a division of Penguin Books Ltd)
Penguin Group (Australia), 250 Camberwell Road, Camberwell, Victoria 3124, Australia
(a division of Pearson Australia Group Pty Ltd)
Penguin Books India Pvt Ltd, 11 Community Centre, Panchsheel Park, New Delhi – 110 017, India
Penguin Group (NZ), 67 Apollo Drive, Rosedale, North Shore 0632, New Zealand
(a division of Pearson New Zealand Ltd)
Penguin Books (South Africa) (Pty) Ltd, 24 Sturdee Avenue, Rosebank, Johannesburg 2196,
South Africa

Penguin Books Ltd, Registered Offices: 80 Strand, London WC2R ORL, England

www.penguin.com

First published 2010
1

Copyright © Michele Gorman, 2010
All rights reserved

The moral right of the author has been asserted

Set in 12.5/14.75 pt Monotype Garamond
Typeset by Ellipsis Books Limited, Glasgow
Printed in England by Clays Ltd, St Ives plc

ISBN: 978–0–141–04826–0

www.greenpenguin.co.uk

For my parents, who never said 'You can't', but instead, 'Why can't you?' And for John, who challenged me to put my money where my mouth was and never let me quit.

Acknowledgements

I'm eternally grateful to Caroline at the Marsh Agency and to Lydia at Penguin. You are fab, both professionally and personally. Emma, thank you, you're exactly as pedantic as I could hope an editor to be. Thanks to Lucinda, for your invaluable advice, which put *Single in the City* on to the road to publication. Kisses to Yasmeen, Josephine, Annabel and Lizzie, my early, brutally honest readers, and to Bellini, who was instrumental in helping translate Hannah's Americanisms into English and has indulged my work-time witterings for years.

I

Every other storefront is a sandwich shop without a low-carb advertisement in sight. Are Londoners really willing to embrace the doughy delights of an Atkins-free world? It's a thrilling prospect for a girl raised in a culture plagued by cellulite bogeymen.

The customers are directing the deli man with the unnerving efficiency of Starbucks regulars babbling coffee instructions.

'Next.'

'Erm.' That stuff in the metal bowl is unrecognizable beneath all the mayonnaise.

'Next!'

'Tunafish sandwich, please.' Is that *corn* mixed in there?

'Bap?'

'Sorry?'

He's pointing to a roll.

'Okay.'

'Butta?' he says.

'What?'

'Butta!'

But a what? 'Oh, no thanks, no butter.' Who puts butter on a sandwich?

'Salad cream?'

Now what? 'Uh, no.'

Carefully he arranges a tablespoon of dry tuna on the roll.

'Um, can I have mayonnaise?'

'Tsch. I did ask.' A pea-sized blob lands judgementally on the flaky filling. 'Salad?'

I don't see any salads. 'No, no salad.'

He closes the sandwich and starts wrapping it.

'Uh, can I please have some tomatoes?'

The lady next to me is staring at me like tomato is a dirty word.

'You didn't want salad.'

'That's right, no salad. I want tomatoes.' There she goes again, like I've said hairy penis.

'Tamaydas?' he mimics. The lady sniggers.

'Yes, please.' I can feel my face going red. Red as tamaydas. Congratulations, Hannah. You're an expat.

What am I doing? I'm living in a room too small to open the closet without standing on the bed, in a city I've never set foot in before, whose language I obviously don't speak, 3,000 miles from everyone I know.

ex·pat·ri·ate

1: (*noun*) A person living in a foreign land.
2: (*verb*) To withdraw oneself from residence in or allegiance to one's native country.

That makes me a noun with slight verb tendencies.

Thinking about it now (admittedly a little late), I probably got carried away with the idea of starting afresh. Perhaps Stacy was right; a new haircut *would* have done the trick. But sometimes we're swept up in a seemingly unstoppable tide of events. Or we get drunk and do something stupid. The verdict could go either way in my case, given that I've just landed upon

England's gentle shores without the faintest idea how I'm actually supposed to build myself a new life. I'm not an expat in the traditional sense. I haven't just finished school, with a network of acquaintances to leverage for a job. This was no overseas posting, with the usual electronics allowance to buy my flat-screen TV and straightening irons whose voltage won't set my hair on fire. I don't have British cousins or a long-time family friend in the city. I arrived at Heathrow with a freshly minted passport, 5,000 dollars and a vague idea that an adventure awaited me in London.

You know how, in any group of friends, there's always one who organizes the nights out, the holidays and surprise parties? That's not me. I'm the one most likely to arrive at the wrong theatre/restaurant/airport and miss the whole thing. So here I am, jet-lagged, with no clear plan beyond dinner.

'Stace? It's me.'

'DO YOU LOVE IT?!' Stacy's been my best friend since we were seven. Being at least 50 per cent responsible for my being here, there's hope in her question.

'I haven't even unpacked yet.'

'How's the hotel?'

Somewhat disingenuously, it declared itself 'charming' on its website. Translation: last habitable during Queen Victoria's reign. Its rooms are perfumed with Eau de Oodles of Noodles[1] and there are dust bunnies[2] in the corners from the Thatcher era. Hookers trading sex tips in the hallways wouldn't be out of place. Evidently this is what a hundred bucks a night buys you in London.

1. Oodles of Noodles = Pot Noodles or any of the ramen-based just-add-water soups favoured by students after a night of binge drinking.
2. Balls of unidentified fluff, often found under beds or anywhere your mother won't notice you haven't cleaned.

'I hate the owner.' Not just because she looks like a slightly less feminine Mrs Doubtfire and has sofas that need flea-bombing.

'How come?'

'She asked me if my husband was joining me. When I said I don't have one, she made that face. You know the one.' Like I'd just confessed to an STD.

'Brutal. What'd you say?'

'Nothing. You know me.' My retorts are subject to long delays.

'You'll come up with something eventually. Have you seen any royals yet?'

'Between Terminal Five and the hotel?'

'Right. I guess it's still early. You could go see them now.'

'Stace, you can't just drop in on them, you know.'

'Well then, what *do* you plan to do?' She sounds disappointed by my unwillingness to stalk the Queen.

'English stuff, obviously.'

'So?'

I made a list on the flight. 'So, have a pint at the pub, go for tea, try fish and chips, ride the big red buses, uh . . .' I guess it's more of a doodle.

'Call me when you get back. I want all the details.'

'Will do.'

'And Han, I just know this is going to be great.'

'Sure.' Stacy's confidence is legendary, if sometimes rather premature.

She wasn't like that when we were little. She was painfully cautious, hanging back till she worked out whether a situation was likely to hurt her or not. Ever the compliant friend, I was her canary in the coalmine. Then fate blindsided her where I couldn't help. Her dad skipped town, leaving them a note propped on the kitchen table. That was the last anyone saw of her vulnerability. Eventually she believed her own bravado and the confidence became a natural part of her. Being the world's cheerleader must get exhausting but I'm constantly grateful to have her on my team. And I think she's happy, as long as she doesn't think too much or dig too deep. As her best friend, it's my job to keep those shovels out of reach. It's remarkably easy – I'm not exactly the poster child for careful reflection. I did, after all, move 3,000 miles out of spite (well, spite and a realization) . . .

Sometimes small events have long-lasting consequences. A simple conversation about my sister's weekend plans set the wheels in motion for me. She told me she was running errands, maybe renting a DVD. She'd done the same thing every weekend for at least two years. This was a woman who used to get arrested more often than she got her roots done. She seemed constantly to be chained to something in protest. What had happened to my cool, slightly felonious sister, the one who was interesting?

'I don't need to be interesting,' she said. 'I'm past all that.'

Chillingly, those were Mom's words. How did that happen? We'd made a pact to be vigilant against the creep of Momness, not to let it insinuate its way into our personalities. And yet Deb believed that her life didn't need to be interesting. And *yet*, who was I to cast stones? I hadn't met any new friends, or tried anything new (or any*one*), or even gone to New York in months. They call it a come-to-Jesus moment when people face their own mortality and realize that their lives haven't turned out as they expected. I'm lucky I didn't have the same epiphany from a hospital bed. In that moment it dawned on me: my life is not a dress rehearsal. At twenty-six I was cruising into a lifelong holding pattern. Is it inevitable? Do we march methodically towards middle age, shedding our sense of adventure, our desire to spread our wings as we go?

It was then that I realized something even worse, something I dread more than running into my ex and his model girlfriend at the supermarket while wearing pyjamas after a three-day ice-cream binge. I was becoming my mother. I once had exciting plans for my life. Now I didn't even have exciting plans for my weekend. Knowing me, I'd have cultivated this vague sense of doomed future indefinitely, dying a bitter old woman in Stacy's basement, if fate hadn't intervened one morning a few weeks later. But that's another story.

Meanwhile, if I'm truly in the grip of destiny, I only need to surrender to the forces at work. Camberwell Green. How idyllic. When I find a nice-looking pub, I'm going to get off the bus and drink my first English pint. This is so exciting! And my mother would wholeheartedly disapprove, which naturally adds to my pleasure. She hates when I ride the bus because, like most steadfastly suburban parents, she suffers from an upwardly mobile contempt for anything that could stigmatize us as *the wrong kind of person*. Incidentally, that list also includes leaving the house with a dirty face or unchanged underpants, and sharing woolly hats with classmates (lest they harbour head lice, aka social suicide). It's no wonder America has more psychologists than dentists.

'How much, please?'

'Pay before boarding.'

'Right. How much?'

'Pay before boarding.'

We're not understanding each other. 'That's what I'm trying to do, if you'll tell me how much the fare costs.'

'Buy a ticket.'

'Okay.'

'Please get off the bus and buy a ticket.'

'*Ahh*.' I may have just run aground on the tip of the cultural iceberg. Who knows what other misunderstandings lie in wait for this lone traveller. And considering that my next of kin, geographically speaking, is the hotel owner, I am definitely alone. This is not a comfortable realization.

The conga line of buses proves the truth of our grandmothers' adage likening them to men.

'Hello. Here's my ticket. Okay?' The driver has either just acquiesced or he holds a blink longer than is normal. In any event, he obviously prefers his customers to ricochet off the walls before settling into a seat. He's careening round the corner at 126 miles per hour. This would never fly with the Health and Safety people at home. I'm thrilled! The passengers wear fixed expressions ranging from 'I'm bored' to 'I'll cut you if you come near me'. A few are sleeping with their mouths open and one teen is singing along with Shakira at middling volume. Actually, he's not bad.

This isn't exactly the sociable scene I'd hoped for. Not that I'm expecting to meet my new best friend, but I'd at least like the *chance* to talk to someone who may know of a good pub along the way. Surely it wouldn't be awful to simply introduce myself to someone interesting, assuming I can find someone interesting. You never know what chance meetings like these can lead to. Consider the case of Joseph Pulitzer, of journalism prize fame. He migrated to America from Hungary as a teenager but, after fighting for the North in the Civil War, couldn't find a job (not because he fought for the North). To occupy his days he played chess in his local library, and there he met an editor for a local German-language newspaper. The editor, recognizing Pulitzer's potential, though probably not his own hand in altering the

7

journalistic fabric of America, offered the boy a job as a junior reporter. From that start, Pulitzer went on to become an influential media tycoon.

There, that woman looks — never mind, she's talking to herself. It's possible that she's got one of those ear doohickeys, but either way she's unlikely to welcome the interruption. Men are out, obviously. It's too easy to be misinterpreted, as in: 'Your idle chitchat must mean you want to be hit on until there's enough evidence to bring assault charges.'

Wait, what about her? She looks normal enough. She's probably a little older than me (in the sensible end of her twenties, as Mom would say) with no obvious signs of mental illness.

'Hi, I'm Hannah.'

She's staring at my offered hand, surprised perhaps that a stranger would leave her own seat to squish in next to her on a mostly empty bus.

'Excuse me, em, I have to go.' Her coat catches on the back of the seat in her rush to leave. It's just my luck to pick someone as we reach her stop, though she didn't look like the kind of girl who'd live in this neighbourhood — by which I mean she wasn't wearing an electronic ankle bracelet. In the time it took me to choose a target to befriend we've travelled from Big Ben and the Houses of Parliament to one of Guy Ritchie's film sets. Perhaps I should have picked a route that didn't involve boarded-up buildings and gangs of skinheads and . . . is that guy getting *mugged*?

The bus stops. The lights flicker on and off. I hope he hasn't run out of gas.

They flicker again.

'Last stop. Last stop.'

Oh, no no no! The ride can't just end; it has to continue its circular route back to civilization. 'Excuse me, sir. Isn't the bus

8

going back towards Victoria Station?' (Read: Won't you please get me out of this suburb cum ghetto?)

'Catch the one opposite.' (Read: No, you stupid American. Find your own way out.)

It's going to be okay. The #185 is waiting right across the mostly empty street. Knocking on the door encourages the driver to ignore me even more intently.

'Come on, open the door!'

He turns another page, not looking up. 'Bus doesn't leave for eight minutes.'

I'm supposed to stand out here for seven and a half minutes while he finishes his article on Playmates of the Year? I'm a fare-paying cust– No, I'm not. I've got no ticket, only a couple jingly silver coins and £20 notes. Those boys are starting to take an interest in my handbag, and they don't look like fashion scouts. Stacy's going to be very disappointed if I get myself killed before I've seen the Queen.

Perhaps the liquor store will let me sleep behind their beer cooler until daylight. At the very least, I can get the proprietor's thoughts on the merits of fortified wine.

'Fifty-five pee.' His eyes narrow when I exchange his potato chips for my note. 'Don't you have anything smaller?'

'No, I'm sorry.'

'Tsch. Nineteen pound forty-five change.'

He knows I'm lying.

The driver is pretending to have no recollection of our earlier chat. 'Ticket.'

'Here, thanks.'

Looong blink. They must be trained to do this, in the same way that civil servants learn to move at the pace of a retreating glacier when faced with a room full of impatient customers. I'm not holding a grudge though, given that my life is in his hands . . . I've been thinking about that girl on the first bus. That wasn't really her stop. In fact, she may still be in Camberwell, unwilling to risk another assault on the ride back to Victoria. I feel bad having struck fear into the hearts of the English public like that.

And now I'm suffering from performance anxiety. Otherwise I'd walk straight through that door. For the record, despite the driver's initial reluctance to welcome my business, he did drop me back at the bus stop that marked the beginning of this misadventure. In front of a perfectly nice-looking pub, olde worlde with an ivy-overgrown sign above the door. Red velvet curtains are drawn across the bottom of the little leaded windows, so I can't see inside. I can hear a noisy crowd though. They're laughing, sharing stories and jokes while I skulk out here in the drizzling afternoon. They've probably been friends for years, safe in that cocoon of companionship that I took for granted. I should be in there, instead of standing out here letting my hair frizz.

I had a friend in college who loved to say: 'If you can dream it, you can do it.' It became my mantra. I assumed it was a pearl of wisdom from some great thinker, a philosopher perhaps, like Descartes. It turned out to be Walt Disney, which in no way diminished the wisdom of the advice. Anyone who can build a Magic Kingdom deserves to be listened to.

But what am I supposed to do when I get inside (after scanning the room meaningfully as if searching for my friends)? I'd feel as conspicuous as a third nipple. Have you ever gone alone into a bar, or sat by yourself in a restaurant? I don't mean fiddling with your phone to look busy while waiting for someone. I mean when they clear away the other place setting and leave you to converse with your cutlery. Having a built-in friend like Stacy meant I never had to. I didn't even go through those first days and weeks of junior high, high school or college[3] worrying that I wouldn't have any friends. God, I may have just moved to a country where I won't speak to anyone who doesn't give me a bill at the end of the conversation.

Maybe this isn't a good idea. I can't see inside without *going* inside. What if it's a biker bar? Or a gay bar? Or they're in the midst of a Nationalist Party[4] rally? It'll be dinnertime in four hours. I should save this adventure for tomorrow. Besides, it's raining, and cold. And I have a pimple on my forehead . . .

And my jeans are baggy at the knees, and it's a Tuesday, and, and, and. Could I be more self-defeating? Think of the great pioneers of our time. Amelia Earhart flew solo all over the world. She disappeared doing it, but that was probably just bad luck. Walking into a bar alone can't *kill* me. At worst, it'll maim my self-confidence. Besides, Walt would definitely do it.

Okay, pimple or not, I'm going in.

At least there aren't any obvious rally meetings, or bikers. The room hasn't ground to a silent, suspicious halt at this stranger's intrusion. In fact, it feels quite familiar. Happy groups of young professionals? Check. Heady blend of pheromones and beer soaked into the carpet? Check. Requisite loner propping up the bar? I don't see anyone alone. Okay, maybe that's

3. American grade school = British junior school; American junior high = British senior school (to about age fifteen); American high school (also called senior high) = British sixth form college; and American college = British university. Is it any wonder we don't understand each other most of the time?
4. That's the America for Americans party. Like the BNP, only full of Americans . . . in America.

me. Free barstool and a cute bartender to ply me with drinks? Check and check!

'I'd like a beer, please!' Cute bartender nods expectantly. 'Er, a Stella.' Thanks to the miracle of modern marketing, Stella has reached American shores, whereas Old Speckled Hen must be a wholly English brand. It sounds more like an entrée than a drink.

'A pint or a Hoff?' he asks.

The Hoff makes beer? 'Uh, the pint, please.'

This isn't bad at all. Safely seated, with a half-dozen magazines from the airport to give me purpose, I'm insulated from the glare of unwanted attention (read: pity). In fact, it's perfect. If they haven't noticed me, then I'm free to observe them in their natural environment. I'm like Jane Goodall living with chimps.

It may have seemed like home at first, but now I see there are important differences. Living here may be like staring at those *Where's Waldo?*[5] books – the more you look, the more you see. The first thing I notice is that everyone is drinking beer from a glass. How civilized. I vow never to drink from the bottle here. Aside from the obvious hazard of chipping a recently whitened tooth (my Christmas gift to myself, and they do look fabulous), it'll mark me out as a foreigner. I also notice that most of the men are wearing suits, so either they dressed up to come here or they're drinking on the job. Even in my Michael Kors black wool belted trench coat that I got half-price last year, I'm a little underdressed. Or, to be more accurate, I'm overdressed. Because the third thing I notice is that the women are showing a lot more décolletage than I'm used to.

5. Called *Where's Wally?* in the UK and *Wo ist Walter?* in Germany, presumably because even German children believe in formalities.

Having come from possibly the most preppy part of the United States, a place where Ralph Lauren and Lilly Pulitzer[6] are spoken of in reverential tones, this display of chesty flesh is unsettling. Tugging my top down in the vain hope that it won't look so nunnish exposes an inch of skin below my collarbone. Sex-y.

I'm sure I'm drinking too fast – it's always a risk with a glass and a cute bartender intent on refilling it. And either the pub's designers overestimated their clientele's co-ordination or they thought only absurdly small people would heed the call of nature, because the ladies room is down a too-narrow flight of stairs way at the back of the bar. I'm getting drunk in London! Mom would have a stroke.

'Sorry!' a girl and I harmonize as I push the stall door into her. Hang on. Why'd she apologize to the woman who just kneecapped her? Come to think of it, that's the second apology I've had from someone I've physically harmed. At the airport, I accidentally ran my suitcase into a woman's heel and she said she was sorry, as if she'd carelessly left her foot on the floor to be run over. They shouldn't be so sorry. It's not like they're responsible for global warming or Starbucks, or super-sizing.

I've never seen such stalls. The toilets are fortressed with six-foot walls, real walls, not flimsy barriers with big gaps where they're bolted together. Here, there's absolutely no risk of spotting a stranger's nether parts between the cracks or standing up only to make eye contact with the girl waiting in front

6. America's ode to the belief that wallpaper can be fashionable when worn as a dress. Lilly invariably combines pink and green in swirly flower patterns, then prints them on all clothing that a preppy girl might need to signal her membership to the lockjaw jolly-hockey-sticks club.

of the sinks.[7] It's a superb experience. I enjoy knowing that it'd take a commando abseiling down the wall to get to me.

I don't believe it. My cosy little corner of the bar has been encroached upon. Some man has piled his coat on my chair. His coat! On my chair! I won't be pushed around just because I'm by myself. He must have seen my glass there. It doesn't matter that it's empty, it's obviously still holding my place. He and his friends have settled in like it's their right to be in my little bar space. And my magazine is clearly – well, I put it in my bag to go downstairs. But even so, he saw me there five minutes ago. I will not be intimidated. No, sir. 'Um, excuse me. I was sitting there.'

'I'm terribly sorry!' he says. And I can see that he really is, terribly. He practically throws his coat on the floor to make room for me, shuffling his friends back a few feet in the process. Wow, he's good-looking.

Now I feel bad about saying anything. It was probably an honest mistake, and it is their country. 'Um, you're welcome to use my chair, for your coat, if you want.'

'Cheers.' He carefully arranges his coat over the back of the chair. Mmm, there's a slightly spicy aroma coming from the wool. He keeps turning around to look at me. Either he's afraid I'll steal from his pockets or I'm better-looking here than at home. I'm not saying I'm ugly or fat or anything. In fact, thanks to genetics, I've got boobs and hips without having to shop in the section for 'curvy' girls. People describe

7. Sometimes it takes a foreign perspective to highlight just how peculiar our own status quo is. For instance, we Americans don't feel any embarrassment at publicly defecating behind shoddily built doors that are as sparing in their coverage as Pamela Anderson's blouses. In other words, the really important bits might be shielded from view, but little else is left to the imagination.

me as 'at-trac-tive', with that little dip in the middle of the word that makes it sound like there's a 'but' coming in the next breath. That's probably because of my hair. It's fuzzy dark blonde if you're being generous and fuzzy light brown if you're not.

'Are you waiting for someone?' he finally asks.

'No.'

'Good. Hello, I'm Mark.'

It's happening. Someone outside the service industry is talking to me! 'I'm Hannah. Why's that good?'

'Because I don't want to get thrashed for chatting up another man's girlfriend.'

'Ah, I see. Self-preservation.' Does chatting up mean hitting on? I hope so.

'Well, it is what makes the world go round.'

'I thought love made the world go round.'

'Maybe love makes self-preservation go round. Do I detect an American accent?'

'You do. I'm from Connecticut.' His bemused expression is not an uncommon reaction to the whereabouts of my home state. 'It's near New York.'

'Ah. Visiting?'

'Nope, I live here. As of a few days ago.'

'Lucky me.'

He's got those amazing dark-blue eyes and black eyelashes that I go nuts for. And full, Brad Pitt lips. He looks older, in his thirties, which is perfect because everybody knows that men need a big headstart in the race for emotional maturity.

He raises his glass. 'I'm glad to see that you're upholding one of our great British institutions.'

'Yeah, I'm a quick learner.' This beer really is going down smoothly. 'What are the others?'

'Fish and chips, cricket, and the seductive powers of the finest lovers in the world.'

Mmm, a cocky, great-looking man. 'I haven't had fish and chips yet. And isn't cricket just lazy man's baseball?'

'It's blasphemy to say that about the greatest sport on earth. They can deport you for it.'

'Psh! How is standing in a field all day a sport?'

He ponders. 'Cricket is a thinking man's game. It's like chess, with sunshine and drink.'

'Is it as interesting as watching chess?' I'd rather watch my nails dry.

'It's not even comparable. We spend days sitting in the sun, drinking and watching the game we love.'

'So you're in it for the tan.'

'And the drink.'

'Hmm, back to drinking.' A theme is beginning to emerge here.

'As I've mentioned, it's one of our great traditions.'

'That's right, and something about being seduced by the world's greatest lovers. Can I assume there are a lot of Italians in London?'

'I am, of course, referring to the British gentleman.'

I might be tempted to believe his description if he hadn't been interrupted by a young man loudly referring to the television by that much-maligned female body part. 'I have to say I hadn't heard that.'

'Really? I'm sure it's printed in the handbook.'

'Is that required reading for American women on arrival? Maybe they're out of stock in Terminal Five.'

'I'll ask my people to have a word with their people.'

'You have people?'

'Don't you?'

'Nope.'

'Ah, but you can make your own people.'

Oh dear. My virtue, such as it is, is about to be seriously compromised. Though I have many strengths, keeping my pants on in the face of wit, let alone remarkable looks, is not one of them. Of course, the fact that I'm getting the prickly sweats, where my scalp goes hot and a shiny little puddle forms on my top lip, is probably not doing me any favours in the seduction stakes. Unless he *prefers* his women with a seal-like sheen. Unfortunately, my body regularly betrays me in such unflattering ways when I really want something.

One of his friends asks if he wants another beer. 'Don't let me keep you from your friends.' Of course I hope I keep him from his friends.

'Let them find their own girls. So, where were we?'

'You were telling me about the great British traditions.'

'And about to buy you a drink. Fancy another?'

Who am I to go against tradition?

'So,' he says over our full glasses, 'here's the obvious question, Hannah from Connecticut: why did you move to London?'

'I was looking for a change.'

'That's it? That's a bold change.'

'Well, uh, I –' Is this the time for warts-and-all honesty? Of course not. I can give him the whole story on our golden anniversary. 'I came to a realization.'

'It must have been some realization.'

'You don't know the half of it . . . Have you ever woken up and wondered what you've been doing?'

'Hannah. Are you saying you black out often?'

'Hah, hah. No. Well . . . sometimes. No, I mean I realized I was on autopilot. And I'm too young to be my mother.'

'I understand completely.'

'You do?'

'Of course. You want to be a participant in your life.'

'Exactly!'

'I think you're brave to move.'

'Or stupid.'

'Quite possibly it's the most stupid thing you'll ever do.'

Huh. And just when I thought this might be going somewhere.

'But so what?' he smiles. 'At least you'll have done it.'

Exactly, at least I'll have done it. This guy totally gets me. His insight, not to mention his gorgeousness, are doing wonders for his chances of seeing me naked . . . Who knows, I may have lucked out here. I could even be on the cusp of a fabulous relationship with the perfect man. An English boyfriend – Stacy'll be so jealous! Though Mom'd never forgive him for moving me permanently across the ocean. And she'd hate me for raising her grandchildren so far away . . .

Hold on. This is why I need Stacy close by. Finding Mr Right is supposed to be the icing on the cake for us, after we land our dream jobs, collect a fabulous circle of friends, see the world and generally be as amazing as Oprah insists we can. Aren't I getting a little ahead of myself? I haven't even found the car keys to get to the store to buy the Betty Crocker[8] mix to make the cake. And I don't bake, so technically I can't even follow through with my own analogy. Besides, I hardly know this man. He could be a psycho. He might be a bum. He may be happily married with kids.

Obviously I'm not going to let something as minor as a complete lack of information stand in my way. Subtle

8. Well-loved fictional baker responsible for the wonderful world of readymade cake mixes. Think Delia in a box.

questioning can peel back the layers of this lovely onion. 'So, aside from beer drinking, sun worshipping and cricket loving, what's your story?'

Or I could just chop it in half and see what's inside.

'My stah-ry? . . . Sorry, sorry! Actually, I really like an American accent.'

'You do?' This is hard to believe.

'I do. I went out with an American girl once. I was absolutely head over heels in love.'

'What happened?' Hopefully she betrayed him, then dumped him, then died. As with vampires, it's better to be safe than sorry when it comes to the spectre of fabulous ex-girlfriends.

'She married someone else.'

'I'm sorry.'

'I'm not. We'd have made each other miserable.'

'Really? Why?' Because you love sex and she was frigid? You're rich and generous and she didn't like jewellery or fancy hotels?

'I guess I thought she was a little neurotic. But I was very immature. When you're young, everything is a big deal, isn't it? That was an age ago. Now it'd probably be different. I wish her nothing but the best. What about you? Is there someone back home?'

'Nope, I'm single. You?'

'Would I be here with you if I weren't?'

'You'd be surprised how many men would.' I'm a little breathless, definitely not used to guys this hot flirting back. Oh, I dream about them. I hope that they will. But they don't . . .

'I'm not at all surprised. Always remember, Hannah, most men are bastards at heart. We're hard-wired like that. Are you working here?'

'No, not yet. What about you? Where do you work?' . . .
Dating has always been like convincing myself that my new
half-price shoes are the best I'll ever own. Deep down, I know
that while the thrill of the discount is strong, they're half a size
too small and not exactly the right colour . . .

'You're intriguing, Hannah – a woman who doesn't want to
talk about herself. Every time I ask about you, you ask about
me.'

'Maybe I'd just rather talk about you.'

'Flattery will get you very far indeed.'

. . . 'So, as you were saying. Something interesting about
yourself.' Mark just might be the most comfortable pair of
Jimmy Choos I've ever seen.

'You're like a dog with a bone. Something interesting. Well,
I've worked my arse off over the last ten years to build my
company. I started in my back bedroom with one account,
which was a family friend, and a thousand-pound overdraft. I
was so nervous at my first event that I was physically sick.'

Why, whenever I ask about a man, does he think telling me
what he *does* counts as interesting? 'I see. Interesting.' And why
do I pretend it is?

'Not really, but you're kind to say so. I know what you're
asking. You want to know my deepest darkest secret.'

'Go on.'

'All right, since you asked.' He's gazing right into my eyes.
'I'm afraid of being lonely. I don't mean being by myself. I
mean having people all around me, but nobody to connect
with. I'm afraid of living my entire life like that, and I'm afraid
of dying without ever having made that connection.'

A man with feelings and fears, and the willingness to disclose
both? Now that *is* interesting.

'Incidentally, my other fear is to be taken advantage of by

women who are only looking for a spectacularly endowed man with epic love-making skills.'

Very funny . . . as long he's not stretching the joke too far.

Time flies when a sexy man plies you with drinks. Much later, the barman rings a big bell and shouts something.

'Last orders,' Mark says.

'Is that for a big tip?'

'Big tip?'

'At home, when someone leaves a big tip, the bartender rings a bell.'

'We don't tip barmen.'

Lucky Brits. If we don't tip barmen, they ignore us for the night or spit in our next round.

'It's the call for last orders. If we want another drink, we have to place our order now. Would you like another pint, or a Hoff?'

'What's a Hoff?'

'Hoff a pint.'

Ah, I get it.

The bouncer is sweeping the night's debris over my shoes to let me know I'm welcome to stay as long as I'd like. 'I guess we'd better go.'

'Probably so. Do I get to see you again?'

He wants to see me again! If I play my cards right, he may even want to see more of me tonight. Which means I'd better not take my usual approach. British men might not appreciate Jeremy Paxman's assertiveness when it comes to conquests. 'Sure, I'd like that, only . . .'

'Only . . . you really do have a boyfriend, and he's a bodyguard with a jealous streak and a fondness for assault weapons?'

'No.'

'Only . . . you've sworn off men?'

'Uh-uh.'

. . . 'You fear I like men?'

'Not likely.'

'Hannah, those are the only acceptable reasons not to see me again.'

'What if I don't like you?' This is technically possible. Not true, but technically possible.

'Ah, but you do like me.'

'How do you know that?'

'You're holding my hand.'

'Oh, right.' That is rather watertight evidence.

'So . . . ?'

So, the only phone where I can be reached is in the hotel hallway beside what might be a needle-exchange bin, and I barely remember how to get back there, let alone what it's called. 'This is embarrassing, but I don't know the name of my hotel.'

'Do you remember where it is?'

'Uh-huh.' Sort of. These streets all look the same – buses, taxis, people and shops selling something called doner kebabs.

'Then I'll walk you there.'

Hand in hand we walk, and walk. After the second time around the block, I can faithfully report that my hotel isn't there. Luckily it *is* on the next block. I may seem to be better-looking in the UK but there's only so much patience a guy I just met can be expected to have.

I've just had a sudden terrible thought. What if he's a bad kisser? This amazing streak of beginner's luck may be about to end in tears. Beggars shouldn't be choosers, but a man this good-looking who can't kiss would be tragic, like ordering the double-chocolate fudge brownie only to find out that it's not moist and delicious at all. The moment of truth has arrived. Mmm. He's off to a good start, hand stroking my hair. Deep eye contact tempered with cheeky smile, so not creepy. The lean-in. Ahh. He's a good – no, he's a great kisser. Rule Britannia!

So much for turning over a new leaf. I want him upstairs with me. I wonder if English girls put out on the first date. Can this be considered a first date? Am I sabotaging my chances with this amazing man for instant gratification? No doubt my answers will differ in the sober light of morning, but right now they are: don't know, no, don't care, in that order. The landlady mimes her opinion of my imminent promiscuity as I lead Mark upstairs. See last answer for response to her look.

I admit it. I'm on the alert for cultural differences. Mark is, after all, the first non-American I've ever been in bed with. Things seem to be moving rather fast, though I can't really blame that on his nationality. I've slept with men who timed sex to coincide with the commercial break in the middle of *SportsCenter*'s 11 p.m. broadcast.[9] I'll choose to believe that Mark just can't keep his hands off me. A little self-delusion can be a great comfort. Besides, he might even be the sexiest man I've ever kissed. Can you blame me for wanting more and more and, yes, please, more?

Within seconds of hearing him come my mind is in fifth gear. For the record, yes, we're face to face. I just have a thing about making eye contact while his are rolling back in his head. I feel a guy should have a little privacy at times like these.

My concern that sex wouldn't translate across borders is

9. *SportsCenter* elicits the same reaction from America's population as smutty magazines do: i.e., lusty devotion among men and unmitigated loathing among women. And airing the same scores and highlights *ad infinitum* only heightens their allure to sports junkies, who apparently need repeated attempts to comprehend them.

unfounded. No major surprises – condoms obviously work the same and he didn't make any weird noises or apologize for anything (as I feared he might, given his culture). But I don't know why I can't just live in the moment. I'm lying beside a perfectly gorgeous man, one I'm confident I can encourage into a repeat performance, and I'm already analysing the night. Worse, now I'm thinking about how pathetic it is that I'm analysing the night when I should be enjoying all the nakedness in my bed. The most important thing is not to say anything stupid. It's not easy. The silence is killing me. Is he sleeping? No, he's looking right at me. Does he want me to say something? He's smiling. I smile back. I should say something. Something breezy and casual. Definitely don't ask him any questions. Guys hate that. Just be casual, say something fun and confident. And not desperate. 'That was great. Let's do it again.'

He laughs, and kisses me.

Occasionally, when the stars are aligned and the gods smiling upon me, I do say just the right thing.

2

When Mom tearfully said 'Have fun!' as she kissed me goodbye at the airport, she probably didn't mean 'Get drunk and have sex with a virtual stranger'. But what fun it was!

'Stacy, I met someone!' Whether I've just paid half-price for perfectly fitting jeans or just had sex with a perfectly fitting man, saying it out loud always sweetens the experience.

'Hannah, it's three a.m. here. Was it the Queen?'

'No, a guy.'

'Prince William?'

'No –'

'Not Jude!'

I wish. All Hugh, Orlando or Jude sightings are to be instantly reported; physical contact documented on film when possible.

'No, his name's Mark. He's English, and he's so gorgeous you can't even imagine. I met him in the pub yesterday and we talked for hours. Stace, he's so funny, and not just joke-cracking funny either, wittily funny. Stace? You still there?'

'Mmm, yes. Just trying to unstick my eye.'

'Mascara?'

'And two sets of lashes.'

There are few women who can get away with fashion statements like these. Stacy tries most new styles (she must have embraced ladylike vamp last night). Blessed with a figure that's flattered in every look from Kate Moss to screen siren, she exercises her creativity the same way a decathlete trains for his competitions. That is to say, with intense dedication to the widest range of endeavours. Sometimes being her best friend does me no favours. It just encourages me to think (wrongly) that I can pull off the same styles.

'He sounds great, Han. See, I *told* you it was gonna be fun. There's nothing to worry about.'

'Not quite nothing. I'm living in a hotel, and I don't have a job.'

'Well, go find one.'

'Just like that!' I don't mean to snap but Stacy's can-do attitude sometimes grates

'How do you expect to get one if you don't look?'

'Who says I'm not looking?'

'Are you?'

'I will.'

'And when you do, then you'll find one. Hey, did he sound like a prince?'

'Come to think of it, he did.' Funny that I didn't have trouble understanding him. Isn't that odd? Maybe my near-religious devotion to *Four Weddings* . . . and *Love Actually* has made me immune to certain British accents. Though if I met someone from one of those gangster films, or *Trainspotting*, I feel sure I'd need an interpreter on hand.

'When are you gonna see this guy again?'

'His name's Mark. I'm not sure.'

'I wonder if the three-day rule applies there.'

I hope not. 'He doesn't have my number, but he knows where I am. You don't think it was too slutty to sleep with him on the first night, do you?'

. . . 'You slept with him?'

Didn't I mention that? 'Well, yeah. You should see this guy, Stace, totally sexy. And he *gets* me.'

But the saboteurs are descending even as I say this. Why should something that feels so physically good feel so emotionally bad? Apparently there *are* women who naturally feel no self-loathing after a one-night stand. I've never met one, but urban folklore says they exist. And let's be honest, this was probably a one-night stand. It doesn't matter that I've mentally picked out china patterns and fretted about where to raise our kids. He didn't exactly propose. Come to think of it, he didn't exactly say he wanted to see me again. Of course he won't want to see me again, except maybe for sex. Guys don't fall in love with easy girls. It's a simple application of scarcity value theory (I took an econ course with Stacy sophomore year so we'd both be done with class by lunchtime on Fridays). When *we* give in, men think we're not worth the effort and we become unworthy of their affection. Yet when they jump into bed with us, we think they're keen, thus making them more desirable. We aren't from different planets; we're from different solar systems.

'You used a condom, right?' Stacy asks, breaking into my self-abusive reverie.

'Huh? Oh, yeah . . . But was it too soon?'

'In what sense? Hasn't it been a while?'

Thanks, Stacy, for reminding me that the most excitement my mattress has seen in the last six months has been a weekly change of sheets. She's right though. In *what* sense? I know that I wouldn't pass up a no-strings-attached adventure just because it's doomed to end. The question is whether our impromptu naked Olympics sealed my fate as what's-her-name, literally the one-night one-night stand. I'd hate to think I'll never have another shot at the gold. 'I mean was it too soon to sleep with him. Do you think he'll get in touch again?'

'I don't know. Maybe they're more sophisticated in Europe.

You know how the French are always sleeping around and then claiming that it's part of their national identity. Wait, where'd it come from?'

'What?'

'The rubber.'

'Uh.' Where had it come from? This kind of attention to detail makes Stacy the perfect confidante. If conversation surgery existed as a profession, she'd be a specialist. 'He must have had it with him.'

'What, like in his wallet?'

'I don't know. I guess so. Why?'

'That's awfully prepared of him.'

'Maybe he was a boy scout.'

'Maybe he likes to have sex with a lot of women.'

Sometimes talking to Stacy is a double-edged sword.

It's remarkable how a little sex can change your outlook. Becoming gainfully employed just moved to the top of my priority list. Without a job, I'll have to go home in a month, a failure living five time zones from the one man who offered to see me naked in the better part of a year. Granted, the little stamp in my passport says I'm not supposed to work, but given that I'm college educated, I have experience, I speak the language . . .

'I'm sorry?'

'Your CV. May I have your CV, please?'

'My CD? I don't have a CD.' Does she think I'm a rapper or something?

'Please detail your work experience on the form.'

'Why don't I just give you my résumé?'

She looks it over. She looks me over. She's not impressed with either of us. 'You haven't fully listed your education.'

'Yes, I have. I didn't go to grad school.' I won't be bullied by an employment agency receptionist, not while wearing my most confidence-building suit (black Ralph Lauren boiled-wool skirt suit with fishtail pleat and patent skinny belt. It's perfect with my moss-green knock-off Jimmy Choo kitten heels with tiny studs – they're comfortable as long as I scrunch up my toes when I walk).

'Where did you do your sixth form?' she asks. My bewilderment must be obvious. 'College?' she tries.

'University of Connecticut.'

'That's university.'

'That's what I said.'

'You haven't listed your GCSEs.'

'My what?'

'Your high-school grades.'

'They're right here.' They should really screen their receptionists more carefully for reading comprehension.

'Are those your A-levels?'

'Well, they're not all As.'

Her sigh says she loves this kind of variety in her job. 'We need the grades from the papers you sat at sixteen.'

'Do you mean my middle-school grades?'

'Perhaps. Employers will want to see all your grades before university.'

If you say so. In kindergarten I excelled at naps and snacktime, rose to top of the class for colouring inside the lines and always remembered to raise my hand for the bathroom before I wet my pants.

'And please fill this out as well.'

Name, okay. Address, I've now memorized. Previous position, PR Junior Account Executive (glamorous-sounding, I know). Age and marital status . . . What are they running, a dating agency? There's no box for none of your business.

'Now, if you'll just stand against that wall.' The camera's flash temporarily blinds me. This can't be a coincidence; the guy at the first agency did the same thing. I told him to fuck off in plain English (that translates perfectly, by the way) and stormed out.

'Why'd you do that?'

'It's so we can put a face with the name. We have a lot of candidates and find this is a good way to be sure we give them personalized attention.'

I'm such a fool. I've happily contributed my bodily fluids at home to prove that I don't have any illegal habits, and yet I freak out about having my picture taken. I fear my sense of employee rights is out of whack. Maybe I should send a snapshot to the first agency to make amends.

I know I have no choice if I want to find a job, but I absolutely hate having to go through this process. I'm terrible at selling myself. Even my college's recruitment drive failed to unearth a willing employer, and we all know complete losers who've managed to get hired that way. Naturally I'd prefer to blame someone else, but I know that my own laziness plays a part. Evidence: my one and only real job resulted from a friend introducing me to her boss in a bar. And don't get me started on my dating record. Being an opportunist at heart (in the positive, non-bottom-feeding sense of the word), I tend to settle for the good-enough that comes my way. It's worked pretty well so far. I think that the Taoists are on to something (I once dated a t'ai chi instructor, so I know a little about it). They believe that the universe works harmoniously and when man exerts his will against the world, that harmony is disrupted. Which can't be a good thing. So maybe I'm not lazy, I'm simply the unwitting disciple of an ancient Chinese philosophy.

I'm not suggesting that I've never been motivated to exert my will against the world. There are women still nursing wounds from past sample sales. But fashion and sex aside, little has the power to overcome my natural inertia. Until now. There's no settling for second best here. Either I find a job or I go home with nothing but a stamp in my passport that cost me 5,000 dollars. That's not much of a choice, so here I sit in the reception area of about the 7,000th agency, hoping for a miracle.

'Hi, I'm Chloe,' says the young woman sticking her hand out in front of me. 'Come through, please.' She's really pretty. And even without the ability to label spot here, I can tell that she's very stylish. She's got long, straight honey-blonde hair, blue eyes and pale skin. London seems to grow more than its fair share of dewy-skinned blondes. It's not quite Sweden, but I find it demoralizing nevertheless. A petty girl might say that most of this golden hue is chemically induced, ergo, the carpet will rarely match the curtains. But that's no comfort when you realize that men don't know a broadloom from a valance. What's more, they don't care.

'So you come from Connecticut,' she says, glancing at my résumé.

'Uh-huh. Have you been there?' As I've mentioned, this is a stretch. Nine out of ten people outside the US can't point to Connecticut on a map. Five out of ten Americans have a hard time finding it.

'No, I've only been to New York City.'

'I like New York. I used to get down there a lot. There's so much going on.'

'I have to admit,' she confides, 'I really go for the shopping.'

'Me too!' Here is a kindred spirit, not afraid to admit that Missoni is more interesting than the Met.

'There's that shop down by the World Trade Center site –'

'Century 21!' What are the chances that this woman, from a different country, knows my favourite store on the planet?

'That's it! The designer section is incredible.'

'I love the jeans. So cheap!'

'Especially in pounds. And the cashmere –'

'What about shoes?'

'IT'S AMAZING!' we chorus.

We observe a moment of silence to give this cathedral to discount shopping the respect it deserves. Without wanting to get ahead of myself (which I've been known to do), Chloe could be my new best friend in London.

Within about two minutes it's obvious that I'm unfit for most of the jobs she's trying to fill, so I can't really hold it against her when she starts making small talk. Interview over, I guess.

'How long have you been in London?' She's more relaxed now that we've established she isn't going to find me a job.

'Just over a week. It's harder than I thought.'

'I lived in France for a year, so I know what it's like.'

'Did you . . . did you feel like everything was very *foreign*?' Yes, I realize how stupid I sound.

'Huh, I did. I spoke a bit of French, but living there was a completely different story.'

'No kidding. I *thought* I spoke the language here but . . . I guess I didn't expect you all to be so different.'

'Really? Different how?'

Uh-uh, I'm not falling for that. No doubt it's intriguing to see how others perceive your culture, but surely I'm not qualified to pass judgement on the English. I've been here about five minutes . . . On the other hand, a fresh view is often illuminating. After all, we don't realize we're loud until some soft-spoken European, cringing and clutching his bleeding ears, points it out to us. But on the other, other hand, telling Chloe that I think her people are scantily dressed alcoholics probably isn't the best way to cement our friendship.

'It's all pretty different.'

'I guess so. Have you got friends here?'

'Nope. But I talk to Stacy, that's my best friend, every day.' Every couple of hours, every day.

'That must get expensive.'

'Nah, I've got one of those prepaid calling cards. It's probably cheaper than calling across town. It's a good thing too . . . it's kind of lonely here.'

'I remember what that was like too. It gets better though . . . If ever you want to meet for a drink sometime . . .'

'That'd be great! I'm free tonight.' I think I have a little crush on Chloe. You know how you get excited when you meet a potential friend, one that you really click with? You trade phone numbers and make plans to see each other again. You plan what you'll wear and spend your time searching out common points of interest. Except for the kissing, it's no different than a date. In fact, it's just as much fun, often with more promising long-term prospects.

'Er, okay.'

She sounds anything but okay. I've just cornered the poor girl into a social engagement with a complete stranger. I must sound desperate.

'Erm, I'm done around six,' she continues gamely. 'We could meet somewhere near here.'

Desperation be damned, I get to go for drinks tonight!

I know by the unladylike belly rumbles punctuating our goodbyes that this was a fateful meeting and could be the start of something great. You see, unlike those whippet-thin girls whose high spirits kill their hunger pangs, my happy-appetite is legendary. Food only loses its magic when I'm low. And while it's been nice these past few months shedding pounds on a diet of forgotten dreams, my belly is obviously about to make up for lost calories.

. . . This is ridiculous. Ordering lunch is a simple process. Order. Pay. Leave. No need for a panic attack.

'Next, please.'

'Turkey and cheese, please.'

'Bap?'

'Yes.'

'Which cheese?'

'That one.'

'Butta?'

'No, just salad cream.' So far, so good.

'Salad?'

Oh god, oh god. 'Just tomahdoes, please.' As in 'Awesome, man. I'd like some tomahdoes, heh, heh. Pass the bong.'

I swear the guy smirks. Is there a medical term for fear of delis? Label or not, I'm developing the condition. If I could turn back time, I'd apologize to all the foreigners I've ever been impatient with, and banish all the 'Why can't you just speak English?' thoughts I've ever had. Hah, that's ironic, considering that apparently I *don't* speak English. Our cultural blunders may not exactly endear us to the Brits, but they should cut us some slack. We don't expect them to tip generously or drawl in American upon landing at JFK.

'WACHOUT!' Someone grabs my coat, yanking me backwards on to the sidewalk.[10]

'Wha–?!'

The van blasts its horn as it ricochets off the kerb and speeds off into the distance.

'You haff to look the other way,' my saviour advises. 'Well, both ways. Those white vans are shoeisheidal.'

Suicidal vans, got it. I'd thank him if my heart wasn't pounding in my throat.

'Where do you come from?'

Deep breaths. 'The States.'

'Ah, I come from Espain. We drive on the right too. Iss very confusing.'

I knew that. It's just hard to unlearn a lifetime of looking left for danger. Sorry, Mom, all your years of training were for nothing here.

'Tha's why they write in the roads.' He points to the tarmac.

Sure enough, it says LOOK RIGHT in big white letters. So I'm not the first pedestrian to have been targeted. 'Thanks.'

'No prolem.' He's smiling as he trots away.

'Wait . . .' It's too late. He's been swallowed up in the lunchtime throng. I wanted to ask him about the crosswalks.[11] Sometimes

10. American sidewalk = English pavement, and I'm proud to say that, in this case, American is more accurate than English. A sidewalk is quite obviously a place to walk at the side of something.

11. Crosswalks (pedestrian crossings) mean business in London. Not only are there stripes painted on the road, they're often raised to guarantee that a car going over them at speed will drop a tailpipe in the process, and they sometimes have blinking yellow lights at each end. They're the tarmac equivalent of those warnings like 'Don't fall asleep on the railroad track'. You just know there were enough 'incidents' to warrant the caution.

cars stop, sometimes they don't. Some people walk across them without breaking their stride, others wait at the edge for cars to stop. I don't know how I'm supposed to cross one without ending up in the hospital. It's this kind of advice that's lacking in travel books. In my opinion, the success of life-saving measures shouldn't be trusted to interpretation by tourists.

There's another one (a crosswalk, I mean; there are tourists everywhere). A man rushes past, practically knocking me out of the way. I'm not kidding. If we were playing hockey, there'd be a penalty. Or a fight.

'You cross on the zebra.' The lady next to me rhymes 'zebra' with 'Debra' as she strides past.

'I'm sorry?'

'You might want to cross the road,' she snaps. 'You're holding up traffic.'

Her look, as if she's just remembered the time she stepped in a rather large and steaming pile of something, reassures me that I'm very welcome in her city.

You know, for all their supposed reserve, Brits can be astonishingly aggressive to newcomers. I vow to walk unafraid across the zeb-ra and to practise saying 'tomahto' so they'll stop sniggering at me. At the risk of sounding like a nutter as I repeat the word on the way to the bar ('tamahto, tamah–. . . tomaahto, toemaahhto'), it seems the least I can do to try to embrace my new culture. I think Chloe, as my first potential friend within the country's borders, will appreciate the effort.

3

There's no sign of Chloe, but with my lingering insecurities about being alone in a bar I've got plenty of company.

'Can I please have a glass of Chardonnay?'

'Order at the bar!'

My mistake. I assumed that a man in a smock, approaching my table, carrying a tray, was here to take my order. How I'd like for once to be the one with the inside knowledge. I wonder if newcomers to the US have the same problem, whether our ways are as mysterious to them. Are they confused by our tipping protocol, or suspicious of our instinct to shout 'Have a nice day' at everyone? Do they hurry away from the Wal-Mart greeters trying to push shopping carts into their hands or stare with disbelief at the cars circling the first few packed rows of a parking lot while acres of empty spaces stretch into the distance a hundred yards away? To think I ever believed that we Americans differed from Brits mainly in enunciation, sophistication and dentistry. Hasn't *that* been the understatement of a lifetime, considering that I've failed to properly order a sandwich, ride a bus, communicate my educational or work experience, cross the street or get a drink in a bar? I've told a man to fuck off for doing his job and, for the record, I haven't had a decent shower in a week because I can't get the plastic box on the wall to produce hot water. When I asked Mrs Doubtfire, she told me it's electric. Her look assured me that she didn't mind explaining because I was obviously retarded. Right, *I'm* retarded. Tell me who thought it was a good idea to run electricity in the shower.[12]

'Stace? It's me. What are you doing?' Cellphones are surely the security blankets of the twenty-first century.

'Ugh, I'm in a phone conference that's been going on for ever. Where are you? It sounds like fun. What time is it there?'

'In a bar. About six o'clock. Do you want to call me back when you're done?'

'Nah, the phone's on mute. They won't notice. What're you doing in a bar? Are you with that guy?!'

I love Stacy's nonchalance when it comes to her job. Despite being some kind of analysis wizard, she's never been one to take employment too seriously. Who do you think I always goofed off with in the afternoons? 'No, no, I met a really nice woman today at the employment agency and she's meeting me for a drink. She's the recruiter, but I don't think she can find me a job –'

'Not with a P/E ratio of eighteen-point-six.'

'Er, I don't know what my ratio –'

'I was talking to my boss. What's she look like?'

'She looks like Reese Witherspoon.'

'Plus the haircut.'

'Well, yes, the haircut.'

'Han, the boss again. Actually, I better call you back. I may have to explain some stuff to these numbnuts in a minute.'

'Sure, no problem. Chloe'll be here soon anyway.' I leave her chanting her unintelligible acronyms to an audience of numb-nuts.

12. We Americans encase our plumbing mechanics safely behind walls, and don't generally use electricity to push water through the shower end. Either strong pipes or greedy lawyers are to thank for this.

But Chloe is definitely not here yet, so I'm justified in continuing my anthropological work, as Dr Goodall would surely do if her interests lay in less hairy primates. It's a sight to behold. You know how a bakery can sometimes overwhelm you with choice? This bar is wall-to-wall cupcakes. I love the men in this city! They're young and fit-looking, a little on the lean side, perhaps, but definitely sexy. And most of them have funky haircuts that are sort of sticky-uppy on top. But most unusually, most of them have their hair. I can't be the only one who's noticed how bald most Americans are these days. And I'm not talking about our fathers or the old men packing groceries at the supermarket. There are a lot of perfectly healthy twenty-five-year-olds with a widening expanse of forehead.

There's a cupcake staring at me. He's perhaps a little geeky, and red-headed, but smiley. Would it be unfaithful to Mark to flirt back? Surely not. He's not my boyfriend or anything. In the name of new beginnings, don't I owe it to myself to spread my wings? I didn't move all the way to London to get seriously involved with the first guy I meet, even if he does tick all the boxes. Though it does feel a little wrong, given how well we got on. It's even possible he thinks we have a future together. Maybe he's in a bar right now, not flirting. In which case it would be unfair. So I shouldn't flirt. Unless he is flirting. He was awfully flirty when we met. Maybe that's the way he operates. He might be a complete slut who couldn't care less about the girls he sleeps with, notching them up on his bedpost as he goes along. That's so typical. What does he care about my feelings? He's just trying to get laid, the jerk. It figures, the first guy I meet in London is exactly like all the guys I've met at home. Talk about being a creature of habit. Just once I'd like to go out with a nice guy. Watch *this*, Mark!

It's not my imagination; I definitely have superpowers in

this country. It takes him less than five seconds to appear at my elbow. 'Pardon me. You must be a thief, because you stole my heart from across the room.'

This is the alternative to Mark? Of all the great guys in this bar, in London . . . in the world . . . I've attracted a parody. Fate is too cruel sometimes. 'I'm sorry, I don't speak English.'

'Wha–? But you're . . . Right, got it. Uh, have a nice evening.' He slinks away, undoubtedly to tell his friends that I'm a bitch. I don't like to be mean to guys, but honestly, sometimes it's for their own good. He will never, ever get a date with lines like that. Only the very handsomest man can get away with cheesiness. In the hands of lesser beings, it's a disaster. I'm actually doing him, and womankind, a favour . . . Though now I feel bad. He *was* trying. I've probably shaken his confidence. Who knows, he might not want to approach a girl again. And he may be a perfectly nice man with appalling judgement in pick-up lines. In fact, wouldn't I *want* my boyfriend to suck at picking up girls? I've got no right to judge another person like that, and to be so mean in the process. I've certainly said enough stupid things in my life. I'm lucky some guy hasn't made me look like a fool in return.

'Um, excuse me.'

'Yeah?' His look suggests he'd prefer minor surgery to talking to me again.

'I just wanted to say I'm sorry, for before. What I said was stupid.'

'It's nice to see you're learning the language.'

'I just didn't expect the line . . . It was a really *bad* line.'

'So bad it's good?'

'No. Just so bad. What's wrong with introducing yourself?'

'I'm Jack.'

'Hannah. Nice to meet you, Jack. Anyway, I just wanted to apologize for being such a bitch. Have a nice evening.'

'Wait! Do you believe in love at first sight or should I walk by you again?'

Some men are simply lost causes.

'Hi,' says Chloe, 'sorry I'm late. Have you been here long?' She's leaning in like she's going to kiss me? Fantastic, she thinks I'm a lesbian.

Mwah, mwah, one for each cheek. Not gay, just European. 'No, only a few minutes.'

'Should we get a bottle of wine?'

'Sure!'

'White or red?'

'Either is fine. Which do you want?'

'Oh, I don't mind.'

. . . 'I'm happy with either.'

'Me too.' Why do we become so indecisive when it comes to voicing our preferences to other women? Perfectly independent, capable women, even leading lights in their chosen professions who make multi-million-dollar or life-saving decisions on a daily basis, get stymied by the question 'Still or sparkling for the table, madam?' Sometimes consensus-building just holds up everyone's good time. 'Er, how about white?'

'Okay,' she says, gathering up her handbag. 'I'll be right back.'

'Wait, I can't let you pay for it.'

'What? Yes, don't worry –'

'No, really –' It's bad enough I bullied her into meeting me in the first place.

'It's fine, Hannah.'

'I insist –'

'Really, I don't mind –'

'Why don't we split –'

41

'But I'm putting it on my card.'

'Then –'

'No –'

'Why –'

'How about if you get the next one?' she says as she goes off to the bar to contemplate why I've nearly wrestled her for the privilege of buying a bottle.

'Well, cheers, Hannah! To your move.' She's just handed me a mixing bowl on a stem, full to the rim. The English *are* very precise in their language; maybe this is their way of proving they are not alcoholics, as in 'I only have a couple glasses a night'.

'Cheers! To finding a job. Which I'm starting to think isn't going to be easy.'

'There's always a chance something will come up.'

'But not a good chance.'

'I'm sorry, Hannah. Employers have a lot of EU candidates to pick from who don't need work permits. It's too bad your old company couldn't have transferred you here.'

'Maybe they would have, if they had an office here . . .'

'Shame.'

'And if I wasn't the most junior on the team . . .'

'Right.'

Since she can't get me a job anyway without a work permit, there's probably no harm in telling her the whole story. 'And if I hadn't been laid off.'

'Is that like being made redundant?'

'Does that mean I'm out of a job?'

'Yes.'

'Then yes.'

My old company announced on a bright Monday morning that Indians speak better English than we do. Following the industry trend, they were relocating my PR job to someplace called Hyderabad. Call me selfish, but knowing that India's future is secure as the world's outsourcing capital didn't exactly take the sting out of the event.

It's fair to say that I can sometimes be dramatic. I don't get pimples and period cramps; I get cancerous tumours and recurring bouts of appendicitis. So I've got a fairly lively imagination, and I have envisioned myself in most scenarios. The Deathbed, for example, is a favourite that I like to invoke after a break-up to picture how gutted my ex-boyfriend would be to lose me permanently. Comebacks is another, where I deliver all the cutting remarks I wasn't quick-witted enough to say at the time. The Firing plays beautifully in my mind. I'm the epitome of good grace, full of sophistication and understanding. My boss, shedding a heartfelt tear, wishes there was some way he could keep me. I'm the strong one, the shoulder to lean on when everyone else falls apart.

So I was called to the conference room where our HR rep and my boss waited to tell me that an Indian PhD would be writing my press releases in future. My boss wouldn't meet my eyes. The HR rep's gaze was full of pity. Nothing prepared me for the humiliation I felt. Not even hearing about my severance package drowned out the horrible feeling of rejection. How was I supposed to go back to my desk and act like everything was fine? I wasn't, apparently. I was to leave the building with my belongings in a cardboard box. My boss mumbled something about confidential files and corporate liability. At that point, I burst into tears, fled the room and called Stacy from the lobby. Call me Gibraltar.

Stacy promised to be there in five minutes. I had visions of fist fights and assault charges. 'What are you gonna do?'

'I'm going to take you out and get you drunk.'

True to her word, we were full of tequila slammers by

lunchtime, righting the world's ills in a single flammable breath. Just before last call, the reality of my predicament spilled back into my consciousness, at which point Stacy uttered four fateful words.

'So change your life,' she slurred. 'You never liked that job anyway.'

She was right. But change my life? 'Just like that?'

'Why not? Start with some highlights or something.' Stacy's entire outlook improves every six weeks with a good cut and a blow dry.

She obviously didn't understand the gravity of my predicament. Even drunk, I knew something was seriously wrong. 'Stace, I'm in a rut. I have no job. I don't like who I've become. And my hair colour is fine.'

'Then why don't you do something big?'

'What's big in Hartford, Connecticut?'

'Who says it has to be here?'

She had a point. With my severance package, I could move to New York, or Chicago or . . .

'London.'

'Huh?'

'London.' She directed my attention upwards.

In front of us was a ten-foot-high British Airways billboard. Nonstop flights to London from Logan Airport. It was literally a sign that I should move to Europe, like I used to say that I would. Like most things do when your blood alcohol level approaches your GPA,[13] it made perfect sense.

---

13. Exam results, usually on a four-point scale. Beware anyone who brags about a 'four-point-oh'; either they studied too hard, to the exclusion of all socialization, or went to a school where underwater basket-weaving was a valid degree course.

'Should I do it?'

Stacy didn't miss a beat. 'Definitely!'

'You want me to move?'

'I want you to be happy.'

'But London's far.'

'Look, if you're gonna make a change, you should do it. There's no sense in being half-assed when it comes to your future. Don't be a coward. You should go.'

I was stung by her words. We'd never been apart. We were closer than sisters. We were soulmates. How could she suggest so flippantly that I move thousands of miles away, like it was nothing bigger than a new hairstyle? 'Well, maybe I'll just book a flight when we get home.' I wanted to scare her, to hurt her, to make her say she didn't really want me to leave. She didn't say anything.

The next thing I knew, it was morning and Stacy was jumping on my bed. 'I can't believe you're going to London!' she kept screaming.

'What are you talking about?'

'London, London, London! Your flight's on New Year's Day.'

And that's what I get for being spiteful during a black-out. . . . 'So, once I got over the shock of having an eleven-hundred-dollar non-refundable ticket on my credit card, it did seem like the right thing to do.'

'Plus there was the sign,' Chloe says.

'Yeah, I'm a huge believer in signs.' At least she's not looking at me like I'm crazy, which means she's also a big believer in the cosmos. Or she's an excellent bluffer, and I shouldn't play poker against her.

'And you're not mad at your friend for pushing you into buying the ticket?'

45

'Well, at the end of the day, I made the decision, even if I don't remember actually doing it.'

Am I mad at Stacy? Not for the reason Chloe thinks. Once Stacy gets an idea in her head she charges ahead with it. When we were in high school, she drove us nineteen hours to Graceland to see Elvis. She'd had her driver's permit for about a week and Elvis had been dead for a couple decades. Our parents reported us to the police as runaways. No, I'm not mad at her for making me buy the ticket. I'm mad that she let me go so easily.

. . . 'But if I don't find a job I'll have to go home.'

'Isn't there anyone you know here who might be able to help?'

'I don't know anyone.' Except for Mark, but I can't very well ask him for a job. Can I? 'Well, I sort of just met someone. He runs some kind of events company.'

'That's exactly the kind of contact you need! Most good jobs don't come through people like me. It's the network you need to tap into. That's where the real opportunities are. We get the postings they can't fill. How comfortable are you with this guy? Could you ask him for a job?'

How much to tell Chloe? Here's my first potential friend in London. Will she think I'm a slut if I admit to sleeping with a man I just met, or will she say 'You go, girl!' or its English translation, leaving me in no doubt that we're kindred spirits and cementing our friendship for ever? 'It's fair to say we're pretty . . . comfortable.'

'Then definitely ask him.'

'What if he says no and that wrecks everything?'

'Then he's a knob.'

'I'm sorry?'

'He's a knob.'

Door knob? Knob of butter?

'A wanker. I think you say dick in American.'

'Yes, we do,' says I, speaking for my nation.

Perhaps Chloe is right about Mark. There's no harm in asking if there's a job for me at his company. Really, I owe it to myself, and certainly to my parents, who paid good money for my college education. My mother would definitely tell me to ask. So would Stacy. And Chloe already has. It's not like I'm coming from left field by asking. PR and party planning are kind of the same thing, if you substitute parties for press releases. I resolve to ask. The only complication is that I haven't heard from him. Not that I won't. It's only been a few days, so he's still within the acceptable callback window. But I don't have his number. All I know is that his company is called M-something events. I remember because I asked if it was named after him (it isn't).

'Chloe, do you know of an M-something events?'

'Not offhand. But hang on a sec.' She whips out her phone. It's one of the flippy ones that Captain Kirk would use, if he was real, and in a wine bar making a telephone call.

'New York office,' she mouths. 'They can check the database . . . It's not a name? Definitely initials?'

'Definitely initials. M and something.'

'It's definitely in London?'

'Definitely.'

'There are four.' She jots down the telephone numbers and slides them over the table to me. I'm in the presence of great power. 'There you are. All you need to do is call and ask for him.'

How easy is that? It couldn't be easier, assuming I knew his last name.

There's nothing like a few bottles of wine to bring girls

together. The best conversations, even with strangers (and sometimes especially with them), revolve around sex, in a kind of verbal swordplay. I suppose this war-story swap is akin to dogs sniffing each other's rear ends or apes beating their chests. It's meant to bond (you're so special, I'm sharing) and intimidate (don't tell *me* about rough times) all at once. So we're drunk. We're strangers. We've degenerated into a conversation that'd win ratings for Jerry Springer.

'You know,' I say, 'I once had a guy want to spank me during sex.'

'Hmm. I went out with a guy who couldn't come unless he sang the lyrics to "Eye of the Tiger".'

Wow. She sees my spank and raises me a crooner. 'The theme from *Rocky*?'

'The very one.'

'I didn't know it was popular over here.'

'It was for him.'

I haven't told many people this, but the ante has been upped. 'Once, a guy I was seeing turned out to be sleeping with his sister.' Ladies and gentlemen, place your bets. We're at the high-stakes table now.

'Oof. What did you say?'

'Say? I didn't say anything!' What do you say to something like that?

'How'd you know?' she snorts. 'You didn't catch them, did you?'

'No.' There isn't enough therapy in the world. 'Actually, it was circumstantial evidence. First, he had this enormous stack of family porn.'

'Family –?'

'You know, mother–son, kissing siblings, that sort of sick crap. Once I found those I started putting the pieces together.

48

I mean, *possibly* a guy could grab one of those off the newsstand by accident, but it looked like he had a subscription. Then I started to notice how jealous he got around his sister's boyfriend. I mean, he really freaked out sometimes.'

Chloe drains her glass and reaches for the bottle. 'That's it? I went out with a guy who made me wear trainers in bed.'

Training wheels? 'What are trainers?'

'Running shoes.'

I take my cards off the table. She's won the pot. 'Pretty ones, like Adidas?' I have my eye on the cutest pair of pale-blue and red Adidas running shoes. Think what a perfect chic urban footwear statement they'll make (there's no rule saying they *have* to be used for running). I'll never have to buy another pair of sneakers again.

'Uh-uh. Black high-top Reeboks.'

'During sex?'

'When else? And he wouldn't let me go to the gym. I broke up with him.'

'Of course. A girl's gotta keep fit.'

By the time the bell rings, I suspect I'm very drunk.

'Will you be okay getting home?' Chloe asks as I trip on the sidewalk.

'Yep, fine.'

'Will you take the Tube?'

If I get into the Underground system, I'll wake up in Zone 6. 'Mebbe a taxi'd be best.'

A kind driver at the roadside stands ready to help. 'Taxi, taxi?'

'Do you know where we can get one?'

'Yes, taxi, taxi,' he says, gesturing inside his obviously-not-a-taxi.

'Does he want to drive us to a taxi?'

'It's a minicab.'

'Like a limo service?'

'No, they're not licensed. It's just a punter with a car. You want a black cab.'

Well, obviously. I may be (very) drunk and (occasionally) naive, but thanks to Mom, even I know enough not to get into a stranger's car that pulls alongside me on the street.

'Here's a cab; we'll share.'

Bless her, she's determined to make sure I don't end up in tomorrow's newspaper. The driver has trouble understanding me when I give him my address, but it's not his fault. I'm speaking California Chardonnay.

'By the way,' she says, 'I'm happy to come with you to look at flats if you want.'

I don't remember telling her that I need flats. I have enough shoes, and besides, I walk better in heels (trips on the sidewalk notwithstanding). 'That's okay, I can't really afford any shopping till I find a job.' Unless those Adidas go on sale.

'An apartment, Hannah. You said you were going to look at apartments. I can go with you if you want.'

I did say that, didn't I? Floating somewhere in the wine is the recollection that when deciding to be optimistic on the job front, I also decided to look for a place to live. Given that Mark could have the perfect job for me, I should at least look around. I vowed to start first thing in the morning. It seems unfair to make such a brand-new friend suffer. 'Thanks very much, but I'll be fine. I'll just blitz through a bunch in the morning and get it done.'

'You may need a little more time than that.'

Why does she look so sceptical? She obviously underestimates my highly evolved hunter-gatherer instinct when it comes to finding things to buy, or in this case, to rent.

4

I'm still optimistic, if tremendously hung over. I officially have a friend in London, this is a gorgeous neighbourhood, the apartment sounds great, my skinny jeans are even a little loose and my Juicy Argyle cashmere sweater is a style favourite. Nothing says 'Make me your housemate' like having covetable clothes.

'Um, hi, I'm here about the apartment?' A Sienna Miller doppelgänger is blocking the doorway. It's not a good start, though it's possible, in a 'perhaps I'll win the lottery this week' way, that she's beautiful *and* nice. It doesn't matter. I'm willing to overlook her obvious lack of flaws when I step inside. This is exactly the way I'd decorate my own place – just Pottery Barn[14] enough to be comfy without tipping over into baby-dressed-as-flower artwork. There's a squishy-looking sofa in one corner, perfect to curl up on with Ben, Jerry and a spoon. If they shift that table over, they could get a reading chair there, maybe with a floor lamp . . .

'The room's a single.'

'That's okay, it's just me.' Although hopefully not every night.

Nothing truly prepares you for the disappointment of dashed hopes. We don't go inside the bedroom. Why? Because it's literally a bed-room. It's maybe, *maybe*, five feet wide by

14. Pottery Barn is the kind of homestore chain where customers say things like 'Wow, that's really *unique*' with no trace of irony . . . a sort of Habitat for country-house/beach-house aspirants.

eight feet long. The only way to get into bed would be to take a running leap from the doorway and launch myself on to the mattress. 'Uh, it's kind of small.'

'We did say in the advert that it was a single. And the rent is very reasonable.'

So people gratefully pay for the chance to live in a submarine torpedo launch tube at the right address. Thanks anyway, Sienna.

South Ken definitely looks like the right address, even if the architecture is a bit schizophrenic. That's something I know a little about. Architecture, I mean, not schizophrenia. I took a course in college when the object of my desire signed up, only to have him drop the class on the last withdrawal day while I was in bed with tonsillitis. I never saw my tonsils or the object of my desire again, but I got a B+ in the class.

The need to crawl under the nearest duvet is taking on a new degree of urgency, but the next apartment is just a block away at number eleven. Lucky number eleven. That was my soccer number, though I only played for a week before it dawned on me that watching *Days of Our Lives* after school was infinitely preferable to sweating in a field. They let me keep the shirt though. There's number two and, across the street is ... forty-eight. I'm in no frame of mind for higher-order thinking, but I'm sure the house across the street from number two should be number three. Forty-seven, forty-six, forty-five ... There it is, across the street from forty-four. What kind of country numbers its buildings sequentially up one side of the street and down the other? How do they assign house numbers if they have to extend the road later? Negatives? Fractions? Are there people living at Twenty-one-and-three-eighths Queen Street?

'Hi, jeez, you're hard to find!' I blurt when a pudgy girl answers the door. I'd be much more comfortable living with this mere mortal. I *knew* this was going to work out.

'Really?' She looks a little doubtful about my mental capacity. 'The bedroom's through here.'

At least I don't have to step on the bed to open the window. 'It's great . . . wooh.'

'Are you all right?'

Her concern is understandable given that my stomach is groaning like an extra from *Jurassic Park*. The force of this painful eruption just drove me to the mattress.

'Fine, thanks, wooh.' She doesn't need to know about my appalling lack of fortitude in the face of a good vintage. 'Sorry. Just a little cramp.' Panting seems to help the spasms. 'Um, where's the kitchen?'

'We don't have a kitchen.'

'What do you mean, you don't have a kitchen?'

'Lucy's room is the old kitchen. But all the appliances are gone.'

'Where do you eat?'

'In the living room.'

'No, I mean, where do you cook?'

'Cook?'

While it's fine to exist on take-outs and dinner dates, I have a feeling that at some point, in a moment of foolishness perhaps, I might get the urge to actually assemble my own food. I'm no Julia Child,[15] but the ability to make an omelette

15. Many of our mothers have Julia Child to thank for their ability to cook French cuisine. She was a celebrity chef on TV decades before that phrase was invented and never saw a cooking dilemma that a little more wine wouldn't sort out.

is a basic human right. To think I was blissfully unaware that I needed to ask whether an apartment comes with optional accessories like a refrigerator.

'Thanks, can I, wooh, let you know?'

'The rent's very reasonable. Only two-fifty a week.'

So I keep hearing. Wait a minute, did she say . . . 'Two-fifty a *week*? You mean per month.'

'Er, no, it's two hundred and fifty pounds a week. But the gas and electric's included.'

So Brits quote their rents in weekly increments to make themselves feel better about lining their landlord's pocket with amounts that most third-world countries consider an appropriate payment on their national debt. 'Thanks, I'll let you know.'

I won't lose heart. And I won't lie down on the sidewalk, which is what I really want to do. What am I *doing* anyway? I can't afford to live here. I'm 3,000 miles from home, with a dwindling bank balance, no job, one friend less than 24 hours old, a seat reserved on a plane in a couple weeks and I may have just gone into labour. Who looks for an apartment under these circumstances? Being optimistic is one thing, but this is ridiculous. I may as well buy a wedding dress on the off-chance I actually do get married somewhere, some day, to someone I haven't yet met. Throw in a couple ponies for my non-existent children.

'Stace, what the hell am I doing here?'

'Aw, Han, I know it's hard getting started, but you owe it to yourself to try to make it work. Otherwise you'll regret it later.'

'I know. It's just . . . I'm being stupid. I mean, who does this?'

'I would.'

'But you're different.'

'I am not! Han, we're exactly the same. You can do this too.'

'Thanks.' I don't believe that. 'I really miss you.'

'I miss you too.'

I don't believe that either. The resentment, never too far away, slaps me. It's been too easy for her to let me go. We're supposed to be a team. We literally haven't made a decision without the other's input . . . or at least I haven't. A memory intrudes. Like most intrusions, it's unwelcome. College admissions. We waited for the envelopes to arrive (dreading the skinny ones, knowing they meant rejection). The daily phone call after school – did it, didn't it? Then one day it did. Stacy got her first acceptance. To her, our, first choice. 'OhmygodI'mgoingtoUConn!'

'That's great! . . . But what if I don't get in too?'

'Of course you'll get in.'

'But what if I don't?'

She was quiet for a while. 'Well, the other schools aren't that far away.'

I did get in but I guess I knew, even though I didn't want to know, that I needed Stacy more than she needed me. With her to lean on, I didn't have to make my own fun, or decisions, or pursue my own dreams. I guess I've been on autopilot in more ways than one. Maybe that's what she's telling me. It's time to live my own life. The waves of betrayal hit me all over again. That's a rotten thing to tell a friend.

'Stace, why'd you let me go?' My heart is thumping in my neck.

'What do you mean, let you go? How was I going to stop you?'

'You could have talked me out of booking the ticket.'

'Hannah, you were so excited to do it!'

She's right, I was. 'You could have asked me not to go.'

'I couldn't do that!'

'Maybe you should have.'

'Why?'

'Because we're best friends. Because you don't want us to be a million miles away from each other. Because you need me there.' I wish my voice didn't shake whenever I get emotional. 'Stace? You there?'

'I'm here . . . Hannah, do you think I want you to be in London? I mean, that I'm happy you're so far away?'

'Psh, you've made it sound like you are.' I know I'm being petulant.

'You're such an idiot. I'm miserable without you. We're a team, like two halves of a . . . I don't know, pick one of those stupid similes you like so much. I hate that we can't see each other. It's not the same on the phone. Honestly, I hope you don't find a job and you come home and we go back to the way things were. But if that happens, I know you'll be miserable. You've decided to do something huge, Han, and I want to back you up on that, only . . . I'm selfish. I also want my best friend back.'

Tears are pricking my eyes. Relief? Yes, and the emotion of missing her. 'I love you!'

'You dope! I love you too. Now, you're going to do this, right? Because if not, even though I'll be happy to have you back, I'll think you're a wimp for giving up.'

'I'm really going to try.'

Of course I can do this. Just think of our founding fathers. They didn't have hotels or recruitment agencies or savings accounts. They had famine and unfriendly Indians and outdoor plumbing, and they started a whole new country. What have I got to complain about?

It's time to push the universe a bit. And I know just where to start.

5

Surely it isn't always considered stalking to track a man down at his place of employment. There are many legitimate situations where this is a perfectly reasonable thing to do. If you're a doctor with his lab results, for instance, then obviously it's expected that you'd get in touch. Or maybe you're a telemarketer with an amazing opportunity, then he couldn't blame you for calling. Perhaps you're with the airline and his flight details to Bermuda have changed (he'll be grateful you've let him know). Or what if you're a friend of a friend who's just moved into town and doesn't know anyone else? Naturally, he'll be happy to chat. I'm about as close to the last category as a girl can be without actually having a friend in common. So it's not stalking.

There's a hiccup in my plan when I call the first company.

'Mark who?' the woman asks.

What am I supposed to say, Mark the good kisser? Luckily my PR training has armed me for these sticky situations. 'I'm sorry,' I tell her, projecting such confidence that she'll naturally assume I'm a client, 'but I didn't catch his last name when he called.'

'When he called' may be a small lie but it's a huge door-opener. Actually, he would have called if I'd had a phone number, so this isn't a lie, it's simply the anticipation of an eventual fact.

'I'm sorry, I'm afraid you have the wrong number. There's no one here by that name.'

'I see.' My tone says I'm very sorry she's putting me out like this. 'Thank you very much. Good day.'

The next two calls go the same way, each time the reception-ist telling me that she's sorry and afraid. Then, open sesame, I've got the right company. 'One moment, please. May I tell him who's calling?'

May she? Of course she may. My lip is sweating. What if he doesn't want to talk to me? What if he completely regrets ever meeting me? What if he tells the receptionist to say he's not there? Or was fired? Or had to have an operation? What if he –

'Hi, Hannah. How are you?'

And the angels sing Hallelujah! 'I'm great! Um, how are you?'

'Fine, busy with work as usual.'

'Oh.' . . . Now what am I supposed to say? I really should have thought this through better. Or at all. It's probably too late to pretend it's the wrong number and hang up. 'Me too . . . I'm fine, I mean. Not busy with work. I don't have a job. As you know.' Surely he's questioning his judgement in women at this point. 'Erm, I met a new friend though. We went out for drinks the other night.'

'Hmm, drinking again. That's great. Should I be jealous?'

Ah. Flirting I can do. 'I don't think so, she's not really my type.'

'I'm happy to hear that . . . So, what are you doing now?'

He sounds even sexier over the phone. 'Nothing. Just hang-ing around . . . trying to stay out of trouble.' Whereas I sound like a dimwit.

'There's no fun in that. Feel like meeting me for a drink?'

'I thought you were busy with work.'

'I'm the boss; I'm allowed to bunk off.'

'When?'

'An hour?'

'I'll have to check my schedule. Hang on.' One-hippopot-amus, two-hippopotamus, three-hippopotamus. 'Yes, I can fit you in this afternoon.'

'Good. There's a Balls Brothers on Brook Street, shall I meet you there at four? You can take the Tube to Oxford Circus.'

'Okay, see you there!'

This almost never happens. Men showing such obvious interest, I mean – I go to bars fairly regularly. He must think we have a future too, otherwise he wouldn't leave work at the drop of a hat, when he's obviously critical to his company, just to meet some girl that he's already slept with. I admit it: if I knew his last name, I'd be tacking it on to Hannah just to see how it sounds.

A date *and* a Tube ride; fortune strikes twice. I love the Tube. I've got my pick of cushioned seats. The fact that there are actual fabric cushions on public transportation speaks volumes for the country's civility. Surely if they can't be hosed down, there must be no need to. So not only is it clean, it has many considerate touches that you wouldn't see anywhere else. Like classical entertainment. Yesterday there was a woman playing her cello for us at the bottom of the escalator. A cello! It's a beautiful instrument, but not the obvious choice for portability. And when the trains are delayed, the man on the loudspeaker cheerfully tells us why, as in: 'The train is delayed because there's impersonator the drain.' Only when the guy next to me muttered 'Bloody top yourself on your own time' did I realize there was a *person under* the *train*. Nausea aside, I admire this kind of honesty in public services.

To be clear, I'm not spying on Mark. I'm killing time looking in the window before I'm due inside. He's standing nonchalantly by the bar, laughing with the barmaid. Is he flirting with her? Surely not, not when he's waiting for me to meet him. Though technically he's only waiting for me because I called him. Isn't there something seedy, and slightly needy, about that? I should be playing hard to get. Admittedly that's hard to pull off now that I've stalked the man. Unfortunately, restraint isn't one of my strongest qualities when it comes to the opposite sex. Whenever my better judgement suggests I don't call, or write or follow, I'm plagued by that little voice that whines, 'But I *like* him.' I'm the girl who, when a guy claims illness as an excuse for not having called in a week, brings him soup.

Catching sight of me at the door (thank god not through the window), he beams me a smile. Definitely the best-looking man ever to see me naked. I'll play hard to get after today.

'Hi!' To kiss or not to kiss. Considering where our lips were a week ago, you wouldn't think there'd be any question. I'm not going to make the first move. I will not, I will not. Unless he doesn't.

Mwah, mwah. I was under the impression that cheek-kissing one's lovers went the way of the corset and the chamberpot (necessary at the time but thankfully no longer in use), but I suppose there's a certain charm to it.

'Come, let's sit down. You're looking well.'

Did I look ill before? He must mean I look pretty. I should, considering the effort I put into my outfit (and in under an hour too). It's not like I'm spoiled for choice, for despite an innate preoccupation with fashion, and several full suitcases to show for this, I have only a handful of good pieces. That's what my mother calls them: 'pieces'. She likes to tell me what 'pieces' 'they're' wearing this season. My limited pieces are what make the decision tricky. Pacing is essential. If I peak too early,

I'll only disappoint later on. But let's be frank, the second date is the most important. On the first date you're generally either 1) drunk when you meet, so the goggles work their magic or 2) anticipating the date, so the rose-coloured glasses do the trick. The second date is when you see each other in the cold, hard light of day. It's very important to be extra-impressive. For this reason I'm wearing my Missoni sweater with skinny jeans. Though it may cause me to have nothing to wear on a third, hopefully dinner date, it's worth the risk.

I'm suddenly nervous. I really like this guy. Plus I've never tried to manoeuvre my way into a job and a man's bed at the same time before. 'Nice place. Is it near your office?'

'No. I just like it here. Stella?'

'Yes, please. A half.' He remembered. I don't want to start looking for signs, but not every man would bother to remember your drink. He's clearly had some training. I wonder who trained him. The American bitch? Many American bitches? Men are works in progress, and it's usually a woman on the construction site. Some, of course, don't even have their scaffolding up. They're the ones you make sure you don't get under.

'So, do you usually sneak off from work to go drinking in the afternoon?'

'Only when I don't have my AA meeting.'

'Drink too much?'

'No, I drink just the right amount. Well, cheers. I'm glad you called.'

'Happy to.' With my hand clasped in his, it's a little hard to concentrate on anything but the fact that *he's holding my hand*!

'Tell me what you've been doing since we last met. Have you had fish and chips yet?'

'Not yet, and no cricket either.'

'Well, it's not the season. That leaves being seduced by the world's greatest lovers.'

Is he jealous? I hope so. 'Is that in season?'

'Always.'

Maybe dropping a few hints will make him think he's got some competition. Rivalry can be a great motivator. Psh, right. Look at this guy. His competition is in LA making blockbusters. 'Nothing that exciting. I've been on the job hunt . . .' Here's my chance. Don't blow it. Mmm. His eyes are lighter blue than the other night. They're wonderful. I wonder if I look different. Maybe . . . maybe I should stop daydreaming and focus on the task at hand. 'But no luck so far.'

'I'm sure it won't take long.'

'I don't know. If I don't get something soon, I'll have to go back home . . . I don't suppose there's anything at your company?' If I smile like I'm kidding, maybe he won't take offence. I'd hate for him to think I'm just after him for a job when I really want sex and a job.

'Well, I think there could be. How're your juggling skills?'

'I'm a great multi-tasker.' I *knew* this was a good idea!

'No, I mean can you juggle?'

'What, literally?'

'Yes.'

'No.' Is it possible that I've literally slept with a clown? 'Is juggling a prerequisite for working at your company?'

'You do know what we do, right?'

'Uh, you're M&G Events. I assume you plan events.'

'Ah, no. We *staff* events.'

'Like the circus?' Oh god, he is a clown. This has to be a new low in my dating career.

'Not always. Can you eat fire?'

'Eat fire!'

'What about your clown skills. How are those?'

. . . 'Right. You're kidding.'

'I'm kidding. We plan events, parties, conferences, store launches and the like. The look on your face was priceless.'

'So given that I can't juggle or walk a tightrope, do you –'

'Or eat fire. I have to wonder what those American schools are teaching these days.'

'Right. Anyway, *is* there something, given my limited acrobatic skills, that you think I might be able to do for you?'

'I think there is. Would you like another drink?' I am the luckiest woman on the planet. Not only is the sexiest man in this bar (possibly in all of London) holding my hand like I'm his one true love, he's going to give me a job. How great is this?

Only . . . is this smart? Hasn't moving here taught me anything? Barrelling ahead and sorting out the consequences later hasn't exactly put me ahead of the game so far. Getting a job should be a decision I make, not an accident I stumble into. In the abstract, it might be a great idea to take a job from an amazingly handsome, sexy man that I've just slept with. But if I do, and I only got the job because we've slept together, does that make me a prostitute? I think the answer is yes. But the question is: do I care?

a) I do care what people think of me, at least some people. I'm shallow like that. The people I care about include the ones I already know, plus anyone I might like to know in the future, like potential friends, boyfriends or employers.

b) But none of the people I might like to know in the future will ever know the circumstances of my employment, unless I tell them.

c) And the same is true for the people I already know. But unless I'm prepared to lie to them all, I'll have to tell them.

d) Ergo, the question is whether the people already in my life will judge me for taking a job from a man I'm sleeping with.

e) Stacy definitely won't. She'd do it in a second.

f) My parents can't judge me, they're my parents. It's in their contract.

g) My grandmother judges everyone, but she's senile, so she'll forget all about it within a week.

h) I'm 100 per cent sure that all the women in the new office will think I'm a slut if they find out, except anyone who's like me and Stacy, and those are the ones I'd want to be friends with anyway, so I don't care about the others.

So there's my answer.

'I will have another, thanks. Make it a pint.'

6

Of *course* I take the job. No sane person would pass it up, not when the alternative is to go home, and certainly not given the fact that I'm going to get paid to attend A-list parties. Granted, I have to plan them first, and I'll need to learn how to do that. And I have to be someone called Felicity's assistant before that, but this miraculous series of events can't be coincidence.

My certainty that I was made for this job almost (almost) offsets the doubts I have about sleeping with the boss. Again. In my optimistic moments, I think, how bad can it be? It was such an amazing night, drinking at the bar, flirting and swapping stories, then dinner at the coolest tapas restaurant I've ever imagined. Then, yes, to bed for a marathon session (I was definitely in contention for the gold this time). It was the kind of night you'd remember for ever. A night like that has to lead to something and who knows, working with Mark might turn out to be the best thing that's ever happened to me. If we fall madly in love, we'll get to spend all our time together. We'll be a team, like Clements Ribeiro (Suzanne and Inacio) or Dolce and Gabbana (before they broke up). And if we do eventually part ways, like Domenico and Stefano we'll maintain an amicable professional relationship. But if I don't take him up on his offer, then I'll have to go back to Connecticut, with no chance to convince him to fall in love with me and no great job to distract me from the first two points.

But the doubt creeps in at night, usually while I'm lying awake listening to the hotel's creaking floorboards, trying not to think about the potential murder suspects wandering the halls. What if we're not as mature as I hope we'll be? What if he dumps me, then fires me? Or he dumps me but doesn't fire me, and I have to face him every day? Or, worse still, what if I'm so terrible at my job that he *has* to fire me? It's going to be very difficult to seduce him when he's seen me bawl in front of HR. Then I'll have to go home jobless, heartbroken and with my self-esteem puddling in my socks . . . Come to think of it, the worst-case scenario puts me exactly where I'd be if I didn't take the job in the first place, minus the self-esteem puddle. So I have nothing to lose. Besides, I'm confident at least in the fact that I was born to be a party planner. I just didn't know it until now.

I'm missing only one ingredient (besides relevant experience): the perfect assistant-soon-to-be-party-planner wardrobe. Nothing says career success like the right trouser suit.

'Sorry!'

The entire population wants to pass me on its right-hand side. We meet, shuffle to my right, meet, shuffle right till one of us hits a building or falls off the kerb. Where does their compulsion to veer left come from, and more importantly, how am I supposed to survive in a city where I'm destined to knock foreheads with everyone I try passing in the street?

It's hard to fathom that ten million people live here. In a ten-mile radius. Do the math – that's about thirty square feet per person. Prisoners have bigger cells. New Yorkers might disagree, but London feels like the most crowded city in the world. Exciting and vibrant, but crowded. There are hordes of people everywhere, all the time, and they all want to be exactly where I'm standing/walking/sitting. Londoners are teaching me some very effective coping mechanisms though.

For sheer passive-aggressive versatility, the tut is already a firm favourite. I first learned the technique when its originator stood three inches behind me and clucked in my ear. I think it's shorthand for 'Excuse me, please, may I get past you?' Sometimes it coincides with a mild but well-aimed elbow, and is almost always followed up with the 'huh'/eyeroll combination ('Thank you very much').

There's Chloe, trying to hold her position against the rising tide of shoppers. 'Ready to shop?' she asks as we air-kiss. Mwah, mwah, darling. It feels very posery, but everybody does it, and not even ironically. I suppose it's no more odd than our compulsion to begin every social interaction with 'Howareya?' when we never intend for the question to be answered.

'Ready as I'll ever be.'

'Do you know what you're looking for?'

What a question. Only rookies try something this important without diligent preparation. I'm armed with every fashion magazine on sale here. They weren't obvious to spot at first, buried under the rubble of crashed relationships and burned-out careers spread over the magazine shelves. Brits are obsessed with *Hello!*, *OK!* and *Tatler*, and aren't even ashamed about reading these odes to sensationalized mediocrity. Not for them the 'I must have picked it up by accident' or 'My sister left it here' excuses that we use. They celebrate their voyeuristic tendencies, revelling in magnificent hyperbole. So, in the midst of all the infidelities and catfights, my fashion favourites coyly waved from the news-stand like old friends. There's *Vogue* – hello *Vogue*! And *InStyle* . . . looking great as usual. *Elle*, always a pleasure, and *Glamour*, where *did* those shoes come from! Thumbing through these British cousins was an epiphany. The styles here are completely different. Can I really reinvent my look in a chain store? Must I no longer settle for the

Gap-Banana Republic-Limited triumvirate of cookie-cutter fashion? It's amazing, stupendous, a life-altering experience . . .

I want to go home. To the triumvirate. These clothes are designed for self-(esteem)mutilation. I can't get the first pair of pants past my knees. Double-checking the size, yes, size eight, is no comfort. I yank. They don't budge. Every pair fits the same way. That is to say, they don't.

I'm trying not to panic. 'Chloe!' I don't know why she looks so embarrassed. I'm the one hopping towards her grasping my pants around my thighs. 'Chloe, what's going on here?'

'You need a bigger size.'

And just when I thought we could be best friends. Of course I don't need a bigger size! The pants are mis-sized, or cut wrong, or this store is known to stock absurdly tiny clothes. 'I'm a size eight!' I'm a little vain about this. Although it's just a number, there was a time in college when I got a little large. Those pizza-delivery people were as persistent as Jehovah's Witnesses. I was back to normal by senior year but the experience definitely left a mental scar, and slightly dimpled thighs.

'You're an American size eight. English sizes are smaller. Try a ten or a twelve.' She's sliding a gorgeous pair of wool boot-cuts over her hips.

Ten? Twelve? Is she mental? Everyone knows there're two important milestones in women's sizes. One: double digits. Two: the dreaded teens.[16] I won't be a double-digit girl again, especially when I haven't had the indulgent joy of getting there. Maybe I should do all my shopping at home. But The Gap doesn't have these pretty clothes and besides, I can't wait

16. Nobody knows why going from an American size twelve to a four-teen is at least twice as traumatic as the ten-to-twelve leap, but then nobody can explain why birthdays ending in 'o' should cause us to melt down either.

that long. Steeling myself, I take a size ten into the dressing room.

It doesn't fit. I can just get the legs over my thighs but something funny is happening around the waist. I've got butt cleavage (builder's bum, Chloe helpfully translates), flashing at least two inches of crack when I sit. You don't even want to know what squatting looks like.

This has been worse than shopping for a swimsuit in mid-winter. At least then there's the compensatory anticipation of sun and sand, and the delusion that a little tan will turn the pale puckered horror in the fitting-room mirror into a body worthy of the *Sports Illustrated* swimsuit issue. I can't face the sight of my thighs stretching that judgemental ridge of fabric across the front of any more pants. Just the idea of a size twelve makes me want to rethink my stance on liposuction. Skirts are much more forgiving and, totally forgiven, I'm now the proud owner of half a dozen. I'll never have to buy a skirt again.

'Don't let it upset you,' Chloe counsels while sipping her skinny latte in Costa Coffee.[17]

Easy for her to say, surrounded by shopping bags full of pants. Size-eight bitch. 'How am I supposed to live here if I can't even find pants that fit!'

'Shh! Pants are underwear.'

'They are not. Underwear is underwear.'

'Not here. You're shouting about your knickers.'

'Oh.' Then I'd better stop doing that. 'Do you think the girls here are shaped differently?' It's a theory I'm working on (cling-ing to). I notice, for example, that Chloe, while willowy of leg, has a gut. And I'm not just saying that out of sour grapes. She's built like a blueberry muffin. Perhaps evolution has created

17. Britain's two-finger salute to Starbucks.

different shapes in different countries. I come from Sicilian stock on my mother's side, and even though my father's family was British from way back, everyone says I look just like my mother. Maybe it's simple genetics at play. I'm not fat, I'm Italian.

'That's probably it. You're built to wear the Italian designers, like Armani.'

'Really, you think so?'

'Definitely.'

Finally, Chloe becomes the friend I knew she'd be. 'Thanks,' I say. 'You did well today.'

'Hmm, yes. Now that I think about it, though, I feel like I already have that zig-zaggy wrap dress. It did seem familiar when I tried it on.'

'Keep the receipt. You can check when you get home.'

'I suppose, though I'm not sure where it could be. Maybe in my wardrobe somewhere. And I've got some things at the cleaners.' She opens her purse and starts pulling out receipt after receipt, smoothing them on the table top. No two are from the same cleaner.

'Well, those boots are great.'

'Yes, I wondered about those too. There might be a pair at home.'

'Save the –'

'Receipt, I know,' she sighs. 'I'll never get around to returning them. The place is such a disaster, I'll lose the bags.'

'Well, if you want, I'm happy to come over and help organize your closets for you.'

'Oh, I couldn't let you do that. The place really is a tip.'

'But I'd love to. And if it'll help . . . Who knows what treasures we'll find?'

'Really? Erm, okay, if you're sure it's no bother.'

'Are you kidding? I love doing stuff like that. It'll be fun!'

71

Truthfully, I can think of at least 972 things I'd rather do than excavate someone's closet, but a woman who can't find a £400 dress obviously needs guidance. Besides, I can tell Chloe is a genuinely nice woman. I want to help her.

While we may not have solved the world debt crisis or global warming today, I feel we've made some important progress.

Now gainfully employed, I'm justified in flying Mrs Doubtfire's nest. And none too soon, since her scant hospitality has worn thin. She now throws her cardboard-flavoured toast at me in the mornings. She's obviously still disappointed at my failure to produce a husband for her inspection. She also thinks I'm an alcoholic, based on the flimsiest of circumstantial evidence. She wouldn't always see me drunk if she'd give me a front-door key instead of making me ring the bell after 10 p.m. The woman has trust issues.

"Annah?' says the man in the doorway.

It's Crocodile Dundee.

'Hi, yes, I'm Hannah. I'm here about the room?'

'G'day, I'm Nathan? This is Syrah, and over there's Adam? He had a beet of a rough noight.'

'Hnn,' confirms the pile of blankets on the sofa.

The apartment is big, pretty and clean. Incidentally, the Australians are also big, pretty and clean. And the bedroom is palatial, with weak winter sun dribbling through its tall windows.

'I love it!'

'How soon can you move in?'

'I can be back here in an hour.'

He laughs. He realizes I'm serious. 'Oh, ah, well . . .'

'Give us a minute, will ya, 'Annah?'

'Sure, Sarah, no problem.' If they don't let me be their

housemate, I'm going to cry in their living room until they either relent or call the police.

'You'll have to put down a deposit,' Nathan advises when they emerge from their kitchen conference. 'Two weeks' rent?'

I'd give them a kidney if they asked. 'No problem.'

'Well then, you can move in tomorrow. Welcome!' Sarah strides over and hugs me. She's squeezing too hard because I swear tears are squirting out.

So my new home is in a slightly down-at-heel white-painted townhouse on a tree-lined crescent near Earls Court Tube. I didn't expect this much green in London, but the English are absolutely obsessed with their gardens. Even borderline slums like Earls Court have them. We Americans may think we embrace the great outdoors, infatuated as we are with our national parks and ride-on lawnmowers. But we're rank amateurs compared to these people. Everyone here, ev-ery-one, regardless of race, colour, creed or class, has a green thumb. Even Chloe waxes poetic about the 'pot plants' that she proudly cares for on her roof terrace. At first I mistook this for misdemeanour drug use, but it was just another translation error. Entire TV shows are devoted to the finer points of caring for one's zinnias and ridding one's tomatoes of garden pests. It must be a reaction to all the rain. The English have found a silver lining in all those clouds.

'G'day!' Sarah doesn't seem the least bit annoyed that I'm on her doorstep with my worldly belongings at eleven o'clock on Sunday morning. She looks like one of those easy-going girls who's never plucked or dyed, waxed or bleached, because she doesn't have to. She's Elle Macpherson without make-up. 'Come on, you bludgers, 'Annah's here. You bidda git off yer arses!'

She doesn't sound like Elle. 'No, that's okay. I don't have very much.' I admit that the mountain of luggage behind me is somewhat undermining my credibility.

'Well, good onya! Perfect timing.' Nathan's tall and blond and square-jawed. I truly believe that the fallen are better-looking than the righteous. What else accounts for Australia's transported population being so much more handsome than England's home-grown one? Not that I'd start anything with him for all the tea in China. Housemates are off-limits. Almost always. 'Heart-starter?'

'Sorry?'

He's pointing to his beer can.

'Uh, sure.' Nobody refuses the kind hospitality of a new housemate, even when that hospitality borders on alcoholism.

'Good, get ya stahted for the Church. You'll come, won'tcha?'

Australians drink to go to church? 'Well, I'm not very rel–'

'Aw, come on, 'Annah. It's cracker!' Adam confirms, which, judging by the rapturous look on his face, means good. He does look rapturous, angelic almost, with cherub-fat cheeks, blond curls and a young boy's optimistic countenance. He could even have wings, though he's a bit too portly to make much progress off the ground.

'Well, why not?' I have the slightly uncomfortable feeling that I may have agreed to live with god-botherers, but I'm willing to suspend my judgement for the moment.

'Ya ready?'

'Maybe I should change.'

'Nah, you're fine,' advises Sarah between chugs of beer, 'though ya may want shoes ya don't care about.'

Why, do we trade them with fellow worshippers at some point?

Oddly, there's a huge group of what look like very normal (read: good-looking and fun) people milling in front of the Tube station as we arrive. 'We're just waiting for a few more,' Sarah tells me. This appears to be a siege in progress. Maybe these young travellers aren't welcome in English churches and collect en masse each Sunday to storm the cathedrals in an effort to exercise their freedom to worship. Though the motive is no doubt worthy, my mother will still be mad if I get arrested today. 'You've got seven quid onya, right?' Nathan asks as the church comes into view.

'Yep, I think so.'

'Good. You can buy a membership at the door.'

Pay at the door? Either this is a very orderly siege or I've completely misunderstood the situation. It must be one of those progressive places where the service is more theatrical. Wait till I tell Stacy that London's churches charge entrance fees. 'Will there be singing?' With the grey sky framing its stone façade and rising spires, the church seems very severe indeed. And it doesn't look big enough for all these people. Maybe that's why they have to charge admission.

'Aw, yeah, all the songs you know by heart.' Sarah over-estimates the rigour of my religious upbringing. I can hum along to a few fervent ditties, but sing them? I don't think so . . . ''Annah? Where're ya goin'?'

'Wha—?' My new housemates are staring at me from the sidewalk. 'Inside?' Based on their bent-double hysterics, I've done something wrong. 'What's so funny?!'

'Over here,' Sarah says, gesturing to the concert hall beside us. 'We're not going to church. We're going to *the* Church.'

The building is cavernous, with a stage at one end and a bar at the other. Sawdust covers the floor. It's the adult equivalent of Chuck E. Cheese,[18] and just to add to the ambience, they're playing one of my favourite songs. I'm not proud of my devotion to Bryan Adams, but there's something irresistible about a catchy tune earnestly sung. I feel the same way about tall, blond men offering me beer. Oh look, there's one now. 'Thanks, Nathan.'

'Cheers!' He necks his can without pause for breath. 'Ah. That's *good*! Whaddya think?'

'This is great!' Parties at noon that don't involve dinosaur-shaped birthday cakes or bickering relatives are rare on my social calendar. 'What is this place?'

You may have gathered that the Church has no religious affiliation whatsoever. It's London's party equivalent of The Beach, a secret passed on among backpackers and expats. Genius struck nearly thirty years ago when a couple Australians were looking for a place to drink on Sunday before the pubs were legally allowed to open. An enterprising publican hit upon the fine idea of charging membership to his 'club', hosted in his bar on Sunday. Despite its popularity, only about half a dozen people in all of London know where the place actually is, the rest being victims of beer amnesia. I can't help but feel that fate had a guiding hand in my choice of housemates. How lucky I was to answer that ad! These seem like good people, friendly and more than willing to include me in their lives. When Sarah drapes her arm across my shoulder to belt out Mr Adams's famous chorus about one particular summer in the 60s, I shout in her ear, 'I'm so happy you're

18. Imagine McDonald's in a shameful threesome with a games arcade and Disney World. The result is a cacophonous restaurant serving mediocre food to overstimulated children who split their time between groping mutant mice in baseball caps and pushing their friends off the rides.

letting me be your housemate!' Yes, that's a little bit of the beer talking.

'Me too. We knew you were awright right away. And Paul had big shoes to fill!'

That's right, I'm replacing a young South African spoken of in reverential tones for his ability to 'skull' the 'amber nectar' without getting a 'gutful of piss'. Alas, Paul's drinking prowess held no sway with Immigration, who kicked him out when they learned he'd been working here illegally. This was a sobering cautionary tale for me, considering that I'm working here on a somewhat informal basis myself. 'They turned him around at Heathrow,' Adam had told me. Not even the chance to collect his belongings. Like a disaster happening somewhere else, it makes you appreciate what you've got.

'Besides,' Sarah says now, 'it's nice to have a girl in the flat.' I'm relieved to know that she's not going to be territorial about Adam and Nathan. Not that a woman who looks like Sarah has much to feel threatened about.

'How long have you known the guys?'

'Just since we moved in. Er, eight months?'

It's going to take me some time to get used to my housemates constantly sounding like they're asking questions when they're not, but this verbal quirk is no stranger than Americans' habit of peppering our sentences with 'like'. I'm the first American the housemates have seen at close quarters. At least, I think I am. What Adam actually said was 'Too right, yer a seppo.' Seppo, septic, septic tank, rhymes with Yank. And I thought English-English was hard to get to grips with. I'm going to need a translator to live with these guys. But they seem to have as hard a time understanding me, because when I asked how they got their work permits they just looked at me blankly.

77

'Did you meet through friends?' What I really want to know is whether Sarah has any first-hand knowledge of her house-mates' bedroom techniques. This information is purely for informational purposes you understand. Well, mostly.

'Nah, we all answered Paul's advert.'

'Good. I mean, it's good that you all get along so well.'

''Nother beer, 'Annah?' Without waiting for a response, Nathan pulls a can from its plastic webbing, pops it open and hands it to me. I'm sure his mother is proud to have raised such a fine host.

'Thanks.' It's kind of hard to drink my beer, what with him dancing me back and forth. He's flirting, of that there's no doubt. I've been to gynaecologists who were less intimate. Unfortunately, my resolve not to start anything with a house-mate is being somewhat diluted by all the Fosters.

Boundaries, in fact, seem to be falling all around us. We've only been here an hour and already everyone is talking to each other, lubricated by free-flowing beer and music we know all the words to. Oddly, despite continual assaults, Sarah isn't paying any attention to the wide array of male talent on tap. Like Sputnik, being in Sarah's orbit might give me more gravitational pull.

'Hiya, this is Gianni and I'ma Paolo,' says Paolo to Sarah's chest. Really? Italians?

'Where do youa come from?' Gianni asks her.

'Gypsies.'

''Scusa me?'

'I come from gypsies.'

'You sounda Australian.'

'Australian gypsies, mate.'

They nod like they completely understand. Either they're the most gullible men I've ever met or they're equally adept liars called Keith and Jamie from London's East End.

'Where do you come from?' I ask Paolo/possibly Jamie.

'I'ma from Italy. You know Italy?'

I know of Italy. Geography has never been a strong suit. 'A little.'

'I come from Pizza.'

'Pizza?' Come on. He may as well say he's from Parmesan or spaghetti with clams.

'*Sì* . . . no, no. Pisa. Likea the tower.'

Oh, *Pisa*. This is one cultural divide too wide to bother crossing.

'Ladies and gentlemen,' the DJ announces in a booming voice as a man in a spandex leotard and cape climbs the stairs to the stage, 'please welcome today's first entertainer, Fartman.' The room goes nearly silent. The man taps the microphone a few times, then aims it under his cape. 'Pth, pth, pth, pth, pth.' He pauses, then squeezes out 'pth pth, pth pth'. It takes me just a second to recognize *The Blue Danube* waltz. And they say classical music isn't accessible to the masses.

'That's vile!' Sarah shouts. I notice, though, that the man holds her attention.

Adam at least has the good grace to look unimpressed by the man's gaseous prowess. He and Nathan are busy anyway, swapping drinking stories of monumental immaturity that, told with an Australian accent, have me in tears. The Irish aren't the only drinkers with the gift of the gab. Sadly, watching Adam, I realize that he's one of those men cursed with devastating teddy-bear qualities. While it's delightful to have him as an SBF (safe boy friend), I'm sure he's tired of being told he's 'too nice' by women. Still, I'm thrilled that he's my flatmate. Every girl should have at least one nice man in her life, to provide a corrective experience against the stinkers she generally dates.

Their beery banter is interrupted by the DJ intoning, 'Ladies and gentlemen, please welcome Miss Butter Cups!' A roar goes up from the crowd. Evidently Miss Cups is very good at whatever she does. The music starts and a nine-foot leggy blonde struts on to the stage wearing thigh-high rubber boots and little else. It figures. The boys get a stripper. We get a gassy man's rendition of show tunes. I'm sure this isn't what my mother meant when she said I should take in the theatre here. It's not that I don't appreciate her obvious talent, but I take issue with breast implants the same way I take issue with a mother who does her adult son's laundry. Both unrealistically raise men's expectations about the women they date.

'Watch this,' Sarah says as the stripper picks up her various bits of dental floss and leaves the stage to thunderous applause, 'they're gonna go white pointers.' A herd of girls are piling on to the stage.

'What?'

'They're gonna take their tops off.'

'Really?' This is *so* not a church.

'Too right. They might even get in the nuddy.'

'In the . . . ?'

'Naked,' she winks. 'I've seen it happen.'

'Are you going up there?'

'Nah, those girls are slappers.'

'What's a slapper?'

Unbeknownst to me, Gianni is listening in. 'A slapper isa sluta, no?' He looks pleased to be so bilingual.

The naked girl parade is the day's finale. It's 3.30. That's 3.30 p.m. Unbelievable as it sounds, this entire day has only lasted a little over four hours. It feels like midnight, and the room is starting to spin. ''Annah, are you all right?'

'Yeah, jus' a liddle tired.'

'We're gonna go on, do you wanna come along?'

'Nah, I'll tek the Tube.'

'Ah, guys, let's go to the Teck insteed.' Nathan drapes an arm over my shoulder. 'We can drop 'Annah off on the way. Come on, pumpkin, we'll getcha home.'

He's my knight in shining T-shirt! Yes, his mother ought to be very happy indeed.

7

My mother doesn't sound very happy at all. 'Mo-om,' (yes, I'm whining) 'I told you I was going to find a job here. I didn't just come for a vacation. I plan to live here.' How can talking to the woman who gave me life have the power to send me back to pre-pubescence?

'I just don't see why you couldn't find a job here at home,' she says. Again.

'Because I have the chance to live in London! Look, I need to call Stacy. I've gotta go now.'

She's obviously still taking my move as a personal insult.

'This is what I raised you for?' she'd said when I first told her. Like I was moving to Mexico to become a drug mule.

'You raised me to be independent.'

'When are you coming back?'

'I haven't left yet.'

'You're not going to stay for ever, are you?'

'Mom, who knows? Are you and Dad going to stay for ever in this house?' I was brought home from the hospital through its front door. The little pen lines charting my growth are still on the doorframe in my bedroom.

'Yes!'

'You can't know that.'

'Of course I can.'

'What if Dad gets his dream job in, I don't know, LA? Then you'd move, so you can't know what's going to happen in the future.'

'I don't like LA.'

'Well, wherever.'

'Why would your dad be looking for a job in LA?'

'I don't know, Mom, he just is!'

'Joe, is this true?'

Poor Dad had looked confused. Even with experience, Mom's random attacks aren't easy to deflect. How do you argue with a crazy woman?

'What if your sister has a baby?'

'Mom, it's a six-hour flight. Pregnancies last nine months. There'll be some warning.'

'What if I have a stroke?'

'Once again, Mom, it's a six-hour flight . . .'

Despite my mother's disapproval, I *am* starting a new job here. And striking the right balance in one's clothing choices is critical. Like the South Beach Diet, it won't work if the combination is wrong. The outfit for my first day has to say I'm super-efficient, bright and capable yet fun, stylish and not afraid of a bottle of wine or two at happy hour. Stacy says tweed is out.

'Even in pink?' My new Chanelesque skirt suit gives me a killer silhouette.

'Not on the first day. You want understated chic. What was everyone else wearing?'

'I have no idea. The only person I saw when I interviewed was Felicity.'

'What'd she look like?'

'She's gorgeous. She's Maltese –'

'Like the falcon.'

'Exactly. Very exotic, shiny dark hair, olive skin, and great curves.' In a bar, I'd hate her on sigh

'What was she wearing?'

'A great suit.'

'Pants?'

I hope so. 'Yep.'

'Designer?'

'I don't know.' Identifying Donna Karan or Kate Spade from across the street is a gift that I take pride in, but being less familiar with English labels, I'm a magician without her wand here. I don't label-spot for snob value, but for purely practical reasons. If a woman has something that I love and I know where she got it, then I can have it too. And though I'm not above asking, it's amazing how jealously some women guard their fashion secrets.

'But not tweed, right?'

'You're right. I need to go shopping again.'

'No, you don't. Let's take this step by step. Describe everything in your wardrobe.'

'The new stuff?'

'Everything. Hang on, let me get a cup of coffee.'

This is why I love Stacy. It's a rare person who'll suffer all of your fashion, beauty and romance crises twenty-four hours a day, and still not screen your calls. Besides, she's being incredibly supportive about my staying here, which I appreciate now that I know she really doesn't want me to. I underestimated her.

trayed her, if only in my thoughts. That's possibly s, because she didn't even get the chance to defend re rules in law against accusation *in absentia*. Not I suspect we've all done it, whether in big

*kno*ake some comfort in the safety of numbers, me feel like an unworthy friend.

ob I know nothing about, in a city I woman I know nothing about, my composure is admirable this morning. Except for the sheen on my lip you'd never know I was about to throw up.

'Welcome, Hannah!' Mark looks super-sexy. What are the chances that he happens to be here, at the elevator, at the exact second I arrive? Talk about fate. Unless he's been waiting for me, because it's my first day, because he can't wait to see me . . .

'Good morning, Mark.' Listen to me. You'd think we were just business acquaintances.

'Here, let me show you to your desk.'

He's just offered to accompany me twelve feet. This has to be a sign, right?

'Felicity, Hannah's here. Well, I'll leave you to it.' His wink threatens to dislodge my breakfast. Definitely a sign.

'Good morning, Hannah.'

'Hi, Felicity!' She's wearing the most superb suit, navy blue with yellow pinstripes and mustard-yellow snakeskin heels. I'm very tempted to ask her where she got them, but we should probably bond first.

'Would you like a cup of tea?'

'Uh, coffee, if you have it.'

'Come, I'll show you where the kitchen is.' Our office is in a converted bank, with big brass chandeliers hanging from two-storey-high ceilings and tall windows all along the front of the building. The conversion was not, however, sympathetic to the building's architectural integrity. Royal-blue partitions dissect the giant room into cubicles. In a sci-fi film there'd be white-coated giants hovering over us with clipboards to document our oblivious progress through the maze.

Felicity and I are the only ones in suits. Everyone else is wearing trendy urban footwear, jeans and funky T-shirt/blazer combos. They all look incredibly cool. They all look incredibly cooler than me. I wonder how many of my skirts are return-able given that a) right now I'm Felicity's mini-me and b) it is an established fact that only Uma Thurman can get away with a skirt and sneakers. That ensemble makes the rest of us look like we save tin foil and think our cats are people.

'This is my mug.' It's a blue glazed cup with a fish on it. Interesting crockery statement. 'And I like my tea strong, white with no sugar.'

'Okay. I like my coffee strong too, with milk and two sugars.'

'That's nice, though irrelevant.'

'I thought we were sharing.'

'I'm telling you how to make my tea. I drink it when I first get in, which is eight-thirty by the way, so you'll have to be here by then in future, and at eleven and three. Don't be late. Any questions?'

I guess telling me where you got your shoes is out of the question.

'Ah, Sam, there you are,' she says like she's finally found him at the end of an exasperating search. He looks disappointed to have been noticed. 'This is Hannah. Hannah, Sam.'

'Hi, Sam, nice to mee—'

'She needs her email account set up. And her building pass. Any more questions?'

Given that Sam now has his back to her, wedging in beside me to concentrate on his coffee, I assume her question is for me. 'Uh, when do you have lunch?'

'I don't eat lunch.'

'Ever?' What normal woman doesn't eat lunch?

'No.'

I swear Sam just muttered, 'Feeds on her hostility.'

'Er, when do I have lunch?'

'Well, whenever you want. I certainly wouldn't dictate when you should eat. You can find your way back to your desk, right?'

'Sure, yes. Sure,' I say to her retreating back.

'Come on,' Sam grins, 'I'll walk you back and set up your email.'

'She wasn't very friendly to you. What'd you do to her?' He looks familiar. Maybe it's his curly hair, *à la* Adrian Grenier.[19]

'She doesn't need to be. I'm the office bitch.'

'Is that your official title?'

'I've got business cards to prove it. You American?'

'Yep. You too?'

'Uh-huh. Long live the colonial empire.'

So my boss is either a slave driver trying to act laid back or a daisy-sniffer with an anal-retentive streak. Either way, my main job appears to be keeping her sufficiently caffeinated. I'm also supposed to make sure nobody gets to her without her say-so. I get the sense I'm to tackle anyone who slips past, which may be why everyone wears comfortable shoes. I also make all her travel arrangements. And book her client dinners. And drinks. The power is intoxicating . . .

I'm bored out of my skull. The phone has rung twice. I can't understand what they're saying because of their accent, and I made one guy spell his last name. S-m-i-t-h. I've familiarized myself with everything on, in and under my desk. I've written a long email to Stacy describing how sweet Mark is and Felicity isn't. My desk is near the ladies room, so I'm running a tally of how many times it's being used and what direction the women are coming from (two corridors meet at my desk).

19. 'Who?' you may reasonably ask if you are not, like me, obsessed with the cable entertainment channels. Anne Hathaway's boyfriend in *The Devil Wears Prada*.

Pouring hot water on a teabag has been the highlight of my morning.

'Um, Felicity?'

She's flipping through a folder that's stuffed with torn-out pages from magazines. I'd give my eyeteeth to do that.

'How's everything? Settling in?'

'Yes, thanks.' I'm going to fall asleep if I get any more settled. 'I was just wondering, is there anything I can do, between phone calls?'

'Have you been on the Internet?'

'No!' Already she thinks I'm a slacker.

'Why don't you do that? I'm sure you've got a lot to take care of, having just moved over.'

'Uh, okay.' What kind of boss encourages you to goof off? She can't be paying me this kind of money just to answer her phone. A monkey could do this. In fact, the monkey would get bored and quit.

In the corridor, a tiny woman is rushing by with a tray full of mugs. Clip-clop, clip-clop, 'Shit, fuck!'

It's a slingback malfunction, surely caused by the misguided notion to wear them with pantyhose.[20] It's like watching a Jenga tower as you pull out one of the blocks. You hope it's not going to topple but there's a sick inevitability about it. The cups splash and shatter across the floor. Felicity rolls her eyes. 'Go and help her.'

'Are you okay?' I say to this diminutive colleague attempting to pick up her dignity from the office floor.

20. Face it, there's just no way to say the word 'panty' without embarrassment. The fact that it is combined with 'hose', thereby increasing the chances that your father will say it to you in a sentence, only heightens the mortification. I'm with the English on this one; 'tights' is much better.

88

'Fuck me,' she says, ''e's gonna make me pay for this.'

'Who?' It's hard to take her swearing seriously when her Irish accent makes her sound like a foul-mouthed leprechaun.

'Mark. That's, like, the third bloody tray this month.'

Seriously? I'm no Olympic champion when it comes to hand-eye co-ordination but that's clumsy even in my book.

'I'm Shivawn, his secretary. You're Hannah, right? I heard you were starting today.'

'Yep, nice to meet you.'

'I've gotta make another batch now. Fancy goin' for a drink at lunchtime?'

'Sure!' She can't mean a drink-drink, can she?

At 12.58, Mark appears at my desk. 'Coming for a drink?'

How I've fantasized about those words. Granted, my fantasy doesn't involve half a dozen co-workers, but it's something. And his look is definitely lingering. 'Love to!' This is possibly the best decision I've ever made.

There's a pub around the corner (though there seems to be a pub around every corner).

'I'll get us drinks.' Mark clearly enjoys playing host. 'What's everybody having?'

'Pint of Stella.'

'Boddingtons, please.'

'Glass of Chardonnay.'

'Me too.'

'Make it three.'

'Hannah?'

'Er, make it four.'

'I'll get a bottle.'

Where are the drinks that lubricate normal American business culture, the Diet Coke, the iced tea? *Drinking* at lunchtime? Our fathers might have sipped their lunches, but this isn't 1972.

And yet here we are. There's not even a hint of pinch-faced disapproval or winking titillation at flouting the rules. These *are* the rules. I can't wait to email Stacy with an update.

Clearly this pub ritual is a) daily and b) a microcosm of wider office dynamics. This could be the most informative glass of Chardonnay I've ever drunk.

'Hey, Mark, I'll get some crisps for the table. What kind . . . ?'

'By the way, Mark, I managed to source that wine for the Asprey launch. Thanks, I thought it was impossible too . . .'

'So after the hundredth time that she changes her mind, Mark finally says, "Sweetheart, if you keep worrying, you're going to need more Botox by dinnertime." Remember that, Mark? I thought she was going to kill you, but she just laughed.'

Look at him. He's the master of all he surveys, organizing the first round and picking up the tab with casual benevolence. He laughs, he jokes, he somehow gives his undivided attention to everyone at the table. You just know that when he arrives at a party, the hosts have to resist the urge to run round the living room whooping, 'Mark's here, Mark's here, Mark's here!' He's a charismatic leader, a Dalai Lama for the party-planning world. I'm incredibly proud that he's practically my boyfriend. I don't usually date guys this assured, this grown-up. This *sexy*.

'Tell me, Siobhan,' he says, 'what we all want to know. How was your date with the barrister?'

'Ugh, Mark. Remind me to add the legal profession to my list of the undateable.'

I'm trying not to be jealous as Mark trains his gorgeous gaze upon his secretary. I'd feel better if she wasn't so tiny, with that sweet pointy face and those sparkling green eyes. I've often wished to be petite, but I'm five foot eight, so it's never going to be a fitting adjective. Instead I get called sturdy. I'm sure it's meant as a compliment, but it conjures up visions of meaty-armed women in housecoats.

'What went wrong?'

'Jaysus,' says the blasphemous elf, 'what went right? The guy shows up half an hour early, *half an hour*, insisting I let him in because it's raining. Like he's made of sugar. Naturally, the timing's perfect. I've just put bleach on my lip, my hair's wet and I've got loo roll stuffed between my toes. So I beg my neighbour to let him in so he doesn't see me. My neighbour, of course, pisses himself when *he* sees me, making the chances of getting off with him in the future nil. Shame too, because he's fit . . .'

'So, the date?'

'Ah, yes. Cipriani's mysteriously lost the reservation – this is eight o'clock on a Saturday, mind you. They're looking at us like we just weed on their floor, my date is trying to bully or buy his way into a table, and all I can think is, I can't believe I bleached my lip for this. By the time we end up at a dodgy Chinese buffet, I'm so hungry I'm considering eating their moo shu cat. It gets worse from there. I would have climbed out the ladies window, but the restaurant was such a dive there *wasn't* a window in there. I checked.'

'You're joking.'

'If only.'

Felicity has been following the conversation with the intensity of a KGB agent sent to keep an eye on things. I wonder why she's here at all, given that she claimed never to eat lunch. She certainly didn't join us so she could talk to me; she hasn't said a word. That's no way to behave towards your new hire on her first day. I think she knows about me and Mark. Did she hire me because she had to? Or did she want to hire me

91

and find out later that she's got something to resent me for? 'Felicity, can I get you something else to drink?' Maybe she's nicer when she's drunk.

'No, thank you. Actually, I have to get back. Excuse me, everyone.'

I'm definitely not paranoid. She hates me. This isn't doing my new career any favours.

'Should I go too?' I ask Sam, who's wearing the expression of a man recalling a very funny joke. He's familiar to me, especially that grin, though that could be because he looks like everyone's neighbour: the guy who'll cheerfully help dig your car out of the snow or come over to kill a spider threatening your mental stability.

'Nah, you may as well stay. Mark's the boss after all.'

'I don't think Felicity likes me.'

'Don't take it personally. She doesn't like anyone. Except herself.'

'You sound pretty bitter. How come you're working here if you hate it so much?'

'Oh, I don't hate it. I don't hate anything really. That's an awfully strong word. Besides, it keeps us in drinks at lunchtime. Another bottle?'

I think I'm going to love this job.

It's only when we stand up to leave three rounds later that I realize there's no lunch in our lunchtime. So strictly speaking, Felicity isn't a liar. 'Come on.' Siobhan grasps my arm as we walk blinking back into the light. 'We can get a sandwich at Pret.'

I'm grateful for her guidance. Technically, I only drank a few glasses of wine, as long as fishbowls are technically glasses.

'So how's your first day?'

Given that I just drank away half of it, it hasn't been bad. Except that my boss doesn't speak to me or let me *do* anything . . . 'Felicity doesn't trust me to arrange the paperclips. Helping you mop up tea was the biggest challenge of my day.'

'At least you get to go to the parties. Be glad you're working for her. I never get to go.'

'Well, I suppose if I plan them one day, then I'll get to go.'

'What?! You get to go to *all* the parties she plans. She always takes her assistant. That's so she has someone to pin all the blame on.'

'Really? She didn't mention anything about it.'

'Well, your predecessors all got to go. And you get your choice of the clothes.'

'What clothes?'

'Feckin' hell, didn't anyone show you around?'

'Felicity showed me where the kitchen was.'

'Who cares about the kitchen? Come with me. You've got to see this.'

She unlocks what I assumed was a supply closet. We've stepped through the back of the wardrobe into a magical place, even better than Narnia! The walls are lined with shelves and rails, which are stuffed with the most gorgeous clothes I've ever seen. 'What is this?'

'The designers send them to us for our clients. It's good PR if they're snapped wearing them at the parties. Of course, most of the stuff never gets sent back, so Felicity uses this as her own private dressing room. And she lets the other planners do the same thing.'

'Oh my god, this is so worth the boredom!'

'Yeah, you don't know how bloody lucky you are. I'm run off my feet with yer man, and I *never* get to go to the parties.'

My man? She knows. I was right. That's why Felicity is being so weird. I'm torn between dread and a strange sense of pride that my boyfriend – I think I can call him that under the circumstances – has already declared his love for me to his nearest and dearest. Or at least to his secretary.

'Do me a favour, Siobhan. Keep that to yourself, okay?'

'Sure, whatever.'

Obviously I need to talk to Felicity. Now that I've had a few days to 'settle in' (and sober up – I've gently declined Siobhan's daily liquid lunch invitations), it's clear that my first day was indeed an accurate reflection of my career path at M&G. By which I mean that in six months I'll be perfectly trained to sit at a desk and do nothing. I deserve the chance to prove myself. More importantly, I deserve the chance to wear the clothes in that closet! It shouldn't matter how I got the job, the important thing is that I'm going to be an excellent party planner some day. I just need to let her know clearly what I expect from this job, and what she can expect from me. Simple as that. I'll be eloquent and confident. We'll have more of a chat, really. She'll assure me that she has big plans for my career and that she liked me from the moment we met. She'll confess that we even wear the same size, a proud twelve, which means we can share each other's clothes and be best friends, except at the sample sales, where it's every woman for herself. Then she'll tell me to take the rest of the day off and give me her manicure appointment at the best place in town.

That's how it *should* go. In real life, I've just stormed into her office in time to hear her say 'I've got this itching . . .' This is not a good start. I can't back out of the room now. She's seen me. Worse, she knows I know about her itching.

'Yes, Friday at one is fine. What *is* it, Hannah?'

From her tone, you'd think I was responsible for her urinary complaint. 'Felicity, I'd like to talk to you.' That sets the tone straight. Pure professionalism.

'Yes?'

'I don't feel that you're using me to my full potential.'

'And?'

'And, uh, well, I'd like you to.' This would sound more convincing if my heart wasn't thumping on my voice box, strangling my words into a squeak.

'I don't think so.'

'You don't?'

'No.'

How do I recover from a flat-out 'no'? Beg? Accuse? Cry? . . . Pretend I didn't hear her and leave the room? . . . 'May I ask why?' I can't believe how cool I'm being. Get me, Miss Fancy-pants Grown-up.

. . . 'I'm not certain about your abilities.'

'But you hired me!'

'There were extenuating circumstances involved . . . and I'm sorry, but I'm not sure how long you'll be around.'

Ah. Extenuating circumstances named Mark. So my boss thinks I'm a fly-by-night whore who won't last longer than the milk in the kitchen refrigerator. This isn't a total disaster. 'But you've seen my résumé. I can do this job. I can do it well.'

I should end it there, case made, and let her realize my value. Don't say anything, don't say anything. She's not saying anything. She's just staring at me . . . Still staring. 'Please give me a chance? I promise I'll impress you if you give me the chance. Please?'

'There's a lot of confidential information here. I can't be expected to trust just anyone.'

Like I'm some party-planning spy intent on committing corporate espionage. 'There must be something I can do to help you out. Anything.' Come on, lady, this is my unsluttiest, most competent smile.

95

'Fine.' Her deep sigh says she's made better decisions in her life. 'Go get the Hermione Withers and Chastity Bates files. Learn them. They're important clients and their events are live.'

I'm going to be a party planner! The long file boxes are heavy in my hands, much heavier than a few boxes of paper should be. That's because they're metaphysically taking on the weight of this momentous event, the day that I launch my spectacular new career. They say, 'These events mark the start of a whole new life for you, new beginnings, new adventures.' They're pregnant with the importance of the task ahead, carrying my entire future in their corrugated confines . . . Oh! . . . There're ashtrays and napkin rings in here.

Nevertheless, it's still a big moment.

'Hey, do you want to grab some lunch?'

'Hi, Sam.' I enjoy sitting here, a modern-day Constantinople, at the crossroads of the great Lavatory Route. 'Um, no thanks. I'd like to get through these files.'

'What've you got there?'

'They're party folders!' I can still hardly believe it myself.

'Well. It looks like you're on your way, then. Do you want me to pick something up for you?'

'Thanks, yeah, if you could. Some soup, please. Creamy. And some bread. With butter.'

'Not watching your weight?'

'That's not polite to ask a lady.'

'I don't usually have to ask. Everyone around here is on a diet. Glad you're normal.'

Hah! He obviously doesn't know me yet. '*They* probably have access to the closet.' They need to eat dust to squeeze into the sample sizes. I'm not sacrificing the buttery joys in life till I get in there.

'Ah, yes, the closet. Is that your Holy Grail too?'

'Of course. Just imagine getting access to those clothes. And shoes.'

'Sorry, as a straight man, I'm afraid I just can't appreciate the allure.'

And once again, how thankful I am to be a woman.

My soup is long cold when Henry, the accountant (in very unaccountant-like orange and brown suede sneakers), materializes. 'All right?'

Has he heard about my talk with Felicity? So much for British discretion. 'Fine, thanks.'

'Staying late?'

A glance at the Piaget watch my parents got me for graduation tells me it's 7.30. Being a steadfast clock-watcher, and someone who is happiest feeding at two-hour intervals, this is unprecedented. The entire afternoon flew by while I've been getting to grips with two of London's It girls. Based on the clippings, they're singlehandedly keeping several tabloids in business.

'Just going through some files.'

Eventually he says, 'Plans tonight?'

'Uh-uh.'

. . .

'Aren't you tired?'

'Henry, do you want me to leave?'

'It's just that I have to lock up, and my girlfriend and I have tickets to the theatre tonight.'

'What time?'

'Seven-thirty.'

'Why didn't you say something?'

'I did!'

Poor guy, he has no way to know that jingling his keys like

an OCD patient cannot speed my progress. In heels this high, I only operate in first gear. 'Can you make the second act?'

'Dunno,' he murmurs over his shoulder as he shrugs into his coat. 'See you tomorrow.'

'See you. I hope your girlfriend's not going to be mad.'

'Thanks.'

His girlfriend is definitely going to be mad.

8

'Sorry I'm late. Are you mad?' I say, peeling off my coat.

'Nah,' says Siobhan, 'I just got here myself. All right?'

'Yes, fine.' Why does everyone keep asking me that? Maybe I should start using under-eye concealer. 'Why does everyone keep asking me that?'

'Sorry, it's just being polite.'

So it's another figure of speech they use, like I found out 'yer man' is. Apparently that doesn't mean my man, it means some token random stranger. It's the Irish equivalent of what's-his-name. So it's a good thing I didn't blurt out anything stupid about Mark when Siobhan said it in the office the other day.

I'm really taking to Siobhan. Not only did she show me the magic closet, she has invited me here, to speed-date with her. Some people may view this as an act of Gen Y[21] desperation, but I prefer to think of it as a free-market sexual economy for the twenty-first century. Besides, why shouldn't I? Keeping up the appearance of singledom has proven easier than I'd anticipated. Mark is the epitome of professionalism . . . Such a shame, considering the desk-clearing fantasies I've had all week. Even so, I am a little ambivalent about being here tonight. It's not like we're exclusive. We haven't had 'the talk' or anything, but there's no denying the connection and I'd

21. Not to be outdone by Generation Xers, those of us born in the last twenty-five years of the twentieth century have our own generational tag. We are the iPhone-Facebook-file-sharing generation.

hate to think he'd be jealous. Okay, that's a lie. I'd love to think he'd be jealous. I just don't want him to find out and dump me. The old Hannah would have put her life on hold waiting for him to declare his intentions. Actually, the old Hannah would've cornered him in the kitchen by now and been led away by security. The new Hannah, the one who moved half-way round the world to seek her fame and fortune, is an altogether different animal. She's calm, cool and collected. And she's a *free agent*. So I told Siobhan that I'd go, but I asked her to keep it quiet in the office. Just in case the old Hannah needs a fall-back plan.

She swears these nights are restricted to professional twenty- and thirty-somethings who aren't a) indigent, b) married or c) pervy, ugly or boring (not really, but wouldn't that be an unbeatable business model?).

The pub is packed with girls in their twenties who look like they meant to go dancing but accidentally walked in here. Siobhan says most people come to these things straight from work. If that's true, then I can faithfully report that British women dress like hookers in the office. Their fashion sense is strangely immune to things like the season, which explains why little blue toes are poking out from strappy sandals on half the women in the room. We Americans obviously aren't suffering enough for fashion. I'm now recalling with mortification the entire winter season that I wore snow boots with my business suits to the office. My face burns at the very thought. Given fashion statements like these, is it really such a surprise that I'm single?

This creeping inferiority complex isn't just because I'm wearing socks tonight. The fact is I'm intimidated by British women's nipples. They're everywhere, which is very discon-certing for an American. Look at 99 per cent of the bras in

Victoria's Secret.[22] They are modestly reinforced against spontaneous nipple erections. Even in that bastion of sexual enticement, they sell sticky breast 'petals' as a second line of defence. This just proves that we did indeed descend from Puritan stock. I bet when the Mayflower sailed the English women onshore cheered as they shimmied out of their under-things. I'm steadfastly in the nipple-free camp on this one, which I fear puts me at a disadvantage among Great Britain's perky bosoms.

'Here you go, ladies.' A young woman is smugly handing out scorecards with her ostentatiously engaged left hand. Nice sales technique. 'Find seats, please.'

Siobhan makes a run for a little table near the front. When I plunk down opposite, she whispers, 'Not here. Find your own table.'

'Fine, suit yourself.'

'I mean we're meant to sit on one side and the boys rotate through each table. They get three minutes.'

So it's a very fast recruitment day with drinks. Hello, my name is . . .

My first 'date' looks very slick. By this I mean he literally has a sheen: on his shoes, his hair . . . his face. 'So,' he says when we've introduced ourselves, 'I'm twenty-six, I own my flat in Clapham, I've been working at Morgan for three years on their equity trading desk; haven't left because they pay me a wodge of money, I graduated with a first from Cambridge, studied Economics at LSE, my parents live in Wentworth, we have a cottage in Devon, I travel long-haul at least twice a year, my favourite countries are South Africa and China, I've been

22. American women's first choice for underwear; picture M&S selling its smalls in a boudoir replete with pot pourri, padded hangers and French love songs.

to five of the seven continents, speak three languages, French and Italian are the other two, I lived in Florence during my gap year, I like film, theatre and the symphony, I like to go clubbing, play rugby, scuba dive, I follow Champions League football, cricket and tennis internationally, and drive a five-series Merc.' He takes a moment to breathe. 'I like Thai food, Indian, Italian, Spanish, Vietnamese and Ethiopian. I hate crêpes and Belgian beer. I only read spy novels and biographies, and prefer English films to American ones. What do you think?' The whistle blows.

I think I'm completely unprepared for this, considering that I don't know what Clapham, Morgan, equity trading, wodge, a first, LSE, Wentworth, Devon, long-haul, gap year or Champions League are supposed to tell me about this guy. And that's in three minutes. 'Uh, I think that's interesting?' I'm playing the odds that I'm right.

'Good. I'd like to see you again. What did you say your name was?'

'Hannah.'

'Jerry.'

Evidently mute incomprehension is a turn-on for the self-absorbed. Nice to meet you, Hard Sell.

If this is the competition, then Mark has nothing to worry about. I wonder if he is worried. I'd love to think he's thinking about me (it's only fair considering the amount of brain power I've used up on him this last week). Do men think about women as much as we think about them? I mean with clothes *on*. Or is it true that when you ask them what they're thinking their minds are literally blank except for the occasional longing for nachos or sports statistic skittering across?

Hard Sell hasn't exactly set the bar high, but even if he had, the guy sitting opposite me would clear it easily. Imagine the lead singer from a very cool band playing at a big outdoor festival. Not technically good-looking (more rough and rumpled than pretty boy), but with the stage presence to nonchalantly hold an audience in thrall.

'Why are you here?' he wants to know.

'My friend Siobhan brought me.'

'I meant in the broader sense. You're American, right?'

'Right. I decided to move over when I was made redundant at home.'

'Adventurous. I like that. What else are you adventurous about?'

'Oh, I'm up for anything!' This isn't true, of course, but I'm not about to mention my limitations. Caveat emptor.

'Really?'

'Sure. I mean, what's the point of living if you're not having fun?'

'Exactly my philosophy . . .'

He seems to like the fact that I'm American. (I did wonder if the American-in-London thing might give me an exotic edge over these home-grown chippies, but I wasn't sure how my nationality would play in Europe. To read the papers, you'd think they've been burning US flags all over the Champs Elysées.) And he's also nice, good-looking and employed. I've frequently settled for one and a half out of three, so this is a definite step forward.

The smug fiancée blows her whistle.

'Maybe I'll see you later.'

'Great!' If this is speed-dating, I don't know why everyone doesn't do it.

Siobhan is giddy with success. She ticked six guys as matches, including Hard Sell. Anyone who tries that hard to impress in a bar, she reasoned, might try that hard in bed. Why didn't I think of that? 'Come on, Hannah, let's go talk to that one – you said he had potential.'

'I can't go over there now. Look at all those girls.' Look at all those cute girls with their nipples pointing straight at him.

'Get in there, lass, or you don't stand a chance.' She clearly doesn't share my fear of rejection. She's literally elbowing girls out of our way. This has bad ending written all over it.

'Hey, hi, American girl.'

He really is cute. Yes, he does have potential. The others are smiling warmly. We hate each other, but smart girls don't bare their claws in front of a guy they like unless they're very sure they've got him. And given that we all met Potential about seven minutes ago, no one is that confident. Far from being a cruelty-free zone, the barbs will simply fly under his radar. The combatants waste no time.

'You're American?' She's got poker-straight blonde hair and sparkly powder on her cheekbones. 'I have an aunt who lives in New Mexico. You certainly have a different sense of style over there. She sends the most god-awful clothes to me for Christmas.' I'm sure the revulsion in her expression isn't meant for her beloved aunt. Come on, Hannah, shake it off, it's just a flesh wound . . .

'Nobody's forcing your aunt to buy shite clothes,' Siobhan reasons. 'It sounds like she thinks they suit you.'

The others laugh. Like Komodo dragons, they're not above eating their own kind.

Sparkle Face feels compelled to fight on. 'What brings you to London?'

'I guess I'm looking for a new life.'

'What was wrong with your old one?' interjects a stick insect dressed like Baby Spice. 'Was it sad?'

Ouch. That might need stitches. Possible answers include

a) it was boring, b) nothing or c) I've slept with all the eligible men in the tri-State[23] area. The first answer makes me look pathetic, the second stupid and the third easy. Hello, rock? Hard place? Don't squeeze too much, please.

'I guess I outgrew it.'

Potential chuckles. Stick Insect opens her mouth, remembers her manners and closes it. Doctor, the patient has made an unexpected recovery.

There's a message from Stacy on the answering machine when I get back to the apartment. 'Hey, it's me. Did you ever get the Rimmel stuff?' I'm becoming her illicit make-up connection, sending unmarked packages of British products home. 'It's Bonus Time at Clinique again, so tell me if you want the free gift and I can buy two moisturizers. You really should use it, you know, that crap you use is going to catch up one day. How was your day? Oh my god, my boss is definitely having an affair with Kara, can you believe it? He pretty much admitted it to Jeff.' I don't have any idea who Jeff is. Or Kara. It's nearly impossible to follow Stacy's conversations at times because she assumes you know everyone in the world she could possibly be talking about. Listening to her is best approached like squinting. You get the gist from the blurry outline of the conversation, without any confusing detail to distract. 'I really wanted to give him the benefit of the doubt but he is, in fact, a complete asshole. And his wife's so nice too. I'm calling to tell you that I think I am going to go out with Tye. I know, he's not much to look at, but I'm getting older now.' We're the same age, not exactly ancient. 'And I need to start thinking about my future. So I'm going to say yes the next time he asks. Shame you're not

23. Refers to the area within a couple-hour commute to NYC. The inhabitants of each town wholeheartedly believe that theirs is the social apex of the region and the others are just lucky to be included.

here, or we could double-date. You thought he was nice, right? And not too ugly?'

Obviously Stacy views the answering machine as a quieter but perfectly valid call recipient.

Shit. Shit, shit, shit. I forgot to tell Felicity about my doctor's appointment. It wouldn't be so bad if I was normally on time, but punctuality is becoming a bit of an issue. Despite the best of intentions, somewhere between towelling off and reaching the Tube platform I lose at least fifteen minutes. It's safe to say my boss and I aren't getting off to the best start.

I'm not sick, by the way. In my continuing education about London's rules and regulations I've learned that you don't simply go to a doctor here when you're under the weather. You make an appointment to register with him when you're well to reserve your place in his waiting room for when you do eventually come down with the flu. So even in illness the English like to queue.

On the plus side, at least the train's not crowded now that it's past rush hour. There are maybe twenty people in the carriage with me. Despite this, it is completely silent. People don't talk on public transport if they can help it. If they must communicate (for instance if a companion's hair catches fire), they'll only do so in a church-like murmur. All foreign residents probably make the mistake of speaking normally once, until the full weight of indigenous condemnation bears upon them and they are silenced. If you want to pick out the tourists, just listen for conversation on a train.

I know the English aren't silent out of polite regard for their travelling companions' privacy, because reading is a team sport underground. On any given morning, half the passengers hold the books, magazines and papers while the other half crane their necks to read them. This is no stealthy over-the-shoulder reading either. They practically rest their chins on their neighbour's lapel. Every morning I'm treated to the coffee breath of the commuter next to me. She's apparently as enthralled with *InStyle*'s spring fashion tips as I am. When I try to shield the article, she just climbs further into my lap to read it. If she tires of reading other people's magazines, she'll think nothing of looking everyone up and down, eventually settling her eyes on some body part or accessory, perhaps as an alternative to taking a nap. I'm sure Londoners don't mean anything by staring so obviously; it's a national habit, like our impulse to introduce at least one sports analogy into every conversation.

I like knowing I can assess everyone's wardrobe without worrying about giving offence here, particularly since London has the most stylish women in the world, in the truest sense of the definition. I realize this is a controversial statement, especially to women in New York, but hear me out. London's glamour pusses aren't all clad in designer labels (it's easy to be rich and stylish), and they don't have that French *je ne sais quoi*. Instead, women here mainline fashion magazines. As a result, the average woman might sport one of at least a dozen distinct trends, from skinny jeans/stripy jacket to bubble skirt/shoe boots, and everything in between. The amazing thing is that most women do. Trendy women aren't the exception here. They are the rule. Case in point: even in workwear, the women manage to stand out. Though bundled up in their winter coats, those coats are trendy, if disappointingly unimaginative in colour. In fact, there's not a bright coat in the carriage. Grey. Black. Blue. Tan. Penis. Blue. Camel . . .

Penis?

No, I'm not seeing things. Yes, the man sitting diagonally

to me has his dick in his hand. He's holding a newspaper with the other, the *Telegraph*, I think. Unbelievable. Who does this? On a train? At 10 a.m. on a Tuesday? He's behaving as if he's simply holding his morning cuppa. He must be mentally ill. Maybe he doesn't even realize he's done it . . . Great, now I've been staring at the offending organ for at least a minute. People probably think *I'm* a pervert. But all seems perfectly normal. Come on, it's not possible that nobody else sees this. We're sitting less than five feet from each other. Everybody stares as a matter of course. I *know* people must have noticed.

Ah-ha. I see you, sir. A man two seats away just glanced up, stared straight at the guy and looked back down at his neighbour's paper. Then another, and another. Everyone on the train sees the flasher, they're just ignoring him. I bet he does this every day. Why wouldn't he, if nobody stops him? I should say something. What if there are kids on the train? They shouldn't be subjected to this. None of us should, for that matter. It's outrageous that he's getting away with this. So say something. Why don't I say something? Because I'm a chicken. And I know the rules . . . But wait, that's the old Hannah. I'm no longer the woman who will be intimidated by a pervert. I'm going to tell him exactly what I think of him. 'Um, excuse me,' I whisper.

He concentrates harder on his article.

God, I hope he's not deaf. This is going to be really embarrassing if I have to mime my outrage.

'Excuse me,' I say louder. 'Uh, that's not very nice. Do you mind putting, ah, yourself away?' I don't mean to be so harsh but he must be told in no uncertain terms.

At least he's tucking himself back in his pants. He's still sitting in his seat, by the way; this guy has balls . . . as we've just witnessed. Now everyone is staring at me like I'm the one with my bits out on the train. I'm not exactly expecting high-fives, or hooked pinky fingers or whatever they do here as a congratulatory gesture, but you'd think there'd be *some* acknowledgement that I've briefly made the world a better place. They look embarrassed. Worse, they look embarrassed for me. The English clearly have a misplaced sense of propriety. It seems they'd rather cut off their own arms than call attention to themselves. It's my mother's worst fear realized. In the early dawn, in Hartford Connecticut, she awakens with a shiver without knowing why.

Now I officially hate the commute.

'Felicity I'm so sorry I'm late I forgot to tell you about my doctor's appointment but I'll stay late and make up the time I promise.' Maybe speaking without pauses will keep her from unleashing the fury that's playing across her face.

'Hannah.'

I knew it wouldn't work. 'Yes?'

'What time is it?'

'Eleven o'clock.'

'And what time are you contractually obliged to be here?'

'Eight-thirty.'

'In what dimension is this eight-thirty?'

'I said I'm sorry, Felicity. I really did forget to tell you.'

'I've had to ask Siobhan to make my tea this morning.'

Mental note: buy lunch for Siobhan today. 'I'm really sorry.'

'I was going to ask you to help me at the party on Friday –'

'Ohmygod, thank you, yes, I'd love to –'

'But I couldn't wait around wondering if you planned to show up, so I asked Anne instead.'

'Oh. Oh, yes, well, okay, of course. I understand.'

'Hannah?'

'Yes?'

'My tea?'

'Okay.' At this rate I'm never going to get in that closet.

Mark has definitely followed me into the kitchen. He can't be this interested in my brewing techniques. Granted, the receptionist just unlocked the forbidden for-clients-only cookie cupboard and freed a packet of Jammie Dodgers, and that kind of news spreads like wildfire through the office. And he's also making tea (as are Sam and Henry and one of the girls from the other side of the office), but it's not like he had to have a cup this very second. There's still a chance he followed me.

'I've been meaning to tell you, Han, you're doing a great job here.'

He's *so* good-looking when he smiles. And I love the Paul Smith shirt he's wearing. It takes a confident man to wear circus stripes to the office. I catch Sam grin in what I assume is a congratulatory fashion.

'I am?' Other than poring over the magical files, my biggest challenge has involved boiling water. You'll understand if I interpret this as Mark being subversively flirty.

'Yeah, Felicity's really happy with you.'

I know this is a lie. Felicity isn't happy with anyone. 'You don't say.'

'Absolutely. You're going to do very well.'

'I hope so. I really want to thank you for giving me the chance.' Let me count the ways I want to thank you . . .

'Just keep up the good work. See you later.'

Either he's developed a facial tic or he just winked at me. That was definitely a coded message. He means *he's* really happy with me. This is amazing.

'Way to go. It sounds like you're in with the boss.' Sam raises his mug to clink with mine.

'Thanks!' Isn't he everything I've ever looked for in a guy? Literally perfect?

'I'm sure it doesn't have anything to do with the fact that you're a pretty woman.'

'What?!' Quite aside from the truth of this statement, which Sam has no way to know is the truth, what an ass. 'Thanks for assuming that I only got this job because the boss wants to sleep with me. That's a very nice thing to tell somebody!'

'I'm sorry. I didn't mean to insult you. I guess I meant to insult Mark. His hiring practices have been . . . consistent in the past. That's all I meant.'

'Whatever. Don't you have somewhere to be?'

I will not let Sam's judgement dull this moment. Not when I might even be a little bit in love. Am I? I don't have much experience with this. I'm in excitement, at least. Desire, naturally. Admiration, affection . . . Is that the beginning of love? How would I know? Everyone says you just do, but maybe I'm one of those people who wouldn't recognize it, like the girls who don't know they're pregnant until they go to the doctor with a stomachache and come home with an eight-pound infant. I hope I'm not that stupid, but you never know until you're in the situation. I thought I might be in love once, in high school. At least I got flustered and blushed and felt sick to my stomach every time Jake came near me. I assumed that was love. Being older now, and wiser, I don't feel like throwing up, but all the other feelings are there.

A monumental realization like this can't go uncelebrated. 'Siobhan, want to go to Selfridges at lunch?'

'For what?'

'Free make-up.'

'Do you have a voucher?'

'Wha–? No. I'll explain on the way.' How can such a trendy

woman not know about free makeovers? Suddenly I feel like Yoda, so happy my wisdom to impart I am.

'I'm glad you took the job,' Siobhan says as we settle into the Tube. 'You're the only one I like there. The rest of them are gobshites.'

I love Siobhan's ability to really bring her opinions to life. It must come from having the blood of Ireland's bards in her veins. And I appreciate that she quickly grasps when I don't have the faintest idea what she's saying. 'Loudmouths who talk out of their arses,' she clarifies. 'They aren't worth knowing.'

'Ah. I had noticed that.' The other girls at the company have done little to impress their warmth upon me. They're not bitches exactly. They're just unfriendly. And I keep overhearing different pairs badmouthing the rest of the team as they come out of the ladies room. And not one has asked me to go for a drink or a coffee, or even enquired about my day. I guess that means they are bitches. 'I'm really glad I met you too. You remind me a little of my best friend, Stacy.'

'Really?' I can tell that she's touched. She does though. She's just as ballsy and sharp, though she has a vulnerable side too. She gets positively weepy over things she reads in the paper (by 'paper' I mean the *Metro*, the city's journalistic equivalent of olives on the table . . . you'll eat them if they're in front of you but they don't replace a full meal). Perhaps surprisingly, her tendency to bawl doesn't come from a negative view of the world or her chance of success in it. No number of epically bad dates, and they all seem to go about as well as her evening with the lawyer, can knock her faith in romance. For Siobhan, the next perfect man is probably just around the corner.

'Yeah. Stacy and I used to sneak out of work at least once a month to get makeovers together.'

'Then I'm honoured to carry on the tradition with you.'

I find the secret of success is not to let the saleswomen guilt, cajole or bully you into buying everything they slap on your face. They might promise you lip-plumping kissableness and lashes lovingly wrapped in magical thickening tubes, but don't be lulled into complacency. Their sales pitch goes straight for your freshly lifted satin-smooth airbrush-effect jugular. Some of those girls could persuade Stella McCartney into a gorilla-fur coat. Over the years, I've perfected a great little noise when they give me the mirror to show off their handiwork. It's the sound you make when you get a paper cut, followed by the tiniest shake of the head. 'I don't know,' I say. 'I'm not sure if it's really *me*.' Then I assure them that I'm very grateful they tried their best, and they flatter me in a last-ditch effort to get me to buy, and we part friends. Unfortunately, they singled out Siobhan immediately. Limping gazelles at dusk on the savannah have had better chances. It didn't help that she blurted out 'I had no idea I could do this!' when she first sat down. So she has only herself to blame that she might now have to get a part-time job to pay off this month's credit-card bill. She looks great though.

Based on Mark's reaction, I must look pretty good too. He's actually lingering at my desk. Subtly, of course. His professionalism really is amazing. He hasn't made a single comment about us or even hinted about wanting to see me again since our second date. No wonder he's the head of the company. I suppose he'd have to ask me when he's sure no one at the office could overhear. It wouldn't do for people to think I'm getting any special treatment. Hasn't he already told me that he's confident I'll be a resounding success completely on my own merit? I love that he's so supportive. Not all boyfriends are like that. Maybe he'll send an email, though if Siobhan has access, he might have to be even more discreet. This is so romantic.

We're practically Tony and Maria from *West Side Story*. The fact that he upholds such standards makes me so proud of him. This is a man of honour.

'Mark?' It's Siobhan stomping down the hall. For a girl who can't weigh more than a hundred pounds she has the heel strike of a water buffalo. 'Your wife called again. She says you can get her on her mobile.'

Come again?

9

Mark is married. And not married-in-name-only either. He's honestly, truly married. Well, obviously he's not honestly married. I sat at my desk for about two years after Siobhan made her announcement, staring at Mark with my MAC Viva Glam VI mouth open. And do you know what he did? He had the nerve to mouth 'I'll talk to you later' and wink! I can't believe this. I cannot believe it. Not after the last time I fell for another woman's husband. I'm not a stupid girl, my married-man track record aside, and I'm generally a decent judge of character. Unfortunately, some men have an extra wily gene that activates when they say 'I do'.

A couple years ago, I met Craig, aka the Scumsucking Cheater, in one of the most romantic ways possible. He asked me to dance at a ball. The Wadsworth Atheneum's charity Christmas ball couldn't have been prettier. We always went in a big group, some with dates but mostly not. Like me, he was with a group of friends. Like me, he was drunk, and like me, he was game for a little post-party action. Within days we were inseparable. Indeed, this was the one time when being easy didn't seem to put the guy off . . . I should have known something was up.

I know that's what you're thinking. My mother (and most of my friends) asked the same question. How could I have dated a married man for months and not known it, given the obvious facts?

Fact 1: he lives with his wife. I agree that this is generally a strong indication of prior commitment. Of course I would have been suspicious if he'd always come home with me or we'd met at hotels. But we usually went to his place, a great little apartment in the south end. And he didn't sneak off in the middle of the night either. Now knowing what I know, I should have looked more closely at the clothes in his closet. I would have noticed that they were suited to a much larger man. The apartment belonged to his friend, who was out of town a lot. How did he manage to spend all those nights away without his wife calling the police? Easy when she thinks he travels for work.

Fact 2: I didn't have his home phone number. The telephone is where most philanderers get caught out. He can't give the girl his home number and any suspicious wife worth her salt will check her husband's cellphone bills (and his credit-card statements for that matter). Scumsucking Cheater had a separate 'business' cellphone. He had his voice on his friend's answering machine, and he had his own business credit card with a statement that went to his office. It was some business he had going.

Fact 3: I didn't meet (all of) his friends. Leading a double life requires a certain amount of discretion in social circles. It doesn't go over well when the wife's best friend runs into the husband out with his girlfriend. But Scumsucking Cheater was blessed with two mutually exclusive sets of friends, one that liked to have weekend barbecues and competitively parent, and another that drank until dawn and slept with whoever they could get into bed. Needless to say, I didn't go to any barbecues.

If he'd conned me out of my life savings on our bigamous wedding day, I'd be perfect material for one of those made-for-TV docudramas. So how did I find out? He met me one night smelling of perfume. I don't wear perfume. That's right. I caught him cheating on me with his wife. Once I started to suspect I wasn't the only woman in his life (though at that point I didn't suspect I was the other woman in it), I did what anyone sensible would do. I followed him. It took a couple weeks but eventually he led me to his house, and his wife. When their front door opened, I stood face-to-face with a perfectly normal, pretty woman. 'Yes?'

'I'm, uh, I know your husband.'

She sighed in a way that said 'not again', and stood aside to let me in. I was surprised that she wasn't surprised.

'How long?' she asked wearily as we stood in her hallway decorated with photos of their family life together.

'Six months. Do you want to kill him?'

She acted like I'd just told her she had a flat tyre.

'Not any more. I want to bankrupt him.'

'This isn't the first time, then.'

'It's the third. After the first one, I wanted to kill myself. After the second, I wanted to kill him. Now I want to get even.'

And do you know the really sad thing? I didn't get to be the breaker-upper. His wife must have ambushed him the minute he walked in the door that night. He never called me again. As I think about it, I've *never* been the one to get the last word in a relationship. Talk about frustrating. There's nothing worse than having a million great shots with no target. Is it any wonder that Final Confrontation is my number-one comeback fantasy?

'I knew it. The fucker!'

As my best friend, Stacy is contractually obligated to be livid at Mark on my behalf. 'What do you mean, you knew? How'd you know?'

'When you first had sex, he had a condom with him.'

'Well, if you knew then, Stace, why didn't you say anything?'

'I don't mean I *knew* then, but it makes sense now, doesn't it?'

'Well, of course it does, now that I know!'

'How do you feel?'

'Hurt. Mad. Sad.' Everybody sympathizes with the wife, and rightly so, but in some circumstances the girlfriend deserves a thought too. Isn't it almost as bad for her, being led on, believing that her search for The One is over, only to find out that Mr Right is somebody else's Mr? Aside from the potential for heartbreak, it's extremely embarrassing. At least Stacy is the only other person who knows about Mark. Without wine-bar access to my normal circle of friends, I haven't suffered from the vocal diarrhoea that usually accompanies a new man in my life. For that, at least, I'm grateful.

'I don't blame you. The fucker. In what proportion?'

'What?'

'How hurt versus sad versus mad?' She's not in banking for nothing. Her mind works best in measurable quantities.

'I guess mostly hurt and sad.'

'Aw, honey, I'm so sorry. There's no way you could have known.'

She's right, though that doesn't make me feel any better. 'But I really liked him, Stace!' Who am I kidding? I really *like* him.

'I know you did, but he's an asshole. He's a cheater, Hannah. You know guys like that don't just cheat women. They cheat everyone. He's probably cheating on his taxes.'

'I don't care if he cheats on his taxes.'

'Yes, you do. That's not the kind of man you want to be

with. You'll get mad in a few days and then you'll feel better. You know you will, right?'

'Yeah, I know . . . Technically, how many days are a few?'

I shouldn't really blame her for laughing, given that I only realized I might be in love a couple hours ago.

'Ugh,' she says, 'I just thought of something. What about your job?'

My job? Oh, right. I've slept with my married boss. Let's see how that's likely to play out. 1: Mark keeps me as his tarty little bit on the side, and as long as I play along I keep my job. When he tires of me, he fires me. 2: Felicity finds out I've schtupped Mark to get my job and fires me, or makes me wish she had. As it is, she's already written me off as a piece of fluff in life's navel. 3: Mark doesn't want to take the risk that I'll blow his cover with the little Mrs, so he fires me. 4: He declares he loves me, announces his marriage is over, we walk down the aisle together and I become the co-head of the company. Admittedly, the last option isn't likely, so all roads lead to unemployment. Without a work permit, I may as well go back to Connecticut and live in my parents' basement. I don't have much choice.

'I'm gonna figure out how to keep it,' I tell her.

'Good . . . How?'

How indeed?

I accept that there's no way for this part of my life to have a happy ending (short of Mark's wife suddenly dropping dead, which I don't think technically counts as a happy ending). The best I'm going to do is to salvage what little dignity I have left. The sassy me would play it cool, like Mark was nothing but a silly diversion. Unfortunately, the real me will probably go psycho on him. I tend to hold it together in the face of rejection only until I've had a few drinks, then I snap. I admit I have a bit of a reputation along the Eastern seaboard as a bad sport when it comes to break-ups. I like to think of myself merely as passionate, though the phrase 'bunny boiler' has been used about me. Quite unfairly. I've never harmed a living animal.

The more I think about it, the more I'm determined not to be the old Hannah. Haven't I grown already? Haven't I done things I never imagined doing? I am a new person. So I'm going to act like it's no big deal, no matter how I really feel. Women in the movies do it all the time. Kate Hudson was unbelievably cool in *How to Lose a Guy in 10 Days* (when she wasn't acting crazy). I can be Kate. I've been practising my seductively aloof smile for when I get the chance to prove my disinterest. If I had a DVD player, I'd rent *The Philadelphia Story*. Katharine Hepburn was possibly the wittiest woman on the planet, and she juggled three men in that film. In my opinion, witty goes a long way towards being indifferently irresistible. And that's what I'm aiming for.

When Mark whispered 'We'll talk later', he must have meant later in the year. He's managed to completely avoid me for two weeks, which takes some ingenuity in our office. It's not exactly Vatican City. I'm regularly camping out at Siobhan's desk these days, but he's cleverly worked a way around me. He phones her from his office to send her on bogus errands in other parts of the building, knowing I can't justify sitting on her desk when she's not even there. Then he sneaks out, the coward. Of course, Siobhan wondered why I'm using her desk as a lookout post, so I had to come clean.

'The wanker!' she'd said, echoing my thoughts exactly. 'His wife's such a nice woman; she doesn't deserve that.' Not the comforting words I wanted to hear. Something along the lines of 'She just became his ex-wife' would have been a better response. 'Did you know, about her, I mean?'

'Of course not!'

'No, of course you didn't. I'm sorry, I didn't mean to imply that you're a home-wrecker.'

I am a home-wrecker, though, aren't I, if unintentionally (and, as far as I know, unsuccessfully)? The longer I go without telling him what I think, the more it looks like I'm prepared to take it lying down. Which is, ironically, what got me into this mess in the first place. So when I got up this morning, I resolved to bring it up myself – which I hate to do, because there's no way to confront a man and make it look like you're snubbing him at the same time. But I can't live in limbo any more, with my anger festering. It's the injustice of the whole situation that really gets me. I mean, cosmically, am I doing something wrong that justifies plagues of married men being visited upon my heart? Maybe I give off some kind of gullibility vibe that says: 'Go ahead and take advantage of me. I'm very unlikely to catch on before you've had your fill of me.' I know I'm being harsh on myself but –

'Hannah! Come in here.'

What now? 'Yes, Felicity?'

'We have a problem.' When she says this, she means I'm about to have a problem. 'With the Withers party. The table cards are wrong.'

I had absolutely nothing to do with any table cards. She can't possibly be blaming me for them. Can she? 'The table cards?'

'Yes. The font is wrong.'

'The font?'

'Stop repeating everything I say. The font is wrong. The engravers used the same font for the table cards and the invitations. Hermione wants Bank Gothic on the cards. They need to be changed.'

'Do you want me to call the engraver?'

'They can't do it.'

. . . 'You want *me* to do it?'

'That'd be great, thank you. Here's the guest list. And here's the seating plan.'

Four hundred and eighty guests? 'Er, okay. Just to check, the engravers can't do it because . . . ?'

'Hannah, I don't have time to explain everything to you. They need to be ready first thing in the morning to go over with the caterers.'

'Okay . . . Felicity?' What have I got to lose? 'Do I get to go to this party?'

. . . 'If you can do this properly, you can go.'

'Can I wear something from the closet?'

'Absolutely not.'

You never know unless you ask. I can live without the clothes. The important thing is getting to the party to show Felicity what I know to be true. I'm destined to be a party planner. So I'm going to do this. It's just some typing, right? And some printing. Of course, it would be substantially easier if I knew how to type using more than two fingers.

'Hannah. Have you got a minute? I need to talk to you about the Withers party.' It's Mark. Standing in front of my desk, acting like we're just colleagues or something.

'Uh, okay. Is this about the table cards?' It's possible that he really wants to talk about the party, considering that the theme was my idea. (Not that Felicity asked for my contribution. I took the opportunity to ambush her in the ladies room.) But surely he'd talk to Felicity directly about the details, considering that she took all the credit for the idea anyway. So this must be his way of getting me alone to talk about 'us'. Huh, as if there is an 'us', or ever was, the bastard. The great-looking, charming, funny, excellent-kissing bastard. I *will* be cool. I *will* be. I am Kate (either Kate, Hudson or Hepburn). At least I look fabulous. Well, obviously. I mean, what girl risks looking awful when confronted with the possibility of facing her ex? I've been dressed to the nines since the day I went to Selfridges. Today is my pink-Chanelesque-suit day.

He closes his door behind us. This is definitely not about the Withers party. 'Yes, Mark?'

He looks embarrassed. Good. 'I wanted to talk to you.'

'So you mentioned.' I'm *so* channelling my icons right now. If I smoked, and had a cigarette holder, I'd light up and blow a smoke ring.

'I just wanted to clear the air.'

'About?'

'About us.'

'Mark, there is no us.'

'I mean, what happened between us.'

'That? It was just a fling.' Look at me, steady as a rock.

He's staring at me like I just told him the test results were negative. Honestly, he could show *some* regret over the fact that he'll never get to see me naked again. 'So, we're good?'

'We're fine, Mark. Is that all?'

'You won't mention it to anyone?'

'Of course not, don't be ridiculous. Mark, it was just a fling.'

'Good.' He's staring at me. Still staring. Don't you dare say anything, Hannah. This is the perfect Final Confrontation fantasy come true. 'Right then,' he finally announces, 'I guess we'd better get back to work.' Is he about to say something else? I wait. He stares. I smile. He smiles. It starts to get ridiculous. I leave.

He's watching me leave the office. I can feel his eyes. I'm drunk with the power. This is incredible. The 'treat 'em mean to keep 'em keen' philosophy really does work with some guys. Now I see that all those men in love with cold women aren't dim-witted, they're simply the spoils of a calculated strategy. What a realization this is. If I had it in me to use malice to my advantage, I'd probably be married by now. But you know what? I don't want to be mean, even if cruelty *is* catnip to a certain breed of man. As for Mark, there's some consolation in knowing that I've just successfully completed my first adult break-up, and I don't have to worry about my job. *And* that he'd jump me if I gave him the chance.

Now I know what the expression 'hollow victory' means, as in: See, I *told* you the test results were wrong; I *do* have cancer! What good is it to have the perfect break-up when it means that you're broken up? Oh, I know, self-esteem, empowerment, etc., etc., etc. I don't care. I'd rather have Mark . . .

I'd also rather have about twenty more hours in this day, which will end in exactly twelve minutes. Thank god for Sam's persistent guilt complex. He's been stopping by my desk at least twice a day since suggesting that I was the office slapper. When I told him I was pulling an all-nighter, he stupidly offered to help, assuming I had a clever plan to actually do what I've promised. Given that I may have overestimated the ease with which I would a) learn to type and b) print 480 table cards, my plan was more nebulous than he probably hoped. What became immediately apparent was that there's a reason we hire engravers to do these jobs. Of course thick card can't be fed through our printers, and something told me that Hermione Withers, a woman so concerned about the social implications of matching fonts, was unlikely to be happy about sticky labels instructing her guests where to sit. Not that I know how to print those either.

Luckily, my dad didn't pay for college for nothing. I've

devised a brilliant, if somewhat time-intensive solution. By buying every type of card sold at the stationers, I found one that *is* Xerox-friendly. I'm typing one name per page, which I'm printing out and cutting to the right size.

In actual fact, Sam is very little help. With only one printer, even using two computers isn't speeding things up much. But I appreciate the company. He's pretty interesting for an American.

'You mentioned before that this was a school job. Where do you go? Shit, that doesn't look right.' I'm on guest number 137. In other words, at this rate I'll be done just about the time that the cleaners arrive.

'It's for my doctorate –'

'Hand me another card. Please.' Henry didn't want to give me the office keys, or the crash course in what to do if the police come while I'm trying to set the alarm, but I was very persuasive (I cried). 'You're studying to be a doctor?'

'Nah. An academic. I don't go to classes or anything. It's not that kind of programme.'

'Sam, is this the kind of school where you get your diploma through the mail after only ten easy payments?'

'Something like that. Anyway, I have about six months left, then I defend and hopefully then I'm done.'

'What do you defend?' Is there a martial-arts component to PhDs? Imagine ninja doctorates.

'My professors read my thesis and pick it apart, but hopefully not too much. I might have to do some more work, or they might pass me.'

'But you won't fail?'

'It's unlikely. There, this one looks . . . er, is this name right? F – F – A – R – Q – U – U – H – A – R – S – O – N? How do you even say that?'

'Let me see. Crap.' This is literally going to take all night. 'Hand me another card.'

. . . 'I've been working with my mentor for two years on the thesis. If there was something fundamentally wrong with it, I hope he'd have told me by now.'

'He wouldn't be much of a mentor otherwise. Then what'll you do?'

'Find a real job.'

'You don't want to work here for ever?'

'I can't lie to you, I'll miss it. The low pay, getting bossed around, the chance to unclog my colleagues' toilets . . . You don't get that kind of glamour everywhere.'

'You're looking for glamour, then?'

'Nah, but it wouldn't be bad to win the Nobel Prize some day.'

'I'm glad to see you have modest goals.'

'It's possible. I have a professor who won one twenty years ago.'

'For what?'

'Economics. Contractual and constitutional bases for the theory of economic and political decision-making.'

What I hear is 'Economics. Blah and blah, blah for the blah of economic and something decision-making'. 'I see. Interesting.'

'Only to other economists.'

'Is that what you'll be, then? An economist?'

'Political economist.'

'Meaning?'

'Meaning that I'll get to go to countries with emerging political systems and advise them on how to do it better.'

'So you'll be a know-it-all.'

'Already am,' he declares. 'Why are you doing this?'

I assume he means the question in the broad sense rather than the immediate one. Because, obviously, I'm sticking the letter opener into the side of the printer to get it to stop making that noise. 'If I can prove that I'm reliable to Felicity, she'll let me plan parties.'

'Is that your ambition? To plan parties?'

'Is that so preposterous? You sound like I want to blow bubbles for a living. Hit the print button.'

'The world doesn't need another party planner.'

'But it needs another economist?'

'Economists solve real problems. You . . . solve seating problems.'

'Then why are you bothering to hang around with me, if you think I'm so stupid?'

'I don't think you're stupid, Hannah. That's the point.'

'But you think my ambitions are stupid.'

'I just suspect you could do more if you wanted to.'

Just what I need, tips on getting ahead from the office boy. 'Thanks. Next time I'm looking for career advice, I'll be sure to ask you. Meantime, if I don't get these finished, I won't have a career to advise about so come on, less talking, more working, please.'

'It's still jammed. Here, let me –' Sigh. 'Sticking that in there won't unjam it.'

'What are you, the Xerox expert now too?'

'You need to take the jammed paper out of it. Get out of the way, please, and let me have a look.'

Sam is developing a real knack for pissing me off.

The answering machine is blinking when I drag myself from bed, still in mid-REM, to begin the day of my first party. Stacy has taken to calling after her nights out, but the housemates insist they don't mind. That's because their friends phone at all hours. It's a side effect of living with people who come from the other side of the world.

'It's me, just got home from my date. Yes, home; before you ask, it's only midnight. Tye was a perfect gentleman. We had fun, he's nice and after a few drinks I hardly notice his eye.' When Stacy said he was ugly, she wasn't kidding. A ginger man with a lazy eye is never going to be a lady-killer, at least in the non-literal sense of the phrase. 'He wanted to go to Black-Eyed Sally's but BBQ is just stupid on a first date, isn't it? Can you imagine what'd end up in my teeth? So we went to Peppercorn's; it was good. I didn't order the spaghetti, for obvious reasons, and we drank quite a bit, come to think of it. But I don't feel drunk. Although I think my tolerance is lower than it used to be. Remember in college when we used to drink a couple cases a weekend? If I did that now, I'd pass out. Anyway, he's a decent kisser. Nothing too dramatic, just a little tongue. He had pretty tight jeans on; I think he might be nicely hung.' God, Stace, not on the answering machine! 'Worth a second date. I'd love to give him a makeover. With darker hair, he'd be much better-looking. Does that make me shallow? Okay, email me tomorrow.'

10

Imagine, if you will, the most glamorous Roaring Twenties soirée. Beautiful women step from antique chauffeured cars, walking advertisements for Cartier and De Beers. Men in tails escort these bejewelled flowers proudly along the red carpet, giving the paparazzi photos that will put their kids through college. Inside, a twenty-piece band plays softly in a glittering gold ballroom, the grandest in the city. Liveried waiters gracefully dance trays of vintage champagne and cutting-edge canapés between the guests, whose voices are raised in delirious excitement at the grandeur of the event. And the guest of honour is so happy that our next two years' party-planning revenues are guaranteed.

Now glimpse reality. I'm going to throw up. I've got butterflies the size of parrots in my stomach. I've already been to the bathroom twice to stuff toilet paper into my armpits. And it's not even seven o'clock. Felicity is screeching in my ear through one of those little headsets that looked like such a good idea in the opening scene of *The Wedding Planner*. 'Yes, Felicity, what is it?'

'The singer! Get over here!'

Now what?

We've lost the band leader. Literally lost him. The saxophone guy says he was in the kitchen about an hour ago. I try the kitchen. 'Last time I saw him, he was pouring himself another drink,' offers one of the caterers.

'Just great. Which way did he go?' He points to the back

door. I'm really not dressed to walk London's streets looking for a drunken singer. What does Felicity think I am, a bloodhound? My Jimmy Choos (hot-pink satin, very stylish, to match my dress) have made the balls of my feet numb. I have no idea in which direction he may have staggered. And come to think of it, I don't even know what he looks like.

'Felicity, I can't find him.'

'Well, you'd better find him!'

As if I carelessly misplaced the guy. 'I'm not telepathic, you know. I don't even know what he looks like!'

'Ugh! Useless cow.'

The saxophonist is still awaiting instructions. I've got an inspiration. 'Can you play instrumentals?'

'I'm sorry?'

They really struggle with my accent here. 'Can – you – play – music – with – no – words?' He's staring at me. Oh, right. By definition a musician plays music with no words. So shoot me. I'm no Beethoven. 'I mean, can you play stuff that's supposed to have words so at least the guests will recognize it?'

'What are you talking about, Hannah?' Felicity barks. 'Don't you think Hermione is going to notice there's no singer?!'

Tell me why I stayed up all night for the chance to get screamed at by my boss? 'Well, I don't know what you want me to do!' I say, storming off. I admit it isn't the most mature response to a crisis, but it beats my instinctive reaction, which is to cry. Unfortunately, as soon as I get to the kitchen I start doing that too.

'Why don't you get another singer?'

'Sam! What are you doing here?'

'Same as you; I'm working. Why don't you just get another singer? From one of the West End shows.'

'Just like that?' This party was nearly a year in the planning.

'It's worth a try. It's better than crying.'

'What do you know?' Now he's an emotional counsellor too.

'I know it's better than crying.'

'Fuck off.'

'Suit yourself.' He picks up his tray of glasses and pushes past me. 'Try *The Rat Pack*.'

Felicity is wearing her expression that says she enjoys the odd seal pup with a side of babies for breakfast. No chance she's found the singer, then.

'Um, when's Hermione getting here?'

'She's due at seven. Oh Christ. Who's going to sing "Happy Birthday" to her?'

I'm not generally a great thinker on my feet (hence my need for comeback fantasies) but miraculously another bolt of inspiration strikes. 'We could have her best friends sing karaoke-style!'

'What are you, thick?' she hisses. 'Do you think Hermione's parents have paid the equivalent of a down payment on a French chalet to hear her drunken friends slur "Happy Birth-day" down the microphone?'

I admit that sometimes my ideas don't stand up to scrutiny. 'Um, how about getting one of the singers from the West End to stand in?'

'Who?'

What did Sam say? Rat bag? Flat pack? No. '*The Rat Pack*?'

'I saw that, it's fantastic!' Now I'm afraid she might kiss me. Instead, she flips open her phone and punches in a number. 'Carol, hi, Felicity. I need a huge favour. Who's representing the guys in *The Rat Pack*? Yes, Frank. And Dean. I see. What about their understudies? Well, can you find out? I need one of them to fill in for me. Tonight. I know, I know. I don't care

131

how much it costs. No, of course don't tell them that. Thanks, I'll call back in five. You're a star.' Five minutes and thirty seconds later she crows, 'We've got Frank!'

As if in response, a bloodcurdling scream erupts from the foyer. Felicity, in more practical shoes than I, is first on the scene. Hermione has just arrived and she's in full hysteria. 'Didn't you vet the dresses?!' she's screaming at Felicity. Vet the dresses?

'I, ah, no, Hermione, I didn't think –'

'I'll say you didn't fucking think. Now my party is ruined!'

'What's going on?' I whisper to a young woman standing with her mouth agape.

'That girl,' she points an emaciated finger, 'has Hermione's dress.'

Sure enough, a stunning redhead is wearing the same Christian Lacroix black and champagne tiered-silk number. Frankly, she looks better in it. 'Who is she?'

'Lord Darlington's daughter.'

It figures. She couldn't be some nobody who'll let me stuff her into a broom closet. The birthday girl now hates Felicity with an intensity normally reserved for girls who trump her on handbag waiting lists. She's not going to listen to a word Felicity says. 'Let me see if I can help.' What have I got to lose? My job. My self-respect. My teeth.

What do I say, what do I say, what . . . to . . . say. It's not like I've had to avert disaster in real-time like this before. I suppose I could just tell Miss Darlington that she has to change her dress. But what if *she* throws a fit? Hysterics in stereo. No. Think, Hannah, how would you want to be told. Deep breath. Ready. 'Hi, I'm Hannah, the party planner, and I just had to come over to say that you look fabulous!' She's positively glowing. Kindness and joy practically ooze from her pores. Or they would if she had pores. Must find out where she gets her facials. 'That is an absolutely gorgeous dress, and,' I continue in a conspiratorial whisper, 'I have to say that you look so much better in it than Hermione.' I smile sincerely, letting that little fact sink in for a few seconds. 'Are you all right?'

She's now the colour of the tablecloths. 'I didn't mean . . . I don't want . . . Oh my god. Where is she?'

I put a consoling hand on her shoulder. 'Oh, I didn't realize you didn't know. Oh dear, this is terrible. I suppose you could always change if you wanted to.'

'But we've come from Surrey! I'll just have to leave.'

What a shame! I mean that, I'm not being sarcastic. Here's a perfectly nice girl who's probably been looking forward to this party for weeks and now she's going to have to miss it because the hostess, who is a bitch on heels, chose the same dress. She doesn't have a monopoly on it. In fact, there're half a dozen others that would have worked as well. The Dolce collection alone has three . . .

'I don't think you have to leave. Stay right there.' As I find the number for Selfridges' personal shoppers (one of the mandatory numbers Felicity programmed into my speed-dial, along with Berry Brothers wine shop and the ambulance service), I realize that I've been in training for this moment my whole adult life. Why else would I have the god-given ability to memorize runway collections with almost perfect recall? 'Hello? This is Hannah Cumming, with M&G events. I hope you can help me. Do you have Dolce and Gabbana's dove-grey and silver sequinned drop-waist dress in stock? In size . . .' I hold my hand over the phone. 'Ten? Great, I'll send someone over now to get it.'

'How did you know . . . ?' She's staring at me.

'Oh, it's nothing. I like to keep up with the trends. Trust me. This dress will be even more beautiful on you. Now, if you'll excuse me, I need to get someone to go pick it up for you.'

And I know just who to send. I'll show him what's better than crying. 'Sam, I need you.' He's carrying a tray of glasses and doesn't break his stride.

'I'm busy. Can I –'

'*I'm* sorry, but I need someone to go to Selfridges and pick up a dress.'

He sets his tray down and walks back. 'And?'

'Well, I can't go, so someone has to, and I thought . . .'

'Yes?'

'That you, um, could.'

'Hannah, I'm not sure who you think you are all of a sudden, but I'm here to do my job, not your shopping.'

He might tower over me, even in my heels, but he's not intimidating. For god's sake, he's got curly hair. He wears a smock to work. Besides, it's *Sam*. 'Look, if, as you say, you're here to work this party, it's part of your job to make sure everything goes smoothly. If that means going to Selfridges, I think that's a fair request. If you have a problem with that, you can take it up with your boss. Either one of them.' I must be channelling one of the Kates again.

He's wavering. 'Fine. Give me twenty quid.'

'Why?'

'For the taxi. Unless paying for *that's* part of my job too.'

'Oh right, okay.' I only have twenty pounds on me. 'They're on the second floor. Tell them it's for M&G. Uh, here, in case they need a credit card . . . Thanks,' I call to his retreating back. 'Wait, Sam!'

'What?'

'Can I have your phone number?'

'Isn't that a little forward? We've only known each other a few weeks.'

'In case I need to get hold of you on the way.'

'Why, are you going to ask me to shop for shoes too?'

'Don't be ridiculous,' I grin, 'I wouldn't trust you to choose shoes.' At least he doesn't look thunderous any more.

Within an hour, Miss Darlington is resplendent in her new frock and once more mingling among the beautiful people. Frank's understudy showed up on time and sober, and the crowd loves him. Hermione's guests are even dabbling in carbohydrates. You go, girls, one mini brioche won't give you love handles. I was wrong in my initial impression of Londoners. All those sandwich shops must be kept in business by tourists and men. Between the New Atkins devotees, South Beach fans, SlimFast point-counters and caveman enthusiasts, planning the menu must have been a minefield. There is literally no safe food any more. I heard there's a chef in Spain who serves flavoured air in his restaurant. Reservations are booked up six months in advance.

By 3 a.m., when the party starts winding down, Felicity tells me I can go home. That's it. That's what she says. 'You can go now.' Not one word about the table cards, about the wonderful job I did on my first party. Not even a thank you. Isn't saving her party, three times, enough to earn a little respect? I'd love to summon the energy for anger but I'm so exhausted I'm weaving in my stilettos. Thanks again, Felicity, for last night's contribution to the bags under my eyes.

And I have no money to get home. I hope Sam has change from my twenty. He's not in the ballroom. 'Try the kitchen,' advises one of the waiters.

He's elbow-deep in soap suds.

'Um, hi. Listen, thanks for going to Selfridges for me. It saved the night.'

'No problem. Who knows what catastrophe might have ensued if two girls were photographed wearing the same dress.'

I can do without the sarcasm. 'Whatever. Um, I was wondering if there was any money left over from the taxi?'

'No, why?'

Suddenly the thought of walking miles in heels at 3 a.m. is too much for me. 'I don't have any money!'

'Wait half an hour and I'll give you a ride home.'

'Really? Thanks.'

'Wait. Where do you live?'

'Earls Court.'

'Okay.'

'What were you going to do, take back your offer if I lived too far?'

'Depends on how far away you lived. Give me half an hour.'

Honestly.

Good to his word, he emerges from the kitchen half an hour later, catching me rubbing my feet. 'I don't know why women wear such stupid shoes.'

'These shoes aren't stupid!' What a thing to say about perfectly innocent footwear.

'They're completely impractical, you can't walk in them and they probably cost a fortune.'

'What would you prefer we do, tape old tyre rubber to our feet?'

'It'd be more practical.'

'Maybe we're not interested in practical.'

'Apparently not. Come on, hop on.'

He's kidding, right? When he offered me a ride, I assumed he meant in a car. 'A moped?'

'It's a Vespa.'

'Isn't that Italian for moped?'

'Do you want a ride or not?'

Since beggars can't be choosers, with my dress hiked up, I can just straddle the seat. I'm very aware that my crotch is up against his backside. As we pull out on to the Strand, I shift back to get some distance between our genitals. This is practically obscene, especially considering the thong that I'm wearing. He speeds up, I grab his sides tighter and the wind catches the front of my dress. Before you can say 'flasher', my dress is over my head and we're speeding through traffic. I can't let go of his sides for fear of falling off. 'You all right?' Sam yells through the wind as he peers from his rearview mirror.

'Fine, thanks.' Central London now knows I didn't keep my wax appointment.

Twenty humiliating minutes later, we pull up in front of my apartment. 'Thanks,' I mumble as I smooth down the front of my dress. Small civilities are important at moments like these.

'No problem. Aren't you going to invite me in?'

'What? I . . .' It hadn't crossed my mind. Do I owe him a drink or something? Or something? Just exactly what is he implying?

'Well, I assumed when you flashed me –'

'What!'

'That you might be interested in getting together.'

'First of all, I did not flash you because I like you – I did not flash you!'

'I think you did. Are you sure you don't want to go out sometime?'

'Look, charming as your proposition is, I don't think we're exactly *simpatico*, do you?'

'That did cross my mind. But I think you're pretty, and you've got fight.'

'And you like to date pretty fighters?'

He shrugs. 'I guess it's my thing.'

'We don't even know each other.'

'What do you want to know?'

At 4 a.m., I don't have the will for banter. 'Nothing, really.'

'Then how are we going to get to know each other?'

'I guess we're not. Thanks for the ride. I'll see you on Monday.'

As I turn the key in the lock, I hear him say, 'Wyoming.'

'What?'

'Wyoming. I'm from Wyoming.'

Is that one of the square states in the middle? 'Thanks, Sam. Goodnight.'

Really. As if I've moved 3,000 miles to date a busboy from Wyoming.

I'm on the rebound, with Mark still rattling around in my head. I know the 'experts' say I should take a break from dating, have a little me-time to focus on what I want out of life and love. I've tried that. It doesn't work. I just mope around making ill-advised beauty choices and annoying my friends with long self-absorbed, repetitive conversations. I don't care if it's politically incorrect. The best way for me to get over a man is to get under another one. A sexy date trumps a seaweed mask in self-imposed exile any day.

Potential may be the perfect balm to soothe my wounded heart. Under normal circumstances, I wouldn't be so optimistic, given the astronomical odds against meeting the love of your life on a speed-date, but I think we can agree that these are not normal circumstances. And Potential isn't your normal man . . . at least, he isn't *my* normal man. Not only is he interested (not always a given when it comes to the objects of my desire), he compounds his allure by being the most English Englishman I've ever met. Granted, my sample consists of Mark, London cabbies and Henry, our office accountant.

'I know him, hnn. He was at school, hnn, with my brother.'

When Chloe suggested that we get massages together, I naively thought she meant at the same spa. We're in the same room. Naked, being kneaded, in the same room. I was right. English women's nipples are just the icing on the proverbial uninhibited cake. I'm only here because she insisted on doing the legwork to find the best masseuse in town. It's her way of saying thank you for running her extra keys around last week when she locked herself out. It was no big deal, I just had to stop home to get them and go to her place. I'd hate to know how she'd thank me if I helped her out of a real jam.

'Which school?' It could be one of the two I've heard of.

'Eton.'

'So he's rich!'

'Or upper class. Few are both, hnn. He's probably from an old family.'

'How do you know?'

'Double-barrelled surname.'

'What?'

'Two surnames.'

So hyphens in England are a sign of breeding, not feminism. It must get a little unwieldy after a couple generations of marrying well. Imagine the poor teachers at roll call. Penelope Spencer-Wessex-Salisbury-Churchill-Gladstone-St John-Smyth? Here, miss. Without wanting to jinx my chances at this early stage, I can say with 100 per cent certainty that I'd take his name if we got married. Giving up my own will deprive me of nothing but mortification. Just try being a twelve-year-old girl called Cumming when the boys in your class learn about sex. I heard more heavy breathing in my formative years than a phone-sex worker does in her whole career.

'Take as long as you'd like to relax,' croons my magic-fingered masseuse, handing me a little bowl of flower-scented water, 'and when you're ready, you can get dressed and someone will take you down to lunch.' Do I drink it? Once bitten, twice shy after an embarrassing finger-bowl experience last year.

What a nifty way to spend ninety minutes and most of a day's pay. I can't imagine ever feeling stressed again. I don't even care that my towel fell off when I got up. Nudity be damned, that was wonderful, and the perfect way to prepare for my third date with Potential. That's right, my third date. But I will *not* stupidly crow to all my friends about him until he's officially my boyfriend, in case my inclination to vocalize good fortune proves too tempting for fate. That's at least half the reason why I haven't told Chloe till now. The other half is because there wasn't much to brag about from the first two dates. I didn't have a bad time, but I don't have the prickly sweats either. It's not helping that we haven't even kissed, but I will not be disheartened. Some people just need a few dates to hit their stride. Besides, we're a multicultural couple. That can't be easy for him. Plus I'd hate to give up when he's so obviously . . . rich.

Perhaps finding out that he's practically a lord is colouring my view, because Potential looks the epitome of the English country gentleman when I spot him in the pub. And he's not flirting with the barmaid, which is a plus given recent events. His longish hair curls around his ears, though it's hard to make out the style because it's adorably windblown. He's the right height to complement a girl's rural fashions (wellie-tall rather than Manolo-tall) and he has at least a two-day stubble. This unshaven look is incredibly sexy, though I confess a hopeless attraction to George Michael too. His jeans look honestly old, not Gap made-to-look-old old and he has a little hole in his sweater that he's got his finger stuck through. There's a collared shirt under there too, sticking out on one side of his jeans where he forgot to tuck. Very absent-minded professor.

'Hi.'

'Hey, America. You look nice.'

'Thanks. What's with you and these old pubs?' We're in a run-down boozer where half a dozen regulars are having trouble focusing beyond their beer mats. When Potential said drinks, I assumed he meant cocktails in a trendy club. I don't know why I assumed this. Our first two dates were in equally morose surroundings. So it's my own fault that I'm over-dressed. Chloe and I crisis-shopped after lunch for a beguiling unwrappable outfit, critical when there's a chance you'll be in flagrante delicto with someone. Skinny jeans might be stylish, but try getting them off while lying down. Diane von Fursten-berg was the only sensible option.

'They remind me of home.'

An intriguing glimpse of home life. We haven't had the whole how-dysfunctional-is-your-family conversation yet. 'Oh? Is your town very old?'

'Erm, the whole country is very old.'

'Right.' Duh. 'I mean, do you come from a little village?'

'Yeh, it's small enough to fit everyone inside for lunch.'

'You invite the entire village for lunch? You talk like you own it. Hah, hah, hah.' Oh my god, he owns a village. I'm a little short of breath. 'Do you go home very often?'

'Most weekends, eck-tually.' He's got one of those accents that ambushes my ear with odd pronunciations like this.

'I'd kill myself if I had to be around my family that much.'

'Well, we don't see much of each other. It's a big house. Maybe you'll see it sometime.'

'Isn't it a little early to meet the parents?'

I shouldn't fault him for looking confused. Not everyone gets my humour right away. 'They're not there now. It's winter.'

So rich Brits, like geese, follow seasonal migration patterns. 'I'd love to see it.' What will I wear?

The restaurant Potential has chosen is as old as the Declar-ation of Independence. So, it appears, are most of its clientele. The decor brings to mind Miss Havisham in her faded wedding dress, with tonight's specials stuffed and mounted all over the walls. The waiters are identical, septuagenarian, penguinlike in their attire and manner. 'This way, madam, sir.'

'What a cool place.'

'Mmm.'

'The food looks, er . . .' The menu reads like the ingredients in a questionable hot dog.

'Mmm.'

. . .

Why, when he held my hand all the way here, is he now sitting silently slumped in his chair? It's possible that PDAs aren't the done thing in restaurants. I mean public displays of affection, not those little hand-held computers. Nobody else is holding hands, but then most of them probably no longer have their own teeth, so they can be forgiven if the romance has worn off a bit. Yet this isn't the behaviour of a man contemplating our future together. It isn't even the behaviour of a man contemplating dessert together. The shine's come off the penny already. I knew it. I don't exactly radiate that worth-the-wait vibe. I blame university for the fact that I'm more Wal-Mart than waiting list. In school, I hardly ever dated. I got drunk and made out with cute boys. After four years, alcohol-induced allure is a hard habit to break, so I'm woefully unprepared for seduction that doesn't involve half-price drinks. I'm sure my dates *would* have wined and dined me if they thought they needed to. Obviously they didn't. I mean seriously, who looks at a price tag and says, 'Go on, charge me an extra fifty.' . . . But that was the old Hannah, not who I am now, right? I can be a sex bomb if I want to, a real-world Dita Von Teese.[24] Just watch me.

24. That famous burlesque star who is known to bathe publicly in a giant glass of champagne.

To my relief, he doesn't snatch his hand back when I reach for it over the tablecloth. My mother is wrong. The way to a man's heart isn't through his stomach. It's through his ego. Show me a guy who talked about himself all evening and I'll show you a guy who thought he had a great time. 'Tell me, what's your idea of the perfect day?' Yes, of course I feel ridiculous fluttering my Xtreme Volume eyelashes (Chloe swears by it. The mascara, I mean, not the slutty eye contact), but my question is going to tell me volumes about Potential, including whether he's into me or not.

His lazy, beautiful smile proves that not all Englishmen have wonky teeth. 'It would have to be at the house. We'd get up late, have some breakfast, then go for a walk. Maybe we'd pack a picnic hamper in summer, or else go to a lovely old pub in the village. Winter's my favourite time because you can sit by the fire. We'd read our books before dinner, and drink some nice wine from the cellar. How does that sound?'

It sounds like I could be in love one day. At least he's not one of those guys who defines perfection as a day out drunkenly watching football with his friends (or at least he's savvy enough to tell me he's not one of those guys). I'm more likely to win the lottery than ever get that kind of man to stay for breakfast. I was right not to give up on him after the first lacklustre dates. He's obviously got a romantic streak, as evidenced by his picnic and pub ideals. He's well rounded, based on the fact that he likes books and wine, and old-fashioned, proven by our presence in his stately home. And into me! Otherwise why would *I* be there at the start of his perfect day? 'That sounds great . . .'

The ensuing silence is occasionally punctuated by his chewing. I'm sure he'd ask about me if his smoked salmon didn't require such undivided attention, what with all the lemon to be squeezed. In a movie, there'd be a clock ticking loudly on the wall to help me keep track of the minutes stretching out. I don't mind working hard for some things, but I draw the line at food and dating. I should no more have to dig meat out of a lobster's claw than I should have to spend an evening pulling conversation from my date.

It is the cheese at the end of the meal that inexplicably loosens Potential's tongue long enough to tell me it's his favourite. I beg to differ. A lump of blue goo that smells of dirty socks isn't even cheese. And anyway, the only way that cheese is dessert is when it's followed by the word cake.

'Thanks for dinner. I had a nice time.' Courtesy demands this lie. On a positive note, it did give me a few hours for uninterrupted contemplation.

Dad's always said there's no shame in failure as long as I've done my best. It's untrue, but I appreciate the sentiment. I did try, listening as if spellbound to his single contribution to the conversation, making witty and charming attempts to extract more participation from him. Plus I hardly even made a face about the cheese. Yet here we are, walking towards the Tube station. I charged a £300 dress on my credit card. It's unfair to have to pay off a bad date in instalments.

'Did you?'

He sounds uncertain. Not incredulous, as in 'I did everything but pee in your soup and still you won't get the hint', but truly uncertain. Have I completely misinterpreted his silence? He may not be uninterested, just shy. A bashful prince, like Shrek, only not green. My new lingerie may show a return on investment yet. 'Yeah, the restaurant was great.' Offal and cheese and silence and geriatric table companions aside. 'And you're, well, you're cool too.'

'Cool . . .'

He thinks I'm a geek.

145

'Cool enough to maybe go out with again sometime –'

'I'd love to!' Admittedly, my enthusiasm isn't very cool. Think Dita, think Dita. 'It would be nice to get together. Again. Sometime. Whenever.'

'Well, how about . . . A few of us are going down to the house this weekend and, well, normally I wouldn't, but, em, well, when you said you were up for it when we met . . . Would you like to come?'

Today's Wednesday. As if I'd just take off at the drop of a hat, as if I'm the kind of girl who'll swan off for a sleepover with a virtual stranger. Like I don't already have plans for the weekend. I have morals. I have a social life.

'I am, definitely up for it!' Who am I kidding? I'd planned to buy a space heater this weekend.

. . . 'You are?'

'Totally!'

'God, I love how direct you Americans are. Perfect. Shall we say one o'clock, Saturday? I'll pick you up.'

'Great!' . . . I'm practically puckering with my eyes closed. I can't give him a stronger signal without humping his leg.

'G'night, then.'

'G'night.' This is ridiculous. I'm an adult. If I want to kiss him, I should just kiss him. It's not like I've never launched myself on a man before. What would Dita do?

Before you can say striptease, he's got his tongue in my mouth. The least I can do is show my support for his efforts. My tongue tickles back. Mmm. We're grappling and kissing while London's revellers stream by. I'm a little embarrassed. What must everyone think? Who cares – there's a handsome man on my face! This is sexy. I wonder how far away he lives. I'm ten minutes by Tube. Can we navigate the escalators in this position?

Wait a minute. Have I learned nothing this last month? Repeat after me: boys don't date easy girls. They sleep with them, and then toss them aside. I can't jump into bed with Potential the first night we kiss just because he's bought me dinner. Unless I want another one-night stand. And I definitely don't. 'All right, then. Thanks again. See you Saturday.' I'm trying not to pant as I say this.

'Wha–? Really?'

'Really. Goodnight.'

'Uh, okay. 'Night, then. See you Saturday.'

Exactly how does one prepare to meet one's future husband's best friends? I have no idea, but I do have forty-eight hours and Stacy at two pee a minute to help me figure it out.

'Oh my god, how exciting!'

Stacy is beside herself with glee at the thought of the manor-house wedding. I know she's envisioning a dalliance in the stable with a morning-suited usher. I'm not excited yet. I'm still scared. 'But I've never been to an English country house.'

'You've been to a regular house, haven't you? What's the difference?'

I don't know. That's what I'm afraid of. 'What if his friends are mean?' If they hate me, Potential will dump me.

'What if they're wonderful?'

If they're wonderful, I'll spend the whole weekend wondering if he's slept with any of them.

'You're worrying too much about the wrong things. What are you going to wear?'

Much as I love my friend and admire her fashion sense, her forte in themed ready-to-wear extends only to cruise collections. She's impeccable in the Hamptons and Newport, but her idea of the country is any place where her cellphone reception is patchy. And I'm not falling for Ralph Lauren's tally-ho view of what Brits wear at home. The man started life as Ralph Lifschitz in the Bronx, for god's sake.

I wish Chloe was in town. Being born into this fancy manor-house life, she'd know exactly what to bring. But she left for the Alps this week, as fancy manor-house people do here in February, and her cellphone just rings and rings. She warned me when we first met that she has a habit of letting it run out of juice or dropping it in the toilet. I thought she was joking until I went to her apartment to wade through her closets and witnessed the chaos first-hand. She wasn't exaggerating. It's remarkable, really, for such a well-put-together girl to be so incapable of managing the details of her own life. She insists there's a method to her madness, but the frequency with which she loses her keys, Oyster card, lipstick, shoes, car . . . makes me wonder. She's just as untidy in her personal life. She always likes at least two men at a time and can never seem to remember where she's left them either.

12

'Hannah, great, you're here.' Mark sounds truly grateful. 'Thanks again for helping out. You're a star. Ah, just make sure the nametags are organized so you can get to them easily. Thanks again for this. You look great, by the way.'

'No problem! Glad to help! I'll just get that sorted!' Why do I sound so grateful for the chance to alphabetize? I need to calm down. I've got the prickly sweats. What *is* it about this guy? My fantastic stand in his office should have given me closure, but it's true what they say. There's a risk of relapse as long as the temptation is there. Maybe they make a patch or something.

Sam is creeping around in his apron again. 'What are you doing, following me?' I say.

'Hmm?'

'This is the second event in a row.'

'I know. I work for the catering company. I thought we covered that last time.'

'I didn't realize your ambitions were so lofty. Office slave *and* busboy. You're really reaching for the stars. To think I just want to be a party planner.' Yes, I am still aggravated by that early conversation.

'Don't put yourself down. At least you're not just blowing bubbles.'

It's not easy arguing with someone who never gets mad back. 'Do we always hire the same company to cater?'

'Pretty much, yeah. Mark and my boss have a thing.'

'A thing?'

'Yeah, listen, gotta go or the crowd won't get their salmon en croute for lunch and the world as we know it will end. See ya later. By the way, I'm sorry to see you're not dressed up today.'

'With stupid shoes? Very funny.'

'I'm not kidding – you scrub up nice.' He flashes a grin and heads back to the kitchen.

Mark and the catering boss? A thing? What kind of thing? Sam must be made to talk.

The conference has to do with banking, blah, blah, blah. There's enough coffee to caffeinate an army. I'm so wired by lunchtime I'm seeing double. I don't mind. I'm seeing double of Mark. He's hovering at the back of the room, ready to jump to the rescue in case of projector malfunction or other technical calamity. I love that he's a CEO who still gets his hands dirty. Every time he catches my eye and smiles, my upper lip sweats. No man has ever had a physical effect on me like this. Granted, sweating isn't as nice as some of the other spontaneous physical effects he could bring out. God, I wish he wasn't married.

'Sorry?' He's standing right next to me.

'Um, nothing.' Tell me I didn't say that out loud.

'I heard you, Han . . .' he's chuckling now, 'to tell you the truth, I think about you a lot. That's not normal for me . . . It was kind of fun, wasn't it?'

. . . 'Yeah. It was kind of fun.' In all honesty, on a scale of one to I love you, it was more than kind of fun.

'It doesn't have to stop being fun.'

Yeah right. 'Tell your wife that.'

'I don't need to. My wife and I have an arrangement.'

'Look, Mark, I'm really not interested in being anybody's other woman, but thanks, I'll let you know if I ever want to apply for that position.'

'Hannah.' He takes my hand, looking around first, and sighs. I don't like the sound of that sigh. 'I'm sorry. I'm afraid I hurt you. You probably think I should have told you I was committed.'

'Married, Mark, you're married. Can't you even say it now?'

'Of course I can. I *am* married. To a woman I don't love, who doesn't love me. What I'm trying to say, obviously not very well, is that I didn't tell you because you never would have given me a chance.'

'*That's* your defence?!' I snatch my hand back. 'That you lied because it was the only way to get me into bed? Thank you for confirming everything sleazy I suspected about you.'

'You're right, I deserved that. I did lie, by omission, but it was because I saw there was something between us, and I didn't want to give up the chance to see if it was real. Is it?'

I know I should walk away. Fool me once, shame on you, fool me twice . . . who's the fool? 'How should I know if it was real?'

'Would seeing each other again help you decide?'

'You're asking me to have an affair with you?'

'I'm asking you to give me a chance.'

'Why are you still with your wife if you don't love each other?'

'It's my mother.'

'You married your mother.'

'Hah, hah. She lives with us. She loves Julia, and she's not well, and it just seems kinder to live our separate lives but keep the illusion of a marriage at home.'

'Do you have kids?'

'No. That's not even a possibility.'

'Why? Did she have you fixed?' I know I'm being cruel, but surely he deserves it.

'We don't sleep together.'

'Doesn't your mother notice?'

'No, she doesn't sleep with me either. Ah, finally, a smile. You can't hate me completely if you're smiling. Here, I'll make it easy for you. No pressure. Give me your mobile.'

'Why?'

'Just – thank you. Here, here's my number. Call any time. Okay?'

Something tells me his wife doesn't have this number. What am I thinking anyway? Didn't I already make this decision? 'Excuse me. I have to check on lunch.' Where the hell is the kitchen in this place? My knees are actually shaking. I thought that only happened in cartoons. How did I let him get to me like this? I'm not in love with him. Am I? No, almost certainly not. That'd be crazy. I made this decision already.

As usual, the kitchen is manic. At least one dish hits the floor every five minutes. I won't tell you what they do with that food – anyone who's worked in a restaurant knows well enough. A sunny corner at the edge of the mêlée beckons. I've decided I like kitchens. I like their heat and noise and the camaraderie in which everyone works. Nobody minds that I'm picking my lunch out of their morning's efforts. Sam hurries through a couple times before grabbing a plate of salmon and fixings and squishing in next to me. 'Having fun?'

'It's a ball. What are they talking about out there anyway?'

'Well, you see, ehem,' he says in a remarkably lifelike nerdy voice, pushing imaginary glasses up his nose, 'it's all about risk assessment, and risk control, and risk abatement, so the party of the first part and the party of the second part . . .'

'It's pretty dire.'

'It's my best accent.'

'I mean the conference.'

'Just be glad you don't have to go to these in your field,' he says. 'Though what would that agenda look like? The napkins of the future? Getting the guest list wow-factor? . . . Calligraphy and your table cards?'

'Don't mention table cards. Besides, you should talk. What's the hardest thing you have to do here? Stir the spaghetti Bolognese? Make strong coffee? I wouldn't throw stones.'

'Fair point. I withdraw my judgement. By the way, have you thought about going out with me?'

'Do you mean in a positive way?'

'Funny girl. I'll take that as a maybe.'

I'd have to sedate Stacy before telling her that I'd moved all the way to London to date an American office boy who washes dishes in his spare time. 'I'm seeing someone.'

'Who, Mark?'

'No!' Definitely not Mark. 'He's my boss. Besides, he's married.'

'That doesn't stop him.'

'Isn't he dating your boss?'

'I hope not. She's his sister-in-law.'

'That would be awkward.' So if I don't care who he's dating, why am I so relieved to hear this from Sam?

'Tell me about the guy you're seeing.'

'That's none of your business. Please don't push me for details. I don't lie well under pressure.'

'Is it serious?'

'I don't know.'

'It can't be, then.'

'I said I don't know.'

'If it's serious, you'd know. Let me know when you're not seeing him any more.'

'You're quite the pessimist.'

'Realist. I can –'

'*This* is cosy,' says the slender girl who's suddenly standing in front of us. She leans in to kiss Sam, her long hair shielding their intimacy in a glossy curtain. What I wouldn't give for those polished tresses.

'Oh, hi. Hannah, this is Janey. Janey, Hannah.'

'Hello.'

She's not even looking at me. 'Hi.' I've met warmer bowls of ice cream

Sam at least has the grace to look uncomfortable that his girlfriend interrupted his dating efforts. 'Janey and I, uh, work together. We're, ah . . . Actually, I need to check on the, the coffee. 'Scuse me.'

'I'll come with you. Pleasure to meet you.' She smiles, with no trace of the emotion reaching her eyes. Who is this English muffin? She's clearly staking her claim; I wonder how long she's been prospecting.

'Let me help you with your bag, erm, your bags. I did say it was just the weekend, right?'

Potential's concern that I plan to squat in his ancestral home is warranted, bearing in mind that British Airways' baggage allowance is smaller than the bags he's trying to fit into the trunk.

It's not that I didn't recognize how ridiculous my preoccupation with others' judgement was when panicking about what to wear this weekend. I just never noticed such an obvious self-abusive flaw in my character before coming to London. Maybe it's like leg hair – we all have it, but we only notice it when it's exposed or rubbed up against. Either I'm incredibly unexamined (that's very unlikely given how neurotic I am) or living my entire life among old friends means I've never had to bare my legs, so to speak. I guess that, also like hairy legs, it's not something I'm going to avoid without a lot of time spent with a therapist. Whether laser or psychotherapy, it'd be a painful cure.

My placement in the car isn't building my confidence. If I'm the future girlfriend, shouldn't I get the front seat? There's a guy already there making it clear that he plans to be Potential's co-pilot. So we're a car full of retirees, husbands in front and wives, plus an extra, in back. Exactly which one of us is supposed to be the extra? Poppy, Jools and George all went to Cambridge with Potential, they tell me. That's why they talk through a mouth full of marbles (they don't tell me this . . . I'm making logical connections). This is a different dimension, where friends are called chums and phrases like 'faabulous dahling' are uttered without sarcasm. I knew it. My twenty-seven wardrobe changes aren't going to compensate for being so far out of my element. They're friendly enough though, asking about me at first before settling into reminiscences about places I've never been with people I don't know. It's as interesting as looking at someone else's vacation photos. I'd be content to sit quietly staring out the window if it wasn't for the funk building up in the car. I can't tell where (who) it's coming from.

'Um, do you mind if I crack open a window?' This might turn into a very long weekend.

'That's a lovely dress,' Poppy says. 'Is it Prada?'

'Well spotted.'

'Very nice. I always like the Italians.'

I bet they don't know about the sample sales to which I owe most of my wardrobe. Finally, a system I have mastered. 'I'm sure they have them in London too, you know, at the end of the season when everything is like 80 per cent off? I shopped them all the time in New York. You get the greatest stuff so cheap.'

'Mmm, well, I don't really . . .'

Of course, these girls don't shop in bargain basements.

'I just never seem to get round to buying new clothes,' Jools says. Old clothes seem to be a point of honour among this set. Potential's ensembles have always looked slightly moth-ridden. Yet I can see that the girls are clad in designer wear. Perhaps they hang their purchases like game until the stench of newness wears off and they're sufficiently aged to be worn in public.

We must have taken a wrong turn somewhere because we're on a Merchant Ivory film set. Emma Thompson and her corset might come along any minute. Sweeping lawns stretch away into the distance, dotted with pines and spiky twisted trees out of Dr Seuss's[25] imagination. More trees, possibly planted by Anne Boleyn, line the driveway. When I say driveway, I mean the private road that we drive on for at least five minutes before getting to an enormous grey stone house. If a butler called Jeeves has the liveried help lined up outside the front door to greet us, I'm calling Stacy.

'I hope you like it,' Potential mumbles from somewhere beneath my luggage.

Of course he likes me. He wouldn't have asked me here, to his house, *to meet his friends*, if he didn't see a future for us. Sitting in the back seat was no big deal.

'Gregory can show you to your room.' He's much less shy now in the company of people depending on him for their livelihood. 'Once you've settled in, come down for a drink.'

25. Dr Seuss wrote the kind of children's books that all parents know were written under the influence of mind-altering drugs, ensuring that all children love them.

'Okay, thanks. Oh, hang on a sec.' It's my phone. It's Chloe. How am I supposed to pump her for information when everyone's standing here? 'I'm just going to, em, take this. Won't be a minute.'

They must be wondering why I'm striding towards the tree line when I'm obviously not a botanist. 'Chloe, thank god you called!'

'Well, I saw that you'd rung, so I wondered if it might be urgent.'

She's being kind. Stalkers on trial have made fewer calls than I've made to her cellphone in the last three days. 'Potential has asked me to his house!'

'You mean his flat? When?'

'No, his house-house, his stately house. We just arrived.'

'Oh, well, brilliant.'

'What's that? You're breaking up.' Odd silent gaps are interrupting my crisis. 'And no, it's not brilliant! I'm way out of my depth here.'

'Phone's beeping, low battery. I can't think where I left my charger. I thought I packed it.'

'I need your advice, Chloe.'

'Of course. About what?'

'Everything! You should see this house. It looks like a hotel. And three of his friends are with us.'

'You're with his friends?'

'Uh-huh.'

'Ah, I see. Okay, well in that case, definitely don't look –'

'Chloe? Hello? Hello?' Would it be *so* hard to make a phone battery that lasted longer than a good night's sleep?

Definitely don't look, she said. Don't look what? Like a slut? Like a grandma? Under the beds?

Jeeves (because who ever heard of a butler named Gregory)

is waiting to carry my bags up to a sweet little room on the second floor done all in blue. It's on a hallway with half a dozen other doors, meaning that the Lakers *and* the Knicks could probably sleep over if they wanted to have a basketball tournament in the back yard. Just to put things in perspective.

'Settling in' in English must mean 'freshening up' in American. Given that I have most of my wardrobe with me, it's a bit of a shock to have overlooked an important variable like heating. Maybe that's what Chloe meant: definitely don't look for comforts like a functioning circulatory system. My lips are blue and I've lost feeling in my fingers. I've been in walk-in freezers warmer than this. Though there's no way to prevent hypothermia without tipping into bag-lady couture, surely my intention to seduce calls for form over function. My padded bra has its work cut out for it.

'Wow, you're dressed up,' Potential remarks when I finally find everyone.

Wow, you're all in the same thing you wore in the car.

'Have a drink?'

'Sure. White wine?'

'Uh, I'll see what we have.' Everyone has mixed drinks poured from the little bar on the sideboard. I've probably just sent him on a wild-goose chase looking for anything under 100 proof. Yet I'm sure he said his perfect day involved a wine cellar. Was he lying about the cellar? Maybe he's lying about the whole thing. How do I know that this is really even his house? Maybe it's his friend's. I'm checking his suits when I find his closet. What if he's a pathological liar? He's probably married with kids. God, I should have asked. You take your eye off the ball for an instant and look what happens –

'Here you go.' He hands me a chilled glass. 'I hope it's okay; it's a new case.'

Okay, it's probably his house.

While I was playing Marco Polo[26] to find my hosts, I took the opportunity to have quite a thorough snoop through the place. You know how most houses have a living room that nobody ever goes into? It's the room with the impractical carpet and no TV that your mom uses when her lady friends visit. Potential's whole house is one giant unlived-in living room. Velvet ropes wouldn't be out of place, and earphones explaining in six languages that Henry VIII once slept there. I suspect the family only lives in a few rooms, to keep from freezing to death.

'Crispy, as you're up, I'll have another, please.' From Jools's gesture, I take it she's talking to Potential. I guess that's short for Crispin. At least I hope so, since that's his name. They all have nicknames, aside from Poppy, who'd have a hard time making her given name any more ridiculous. Maybe Potential will make one up for me. My dad calls me 'Hannah Banana', though I don't plan to share that.

'So, Hannah, we're intrigued by you.' George's sneer recalls some of Hannibal Lecter's more memorable scenes. 'Tell us, did you run away from something veddy teddible back home?'

'Uh . . .' What kind of question is that? Redheads are supposed to be friendly. That's how they compensate for being redheads.

'Shuttup, Georgie, you prat.' Poppy obviously has a background in diplomatic peacekeeping. 'He's always stirring. It's

26. A game that only children, with their absolute sense of fairness and fun, can play without cheating. It involves a child, with eyes tightly closed, chasing friends round a pool in a bat-like manner, guided by their hollered response 'Polo' to his shouted 'Marco'. They play until they are pruney, and generally long after they've all relieved themselves in their watery field of battle.

because he doesn't have any life of his own.' By holding her glass up, she's just drawn Potential off the sofa to pour her another drink. Now *that's* Dita behaviour.

'Ouch. You wound me.'

'Poppy's right, Georgie. Maybe if you got yourself some new friends, you'd have something productive to occupy your thoughts.'

'I would, but I can't stand the class of people out there these days.'

'The commoners?' Jools offers.

'I'm not interested in anything common.'

'Except seck-sually,' Poppy says.

'You would know, my dear.'

Potential laughs. 'Don't scare Hannah off, talking about sex and commoners.'

'Which do you prefer, Hannah?'

'What?'

'Sex or commoners?'

George is determined for me to hate him.

'Don't answer that, Hannah.' Potential actually sounds a little protective. 'George, I'm going to make you sleep in the gare-odge if you keep this up.'

'I apologize for Georgie,' says Jools. 'He doesn't often get to meet new people. For obvious reasons.'

'Sorry, Crispy, don't mean to scare off your little piece of rough.'

'George!'

Ruff? Ruffle? I'm in the twilight zone.

Just to reinforce his role as head of the welcoming committee, George steers the conversation to TV they watched as kids. My most useful contribution will be to have a nap here on the table. For two countries with such a 'special relationship', culturally we have nothing in common. They might not even know who Bugs Bunny is.

'Did you have Saturday morning cartoons?'

'Of course. We are a first-world country, you know,' George says . . . You arrogant cultural imperialist bitch, his look emphatically adds.

'I just wondered what shows you had as kids.'

'*Blue Peter*!'

Which sounds vaguely pornographic.

'*ThunderCats*! Or *Button Moon*!'

'*SuperTed*!'

Ted is no name for a convincing superhero. 'What's *SuperTed*?'

'He's a magic teddy bear,' Potential explains.

'Did he fight crime?'

'He fought Texas Pete.' At least Potential now looks like he too doubts Pete's defensive capabilities.

'Texas –?'

'Texas Pete, the evil cowboy.'

Of course. 'Did he have superpowers?'

'He flew.'

'Did he foil plots to end the world?'

'No,' giggles Poppy, 'mostly he lazed about in his treehouse with his friend Spotty.'

'Hannah, ours is a kinder, gentler existence,' George explains. 'We don't think everyone is out to get us.'

Huh, in your case, George, you shouldn't assume we're not.

Gregory comes in to tell us that dinner's ready. Actually, he says, 'Dinner is served.' I swear to god.

I'm not proud of self-medicating but getting drunk does take the edge off the evening. It's not that I dislike them. Well,

I dislike George. I don't have any idea what the others are talking about. Everything is an inside joke and it's abundantly clear that I'm not on the inside. However, by the time we've pushed our plates away, at least I've got the hang of their banter. If I make everything a sexual innuendo, they think I'm witty. The more booby comments the better. I now understand the Brits' reverence for Benny Hill.

My smutty repartee is working its magic on Potential too. He's even holding my hand now. 'Come on, Hannah, it's a gorgeous night. Let's take a walk.'

'Sure, okay.' Why not? Walking may lie somewhere between leg waxing and vacuuming on my list of favourite activities, but I'm so grateful to get out of this Laura Ashley igloo that I'd walk to Wales right now for the chance to reintroduce my limbs to their circulatory system. A chorus of jibes worthy of pre-pubescent boys follows us into the garden.

'I hope you don't mind a walk.'

Maybe this was the subject of Chloe's caution: definitely don't wear taxi shoes because you're going to be force-marched outdoors. 'Of course not. It's a nice night.' Fortunately for my toes, which are going numb in shoes that are half a size too small (but so cute), his idea of a walk involves a very civilized path around the yard. Given the size of the yard, this could take half an hour. Still, it's snuggly with his arm around me.

'Thanks for coming down. It's very brave of you, you know.'

'Oh, I don't think so. I like your friends.' At least, theoretically, I could grow to tolerate them given enough time.

'They're a lot to handle at first. But you're American, I knew you'd be all right.'

I love that he loves that I'm American.

'Come, I have something to show you.' In a little thicket, I can just make out the frame of a house. A miniature house. 'Come on.' He's dancing me towards the door.

I know you know where this is going. So do I, and I have to say that doing it in the great outdoors isn't one of my fantasies. Not when there are perfectly beautiful four-poster beds in the house, and definitely not when it's our first time. 'Ah, actually, I'm not such a big nature fan,' I say, extricating myself from his embrace. 'Do you mind if we go back in the house?' And tear each other's clothes off, obviously.

'Uh, sure, okay. Whatever you want.'

I like the sound of that!

'That was fast.'

'Georgie, don't be rude.'

'I'm just stating a fact.'

Nobody is bothering to talk over the blare of the TV. With Poppy and Jools draped all over the sofa, Potential and I are forced into separate chairs.

''Nother glass of wine, Hannah?'

'Sure, thanks.' This isn't even close to the romantic evening I had in mind. For one thing, there are three too many people in the room. For another, I'm more than lunging distance from the object of my desire. It's an uncomfortable flashback to late nights in a guy's room during college, ostensibly watching TV, in reality waiting for his room-mate to fall asleep so we could jump each other. This time it's me who's falling asleep, thanks to my impressive assault on the wine cellar tonight. They've beaten me. Intentionally or not, Potential's friends are foiling my plans for passion.

Judging from Poppy's smirk, I may have just snored myself awake. 'I'm turning in.' Short of turning the lights off and calling last orders, I don't know how to more strongly signal my intentions.

'Okay, Hannah.' Potential stands, finally getting the hint. He kisses me. 'Goodnight.' He sits down again.

That's it? What kind of man invites a perfectly sexy woman away for a weekend and then doesn't make a move? I didn't force him to ask me here. He volunteered the invitation out of the blue. He must have liked me or he wouldn't have asked. And we haven't seen each other since Wednesday, so I know I didn't piss him off between then and now. I was even polite to his odious friend . . . Unless he did like me, but upon reflection he's gone off me. Four dates was all it took for him to realize he doesn't want to get involved. I feel a little sick. How many times have I gone out with a guy a few times and never heard from him again? Lots. This just confirms my suspicions. I'm fundamentally unsuitable for the long haul, and this obviously isn't working. I've been kidding myself, thinking I'd have a fabulous relationship with some stranger I met on the rebound. Really, what are the chances of that working out, when we're so fundamentally different? I know virtually nothing about him . . .

Maybe I'm better off sticking with what I know. I do, after all, already have an offer on the table, right? I realize I've made it sound like there's no way I'd take him up on it, and I wouldn't even consider it if not for a particularly troublesome character flaw making me covet what other people have. Knowing he's attached gives him a female 'stamp of approval' that's perversely appealing (perverse because he'd be cheating to go out with me; not exactly a desirable trait in a boyfriend). Still, wouldn't it be so easy, and so tempting, to plug back into the world I know? Who hasn't done it, whether old home, old friend or old boyfriend? I think I understand what long-standing prisoners go through, dreaming of a different life only to be let out and then have to face the fact that maybe they can't do it after all. I want to reoffend, to be let back inside, where at least it's safe . . . Dating a known quantity has its advantages. They say the devil you know is better than the devil you don't. At least I can anticipate the problems. Besides, maybe he'll surprise me. I can't deny we have some weird connection.

What's that? There's a little voice that sounds a lot like the new Hannah. Don't settle, she whispers. And don't give up on Potential. He wouldn't have asked you for the weekend, with his friends, if he didn't like you. Everyone knows boys don't let their friends within ten feet of a shag-buddy. He must see the potential for a future. He's just taking things slowly because he wants everything to be perfect. Even the most fervent optimist couldn't have called this day perfect. Obviously he's a gentleman, planning to make his move later. Or perhaps . . .

Perhaps that bit in the playhouse *was* his move. Is it possible he has just one move, and he thinks I rejected him? Surely he's not that sensitive. Is he? I need clarification. Obviously I can't go back downstairs now that I've made my exit. And I don't know where he's sleeping, so unless I want to risk walking in on Jools, or worse, on George, I can't very well go sneaking into bedrooms. I could text him. Would that look desperate? Absolutely. Not that my pride is my main concern at times like these – there's also no signal in the house, so unless I want to go back outside to the tree line . . . Think, think, think.

How about if, before everyone comes upstairs, I find his room and leave him a playful, sexy note? I'm sure that's exactly what the Kates would do.

Since he grew up here, there has to be one room filled with boy junk. No mother redecorates her son's room if she doesn't have to. I'm guessing it's at the top of the house, as far away from his parents as possible. The stairs are unnervingly creaky. Potential had no chance of sneaking in late as a teenager. I'm sure my footsteps aren't actually that loud, it's just that it's graveyard-quiet up here. I'd never get used to that. I grew up claustrophobic, constantly tripping over a very vocal family. Everything is too spread out in this house. I'd redecorate and put my bedroom on the first floor. And I'd definitely open up those other rooms so they were livable. What's the point of having a mansion if you're going to live in a couple rooms like a poor person?

This must be it. There are band posters all over the walls and at least a dozen upright video games, a sort of nerd's time capsule from 1993. I hope Potential isn't some kind of Oasis-obsessed computer freak. I dated one of those in college (a computer freak, I mean; I have nothing against the band). Ultimately there wasn't room in his life for both Game Boy and me. I'd hate to be beaten again by an electronic device. There's his desk. It's stuffed with papers. I'm not snooping. I'm looking for something to write on. Some look like letters. And I'm looking for a pen. Old girlfriends' letters? Current girlfriend's letters? This pen doesn't work. Perhaps there's another folded inside one of these letters.

Deny it if you like, but it's a rare girl who wouldn't read her boyfriend's letters if she got the chance. The only thing stopping me from reading them is the fear that I'll get caught. My chances then of becoming Lady Potential would substantially diminish. On the other hand, forewarned is forearmed (they're addressed to 'Pickle'). Didn't I resolve not to get involved with another attached man? What if Potential is hiding a girlfriend? (There are at least half a dozen letters here.) I owe it to myself to find out the truth (they're dated two years ago). But it's wrong, I know that. As I scribble my note – inviting him to see more of me without making any promises – I resolve not to pry. What a grown-up I've become! Maybe it's the move, or my new job, or the fact that I didn't go psycho on Mark. Whatever the reason, this transformation is remarkable. I've achieved a new level of personal growth. Good for me.

'Oh my god!' I've just run into Jeeves in the hall. Literally. When I put my hands out to keep from stumbling, I hit him in the balls.

'Terribly sorry to have frightened you, miss.'

'Uh, that's okay.' I've felt up the butler.

'Can I help you find something?'

'I was, ah, looking for the bathroom.'

'It's on your floor, miss.' He knows he's caught me. 'Shall I show you?'

I follow him meekly back downstairs to the bathroom, which is next door to my bedroom, by the way. I'm trying not to give off petty-thief vibes, but I'm sure he'll count the silverware when I leave.

13

You know what they say about best-laid plans. Sometimes nobody gets laid. The sun is gamely trying to penetrate the wine fog in my head. It's sometime between 9.30 a.m. and 3 p.m. People talk about the rain in England, but nobody mentions that the sun barely comes over the horizon this time of year. A glance at Piaget tells me it's technically still morning. A glance at the empty side of the bed tells me I'm technically still unsatisfied. As if I need the reminder. Potential must have read the note and laughed. Or worse, he cringed. Either way, I look like a fool. I've got to get out of here. I'd fake a gallbladder attack if I had any idea where my gallbladder might be. I could hitchhike back to London, but I don't get the feeling that the English are comfortable offering strangers rides in their cars, given that they won't even speak to them on trains, and we're at least thirty miles outside the reach of my Oyster card. Damn this idyllic countryside. I don't know what the English see in it. Chloe talks like Nirvana rests just outside the M25. It sounds like she grew up in a very rural place, which explains her vegetarianism. She doesn't have an innate love of greens, or empathy for God's small creatures. Her father served her pet lamb to the family for dinner one fine evening. Over dessert, he casually mentioned the provenance of those chops and her aversion to meat was born. Honestly, with her parents, it's amazing she's this well adjusted.

George is in the kitchen, waiting to fulfil his ambition to be the world's most loathsome man. He and Potential look like they've slept in their clothes. This is taking the capsule wardrobe a step too far, though Potential is still adorable in his lord-of-the-manor furry cardigan and wide-wale corduroys. If I don't make eye contact, we can both pretend this never happened and I can thumb my way home after breakfast.

'Hey, you,' he says as he rushes, actually rushes, to me.

What's this? Now I'm even more confused. If he *is* into me, why didn't he come to my room last night? And if he isn't, why is his tongue in my mouth?

'Shoot, Hannah?' George says. He's washing down bites of toast with what looks like a gin and tonic.

'I beg your pardon?' It's the weekend. A girl shouldn't be penalized for sleeping in.

'Do – you – shoot?'

Unless he's referring to pool, I don't. It's not something we get much chance to do in Hartford, Connecticut. Shoot*ings*, well, that's another story. I'm not against the concept of hunting, considering how much of its proceeds I eat and wear . . . I've coveted a chinchilla jacket for six months now. I don't suppose they're indigenous to the Surrey countryside.

'What are we shooting?'

'Duck. Ah, girls, ready?'

Well, I'd look stupid in a duck jacket, but I'm game.

Looking at Jools and Poppy, I realize that *this* is where Ralph Lauren should look for his inspiration. They have the chicest little ensembles, pretty plaid blazers and the most adorable tweedy pants and tall boots you'll see outside Chanel's fall/winter heritage collection. Jools even has a cap.

Potential hasn't failed to notice my envy. 'Come on, Hannah, we've got some gear here for you.' They have an entire shed devoted to blood sports. Just imagine how stunning I'll look in a tweed shooting jacket. Maybe there's one in pink. 'There you are. It may be a little big, but it'll keep you warm.'

I'm holding an armload of combat-green oilcloth.

'You'll need those,' he says, pointing to clunky green rubber boots. 'The tracks are muddy.' Plonking a hat (brown and ugly) on my head, he looks pleased with his work.

I look like Elmer Fudd.

'Cheer up, old girl,' George pipes up. 'It's not about style.'

What nonsense. Of course it is.

The dogs are bounding ahead of us, stopping every few minutes to check that we're still enjoying their game. (At least dogs are the same here, although I suppose they don't understand English in other countries. Imagine that. You say, 'Sit, Pepper!' and Pepper says, '*Qué?*') It's exciting to carry a gun, though I'm a little worried about shooting someone (George would be my first choice). This is one instance when I'm not tempted by the urge to embellish my abilities. Some might say I've lied about certain skills in the past. I maintain that from a theoretical point of view, skiing didn't *look* that hard. From the top of the mountain, the view was a little different and I'm very grateful for safety nets at the edge of slopes.

Potential doesn't seem to mind my lack of shooting expertise. It's sexy letting him teach me how to hold a gun. And either he's carrying his cartridges in his front pocket or he thinks so too. This makes his no-show last night even more mysterious. I can't imagine what happened. Except that I didn't sign the note. Maybe he thought it was from Jools or Poppy. If so, he must be mortified that one of his long-time friends propositioned him. It's a person's worst nightmare to have a friend suddenly get a case of the wish-you-were-nakeds. I wonder which girl he thinks it is. It must be Jools, since Poppy and George obviously had a thing. That's why he's been so attentive this morning. He feels guilty by proxy. Just how guilty, I wonder? What if he took Jools up on my proposition? What if they spent the entire night having sex and laughing at me? That two-timing bastard!

'Hallo, hold up!'

'It's my brother,' says Potential.

'Well, hello.'

'Alfie, this is Hannah. Hannah, my brother Alfie.' He's even better-looking than Potential. And I bet he's nice and charming and funny and he hasn't just slept with Jools under my very nose. Just as I'm beginning to wonder how I might successfully transfer my affections to him without seeming fickle, Potential says, 'Good luck getting into your room, Alfie. Mother's had all the video games put in there while they redo the games room.' He rolls his eyes at me. 'Mother insists on keeping all of our old games for the grandchildren she hopes to have one day.'

So he didn't get my note. Thank god. He didn't sleep with Jools by mistake. There's no reason to hate him. In fact, he has no idea that I even extended the invitation to make a dishonest woman of me. He's probably second-guessing every move he made, wondering if he's done something wrong. I have nothing to worry about. It's Alfie's room I left the note in . . . which means I've just propositioned my boyfriend's brother.

You may wonder if I often get myself into this kind of situation. In fact, I have a history. Sometimes I get away with it, like the time I crank-called a boyfriend's ex-girlfriend, who star-69ed me back,[27] forcing me to invite her to a hastily assembled surprise party for him. But sometimes confession

27. America's 'call return' service, like Britain's 1471, is marketed ostensibly as a handy way to get in touch with loved ones when you miss their phone call, but is in fact used almost exclusively by the victims of teenagers' crank calls.

is the only viable option, like when you prepare a romantic Valentine's dinner only to realize you've dropped a Band-Aid[28] off your finger somewhere in the process. I fear this is one of those Band-Aid-in-the-salad occasions.

We've come to the lake where the ducks are supposed to be, but nobody has told the ducks that they're expected. Actually, this hunting expedition has been a little pointless so far. It's just a walk in the woods with dogs, and weapons. Why not just leave it at that and stop by the food store for steaks on the way home?

KAWAAAAAGGHH!

'What – what the hell is that?'

'Duck call.'

It sounds like someone breaking his guitar onstage. Though no duck in its right mind should be attracted to that, fortunately for meat-eaters, ducks are not the smartest animals in the kingdom. Here they come. We all scramble to take aim and shoot. Ready. Aim. Fire . . .

Take safety off first.

Readyaimfire.

'Well done, Hannah!' Potential calls, striding over. 'I think you got one.'

Did I? 'Do you think I really shot one?'

'You did. Poppy got the other one. Congratulations! Look. Drop it, boy. Good dog.'

I shot a duck. My very first time. I shot a duck! I burst into tears.

Alas, I realize that I'm no hunter. Hypocritical as it is, my

28. Through the miracle that is modern marketing, everyone knows what a Band-Aid is, but no doubt our tendency to use brand names as proper names is confusing to non-English speakers. Surely Tupperware is a mystery to those who don't know what a 'tupper' is (i.e., everyone).

interest in meat extends only to the kind that's safely devoid of any animal characteristics, packaged in cellophane and sold in the supermarket. It's for the greater good that most of us have no interest in shooting. If we did, there'd be no animals left after a while and we'd have to start shooting each other to fulfil our bloodlust. My squeamishness simply helps foster a well-balanced ecosystem.

I've got to get Potential alone, to explain about last night. I'm now walking so slowly, dragging on his arm, that he probably thinks I've had a stroke. 'I have a confession.'

His face turns thunderous. Not a good start. 'What is it?'

'It's about Alfie.'

'God, I knew it. You know, this would actually be funny if it didn't happen so bloody often.'

'What are you talking about?' I can't believe a string of girls have accidentally left a love note for Potential on his brother's bed. Surely not more than two.

'I'm talking about you and Alfie.'

'Me and Alfie?'

'Just say it. You prefer him to me. Fine.'

'No, no. I left a note in his room. For you. And I think we should get it before he finds it.'

'What?'

Patiently, I explain again.

'What did the note say?'

Ay, ay, ay. 'Come on, I'll show you.'

It's impossible to tell from his expression whether he's aroused or mortified by what he's reading. Now I'm embarrassed. 'I'd had a little bit to drink.'

'How do you feel now that you're sober?'

He's hitting on me. I love it. 'I feel like I'd write the note again.'

'You don't need to write it. Come here.' I can taste the whisky he's been sipping all afternoon from his hip flask. 'Let's go to my room.'

I'm trying not to think too much during this, the consummation of my future as a lady, but, while the kissing is all right, there's a lot going on that demands my attention. For one thing, he's rubbing my breast like he expects a genie to emerge. I gently move his hand to my ass, just to give him something else to focus on, but within seconds the palm is back, keen as ever. To distract him from his polishing I unbutton his shirt. A slightly sour odour wafts out. I'm a little particular when it comes to cleanliness, but I can't really judge him when he's been out walking in wool all afternoon. I'm delighted to see that, though slender, he's sinewy and not too hairy. I once went out with a guy who was gorgeous until I unbuttoned his shirt and found a Wookiee[29] lurking beneath.

He's been fiddling with my turtleneck for ages and there's no easy way out of it except to wrestle it off. *Now* I understand Chloe's advice: definitely don't look too rugged because you're going to be seduced! We sit on the bed, still kissing, still fumbling. I feel his hand in my hair. I love having my hair played with. But as his hand moves to the top of my head, I realize he's not interested in the smoothness of my follicles. Our battle starts gently enough, Potential's palm pushing down ever so slightly, me nudging back. But within minutes he's practically got two hands on my head. Generally, I'd be out the door by this time, but to be honest, I'm curious to see what he's got down there. He's obviously very anxious to show me. Without making any promises, I unzip his cords. He pulls his pants down so fast I almost fall off the bed.

29. Like Han Solo's shaggy sidekick in *Star Wars*.

Holy mother of all things sacred! I've never seen or smelled anything like this. I won't go into malodorous detail but Port-a-Potties on the last day of a chilli and beer festival have smelled better. And, please forgive my naivety, but what am I supposed to do with that thing? Imagine a boiled pork sausage that you forgot to poke with a fork. The thing that came out of Kane's chest in *Alien* was more appealing.

'I'm sorry, I, uh . . .' God, he stinks.

He releases my hair. 'What's wrong?'

'I can't.'

'You're kidding.'

'No joke.'

'But, you're American.'

'What's that got to do with anything?'

'You Americans love giving blow-jobs.'

'Do we?' If I needed another reason to pull my turtleneck back on, being told my country is full of dick-sucking sluts is it.

'Yeah, everybody knows that.'

'Really. How many Americans have you gone out with?'

'Well, one. But come on. Come *on*.' He makes a half-hearted attempt to put his hand back on my head. I slap it away. Is he kidding? 'Fine. Whatever . . . but I have to say, you're a bloody tease.'

'What!?'

'Psh. Come on, we met *speed-dating*. People go to those nights for one reason.'

'To meet people.'

'To meet people to shag.'

'That's not why I went.'

'Well then, you're the only one. And bollocks, by the way. You told me you were up for it.'

175

'Right, I was up for spending the weekend with you.'

'Whatever. I'll drive you to the station if you want.'

What do you think? Three hours later, I'm back in my apartment, spilling my mortified guts to Stacy.

She's having a hard time adjusting to the fact that she's not going to be a lady-in-waiting. 'Maybe it was a one-off. You said yourself he was out in the woods all day.'

She's missing the point, or, to be accurate, the skin covering it. 'It was disgusting, Stace. Just not appealing in any way.' I'm actually having flashbacks.

'Do you think there was something wrong with him? Maybe they don't all look like that. I know! Google it!'

'What, foreskin?' I'm shuddering at the very thought of seeing a variety of stuffed squid hanging off the fronts of otherwise perfectly normal men. I'll happily live out my days without doing that research, thanks. 'It's just not going to work. Besides, we didn't part on friendly terms. And he's a head-pusher.'

'God, like that guy Chuck, remember?'

Chuck was one of Stacy's college boyfriends. 'Remember?! You sent him to the hospital for stitches.'

'I did warn him. Many times. Besides, I didn't even bite that hard. I wonder where he is now.'

I bet he's married to a woman with dentures.

14

Obviously I've called the London Council together for the local view on this development. I'm sure Siobhan would contribute more if she hadn't just fallen off her chair laughing.

'Oh, Hannah, I'm sorry.' Chloe has to stop to take another breath. 'It didn't occur to me to warn you!'

'I just didn't expect the uncut version.'

'That's just the way they all are,' Siobhan declares, able to draw this rather sweeping conclusion from her body of research on the subject.

'But it was so ugly!' I shudder.

'Aren't you over-reacting, just a bit? I have to say it's not usually that obvious once it's, em, aroused. What, exactly, did it look like?'

. . . 'Imagine a really fat guy, a *really* fat guy, in a too-tight wetsuit. There was actually a crease in it, like circulation was being cut off.'

'Oh, that's not normal.'

'Not at all.' Siobhan is shaking her head with a look not dissimilar to my original reaction to the event. 'I didn't realize Americans were all . . . trimmed. Isn't that weird, Chloe?'

'I think so.'

You know what they say about assumptions. If I can't take something as basic as anatomy for granted, imagine what other surprises my foray into the UK dating scene has in store for me. 'But the BO, I mean, what's that all about?' Granted, we Americans are obsessive about body odour. But I feel that a

177

country whose citizens have the right to vote should adhere to some basic level of personal hygiene.

'Oh that,' says Chloe. 'It comes from school. You know, they're only allowed a couple of baths a week, unless they play sport.'

'Yeah, it's always worth asking if a bloke was sporty in school.'

My view of Hogwarts is now for ever altered. No wonder Harry plays Quidditch. 'By the way, Chloe – what was that advice about "definitely don't look . . ." Your phone cut out, so I didn't hear it.'

'Er, I don't remember . . . Oh wait, yes I do. I just said definitely don't look like you're trying too hard to dress up. We never do in the country. I assume it's the same in Ireland?'

'Sure, but we spend all day digging up the potatoes in the fields, remember, so we don't have much reason to dress up. Or wear shoes.'

'That Celtic wit continues to astound.'

When Chloe and Siobhan first met, I was a little alarmed at the seemingly antagonistic repartee they developed within minutes. It wasn't till Siobhan explained a little of the history between the English and the Irish that I understood, though it didn't set my mind at ease. What I didn't realize (until Chloe told me) is that Siobhan, despite her field-hand declarations, actually comes from Irish gentry. So they can afford to tease each other like this without risking an international incident. 'Chloe, do your dates ever smell?' I have a hard time imagining this stylish woman in bed with a stinker.

'God, no! I date middle-class boys. Most of those are trained to wash. Or sporty ones. I'm afraid this is a feature of some upper-class toffs. They don't give a toss what anyone thinks of them. I'm so sorry, petal.'

Right, mental note. No more dating upper-class toffs unless I can verify that they bathe. But hygiene isn't the biggest issue here. I didn't foresee this circumcision setback. I've been driving an automatic my whole adult life and now I'm expected to operate a manual transmission. Just like that. Without even a learner's permit.

I know what you're thinking. Mark and I were naked together. More than once. How did I, who am keenly observant, miss something as obvious as foreskin? I swear I wasn't that drunk. I'd have noticed a Shar-Pei in his trousers. Maybe he's Jewish. Or maybe, as Chloe said, it isn't a problem as long as he's aroused. Which he was. I guess I have two choices. Either I embrace the Torah or I make sure my dates are so turned on that the issue doesn't come up. Or down, or whatever. Either way, I will not let a little extra skin foil my search for true love.

However, this does beg the obvious question, once again. Why am I putting myself through all this, now limiting my options even more narrowly, when I have an obvious alternative who's already interested? My mother would say, 'A bird in the hand is worth two in the bush.' Okay, I'll stop bringing it up. I'm just telling you what my mother would say.

I think Felicity is finally warming to me. She hasn't given me her manicure appointment (or told me where she shops) but she's letting me help with the Tory dinner. At least, she's letting me attend so she has someone to scream at if anything goes wrong.

I'm late. I'm panicked. Everything in my wardrobe makes me look like the Slovakian national shot-put champion.

Sarah bursts through my bedroom door. 'We're goin' out, wanna come . . . ?'

I'm standing in front of my closet in Spanx and a bra that could support a work crew of six.

'Mate,' she exclaims, 'are you all right? I think your pants are too tight. There's a vein poppin' on your forehead.'

This is hilarious coming from someone whose most stressful moments involve answering the question ''Nother beer?'

'Nothing fits. I think I've gained weight.'

'It's the Heathrow injection!'

'The what?'

'Nathan, get in here!' she calls into the hallway. ''Annah wants to know what the Heathrow injection is.'

Oh god. Where's my robe? All humiliating topics are fair game for group discussion in our apartment, sorry, our flat. My ass is about to become one of them.

'Nathan, now isn't really a good –'

He ambles in, pushes aside the mountain of clothes and throws himself on my bed. 'That's what Aussie girls get when they land at Heathrow. It makes their arses blow up fat as a teeck.' Fat as a tick, thanks very much.

'Not just Aussies.' Sarah looks pointedly at me. Australians are known for many things. Tact isn't one of them.

'Okay, fine, thanks for the definition. Now get out, please. I have to find something to wear.'

I want to crawl into my closet. I can't believe Nathan has seen my Spanx. This is worse than the time he caught me bleaching my lip (I told him it was extra-strength moisturizer, but he looked dubious). He's been privy to too many of my grooming habits not to officially be in the undateable friend zone now. It's probably better this way anyhow – at least I can relax. Who cares if he sees me wearing stilettos with thick socks or my ultra-moisturizing gloves? Finally I'm free to eat pints of ice cream in front of the TV. I've been kidding myself anyway, harbouring a crush on a man who bed-hops like a rent boy in his prime earning years. Plus the other day, he farted on the couch and didn't even look embarrassed. In fact, he said, 'Aw, *that* was a ripper!' That's not the statement of a man who wants to impress a girl.

Sadly, gas wasn't historically a romantic deal-breaker. I fear my list of boyfriend requirements has been too modest. A funny, fun, smart man who wasn't afraid of commitment or my foundationwear ticked all the boxes. But I've realized something these last few months. The real problem isn't the men I'm finding. It's the men I'm looking for. Names may change, but I've gone out with the same guy for ten years. He's Fun Guy, the guy everyone likes. He's the one his friends can count on to drink all weekend, the one so emotionally stunted that he's incapable of admitting he actually has feelings. Shedding a beery tear when his team wins the championship doesn't count. I deserve someone who will listen, share and gossip, someone who doesn't think farts are the height of humour. I want a man who isn't afraid to talk about his feelings. In short, I want my boyfriend to be just like my girlfriends, with a huge penis.

What would my list of perfect boyfriend requirements look like?

1. ~~He cooks.~~ He cooks well. And doesn't use too many chillies.
2. He cleans. Or pays someone to do it for him.
3. He holds my hand in public, and gives me lots of compliments. But not too many, or they'll lose their impact.
4. . . .

That's very helpful. I've just described an affectionate house-keeper.

Perhaps a list of warning signs to help weed out unsuitable boyfriends is better. From previous experience alone, I can come up with a list in seconds. Section I: Things the Perfect Boyfriend Would Never Say. Tick all that apply (even if said in jest, or to a friend that you found out about later, or while under the influence of alcohol or other mind-altering substances):

1. I didn't sleep with her – we just fooled around.
2. I don't mind that your thighs wobble.
3. Are you going to wear that?
4. But I tell my mom everything.
5. You know you can wax that off if you want to.
6. Are you going to look like her when you get old?
7. Maybe you should lay off the Chardonnay.
8. I'm not saying that she's prettier than you – just different.
9. Tomorrow I'm having dinner with my ex.
10. Last night I had dinner with my ex.
11. I bought this for you. It'll help with those little lines around your eyes.
12. How about a quick blow-job before we go?
13. I don't know anyone who's happily married.
14. Look, this obviously upsets you, so next time I won't tell you about it.
15. You have too many shoes.
16. The dinner was lovely. Was that beef or chicken?
17. No, honey, you're not fat. You're just bloated.
18. What do you mean, appliances can't be Christmas presents?

19. I thought about buying you sexy underwear for your birthday but thought à gym membership would be more useful.
20. You're just like your mother.

Ticked only one? With the proper training at Boyfriend School your man is probably salvageable. Ticked three or more? At some point in your relationship, he's going to point out your hairy lip/legs/underarms in public and fart unapologetically on the couch.

Of course, I'm thinking about him again. And while the sad fact is I know he wouldn't be good for me, I also know he's not the kind of guy to fart on the couch. Couldn't that be enough, at the start?

'What are you wearing?' Felicity demands when she sees me.

What I'm wearing is a floor-length raspberry rough-silk (very) fitted dress that I got half-price at Ann Taylor last year. I give her as much of a twirl as the dress will bear. It's her own fault if she doesn't like it. She still won't let me near the closet.

'This is a business dinner! I didn't think I had to tell you how to dress.'

Given the facts, she certainly should have. We're gathered, by invitation, in the grand ballroom of a stately home for a champagne reception with canapés, followed by dinner, a few speeches and dancing. Throw in bickering in-laws and a drunken bridesmaid and it's practically a wedding. What did she expect me to wear, tweed?

She's wearing tweed. And sensible shoes. 'Ugh, it's too late for you to change.' I get the feeling she's not just talking about my dress. 'Go and check on the champagne . . . and make sure the table cards are all set up. And Hannah, please try not to muck things up!'

I'm constantly letting Felicity down. I wish I didn't, and not just because disappointing your boss is a poor route to career advancement. I crave the validation. Can you blame me, when I was fired from my first job and got my second under sexual pretences? I haven't exactly built sound work credentials so far.

'Nice outfit. What are you dressed for?' It's Sam.

'Coming from a guy wearing an apron and gum-soled shoes, you'll excuse me if I don't crumble into tears at your cutting sarcasm.'

'Didn't Felicity mention that this was a business dinner?'

'No! I mean, I knew. Don't you have work to do?'

'I'm on my –'

'Hi, Sam.' Janey may have microchipped him. She certainly has a knack for knowing when he's talking to me.

'Hey, you. Remind me to give you something later.'

'Give it to me now,' she says suggestively, eyeing him from beneath thick, super-long lashes. What kind of supplements does this girl take? 'I'm here for another hour, just for the drinks reception.' She should realize that standing there with that look on her face is just encouraging me to flirt with Sam, simply for the joy of being responsible for her insomnia tonight. 'Will I see you after?' she purrs.

'Gonna have to study but come on, I'll . . .' As they amble out of eavesdropping range, my mumbled 'See ya' meets with no response.

Far be it from me to lecture on manners, but that's just rude, to walk away without a goodbye.

The guests arrive in an enormous wave at 7 p.m., as demanded by the invitation. One after another, the women shed their coats to reveal business suits. Apparently Tories are Conservatives in both the upper- and the lower-case sense. Which means I do look like a hooker. And judging by the leers, I'm not the only one to think so. Just perfect. At least if I sit behind the nametag table, I'm hidden from the waist down. Short of donning a tablecloth there's not much I can do about the rest of me. Under normal circumstances, I wouldn't mind having a few extra pounds settle into my décolletage, but my dress is unforgiving. Breathing in results in a sort of squeezed water balloon effect.

'You! We have white space!' It's the photographer, a man who doesn't understand that skinny jeans on men are as inappropriate as lumberjack shirts are on women. 'We can't have white space!'

'What are you talking about?'

'At the tables. There are three empty chairs on the tables at the front.' Clearly he's one of those hysterical artistes who fall apart when the light goes wrong or it's too humid for the lens. You'd think he was shooting a feature film for Spielberg, not a Tory propaganda video. Annie Leibovitz wouldn't behave like this.

'What would you like me to do?' Spontaneously give birth to a litter of Conservatives?

'You have to fill those chairs.'

'Why don't you just take the chairs away?'

'Uneven place settings? At the front? I don't think so. You!' He spots Felicity. 'Your table plan is wrong.'

Heads down, everyone, and shield the children. In my short career, I've learned that there are a few things you don't say to a party planner: 1) I love the theme, I saw the same thing in *Tatler* last month; 2) Are you sure these oysters are fresh?; 3) I don't think I should have to tip the caterers when

I've paid that kind of money; and 4) You've fucked up the seating plan.

'What do you mean?' Felicity asks with a perfectly raised eyebrow that adds 'you odious little troll whom I'm not above running down in an alley'. I'm in awe of her ability to reduce people to quivering masses in seconds (as long as it isn't aimed at me). The English really are masters of disdain.

But this photographer didn't climb to his prissy heights by being weak. Plus he's English himself. 'I mean that three of your *confirmed* guests haven't turned up and their chairs are empty, which will look terrible on film.'

'Hannah. Who isn't here?' Three badges sit accusingly on the table. Unless there are unlabelled guests inside, the photographer is right.

'Did you confirm these guests?'

This is hardly the time to start pointing fingers. How am I supposed to remember whether they confirmed? They all have names like Pilkington and Tomlinson.

'Ugh, never mind. Hannah, go to the table.'

'And do what?'

'Sit down.'

Oh god, oh god, oh god. What am I supposed to say to these people? Am I supposed to pretend to be Mrs Pilkington? Of course not. They'll catch on to my accent instantly. Felicity has just pressed one of the waiters into service. He rushes off into the kitchen and returns a few seconds later *sans* apron to take his place among the Peers. Felicity settles herself into the third seat.

'Hannah Cumming. Nice to meet you,' I beam to the man on my right.

'Oh, er, ehem, well, uh . . .' You'd think I just tried to hand him a trout instead of my hand. I'm not sure why people who could teach Miss Manners[30] a thing or two can't make smooth introductions. 'Yes, uh, George Whittington,' George Whittington MP says to my breasts. Sir, those are my nipples, not my pupils. The woman I assume to be the long-suffering Mrs Whittington is shooting daggers at me from across the table. As if I'd steal her middle-aged, socially inept husband. 'You must be a Yank,' he says accusingly.

No kidding. What tipped you off? Was it my accent or the fact that I revealed my name without stammering? 'Yes, I am.'

'Fascinating.'

'Why?'

'Pardon?'

'Why is that fascinating?'

'Well, ah, I can't imagine what a Yank is doing at a Tory dinner.'

'Oh, that's easy. I'm the party planner! Well, assistant party planner. And there's an empty chair at this table, and the photographer doesn't want white space, so here I am.'

'Yes, I didn't think you looked like a Tory.' He's eyeing me up like a party favour. There's a saliva ball in each corner of his mouth. When he talks, a snotty string of it stretches between his lips. Nice catch, Mrs Whittington.

What can I possibly say to this hygienically challenged man? 'Nice weather we've had.' Talk about a cliché. But in an equally clichéd Pavlovian response, he starts waxing poetic about the finer points of English weather. How can forecasts that don't vary beyond some combination of warm/cool and wet/dry

30. Judith Martin, aka Miss Manners, has dispensed etiquette advice to confused Americans since the 1970s. She always gives excellent guidance, like how to be gracious when the host has just sneezed into your soup at a dinner party.

hold anyone's interest for long? England has hardly any of the spectacular weather patterns that excite the rest of the world, though there was a hurricane once, and every so often a mini-tornado tears the roofs off a few garden sheds in the Midlands. I think weather is just an excuse for Brits to talk to each other. It's the only way to strike up a conversation for people who think giving you their name is akin to telling you about their last bowel movement.

Just as we lapse into silence, a man stands up at the next table. 'Lords, ladies and gentlemen, may I have your attention, please.'

The only thing worse than listening to someone else's speech is having to make your own. It was the one part of my old job that I absolutely hated (aside from getting fired, obviously). We mostly did boring company PR, but there were a few very rich clients who paid us to manage the scandal they brought upon themselves. I once had to make a statement to the press that started with 'What two consenting adults do in their private home . . .'

'So without further delay, let's begin tonight's discussion. As you all know, the topic is immigration and what should be done about it. Who'd like to start?'

George Whittington clears his throat and says, 'I wonder if our American guest would like to say a few words?'

I most certainly would not like to. Surely this isn't part of my job description. I'm getting confusing signals from Felicity. She's smiling through her I'm-warning-you face. I recognize this look from my mother's well-worn catalogue of threatening body language. Finally she mouths, 'Go on.'

If you say so. What do I think about immigration? What do I think? What – do – I – think? Let me see . . . Everyone in the room is staring at me. Get up, Hannah, and don't breathe in or your boobs will fall out. 'Ehem. Well, as an immigrant, I say I'm all for it!' Heh, heh, heh. The room is silent. 'And, um, well, my country was founded by immigrants and look how successful it's been . . .' More silence. Is that a tumbleweed blowing between the tables? 'Er, and I think that if you let the immigrants in, they'll work here and be product-ive members of society.' Yes, that's better. 'And I don't think they'll take jobs away from English people, like some of the newspapers say. Um, they'll do the jobs that the English people think they're too good to do. So the job gets done, the immi-grant makes his contribution and the lazy bast– uh, people who would rather stay on welfare can do that too.' Are those the cries of vultures circling above? 'Uh, and of course it's not just fruit pickers we're talking about. What about the ones who work in the banks? They've changed the way English bankers work. Well, heh, heh, at least they *do* work now! They really needed a kick in the pants to wake up and realize it's not the nineteenth century any more.' That may be a man coming towards me with a big vaudeville hook. Perhaps it's time to sit down. 'So it's good. Ah, thank you.' A few kind souls limply clap. George Whittington looks very sorry to be sitting next to me. Then a man to my left gets up, clears his throat and argues that immigrants are pond scum and should under no circumstance be allowed into the country to ruin its English-ness. The guys at the next table whoop their support. I think I might throw up.

Sam appears as I'm weaving between the tables on the way to the bathroom. 'Considering a future in politics?'

'Shut up.' I'm trickling tears. I can't believe I've screwed up again. What an unbelievable confluence of events led me to my speech. Think of all the if onlys: if only I'd confirmed the guest list, if only the photographer hadn't had a tantrum, if only Felicity sat me at another table, *if only I'd kept my big mouth shut.* I can't go back to the table now. I'll have to sit in the kitchen.

'Well, at least you didn't insult the Queen.'

'No, just welfare recipients and the privileged class.'

'That was an impressive one-two punch.'

With my head in my hands maybe he won't see that I'm crying. 'Why do I always end up in these situations?'

'Do you give inflammatory speeches a lot?'

'Making a fool of myself. This isn't the first time.' By a long stretch.

'There's nothing wrong with speaking your mind.'

'Tell them that.'

'What do they know, they're politicians. Listen, I'm guessing you won't be asked to join them for any after-parties. Do you need a ride home tonight?'

I'm very tempted, but given that my dress is essentially a sausage casing, the only way to sit on his moped is sidesaddle. Even if I was prepared to hike it over my ass, there is a slight issue in that to avoid unsightly panty lines, I'm going commando. 'No thanks. I'll get a taxi.' I wonder if Felicity will believe I've had an attack of food poisoning, or malaria, and let me leave early. Can a person be fired in the UK for her political views?

My mascara has run through my bronzer to pool along my jaw. Bleakly, I try to fix the mess between waves of humiliation. Occasionally I'm joined at the mirror by a tweedy lady who studiously avoids looking at me. It's impossible to say whether it's my speech or her abject fear of making eye contact that makes her so rude. Just as I get my lipstick right, having chewed it all off during my speech, Felicity walks in.

'Em, Felicity, I'm not feeling very well.'

'It wouldn't have anything to do with your little speech, would it?' She's blotting her perfect red lipstick. She really is one of the most beautiful women I've known. Shame her personality doesn't match.

'No, no! I, uh, feel like I have a fever.'

'Because what you said is right.'

'You're kidding.'

'Don't look so surprised.'

'Well, I just didn't think' – you had a heart – 'you'd agree.'

'Oh, I do, except for the American rah-rah flag-waving. We don't go in for that kind of boasting.'

'That? That wasn't boasting!' If she wants to hear boasting, she should listen to my mother talk about us kids.

'Well, I'm afraid it sounded like it. We'd never say that we think our country is great, or that we're the best at something.'

They have a lot to be proud of and yet these are people completely incapable of taking credit for their accomplishments. Just try telling an Englishwoman that you like her hair or her dress, let alone her country. She'll either disagree with you or tell you yours is better. Maybe it's a consequence of their empire shrinking to the size of Bermuda. 'Felicity, I need to ask you something.' What have I got to lose at this point? 'Do you think I did a good job on Hermione's birthday party?'

She looks surprised. 'Yes.'

'Then why didn't you say anything?'

'Isn't it obvious?'

'No, it's not.'

'I mean, isn't it obvious that you did a good job? Why do I need to say anything?'

To be nice. To be human. 'I'd like to have some feedback.'

'I just gave you feedback.'

'That was feedback?'

'I answered your question. Yes, you did a good job.'

I could wait for more but she's obviously exhausted her meagre supply of praise. It's better than nothing, but she's still not getting my nomination for coach of the year. Even so, and despite tonight's disaster, I feel like I've won the lottery. The pay-out might only be ten bucks in soon-to-expire coupons; nevertheless, technically, I'm a winner.

15

I feel like a reformed smoker. Having kicked the habit (in this case an unhealthy crush on my flatmate), I've substituted one craving for another. The craving's name is Barry. He's a thirty-year-old investment banker, he told me over the Easter for Orphans dinner that the flatmates organized for all us transplants without families here. There are worse ways to spend the holiday than lounging at a table full of food, wine and Antipodeans. Stacy was at her cousin's house, the one who married 'that Mormon' (that's what the family calls him. It's more a reflection of their feelings towards him than the belief that there is, in fact, just the one). Her poor cousin has been pregnant for the better part of fifteen years, giving their house the restful quality of a prison in revolt.

'What, exactly, do you do?' I asked Barry. I have investment-banking friends in New York. Their jobs seem to involve working late and going out to dinner a lot.

'I mostly raise capital for tier-one and -two firms, you know, debt origination, equity flotation, bridge loans.'

I heard mostly blah, blah, blah, blah, blah, you know, blah, blah, blah, loans. Nobody works in fields where they speak English any more. 'Ah. And how do you know Nathan?'

'He's working on my flat. I bought it last year. It's a total renovation job.' When Nathan isn't busy augmenting his sexual track record, he works on construction sites to top up his beer fund.

Sarah offered, ''E's single, ya know, 'Annah. Aren't ya, Barr?'

I may have mentioned that my flatmate has the tact of a seven-year-old. This is because she's one of those rare girls who are exactly as they appear. For instance, she really is uninterested in the men that flock to her every time we go out. I love this about her, of course, since going out with her is like chumming the water. She can afford to be magnanimous; she's got a serious boyfriend back in Australia. I don't know how they make it work, since he hasn't been able to visit yet and she's been gone almost a year. It must truly be love. I could never have a long-distance relationship.

'Uh, yes, I am. Single,' Barry confirmed, glancing back and forth between Sarah and me. 'I had a girlfriend for a couple of years but she, ah, ran off with my boss.'

'How terrible!'

'Mmm, it really gutted me, you know? I was depressed for months. It's hard to see how you're going to get over it, but eventually you do.'

'Is he still your boss?'

'Yeah.'

'Do you still hate him?'

'Nah, we're okay now. When it's not meant to be, it's not meant to be.'

Without wanting to jump the gun, Barry may perfectly fit my new criteria for a suitable boyfriend. He's mature – thirty; not poor – as evidenced by his home purchase; he's ambitious and smart – proven by his unexplainable job; he's sensitive – a Neanderthal wouldn't share his heartbreak with virtual strangers over dinner; and philosophical – *que sera sera*. He's also sometimes funny. At least, I think he was being funny. It was hard to tell because he's completely deadpan. And English. I didn't wring much out of him in the way of interests. Every time I asked about him, he asked about me (how much do I love that?). He did let slip that he likes football (he means soccer, not the NFL[31]). Oh, and he's Jewish. Three cheers for circumcision!

So having decided that Barry is exactly the kind of guy I want to date, and establishing that there's no Mrs Kaplan, I simply needed to convince him that he couldn't live without me. As I've mentioned, I'm not particularly skilled in this art, tending to take an if-I-flaunt-it-he-will-come approach. And it does work. When I have flaunted, they have come. But they've always left soon afterwards. Now, not only do I want more, I want more from a completely different kind of man. This is no Fun Guy (not to say he's not fun). He's like an exotic, well-paid bird. If I move too fast, I'll scare him off. Convincing Barry that I'm the future love of his life necessitated a few modifications to my approach. These were my promises to myself.

First, I won't act needy, clingy or otherwise insecure. This is very difficult for needy, clingy or otherwise insecure girls like me, but I'm reliably informed that it's a deal-breaker unless you're Pamela Anderson. In practice, it's all about suppressing urges: the urge to bitch (about his old girlfriends, beautiful friends or random strangers on the street); the urge to stalk him (to work or any place else); the urge to call (email or text) every ten minutes; the urge to snoop (I'm bound to find something to make me even more insecure); the urge to fish for compliments; or the urge to initiate public displays of affection. As much as I want to drag on his leg when he leaves the room, I will resist the temptation.

31. The National Football League is the equivalent of the Premier League in the UK, except that it is for American football, not soccer. Incidentally, it's called 'American football' by everyone outside America and 'football' on home turf, in much the same way that the Swedish massage is called simply a 'massage' in Stockholm.

Second, I will be mysterious. This doesn't mean disappearing in the middle of dinner with the whispered explanation that I have to meet an informant, but being a little coy never hurt anybody. Historically, upon meeting a guy I liked, an information-overload trigger was flipped, causing me to give him my life story in an evening. Sometimes, less can be more.

Third, I will not be easy. A good rule of thumb might be that if I don't know his last name, how many brothers he has and his favourite ice cream, he doesn't get to see me naked. I know they may not sound like big goals, but a girl's got to start somewhere.

The fact that Barry is here, at my front door, is surely testament to my progress. Generally, I meet my dates out, though not always officially. I say meet, you say stalk. He kisses me very properly on both cheeks.

'These are for you.'

It's the most gorgeous bouquet I've ever been given. 'Thank you so much!' You can tell a lot about a man by the flowers he chooses. Carnations, for example, are gnarled pods of everlasting foulness. It figures that the ugliest flowers on earth don't wilt. They tell a girl, 'Not only are you not worth much, but I don't want to have to do this again for at least a month.' I'm not saying that all gas-station flowers are suspect. They could signal an impulsively romantic nature. But in my experience, they're a panic-buy after the guy's done something he hopes flowers will fix.

'You look beautiful,' he smiles, eyeing my new apple-green silk tank dress. 'Ready to go?'

I've been ready for two hours. 'Yep. Where are we going?'

'Hakkasan. Do you like Chinese?'

'Sure.'

'Good. I hoped you'd like it. It's a very trendy place.'

Seriously, how cutting edge can an egg roll be?

Well, let me tell you. It must be cool because it's in a base-ment off a little alley that smells of pee. Everyone knows that in cities, dank airlessness and the waft of urine are the hall-marks of a great night out. And once we navigate down the dim stairs, all traces of homelessness recede into an Eastern fantasy. The dark latticework room dividers are very Frank Lloyd-Wrightesque, if Wright had worked in Shanghai instead of Chicago, and somehow the lighting manages to illuminate all the unimportant parts of the room, like the ceiling and the little spaces under the tables, leaving walkways and anything at eye level plunged in darkness. And we're surrounded by glowing blue walls. Picture a beautifully illuminated fish tank, from the fish's perspective. I'll never find my way out if I get drunk.

Speaking of which, the cocktail menu offers drinks like raspberry and lychee martinis. Delicious *and* nutritious? Make mine a double. We're surrounded by men and women who don't suffer clothing crises or bad-hair days. It may be a trick of my American eyes, but London is teeming with uber-trendies. New Yorkers are certainly better groomed, but Londoners make up for their chipped nails and unwhitened teeth with very cool clothes.

Uh-oh. I'm starting to get the tiniest, niggling concern. My lip isn't sweating. I know I've made this sound like a bad thing, because it's unsightly and uncomfortable, but it does tend to happen when I'm nervous. And I'm nervous when I really want something. Is this a sign? . . . No, Hannah, this is an adult relationship. If I go through life letting my glands make my decisions, I'm going to end up with the same guy that I've always dated. And I've firmly agreed with myself that that isn't what I want. Besides, Barry ticks all the boxes. Plus he's good-looking. He's got all his hair, which is mostly light brown with some blond that probably gets lighter after a week at the beach, a sort of ruddy complexion that implies that he's been at said beach, and big brown eyes. I'm being too harsh. In fact, he's downright cute, and that's not just the lychee martini talking.

'Hannah, thanks so much for coming out with me tonight.'

I'm crazy to be worried. He is really rather handsome. 'Thanks for asking! This is an amazing restaurant.'

'You must go to places like this all the time,' he says.

'No, in fact, I never do. I haven't yet, in London.'

'You're kidding! But you're so . . .'

What? I'm so what? Easy?

'Great. I can't believe you're not constantly out on dates.'

Nobody has ever said that to me. Is this how adults talk?

'Well, you flatter me.' Please flatter me some more. 'Have you ever gone out with an American before?' In other words, do you have high expectations about our willingness to go down under the table?

'Nope, I've pretty much always dated English girls. Jewish girls, but English.'

'Uh, I'm not Jewish.' I'm barely even Protestant.

'I figured that. I don't mind.'

'Hmm. How about your parents?' Not that I'm suggesting he introduce me to his parents. We haven't even ordered appetizers yet.

'They wouldn't mind. They just want me to be happy.'

This, I know, is unlikely to be true. I dated a Jewish guy once. When he took me home to meet his parents, his mother laid newspapers on the floor throughout the house. He finally admitted she did the same thing when his father brought home Chinese or other unsanctioned food, so that it wouldn't contaminate their table. Apparently, God doesn't mind loopholes. I'm trying not to imagine having sex on Barry's mother's kitchen table with the *Sunday Times* headlines tattooed on my ass.

'Em, have you dated outside the faith before?' It's best to lay the cards on the non-kosher table. I don't plan to be the other woman again, especially if the other other woman is his mother.

'Sure. But to be honest, I wasn't on the market for a couple of years, and now, with working long hours . . .'

Right, investment banking and the mysterious ex. 'So what do you do for fun?'

'Fun?' He's looking uncertain. 'Ah, I really like football. I mean, your soccer.'

'You're not a hooligan, are you?'

'I'm Jewish.'

'Of course.'

'Do you follow it?' he asks. 'Football, I mean soccer?'

I saw a World Cup game once. And I think our girls may have won a medal in the Olympics. 'Sure.'

'You do? Most women I know hate football. Who do you support?'

I wish he'd get off this line of questioning. 'Who do *you* support?'

'Arsenal.'

'Me too! What a coincidence.' It's a harmless lie. Not once have I had to prove my allegiance when feigning interest in a sport.

'Have you been to a match?'

'No, but I'd like to.' How bad can it be to watch fit men run around in shorts for an hour? It's not like I'm committing to cricket, where matches can go on for five days, then end in a draw.

'Well, maybe if you're still talking to me in August, I'll take you to see Arsenal play.'

What's this? A statement of future intent? On a first date? This is an unprecedented show of interest.

Nothing on the menu looks like Chinese food. Where's the chop suey?

'You said you haven't been here before?' He's looking right into my eyes.

'Nope.'

'If you like, I can order for us.'

This is obviously a man who's used to being in charge. While I'm not generally keen on dates choosing my meals, he makes the offer sound chivalrous rather than cheesy. But if he says 'and the lady will have . . .' I'm going to rethink my judgement.

'Sure, go ahead.'

'We'll have . . .' He orders four or five dishes that sound great. And already he's 'we'ing!

As soon as the waiter leaves, Barry returns to my favourite subject: me. He has a real knack for making me feel comfortable. So comfortable, in fact, that before you can say 'perfect date', I've confessed all kinds of embarrassing things, like my fashion-magazine addiction.

'I like that you're so committed,' he says.

'I'm obsessive.'

'I think it's adorable.'

Is it possible that I've finally found the man who thinks I'm quirky rather than weird? I've always fancied myself along Meg Ryan lines, but I'm afraid I come across more Joan Cusack. This is fun. And easy. That's a good sign. The real test will be whether he can have a decent phone conversation. I haven't found a man yet who can, which is down to a fundamental difference in objective. They have the frustrating habit of using speech only to convey information.

Dessert is a deep-fried tower of something with green-tea ice cream on top. 'Oh shit.' In trying to get the right ratio of ice cream to tower, I've just deposited the frozen dairy ball into my lap. And right on the part the napkin isn't covering. If I lob it quickly back on to the plate, will he notice? Things like this don't happen to Meg.

'Oh, Hannah, they shouldn't have put so much ice cream on top.'

I'm not sure we can blame this on the chef's heavy-handed scooping, but I love that he's trying to tell me it's not my fault. 'It's okay. It needs to go to the dry cleaner anyway.' My poor dress. I hope London's dry cleaners are used to slightly clumsy girls with a fondness for delicate fabrics. If not, I'm prepared to ship it to my miracle dry cleaner at home, where it will take top priority – my custom over the years has nearly paid for her lake house.

'Waiter! Your dessert fell over and now my date has ice cream on her dress.'

'Barry, that's okay –' He shakes his head.

'I'm terribly sorry, madam. If you'd like to give us the bill, we'll be happy to pay for the dry cleaning.'

'Thank you,' says Barry. As the waiter walks away, I catch him looking at me suspiciously. He knows this was no dessert malfunction.

'Thanks, Barry, but you didn't have to do that.'

'They shouldn't have given you an unstable dessert. These restaurants all try to be clever. Their food can be dangerous.'

Okay, so he hasn't exactly slain a dragon for me, but his chivalry is delightful.

His gallantry extends right to my front door. 'I'd love to see you again.'

'I'd like that.' And I would too. My stomach may not be somersaulting but this was a nice evening.

'Great. How about Saturday?'

'Sure!' . . . Why did I say sure? A Saturday second date? That's a little presumptuous. Besides, I'm mysterious, an enigma. I should have said I was busy. Even though I'm not. 'I mean, I'll have to check my calendar.'

'Oh. Okay, sure. Well, if you're free from about noon, I'll plan a surprise.'

I'm a sucker for surprises.

Just as I'm beginning to fear his manners are *too* good, he leans in to kiss me. And you know how there are two, maybe three kissers in your life that stand out as remarkable, the kind of kisser you'd give your left arm to have constant access to? Well, Barry's not one of those. He's not bad, just sort of soft-lipped and slow. I will not say boring. I – will – not – say – boring. He's fine.

'Hiya! Back so soon from your date?' Sarah is stretched on the sofa with her legs over Nathan and her feet on Adam's thigh. The fact that my flatmates often pile together like puppies was disconcerting when I first moved in. It's never easy breaking into such close camaraderie, but they've welcomed me with open hearts, open arms and an open spot on the sofa. Plus they've never seen each other in the nuddy, so there's no weird sexual dynamic to worry about.

'What do you mean, so soon? It's –' Piaget says 10.15. That can't be right. Does England have a daylight saving time that I don't know about? 'I thought it was later.'

'Hah, date that bad?' Adam says from under the pile of flatmate. 'Poor Barry.'

'No! It was great. He's really nice.'

'Yeah, he's a good bloke. Not boring, though?'

That's not fair. Just because I didn't spend the night doesn't mean Barry was a bad date. In fact, it was the most perfectly executed date I've ever been on. Flowers: romantic. Choice of restaurant: the perfect combination of buzz and intimacy. Conversation: flowing. And all about me. Hmm. We did only talk about me. Other than his Jewish Arsenal fan status, I still don't know anything about him. That won't work if I'm going to stick by my newly imposed rules. I'll at least have to find out his favourite ice cream … I'm kidding. This is a guy worth getting to know. I promise to ask all about him on our next date.

16

Felicity has just given me my first account! I'm so grateful I could hug her, until I catch her expression. Okay, not a huggy person. Noted. Nevertheless, this is exactly the break I've been waiting for. She's going to regret not taking a chance on me sooner. And you know what? Despite the cold reception, this is so much more satisfying than praise. Just one thing is bothering me. I'm not crazy about the project. The former Mrs Read-Hutchins wants us to throw her a divorce party. In my family's social circle, relationship failure isn't something to be celebrated with crab puffs.

'Tell me again, Felicity, what's the point of this?'

'It's a rite of passage, a way to mark the start of her new life.'

'Then I take it there'll be no ex-husband on the guest list?'

'Oh yes, he'll be there. Their divorce wasn't acrimonious.'

'Any ideas for themes?'

'Hannah, this one's all yours. If you want to come up with some ideas, I'm happy to give you my opinion. All I can tell you is that it's the end of an old life and the beginning of a new one. You might try tongue-in-cheek humour.'

'When do we meet with her?'

'We don't. She's in St Barths. It's all up to you. Here's the guest list. Surprise her. By the way, it's eleven o'clock.' She hands me her fish mug.

I'm shooting to the top of the career ladder all right.

So I have to plan an ironic divorce party, which I've never

heard of, for a woman I've never met, in a country where I'm not generally considered ironic or funny. No sweat. I simply have to put myself in the stack-heeled Pradas of a fifty-year-old English divorcée. Based on what I know of divorced women, she's at least a little bitter. My mother's friends all are. Their reaction to hearing their former husband's name ranges from mild annoyance to uncontrollable oath-swearing on his decapitated corpse. That's Mrs Miller, but she also set fire to Mr Miller's Porsche while he was in it, so her reaction is probably outside the norm. I won't go far wrong if I set the theme somewhere between black armbands and pin the penis on the husband.

Meanwhile, I have a more pressing social engagement to contend with. Being the font of all English knowledge, naturally Chloe is the obvious choice to help me figure out what Barry's surprise date could be.

'You don't think it's a balloon ride or rock climbing or anything like that?' I don't like the idea of falling. And I hate the idea of the stop at the end.

She laughs. 'No, that's something you Americans would do. He's probably taking you to a nice restaurant.'

'That's not a surprise. He's taken me to a nice restaurant already.'

'Maybe he's going to take you to a crap one, then. Surprise!'

'Very funny. Come on, think, Chloe. This has important implications for my wardrobe.'

Sobered by the truth of this statement, she ponders. 'Maybe it's a picnic.'

'It's freezing outside.' Despite the calendar insisting that it's April and the flowers believing the calendar, going outside still involves three layers and an umbrella.

'Mmm, you're right, too risky. Maybe tickets to the theatre?'

'Speaking of the theatre, how was your date?'

'It was wonderful.' Her latest suitor scored tickets to *Avenue Q*[32] that included the cast party afterwards (with the actors, not the puppets). 'Thanks for suggesting it.' Siobhan took me to see it for my birthday. 'And thanks so much for the tip on those shoes. You were right, they were perfect.' I think I've become Chloe's fashion adviser, which is only fair since she's my relationship counsellor. 'I don't think it's a theatre date. It's a daytime date.'

'Matinée?'

I hope not. It's not that I don't like the theatre; Siobhan's birthday surprise was wonderful. But it's generally risky to leave a decision about how to spend two-plus hours in the dark to someone else.

I'm no less in the dark when Barry picks me up. At least there's no picnic basket or abseiling harness in sight. 'You're beautiful,' he whispers, gently kissing me on the lips.

I could get very used to this flattery, though in this instance I think there's some basis for it. I am the epitome of a demure English rose, with flowing skirt and strappy wedges. I even contemplated a hat but didn't want to risk tipping into parody. In any case, my ensemble covers me for every eventuality except walking, which, if our relationship is going to work out, Barry will be well-advised to limit anyway. 'Thanks. So where are we going?'

'Vinopolis.'

'Where?'

'It's a wine-tasting. You do like wine, don't you?'

Do I like wine!

Vinopolis is a museum for drinkers. It charts the history of

32. *Avenue Q* is the very funny, very smutty puppet musical modelled after *Sesame Street*, much adored by anyone whose appreciation of irony stretches to puppets having sex and Nazis extolling racism in song.

wine around the world, with ample stops to sample the local product. If all museums had this sort of thoughtful set-up, we wouldn't need to despair about the state of American education. We might become a nation of alcoholics but we'd know our way around a map.

When we get out of the taxi, Barry grabs my hand. If this is what being the object of affection feels like, I don't mind being objectified.

'Here you go.' He's holding a headset.

'Uh, no, that's okay. I'll just read the little plaques.'

'But you'll learn a lot more this way.'

No doubt this is true, but I'm not going to wear them. Remember, I vowed to talk to my date. 'No, really, I'm fine.'

'Are you sure?'

'Yep, thanks.'

He kisses me on the nose and adjusts his own headphones. Well, *now* how am I supposed to talk to him? I guess I could ask him to take his off. But that's not fair. Look how engrossed he is in the tour. He's stopping at every display . . . What's he listening to? He's taking for ever. I can read the board in two minutes. Maybe I'm only getting the Reader's Digest condensed version. Perhaps he's learning all kinds of wine secrets that I'm not privy to. For once I don't care if I'm missing out. My stomach is rumbling for lunch and we haven't even left Europe.

After about 600 years, we get to the first wine-tasting table. 'Wasn't that interesting about Portugal?' he says.

Was it? I can't remember. 'Uh-huh.' This isn't a lie, per se, since I'm sure that whatever the Vinopolisians had to say about Portugal was fascinating. In any case, it's a harmless fib that I'm unlikely to get caught out at.

'Which part did you like best?'

'Uh, the Italian wines?'

'Me too. Here, let's try one.' He hands two tickets to the girl at the table and takes two little glasses. 'Cheers.'

My belly grumbles in response. 'Sorry.' This is no ladylike gurgle. The Concorde taking off caused less disturbance.

'Are you hungry?'

'A little.'

'I'm sorry, I didn't realize! Let's go have lunch, then.'

'Don't you want to finish the tour?'

'Not if you're hungry. We can come back after lunch if you want.' He takes my hand again and leads me to the restaurant. My hero.

Headphones safely stowed, I finally get the chance to talk to my date. By the time we're sipping our coffees, I'm convinced he's the nicest man on the planet.

Barry David Kaplan was born and raised in North London, within sniffing distance of the kosher bakeries in Golders Green. This, he confides, accounts for his greater than normal sweet tooth. Either he has an iron will or he works out a lot, because his love of the *rugelach* doesn't show. On a scale of one to ten bodywise, he's at least an eight. He has one brother, older, named Gabe, who used to beat him mercilessly until Barry punched him back and knocked his front tooth through his lip. He still feels guilty about it and hasn't hit anyone since. He says he'd only use his fists again to protect someone close to him. Talk about a knight in shining armour! *And* I bet he'd never fart on the couch. When I asked him what other deeds of derring-do he's performed (kidding, of course), he told me he volunteered every summer in high school and college to build houses in third-world countries. And now he's a mentor to some kids from a council estate.

I can't claim any charitable acts of my own. I can't even count the ones on my résumé, because they're lies. Barry puts me to shame. He's an investment-banking Mother Teresa. He was just promoted last year, he says, so he thinks his boss is pretty happy with him. This is the same boss who's schtupping his ex. I asked him again if he's bitter about that, but he wishes them the best of luck. If I'd been in his shoes I'd say the same thing, but I'd be secretly trying to poison them. Mental note: check his medicine cabinet for toxic substances . . .

This really may be the perfect man. 'Is there *anything* wrong with you?'

'Are you kidding? What's right? I'm hopeless.'

'I don't believe it.'

'Oh, it's true, believe it.'

'Example?'

'Well, I wasn't a great student. Or great at sports.'

'But you play football.'

'I'm not very good.'

I hope he wasn't the kid who was always picked last. The thought of team captains fighting on the playground over who had to take little Barry makes me sad. 'But at least you play.'

'I do love it. But I'm hopeless at other sports.'

'Well I'm no . . .' I can't even think of a sportswoman. *That's* athletically challenged. 'No good at sports either.'

'And I hardly ever read books.'

Is that a bad thing?

'Or go to the theatre.'

Which I'm glad to hear. 'Movies?'

'Yeah, I love films. Do you?'

I assume he means romantic films, which are the only kind I see without coercion. Now, on to what I really want to know. 'Relationships?'

'Ah, case in point – my ex running off with my boss.'

'But that's not your fault. She's a bitch.'

'Thank you. She is kind of a bitch.' He has a nice laugh.

'Other relationships?'

'Hmm. Yes, I had a girlfriend at school.'

'For how long?'

'Two years. And I had a college girlfriend, also for two years.'

'And your ex?'

'Uh, two years.'

'What do you do to them on your two-year anniversary?'

He rests his chin in his hand. 'I can't think of anything out of the ordinary. I bring her flowers, we go out to dinner, I give her a gift-wrapped human heart, then dessert, dancing . . .'

'Hah, hah.' See, I told you he has a sense of humour.

'I have a theory that there are make-or-break deadlines in relationships. I think I just hit the same one every time.'

A man with relationship theories? I've never heard of such a thing. 'What are these deadlines?'

'Well, there's the first date, obviously. Then I think there are decision points around a month, six months, a year, two years. And maybe after that, though I've never made it that far.'

'So we passed the first-date hurdle.'

He takes my hand across the table. 'I'm very happy about that.'

'Me too.' And I mean it. I could really grow to like this guy. Maybe I don't have a sweaty lip yet, but he is really perfect for me. More importantly, he's the kind of guy I should be dating, not the kind of guy I have been dating, and he'll be good for me.

'Stacy's been calling,' Adam informs me when I stumble back into the apartment, slightly the worse for wear from my culturally enriching afternoon. 'I let the machine get it the last time.'

'Thanks. Sorry she calls so much.'

'Not a worry, cupcake. You're lucky having a friend like her.'

'Han,' booms the machine, ' your phone's not picking up. Are you out of juice again? I had sex with Tye last night. I even slept over. You know I never do that. But he was so sweet, I couldn't say no. Besides, I'd already told him I was sleeping in this morning. Didn't plan to do it in his sheets! Hah, hah. But we had a really nice time, and I did drink a bit. But that's not why I had sex with him. Han, he's not a bad kisser. He's no Greg' – Greg's the one who got away. I think they actually only had sex once, but she mooned over him for years. Then he went off and married a Japanese woman he met on a cruise with his parents – 'but he had some moves. And he likes oral sex, yay! I mean giving, not getting. Anyway, call me. By the way, the answering machine is in your bedroom, right?' No, Stace, it's in the living room, delighting my flatmates at the moment. I can't begrudge them Stacy's dating exploits, given that Sarah's sexual opportunities are 10,000 miles away and Adam's are possibly non-existent.

17

We haven't had sex yet. Should I be worried that we haven't had sex yet? I don't want to jump to conclusions, but first Potential, and now Barry. It's not like I haven't given them ample opportunity. I can't have turned undesirable in only six months. (I don't include Mark's interest, because he's a horny bastard who can't be relied upon to uphold standards.) And yet . . . I haven't been whistled at once here. Not even by builders, and while I'm not looking for that kind of attention, it does seem to be a universal benchmark. Maybe my appeal doesn't translate well across the ocean after all. Or maybe the explanation is more complex.

Do I really want this to work with Barry? Remember, I wasn't overwhelmed on our first date, and though I'm really growing to like him, I can't deny that my mind is often hijacked by you-know-who. I'm afraid my preoccupation is getting stronger and I don't know what to do about it. It'd be much easier to put him out of my mind if I didn't have to see him in the office. Like mercury poisoning, toxicity builds up with prolonged exposure.

'Without wanting to pry too much into the details, and please don't feel the need to share them with me, tell me the facts.' Chloe's talking about my relationship with Barry. I haven't confessed my other thoughts to her or anyone else. I can imagine the response. I've been asking myself the same question. Why would I let myself fall for the same kind of guy I could have fallen for at home, a guy who is already with another woman? If I'm just going to do that, I should have saved myself the airfare.

This verbal autopsy is being made easier by the copious amount of rosé we've been quaffing. I didn't know pink wine existed outside of Ernest and Julio's screw-top jugs. Moving to a new country really does expand one's horizons. The French are actually quite proud of it (but then, the French are quite proud of everything they do). In a tribute to their Gallic cousins, Londoners all over the city tipple the pink stuff at the first sign of summery weather. For Chloe's benefit I'm recounting each date in detail. After Vinopolis, Barry organized go-cart racing, for which I have to give him credit for originality. I didn't mention that I'm not a great driver, but within half an hour I didn't have to. Luckily everyone involved wore seat belts. Then we went to a special late evening at the Victoria and Albert museum, which was much more my speed, so to speak. A little jazz band in the foyer accompanied our roam around the museum with wine glasses in hand. It seems that the English do like to combine museums with drinks. I'm not sure that Cabernet and priceless textiles necessarily go together, but I suppose those thousand-year-old Bedouin carpets must have seen a few spills even before I got there. We had a late dinner at the same restaurant Potential took me to (which of course I didn't mention). I still didn't touch the fetid cheese. And then dinner at his place. I nearly fell off the chair when I tasted his cooking, not being used to guys making edible food that doesn't come from the freezer. We drank two bottles of wine and ended up making out on the couch. But no matter how *Basic Instinct* I tried to be, he just wouldn't move past the kissing. Finally, he stopped altogether and told me he'd have to take me home.

'It sounds like he's just taking things slow. He's a real gentleman.'

Real gentlemen are over-rated. I want to be ravaged.

'You know he's gagging for it, right?'

I assume this means he wants to have sex too. 'Ah, physically speaking, I don't think there's any doubt about that. But why doesn't he make a move? I mean, I'm throwing him every signal I can think of.' Short of stripping off and straddling him, I don't know what else to do. 'Maybe I should ask him what's wrong.'

'God, no!'

'Why not?'

'Hannah, we just don't do that. He'd be mortified.' Chloe believes that less is more when it comes to talking to her boyfriends.

'Well, what do you do when there's a problem?'

'We go to the pub, get drunk and ignore it. We might give each other the cold shoulder if it's really serious.'

And to think, we Americans spend all that money on couples counselling when all we really need is a good bartender. 'Don't Brits *like* sex?'

'Of course we do. We just don't like to talk about it.'

So I'm at a loss, caught between a rock and a hard-on.

True to her word, Felicity has left Mrs Read-Hutchins's soirée completely to me. And she's been nothing but supportive of my plans. Perhaps I've misjudged her. Last week, I found out that she's up for partnership, so I guess it's understandable that she took credit for Hermione's party. She did do a superb planning job, and couldn't have anticipated the drunken bandleader or unfortunate dress clone. My little contributions were merely Band-Aids on an otherwise healthy patient. I'm proud of my graciousness. Maybe I'm mellowing with age.

I've booked the perfect venue for my career debut. The Crypt at St Martin-in-the-Fields may technically be a restaurant, but is literally a crypt. Brits don't have the same squeamishness about the dead that we do. They're happy to live their lives right on top of the dearly departed. Just look at all the playgrounds in the cemeteries here. I guess in a millennia-old country that's smaller than Texas, eventually a certain amount of stacking is necessary, like an ancestor trifle with a delicious layer of the living on top. So I shouldn't have been surprised to see weary tourists resting their bones over lunch, and bones, in the Crypt. Tables and chairs stand on marble tablets that start with phrases like 'Here lies . . .' What could be more perfect for a divorce party?

Sam is already in position. He flashes me a smile while manhandling a couple plastic boxes of wine glasses to the bar. 'You look pretty.'

'Thanks.' I'm blushing, but he's right. I'm very Sophia Loren in my swingy dress and heels (yes, *my* dress. Felicity guards that closet like it holds the secret to El Dorado's gold). Pencil skirts just don't have the same allure as a pink silk butterfly-print strappy dress. When I spin around, as I did in my room till I was a little sick, the skirt flares out and makes dippy little waves. It's the perfect dress to be taken dancing in.

'No speeches this time though, right?'

No speeches, and hopefully no screw-ups. There's no way Felicity is going to give me another chance to be brilliant. There she is in the doorway. She's stopped in front of the flower arrangements, obviously stunned by my genius. A giant wreath sits on a stand at the entrance. RIP is embroidered on the sash draping the black roses. It was a little expensive but you won't get much more tongue-in-cheek than a funeral bouquet. Besides, I saved money on the armbands.

'The what?' she says, tentatively picking at one of the black fabric swatches in the cut-glass bowl.

'Armbands. Here, take one.'

'Uh, what is this for?' Her doubt about my ability to pull this off is evident from her open-mouthed surprise. I can practically taste that promotion!

'All in good time.' The impact of the evening depends a lot on the element of surprise.

'Well, it's your show.'

Sam does look cute in his black suit. The staff are all wearing undertaker suits, even the girls. I'd hoped that Janey would look butch but she's obviously wearing her own clothes instead of the institutionally poor-fitting rental I arranged. They're all in character too, coached to say 'I'm terribly sorry for your loss' every time someone puts an empty glass on their tray. The guests are already getting into the theme. It's as if they're respecting the dead, whispering quietly together. Some even look sad. Obviously the decorations are having their intended effect. I couldn't have asked for a better start!

'Who's in charge here?' A thin woman with leathery skin is scanning the room.

'I am! Mrs Read-Hutchins?'

'Formerly. What is going on here?'

I have to say, for a woman who's spent the last month in an island paradise, she doesn't look very well rested. In fact, she looks . . . kind of mad.

'It's your divorce party. What do you think?'

'What do I think? What do I think?!'

Uh-oh. Where's Felicity?

'I think this is the most tasteless, tactless thing I've ever seen! Just what do you think you're doing?'

'Well, I thought I'd go for, uh, tongue-in-cheek humour?'

'Do you find this humorous?'

'Well, yeah. Maybe not in a hah-hah way, but in an ironic way.' If this is any indication of the English sense of humour, then I've been sorely misled.

'Ironic. I see. You find humour in the irony that my ex-husband has late-stage prostate cancer?'

Well now, that would have been worth knowing before I peppered the room with RIP flower arrangements, made the guests wear mourning armbands and, oh god, ordered the cake. A six-foot coffin-shaped cake is about to be wheeled out by pallbearers. It's the second-to-last surprise, followed by the symbolic burning of the armbands and handing out of little urns (filled with candy, not ashes – I'm not completely lacking in taste). 'Uh, I'm so sorry, Mrs – I had no idea.'

'Then someone at your agency left out a very important fact in your briefing.'

Yes, she certainly did. 'Uh, the, ah, death part of the party is just the start.'

'Terrific.'

'No, I mean it's just the prelude to the real party.'

'I'm almost afraid to ask. What else have you got planned?'

A Caribbean theme, of course. After the ceremonial casting-off of mourning clothes, which I still think is a brilliant idea, terminal ex-husband aside, the waiters change into loud shirts and shorts, drape everyone in tropical flowers and serve Piña Coladas until the guests fall over. The Calypso band should be here any minute.

'I suggest we get to the Caribbean party quickly. My guests don't look like they're enjoying themselves.'

No, indeed they don't. The room, I now notice, is completely, deathly, quiet. Everyone is listening to the hostess rant at me. 'Yes, ma'am. I'll get right on it.' Grabbing the bowl of armbands, which thankfully nobody but me is wearing, and tucking the big wreath under my arm, I can just about drag it into the back room. 'Uh, everyone in the kitchen, please.'

'All right, everybody, we have a crisis. Apparently the theme isn't going down well because, well, because the ex-husband is, in fact, dying . . .' I'd continue but everyone is too busy laughing their asses off to listen to me. Now why couldn't the guests see the humour in this? 'Yes, okay, irony aside, we've got to change the theme over right now. Can everyone please change into their shirts and shorts? Sam, can you get all of the black roses out of the room and you, can you put out the tropical flower arrangements?' This isn't a total disaster. There's the Calypso band warming up. Everyone makes little mistakes when they're first starting out, right? This could happen to anyone.

'What should we do with the cake?' Sam asks.

'Oh god, get rid of it.' I can't even imagine the look on everyone's face if that had been wheeled into the room. 'No, wait. Do we have flowers left?'

'Yeah.'

'Let's cut it into pieces and stick a flower into each piece. It'll distract from the brown frosting.'

'You're a genius, boss,' he grins. I search his face for any trace of sarcasm but there isn't any.

'Anyway, you'd better get out there and help the bartender. He didn't look too sure about the blender drinks. I think it's an American thing.'

When I see Mrs Read-Hutchins half an hour later, she's got a hibiscus in her hair and a pink drink in her hand. I catch her eye and there's no hatred in her look. There's no love either. My U-turn might be enough to save the night but I doubt it's enough to save my job.

18

I thought Felicity had snuck out but no, there she is, talking to one of the guests. 'Um, 'scuse me, hi. Felicity, can I talk to you a minute?'

'Is something wrong?' She's the picture of innocence as we move away from the witnesses, er, guests.

'You set me up.'

'Pardon?'

'You heard me. You set me up. You purposely let me make a fool of myself and the agency. I want to know why. Why would you do that?'

She's trying to melt me with her death-ray ice eyes. It's the look that makes grown men whimper. It's the look I admired when it was aimed at photographers and cooks. 'Hannah, I find it remarkable that you can blame me for this . . . fiasco. I gave you full reign, and full responsibility. I had nothing to do with it, as you'll remember. Every one of those ideas was yours. You fucked up.'

'Felicity, you should have told me about the husband. You knew what the theme was and you should have told me.'

'I only knew it was a divorce party. As we were briefed. As I told you. I didn't know what theme you chose. You never told me.'

What is she talking about? Of course I told her the theme. Didn't I? I'm sure I mentioned it when I booked the Crypt. Granted, I did play the details close to my chest because I wanted to surprise everyone, but I know I told her. I'm almost sure of it. Fairly positive.

'Let me give you some friendly advice.' Her voice is most unfriendly. 'In this business, one must learn to take responsibility for all one's actions, not just those that save the day.'

What a bitch. 'Felicity, all I can say is that this is going to reflect as badly on you as it does on me.'

'Don't count on that, my dear.' She turns on her heel, which isn't very stylish (and that's not just spite talking), and goes back to the crowd.

My boss has sabotaged me. What possible motive could she have? I'm no threat to her job. I'm not going to take her partnership away. This disaster has to look bad for her. I don't care what she says, it happened on her watch. It's possible she's just mean. I've met women like this before, who'll almost literally cut off their noses to spite their faces. But that doesn't make any sense. She must have a motive for killing my career. I feel sick to my stomach. Why am I standing here, feeling sick to my stomach? I can simply walk up those stairs and be away from this mess. There's no reason to stay anyway, if I'm just going to get fired on Monday.

It's a beautiful night, with people everywhere on the streets. That's the dangerous thing about the West End – you can't count on the traffic to tell you when it's time to go home. Londoners need those curfew bracelets that convicts wear, getting zapped when last orders are called to make them drop the beer glass and step away from the bar. Sometimes people must be electrocuted for their own good.

Speaking of my own good, I'm craving the reassurance of intimacy. I want to be with someone who'll make me feel better. I don't mean Chloe, or Stacy, or even Barry (yes, I feel guilty about that). Though they'll give me perfectly reasonable advice, I need comfort food right now, not a balanced meal. I wish I had a different reaction to turmoil in my life. But I suppose it's no worse than binging on chocolate, or Cheese Doodles.[33] At least my cravings don't expand my waistline. It's time I stopped kidding myself anyway. I've been thinking about him constantly. Despite *her*. Despite everything. There must be something there. It's time I found out once and for all. I do have his number, though I feel a little foolish as it rings.

'Hi, it's Hannah.' There's a catch in my throat. 'Can you meet me?'

'Hi . . . Where are you?' He sounds puzzled. I don't blame him. No doubt my call is a little unexpected under the circumstances.

'Um, in front of a place called Lupo, in Soho.'

'I know it. I can't get there for at least an hour. But I'll be there as soon as I can.'

'Thanks.'

Don't judge me. I need a known quantity right now.

Did I tell you about the first time I went to New York by myself? I lost my wallet and had to make a collect call to Dad to come get me. I wandered around all day first, trying to think of a better way home. My sister was in California, two thousand miles and three time zones too far away to help. Stacy was with her grandparents in Maine, which was why I was alone in the first place. The trip was my first real attempt at a modicum of independence. I was twenty-two, and losing my wallet didn't exactly foster confidence in my ability to fend for myself. After

33. Favoured snack food of seven-year-olds and stoners, which glow a sort of nuclear orange and may be imbued with an addictive substance that makes girls swallow an entire bag before they realize what they're doing.

exhausting my alternatives (including toying with the idea of begging strangers for the fare), I made the call. I was humiliated, so much so that when I saw my dad, I burst into tears. He must have thought I was scared, or relieved or something. He said, 'Honey, don't worry, you can always depend on me when you get in a pinch.' I guess I'm thinking about it now to remind myself that there's no shame in needing someone else to do what you can't do for yourself.

The only thing I'm going to do for myself waiting here is to drive myself crazy. 'Hey, Sarah? It's Hannah. Where are you? Mind if I come over for a bit? Yeah, I know. I was. I'll explain later. Right now I don't want to think about it. Rupert Street? Okay, hang on.' Thank god for A to Z. 'I'm close. See you in a few minutes.' It's comforting to have flatmates that are always within easy drinking distance.

Their chosen venue is a haven for the Irish-at-heart, or botanists. There's an enormous tree growing in the middle of it. My flatmates stand shaded beneath its branches, ready to lend a sympathetic ear and to buy me a pint. I'll gladly accept both tonight. 'What happened? This was your big night?'

'Adam!' Sarah punches him with the force of a middleweight champion. 'She doesn't wanna talk about it.'

'That's okay . . . it was a disaster. The theme didn't go over well at all, and Felicity is out to get me.'

'You wannus ta have a word with her?' Nathan touches the side of his nose. His bravado is just that. As I've gotten to know them better, I've realized that I shouldn't have judged these books by their hard-drinking, joke-cracking covers. These are people with the depth to be excellent friends as well as the humour to be excellent entertainment.

'That's sweet, but I don't think roughing her up is going to help my cause. No, this is something I have to take care of on my own. Anyway, don't worry. How come you're here? I figured you'd be at Walkabout.'

'Nathan's meeting a taht.'

'Howdaya know she's a taht?'

'Your words, mate.'

'Too right. Up, speak of the divil. 'Scuse me, ladies and gents, there she is. G'night.' He ambles off towards this evening's conquest.

Sarah's right. That girl *is* a taht. 'What about you, Adam?' Winking in exaggerated style should warn him about my next line of questioning. 'Have you got your eye on anyone here?' This who-would-I-go-home-with-if-I-had-my-pick game is one of my favourites. It's harmless, because theoretical. It's fun, because a little smutty. And it's revealing. That's how, for example, I found out that Stacy doesn't mind fat guys.

'Nah. D'ya want another beer?'

'Yes, but don't change the subject. Come on. No one in here? At all?' At least fifty young women stand around us in various stages of inebriation.

'Come on, mate, at a push. Who'd ya do?' Sarah really has a way with words.

He looks embarrassed. 'Well, her. Or her. Or her.'

'The one in the rid top?'

Interesting choices, Adam. They could all be in Sarah's immediate family. Like I said, this game is always illuminating.

'I think we need a shot, don't you, 'Annah?'

Most definitely. Here's to the Aussies, who have once again proven how fortunate I was to answer their ad.

There he is. God, I'm nervous. What if this is a mistake? Something in my gut is still warning me. I'm well acquainted with this feeling. After graduation, my parents got a little desperate when they realized that I might never leave home. Dad's friend runs an injection die-casting company (I know, I didn't know what it meant either – it's how plastic handles and things are made) and set me up with an interview. It wasn't really an interview: Dad must have agreed to let his friend beat him at golf for the next ten years or so, because he offered me a job on the spot. I should have jumped at it, considering the student-loan payments in my near future. That night I tossed and turned, and in the morning I knew, although I had no idea why, that I couldn't take the job. So I respectfully turned it down, and a few months later I got the PR job, which led me to London, and my party-planning job. Trusting my gut was the right decision then. But it's too late to turn back now. He's watching me approach. I can't read his expression. Maybe a little concerned, maybe a little annoyed. I can't blame him there – Piaget says I'm later than planned. 'Hi. You haven't been here very long, have you?'

'Ten minutes or so. You sounded upset.'

'Yeah, thanks for meeting me.'

'No worries, it's just a school job. They're used to us goofing off.'

'Hey, Sam,' nods the bouncer as we pass.

The bartender reaches across to shake his hand. 'Sam, I've got your CDs.'

Who cares if I could have dated him at home? I probably wouldn't have. It's taken London and a lot of growing up to learn to stop doing what I think I should do and instead do what I want to.

'What are you, Sam, a closet alcoholic?'

'Where's the fun in being a *closet* alcoholic?'

'True. How do you know everyone?'

'Sweetheart, so much to learn. There's a seedy underbelly to every city, populated by all the people who serve you your dinner and drinks. Where do you think they all go when their shifts are over?'

They go home to their tiny, condemned apartments to sleep for a few hours before serving me my breakfast. 'Do you know every bar in town?'

'Actually, I don't go out that much.' The last part of his statement is drowned out by a girl yelling hello across the bar.

'Uh-huh.'

'I am glad you called. I figured something was wrong when I saw you leave. But I didn't have your mobile number. And I was elbow-deep in rum punch at the time. Tell me what happened.'

I do, with as much attention to detail as I'd give in a relationship post mortem with Stacy. He doesn't seem to mind that I'm adding a liberal amount of whining and self-pity. Ah, the indulgence of a fresh ear! God, it's hot in here. I'm sweating. The little Chinese fan I found in Soho isn't making much difference. It makes me feel glamorous to wave it around, though my technique is not yet perfect. I still hit myself in the face occasionally. 'What's that smirk for? Haven't you ever seen a fan?'

'You mean since the nineteenth century? I'm kidding, it works for you. I don't know how, but it does. Anyway, the party. For the record, I thought your idea was great.'

'It was supposed to be my big break.'

'It was a big break, all right. You had no way to know about the husband. I mean, what are the chances?'

'About a million to one. Come on, a death theme when the host's husband is dying? Give me a break!' It feels great to laugh, even if I'm laughing over the remains of my career.

What's the worst that can happen? Mark fires me on Monday. So, I'll find another job. Maybe I'll take a couple weeks off first, travel around Europe. I should have left already anyway to get another tourist visa in my passport. Being out of work won't be so bad. Maybe Chloe can find me something . . . 'I just don't get why Felicity'd do that to me. I'm no threat to her.'

'Ah, *that* I think I can shed some light on.'

'Do tell.'

'You and Mark didn't happen to have a thing, did you?'

'Uh, why?' I must be blushing very unattractively.

'Because Felicity is sleeping with him. That's why my boss wants to quit working for the agency. She got wind of his affair and, as I mentioned, he's married to her sister. You can imagine the politics.'

'But that was over months ago.'

'Nuh-uh, apparently they're going at it like rabbits.'

'I mean Mark and me.'

'So there was something.'

How I hate to admit this, given his accusation, and my indignant denial, in the office that first week. 'Yes, but I didn't know he was married. As soon as I . . . Anyway, it's water under the bridge.'

'Maybe not as far as Felicity is concerned.'

'Wait, your boss is going to quit? So you won't be working the parties any more?'

'Or at the office for much longer. I planned to quit soon anyway.'

His statement hits me in the solar plexus. 'Is that because you're almost finished with your mail-order diploma?' I joke, but given this information, I don't feel very merry.

'Uh-huh, I've only got about a month left. Then I get a real job. 'Nother drink?'

'I'm getting drunk.'

'Good. I'll get you another.'

'Are you going to take advantage of me?'

'While you're drunk? While you have a boyfriend? No.'

'Very noble of you . . .' Blimey, as they say. He's some kind of hypnotist. All I did was look at him and he got better-looking. Not that he's ugly to start with. He does have very deep-blue eyes. Blimey. 'Sam? I've been thinking. Maybe we could have dinner sometime?'

'. . .'

'Don't let me force you.'

'What about your boyfriend?'

'He's not my boyfriend. We've been on a few dates. It's not serious.' We're not even having sex yet . . . though can Sam say as much? 'Are *you* serious with . . . anyone?'

'Erm. Well, Janey and I –'

'Oh sure, of course. She seems nice,' I lie. 'Forget it, it was just a thought. Must be too much wine!'

'Well, we could have dinner. Sure we could.'

'No, no, really, it was no big deal. Forget I asked. Excuse me a sec, I need to run to the ladies.'

I will not cry. I will *not* cry . . . I'm crying. It's my own fault. I built this up in my head till it was an actual relationship. And it probably *would* have been, if I'd said yes to him at the start, instead of scoffing at the very idea of going out with an American office boy. As if my mother, the Queen, would have disapproved. I have only myself to blame for feeling like this now. So stop being mad at Sam. What did I expect, that he'd keep trying, or put his life on hold while I decided whether he was worthy of going out with? It serves me right to be sniffling in this stall. And understandable, I guess, given my imaginary relationship, to feel like I've been broken up with. What an awful, fitting phrase that is. To break: to separate into parts with suddenness or violence. To break off: to remove by, or as if by, breaking. Ain't that the truth.

'I wondered if you decided to go home and not tell me. Are you okay?'

'Sorry, you know we girls like to take our time.' I managed to erase the raccoon eyes but between the scrubbing and lack of replacement make-up, I look like I've been swimming laps. 'So tell me about Janey.' I'm not a glutton for punishment; I'm hoping he'll tell me that he doesn't really like her, or at least that she's flawed in some important way.

'What do you want to know?'

'What's she like? She doesn't talk to me much.'

'She's great. She's in school too, doing her degree in child psychology so that she can work with kids.'

It figures. He's dating the nanny from *The Sound of Music*. 'How long have you been together?'

'Not long, a couple months.'

'Right, since that first party when I met her.'

'Er no, we weren't dating then.'

'Oh, I just assumed. I thought she kissed you.'

'That. Yeah, I wasn't expecting that. I guess that's when it dawned on me that she liked me. I'm a little slow sometimes.'

He's not the only one. If I'd said yes when he asked me the first time . . . or the second . . . I did screw this up. 'Well, there's nothing like a new relationship, eh? Listen, I should go. It's getting late. Thanks for lending an ear tonight. I really' – there's that hitch again – 'I really appreciate it.'

'Han, are you okay?'

'Oh sure, I'm just still in shock, about Felicity, and the night and everything. I'll be fine. Too much wine, that's all. Thanks again. G'night.'

I make as decorous an exit as three bottles of wine will allow. Actually, my heel pokes down between two pieces of sidewalk, sending me flying, *sans* shoe, to sprawl in a heap on the ground. It's fitting, since that's how I feel.

19

My career is about to end. Felicity is trying to force me out, and she's twisting everything around to do it. I've racked my brain to remember every conversation I had with her. She's been a very clever bunny. She's right: I never explicitly told her that there was a death theme. However, any intelligent person would have pieced the puzzle together. Let's review the facts, shall we? Party in a crypt, black roses, dressing the waiters as undertakers . . . hmm, any idea what the tone might be? This is a somewhat moot point however, since even if I had a picture of her standing next to the coffin cake, she'd deny all knowledge. And Mark will believe her. So a straightforward presentation of the facts won't work. If I want to stay employed, I've got no choice. This isn't my proudest moment, but I'm desperate. More importantly, I'm angry. I may be easy-going, but there's a limit. Felicity passed it when she set me up. She has to expect that I'll fight back. She'd do exactly the same thing. I shouldn't feel guilty about my tactics when she's left me no choice. Of course I do, a little.

I'm armed with the most deadly combination of weapons: a half-caff skinny latte from Costa Coffee and my navy and pink pinstripe suit with really square shoulders. It makes me look a little like Lauren Bacall, if she had a penchant for Ralph Lauren tailoring at H&M prices.

'Mark, I'd like to talk to you and Felicity this morning, please.'

'Ah, yes, Hannah, that's probably best. Give me twenty minutes to get through some emails.'

Shit, Felicity's already gotten to him. She moves fast. Character assassins are the most dangerous kind but you've got to admire their technique. She probably buttered him up during sex (not literally, I hope) and then put me in the worst possible light.

Felicity smiles warmly when she sees me. 'Morning, Hannah. Fun weekend?'

If you call forty-eight hours of sweating over my future fun, you bitch. 'Yep, great thanks.'

At least Mark has the courtesy to look sheepish when I return to his office twenty minutes and thirty seconds later. Settling back in one of the chairs, I cross my legs and lay an arm along each armrest. I am the picture of composure.

'Nice weekend?' he asks.

'Not really, no.'

'I'm sorry to hear that.'

'I bet you are.'

Ever the perceptive man, he gives up any more attempts at small talk.

Felicity swans in like this is a normal Monday morning brainstorm. 'Right, Hannah. I think we should talk about the Read-Hutchins party.'

'Yes, I think we should.'

'I have to say, it showed a remarkable lack of judgement.' I can almost hear the 'young lady' at the end, which is silent in the language of condescension.

'I agree.'

'You do?' Mark asks.

'Absolutely. Felicity, I wouldn't have expected that from someone with your experience.'

There goes the eyebrow. Luckily, I'm impervious in my pinstripes. 'Me! Hannah, need I remind you that this was your responsibility? You begged me to let you have the account and I gave you full reign. I find it absurd that you now blame me for your failure.'

'I didn't beg for the account. You offered it to me. And you set me up to fail.'

'I set you up? Mark, I told you she was going to try to get out of this.'

'Hannah, hold on. You can't really be suggesting that Felicity purposely sabotaged your first account just to see you fail. That's ridiculous.'

'Not ridiculous. True. She did, Mark, I promise she did.'

'I won't hear any more of this,' Felicity interrupts. 'Hannah, you're fired.'

Oof. I mean, I was prepared for this, but it still hurts. 'On what grounds?'

'What do you mean, what grounds? For failing miserably at the first account I trust you with, for tarnishing the firm's reputation. And for accusing me, your manager, of being out to get you. You're obviously unstable.'

Okay, Kate, Katharine, Lauren, ghosts of girl powers past, don't fail me now. 'I don't think it's a good idea to try to fire me.'

'I don't have to try, Hannah. I just did.'

'Mark, you might want to reconsider.'

'This is my decision, Hannah.' Her voice is starting to hit an odd pitch. 'I have Mark's full support in whatever I do.'

'Mark, Felicity, you aren't in a very strong negotiating position given your, um, extracurricular activities.'

You know the expression 'the silence is deafening'? Maybe it's my heart thudding in my ears that's drowning out all sound, but I swear it really is deafening.

We wait. And wait. I'm wearing my most Mona Lisa smile.

She might have been a blackmailer too. Mark finally cracks. 'What do you mean by that?' he whispers.

'Let me spell it out for you, Mark. I have it on good authority, from your sister-in-law actually, that you're fucking Felicity and that your wife doesn't know. And I strongly suspect that, despite what you told me, she would, in fact, care very much. Felicity, I imagine that other people in the firm who are also up for partnership don't know either, and would also care very much. So let me say again that firing me would be a very bad idea.' I can hear my voice shaking but I can't exactly stop now. And I don't want to stop.

'Are you trying to blackmail us?'

'I don't have to try, Felicity. I just did.'

They stare at me, agog. Yes, they are truly agog.

'Now if you'll excuse me, I have work to do. What's the next project? I think you said the anniversary party for the Patels. Just so I know, Felicity, neither of them are terminal, right?'

I'm shaking before I reach the bathroom door. So much for girl power. It's relief. And adrenaline. And wonder. I can't believe I just did that. It was so satisfying! Terrifying but satisfying. All my comeback fantasies have come true at once. The look on Mark's face. And Felicity, she was absolutely floored. They never expected me to fight back. What a remarkable feeling of self-empowerment. It must be what the psychiatrists call a breakthrough. Plus I still have a job. So this worked out as well as could be expected. Or at least it didn't work out as badly as it could have, though I'm probably not in line for any promotions.

Rationalization is a wonderful thing. I am officially over Mark. Close chapter, move on. In fact, I can do better than that. I'll forget the whole sordid affair; pack it away in a mental box. Call it avoidance, call it denial. I call it peace of mind. I guess there's always the risk that someone will come along and open up all the boxes I've stored away over the years. I pity the therapist who has to deal with *that* mess, but unless and until that happens, I'm perfectly comfortable with self-delusion. Mark is in a box labelled Bad Experience (scribbled over in red Magic Marker with the word Wanker).

Barry hands me a ticket.

'Wimbledon?'

'Do you like tennis?'

'Of course!' To be precise, I don't mind watching tennis for a little while on TV while painting my toenails. I tried playing once but gave myself a fat lip. Those rackets are a menace when you have the arm strength and coordination of a toddler.

'It's the men's final today. And you look perfect. I didn't want to ruin the surprise, but they have rules about appropriate dress. Very old-fashioned. I should have known you'd be perfectly dressed in any case.'

No thanks to you, Barry. I've been forced to apply some broad fashion rules to my dates. Since he's never going to tell me where we're going, I've defaulted to two wardrobe genres: demure in daytime and sexy vamp at night. It's a little constricting, since I have at least half a dozen different looks, but so far it's kept me from being mistaken for a hooker at tea. Only the go-carting threw me off, but it's safe to assume after my reaction that there won't be any more sporty dates.

These tickets must have cost . . . Yep, there's the price right there. Wow.

Barry eagerly grabs my hand. 'We'll have lunch in the hospitality tent first and then watch the tennis. Are you happy?'

'This is the coolest thing ever!' I realize I'm shrieking when he sits back a little bit. 'Sorry, I mean, this is just great!' I lean over and plant a very grateful kiss on him. He really is a good man. I may not feel about him the way I do about Sam, but Sam is a road to heartbreak, with potholes, leading to a dead end. At least Barry doesn't have another woman in his life. Or potholes. Plus he likes me. That's enough for now.

He kisses back. 'I was afraid it might be too much, you know, too early. But then I thought that you might not have had the chance to go to Wimbledon, being American, and the tickets were available, so I thought . . .' He looks sheepish and hopeful at the same time.

'Barry, this is so nice. Thank you.'

The time zone thwarts my ability to make Stacy insanely jealous. Besides, I can't gloat properly with Barry sitting right there. Though he continually tempts me to be myself, there's no way I'm going to show him how shallow I really am. I wonder if he does cool things like this a lot. He must be rich. My boyfriend's rich!

His voice breaks into my reverie. 'There are just two other couples joining us, so it'll be fun.'

'Joining us?'

'Well, yes. Two clients and their spouses. They're my biggest clients, but they're very nice.'

So he's not rich, he's working. I'm sure his clients *are* perfectly nice, but I didn't plan to group date. It's hard enough being sparkling and entertaining to Barry without having to worry about offending multi-million-pound clients. I have a terrible feeling about this.

'Super!' I lie.

I may know very little about how the corporate world works, but I'm sure that client entertainment falls within the wifely realm. Suffering through boring dinners is what they get paid in diamonds and live-in help to do. It's a little early in our relationship to be at this stage. He hasn't even had sex with me and now I'm supposed to be his girlfriend host? I seem to have passed Go without collecting my 200 dollars (pounds!). What will I possibly have to say to his clients? Their wives are probably stay-at-home moms or ladies who lunch. I have aspirations towards both but a working knowledge of neither. I can't even fall back on we-stories because Barry and I haven't had any of those all-important talks yet, the ones where you find out that you have the same taste in random things, like black and white photography or sherbet. And I still don't understand what he does all day at work.

'Barry, I'm not so sure about this. What if they don't like me?'

'How can they not like you? Don't worry.' He kisses me as we reach the table. Thankfully, it's empty. A momentary stay of execution.

'But I don't have anything in common with bankers. I might not have much to say.' Given how well things went the last time I spoke my mind at an organized event, I'm not sure there's much he'd *want* me to say.

'They'll love you. Just be yourself.'

Well, obviously there's no chance of that. I excuse myself to make a frantic call to Chloe. Not to worry, she assures me, three little questions are guaranteed to lubricate the conversation. She should know. She's been to more boring business dinners than she can shake a breadstick at. I can do this. I *can* do this.

A middle-aged woman, resembling a more stylish Margaret Thatcher, approaches our table with a man trailing a few steps behind. 'Glenda, hello! Hi, Nigel!' Barry jumps to his feet with hand extended, ready to pump vigorously. Introductions are made. I'm Barry's special friend today. Puh-lease. Maybe date, friend, even lover. But 'special friend'? Wine is poured, thank god. The three of them settle into a jolly conversation: Yes the weather is perfect for the final. Nope, no rain in sight. The journey to Wimbledon was fine, no, not too much traffic. Damn. That's one of Chloe's questions.

'I like your shoes,' I offer to Glenda.

'Thank you.' She turns back to Barry and her husband.

Now that's just rude. Where's the reciprocal 'I like your' whatever, leaving the door wide open for further fashion observations and the eventual binding admission? You know the kind, the whispered confession: They may look great but they're squeezing my toes numb. I got my skirt on sale. I put my hand through my tights in the bathroom and can feel my left cheek squeezing through. Doesn't she know how this game is played? How am I supposed to bond with the one woman in England who doesn't follow strict protocol?

Barry has immersed himself in conversation with Nigel about Arsenal. I haven't exactly studied up on my favourite team, other than to learn that they wear ugly maroon shirts that remind me of my brief, humiliating stint as a cheerleader in junior high. Glenda is looking at me.

'Do you like tennis?' I try.

'Well, yes. I'd have to, wouldn't I, to come.'

Huh. Not necessarily. 'Do you work?'

Glenda's you-must-be-stupid look has deepened. 'I'm sorry?'

'Are you working?' Have I offended her? This is one of Chloe's sure-fire questions. Maybe she's a hyper-feminist, appalled that I'd even ask.

'Of course I am.' She's mentally reporting me to Gloria Steinem.[34]

'Great. That's great. Where?' If I can get her to talk about herself, maybe she'll stop glaring at me.

'At Grand Met. I'm Barry's client. Will you excuse me? In fact, there's something I need to discuss.' She walks four feet away to join the men. There may as well be a couple thousand miles between us.

She's the client? Of course there must be women clients, since there are women executives. So why did this never occur to me? I'm a disgrace to womankind. My sister would be horrified. It's worse than being stumped by that riddle about the boy and his father who get into a car accident. The father dies and when the son is rushed to hospital, the surgeon sees the boy on the table and says, 'I can't operate on this patient, he's my son.' (Answer for any fellow chauvinists: the surgeon's the mother.) And I thought I'd have trouble relating to a bored housewife. I'm supposed to entertain the house*husband*? Until a minute ago, I didn't even realize that was a viable job title.

As I sit resenting my role in this little charade, another couple approaches. Julian and Jade something-or-other. Instantly, prospects look up. Jade is trendy, really trendy, thirty-something, and Julian doesn't look like he knows how to frown. Best of all, they already know Glenda and Nigel. I feel a little giddy now that the pressure to perform has been lifted. Glenda has disappeared to the bathroom so I have no qualms about using my opening line on Jade. 'I like your shoes.'

'Oh thanks, they're killing me though!' she groans. 'Do you think we'll sit down soon?'

34. She is one of the world's leading feminists, with the marvellous ability to push for women's rights while wearing stylish shoes.

See, Glenda, *that's* how the game is played. 'Mmm, mine are killing too. Why can't designers make pretty shoes that are comfortable?'

'It's a conspiracy to make us buy more.'

'No kidding. I must have ten pairs that I've only worn once!'

'I've got that many that I haven't *even* worn once.'

And thus the metaphorical chest-beating begins. By the time Glenda gets back, nose freshly powdered, Jade and I are practically best friends. She stays with us for a minute or two before drifting over to where Barry and Julian are talking shop.

This isn't so bad. In fact, I'm kind of enjoying myself. Jade is curious about my Americanness and I admit it, I'm enjoying telling her what 'we' think. Being the mouthpiece for an entire nation is a little daunting, but I've had a few glasses of wine and am definitely warming to the task. I guess all expats have their crosses to bear: the Brits have Prince Philip, the Germans have their beach-towels-at-dawn reputation, the French have, well, the Parisians, and we have Iraq. Still, I'm glad when we steer the conversation back to our fashion gripes.

Nigel briefly jolts our repartee but I can't hold a grudge now that I know he actually belongs on our team. I try the last of Chloe's questions.

'Nigel, do you and Glenda have kids?'

'We do! A boy, Nigel, who's six and a girl called Mabel. She's three.'

'How cute.' I'm just being nice. Names like that must constitute cruelty to children in most countries.

'How are yours?' he asks Jade.

'Ever-growing monsters. It's no way to live.' Jade doesn't strike me as overly maternal. Unlike Nigel. 'The middle boy goes to Cheam in the Autumn. Two down, one to go.'

Nigel laughs. He has a really infectious laugh. 'Glenda wants to send ours off but I don't think I can do it.'

'Yours aren't demons.' Jade isn't cracking a smile. 'You don't know what you're missing. Once I ship the last one off, it'll be like the good old single days again.'

'Except for the husband!' I contribute.

Jade shrugs. I guess husbands aren't an impediment to single-dom in her circle.

'We may as well be single now anyway. I'm virtually a single father. I never see Glenda. Occasionally at weekends.'

Jade lowers her voice, smirking. 'You're unhappy about that?'

I can't believe she's being so mean. Okay, Glenda's no Kate Moss but Nigel is married to her. He must love her for some reason.

'Heh, heh, not altogether unhappy.'

She turns to me. 'A piece of advice. As long as the bank balance is healthy, the marriage is healthy. It's not a bad set-up. You should try it.' She nods towards Barry, who catches her eye and raises his glass.

'Cheers to that!' They toast their good fortune at having snagged their workaholic sugar daddy (and mommy).

I don't like Jade any more. I've heard about these women who are only with their men for the money, but I imagined they'd look like Anna Nicole Smith and be married to wheelchair-bound octogenarians. I wonder if this is what bankers' wives wither into from lack of attention. Or maybe they're warped to begin with and gravitate towards rich, absent men. It's the age-old nature versus nurture question. Either way, I don't want to be one, thank you very much. Now I'm in a bad mood. This isn't fun and I'm doing it for a man that I'm not even having sex with. At least Sam wouldn't take this long to close the deal, to use banker parlance. Well, obviously he didn't take this long, as evidenced by his cosy relationship with Janey. The lucky bitch. What if all of Barry's friends are like Jade and Nigel? Is that what I'm signing up for? Am I doomed to be surrounded by women who do nothing but complain about their lives while spending their husbands' money? What a sad way to live. There's no way I'd want Cartier and Harry Winston to replace my husband . . . though I wouldn't say no to a Cartier screw-motif gold cuff *and* a loving spouse.

At least the food looks good and sitting next to Barry gives me someone to talk to. Mmm, asparagus. I love it, bad pee smell be damned.

'Do you know,' Glenda says as the last little plate of green spears is set before us, 'that asparagus is one of only two foods that one should eat with one's fingers?' She looks pointedly at me, sawing away with my knife, as she picks up a spear. I hate her. It's bad enough that *one* has had to learn how to eat like the English to keep them from thinking *one* is a barbarian (Chloe counselled that 'civilized people', by which she means everyone outside America, use their fork in their left hand and their knife in their right – no shifting back and forth to cut). There's no need to point out my culinary faux pas. And I don't have to take crap from a woman who looks like a badly ageing prime minister.

'Really?' I ask, batting my eyes. 'What's the other?'

'Artichokes.'

'Hmm, what about bananas?'

'No, we use a fruit knife and fork.'

Now *there*'re utensils for someone with more money than sense. 'How about bread?'

'Well, obviously.'

'Sandwiches?'

'I suppose.'

'Oreo cookies? Mars Bars? Popsicles? What about potato chips?' I'm certainly not above winning my point with trailer-park favourites.

'Yes, well, the rules weren't designed for your American food.'

Barry asks, 'For whom were they designed, then?'

Pretentious women with overbites.

Glenda at least has the good manners to look like she wishes she'd never introduced the topic. 'Our tastes,' she mumbles. I catch Jade roll her eyes.

Barry laughs. 'I prefer it when people follow their own rules, don't you think?'

My boyfriend is doing battle for me over asparagus – touché. He *is* a good man.

Anticipation is running high outside in the stands. For people who know anything about tennis, this is probably quite an event. 'It must be especially exciting for you that Roddick is here,' Barry says as we take our seats on the sunny side of the court after lunch.

Roddick, Roddick, is he a movie star I should know? Or a fashion designer? Surely I'd have heard of any designer that a thirty-year-old English banker knows about. He must be a movie star. 'It is exciting,' I murmur.

'You're cheering for him, then?'

Cheering for him? I'm certainly not going to make that big an ass of myself in public. 'No, I don't think so.'

Nigel breaks in. 'You're not supporting your own country-man?'

Now I see a few American flags being waved. Fans wouldn't do that for a movie star. Understanding dawns. 'Oh. Well, of course I'm cheering for Roddick, what I mean is I'm not *cheering* for him, if you see what I mean.' His ingrained fear of looking stupid in public should prevent any more probing questions. Now, how to know which one is Roddick? It's not like they wear their names on their shirts. Two girls in front of us have flags. I'll just clap when they do. This'll be a piece of cake.

Tennis, like golf, has never struck me as a spectator sport. It's silly to watch a little yellow ball bounce back and forth over a net. Heads left, heads right, left, right, left. But to my surprise, it's gripping. I'm totally sucked into the game. There's not a sound except the strike of racket on ball and the occasional grunt from one of the players. It's as quiet as a classical music concert or a play, without even the distracting noise of the performers onstage. When I say quiet, I mean qui-et.

Except for that cellphone. I've been in theatres when they've gone off, and once an actor actually stopped his performance while the poor guy scrambled to silence the offensive ringing. Talk about humiliating. A voice booms over the loudspeaker after one of the players (mine, I think) misses the ball. 'Please ensure that all mobile phones are switched off.'

'Uh, Hannah?' Barry whispers. 'Is that yours?'

No, that's not my ring tone. But my handbag does seem to be vibrating. I peek inside and, sure enough, my phone's little face is lit up, trying to get my attention. It's Stacy.

'Hello?' I whisper.

'Hannah, I had to call you! I just booked a ticket to come visit!'

'You're kidding?! When?'

'Thursday! I got the most amazing deal out of JFK. The ticket is, like, five hundred bucks. I'm flying Air India but it must be safe or the FAA wouldn't let them fly into the US, right? Do you think they serve curries and poppadoms on the flight? I'm so excited! What should I pack?'

Barry whispers, 'Um, Hannah, you're not really supposed to be on the phone.' I look up. The guy sitting in the high chair at the net is glaring at me.

'Stacy, I've gotta go. I'm at Wimbledon.'

'Wimbledon! Hang on a sec –'

'No, Stacy –'

'Oh my god, I see you! On TV! You're on *Breakfast at Wimbledon*! Wave to me!'

'Stacy, I have to –'

'Come on, wave! Is that Barry next to you? He's cute!'

I give a little wave. 'I'll call you later.' I hang up.

Okay, on the embarrassment scale that goes from forgetting someone's name to congratulating a fat woman on her pregnancy, this is equivalent to getting your period in white pants and not noticing until the end of the day, after giving a presentation on a raised stage, with no podium.

'Barry, I'm so sorry. I didn't recognize the ring tone. Chloe must have changed it by accident when she was fiddling with my phone. And I don't know how to turn my phone off.' I don't blame him if he dumps me now. After today's performance, it's safe to say I wouldn't make a suitable banker's wife anyway.

'Don't worry, darling. Here's the off button.'

'You're not mad?'

'I think it's kind of funny, actually. And I think you're adorable.' He kisses me and squeezes my hand, which he's been holding since I got off the phone. 'Besides, it could happen to anyone.'

That might be true, but 'anyone' always seems to be me. I know it's completely unfair, but I'm starting to wonder about Barry's frame of mind. I mean, if he constantly thinks I'm funny and adorable when I know for a fact that I'm screwed up and weird, what does that say about him? Maybe he's hiding a horrible dark secret and that's the only reason he's so accepting of my faults. Maybe it's the secret he discloses to his girlfriends on their second anniversary. Nobody is really this nice, are they?

20

We've turned into women whose squeals can be heard by dogs as far away as China. Do I care that we're confirming every stereotype about our homeland's lack of volume control? I do not. Not when Stacy is standing right in front of me!

'Ohmygod, I'm so happy to –'

'Couldn't wait to –'

'– see you, I'm so excited –'

'– get here, the flight was like –'

'– that you're –'

'– six days long but I'm –'

'HERE! YOU LOOK GREAT!' we scream at each other. Of course, having best-friend vision means I'd think she looks great in a sack. Not that she is. She's working pure airport glamour, complete with sunglasses in her hair, ready to whip on in case of paparazzi. You'd think she just finished a spa and make-up day at Elizabeth Arden. This is where having shiny straight hair that's immune to humidity comes in handy. When I landed, I looked like I'd been in bed with the flu for three days. And I smelled like a goat. It's the unglamorous side of long-distance travel that you don't read about in *Condé Nast*; the whiff of confinement doesn't come through in those paparazzi snaps of Kate Moss in Terminal 5.

Stacy smells . . . 'Lovely?'

'Isn't it great? SJP is incredible.' So my friend has landed glossy and clean, smelling as sweet as freshly baked bread. She's going for an Elle Macpherson vibe with a skinny blazer and button-down shirt. And what are those? Stilettos? My feet puffed into mini soufflés on the way over. I'm so happy to see her. And yet. Tiny feelings of inadequacy are snapping at my heels. I'd almost forgotten the feeling. Surprising, given how often it plagued me in Hartford. Am I? Am I jealous? Come on. Haven't I grown? Haven't I proven I can do anything Stacy can? We're equals. Still, I wish I'd worn heels.

'Do you want to take a nap or anything?' I'm just being polite. Stacy is happiest on four hours of sleep a night.

'No way, I want to see London!'

'Thought so. Put on comfy shoes and I'll take you over to Hyde Park, then we can walk to Buckingham Palace.'

'Is the Queen there? Or William?'

'I don't know.' Stacy is convinced the heir apparent would pop the question if only they met. The fact that he'd also be her monarch simply sweetens the deal. 'We'll know from the flag.'

'The flag?'

'They fly the Royal Standard when she's home.' I'm proud to be able to impart this bit of trivia about my city. *My* city. I do think of it as my city, and it's such a nice feeling.

'Or –'

'Then –'

'– WE CAN GO –'

'– shopping!'

'– to Harvey Nicks and Harrods.'

Of course. When Stacy told me she was only coming for a few days, I briefly worried that it wasn't enough time. The museums alone here would take a couple weeks to get through. Then I remembered that my friend takes an anthropological view of culture. She can piece together a view of an entire country based on what she finds in its department stores.

'I have an idea,' she says as we're wandering through Harrods' handbag hall. It's as if we've stepped inside an Egyptian tomb, assuming mummies carried Dior into the next world. It's the most sumptuously tacky public interior in London, possibly in the world. Black and tan marble covers the walls and floor. Everything is painted in gold, with flower arrangements taller than me. Imagine the penthouse apartment of a very old, very famous socialite, the Mafia Don(na) of the upper crusties. Then add about a million fabulous handbags.

'Let's go to Europe,' she says.

'We're in Europe.'

'No, I mean the *real* Europe. France, Germany . . . Belgium.'

Belgium? I'm surprised Stace knows where Belgium is. 'Which one?'

'Why not all of them? We could fly into a town near the border, rent a car and drive all through.'

'Why would we do that?'

'So I can see Europe.'

'But you're in Europe now. Why not see London?'

She rolls her eyes. 'I've already got the stamp here.'

Now I get it. She wants inky credit for her travels. 'It's too much, Stace.' There are times when I don't appreciate her sense of adventure.

'Kaiser Wilhelm did it.'

'Who?'

'Kaiser Wilhelm in World War I.'

'Have you been watching the History Channel again?'

'My point is that we could fly into a city close to the border in, I don't know, Germany, have a beer and a bratwurst, drive into Belgium, have some mussels, then go to France for absinthe and steak.'

'A culinary re-enactment of World War I?'

'Why not?'

'The shopping's not great in Germany, you know.'

'It's not?'

'Nope. Think about it. What's it ever given to the fashion world? Dirndls? Sandals with socks? Karl Lagerfeld? He lives in Paris.'

'Oh.' I can see she's mentally recalculating her credit-card bill.

'Don't worry, there's plenty to buy here. We're going to have a great time in London!'

Tell me again why I thought it would be such a good idea to bring my oldest friend and my newest friend together? We're in a very cool bar that welcomes ladies in need of a refuelling glass of wine before continuing their retail assault. It's been an hour. Stacy and Chloe are barely speaking to each other. I assumed they'd love one another because they love me, that affection was somehow transferable. Apparently it doesn't work that way. Stacy's being surprisingly hostile, and Chloe's being very aloof (not that I blame her; I'd be cold too in the face of this much aggression). This isn't like Stacy. She's usually very friendly and outgoing. I hope she's just jet-lagged. I've been bragging to Chloe about how great my best friend is. She must be questioning my judgement at this point.

I suspect there's only one way to unite them. 'So. Barry,' I say. Now they're eyeing me like I'm a single spoon in the chocolate fondant. Talk about throwing myself on the proverbial grenade, taking one in the gut for friendship.

'Yes, Barry,' Stacy sighs.

'Tell me everything,' Chloe orders.

'The thing is, he's perfect. He does everything right.'

'Except have sex with you.'

'I'll get to that. He does all the right things. He takes me on perfect dates. He says the most complimentary things. Do you know how nice it is to be told all the time that you're wonderful?'

'Is he interesting?' Chloe wants to know.

'Does he make you laugh?'

'Sometimes.'

'Not usually?' Stacy asks.

'Or all the time?'

If this is their idea of a good-cop-bad-cop routine, one of them really ought to start playing the good cop. 'I'm not looking for a comedian, girls, I'm looking for a good boyfriend.'

'Why can't he be both?' Stacy asks.

'Don't you want our opinion?'

'Of course not, I want your approval.'

'We can't approve of someone who won't have sex with you.'

'Right. It's unnatural.'

Sure, now they agree on something. 'Maybe he's just taking it slow.'

'How long's it been?' Stacy knows the answer. She knows all these answers by heart. She's just making me say it out loud as some twisted form of therapy.

'Six weeks. No, seven.'

'How many dates?'

'Eleven.'

'Are you sure his tackle's in good working order?' Chloe asks.

'Huh?'

'Maybe he can't get it up.'

'No, he's definitely got it, up, whenever we're together.'

'Maybe he's so big he's self-conscious.'

Ah, Chloe, you're truly a great friend.

'Wishful thinking. Maybe he's too small.' Stacy's a realist.

'Stop focusing on the physical! Can't he be the perfect boyfriend that I just haven't slept with yet?'

'Sure he can. Only that's called being your friend. Look, I'm just concerned that there's something weird going on here. Don't get mad, I'm only watching out for you.'

'Stacy's right, Hannah. Are you sure this is what you want?'

I must have needed an intervention. It feels good to talk. 'I just don't get it. Aside from the sex, or lack of, everything is perfect. He even wants me to meet his parents next weekend. It's their wedding anniversary . . . What's that look for?' Chloe's eyebrows are nearly touching her hairline.

'Uh, Hannah, are you sure he's not gay?'

'Oh my god, I can't believe I didn't see that!' Stacy yells. 'Of course, that's it, he's gay! He's using you as a decoy!'

'Don't be stupid. He's not gay.'

'How do you know?'

'Well, for one thing he has a hard-on the whole time I'm with him.'

'That is rather strong evidence.'

'Fine. Then how do you explain his reluctance?'

'I can't. And I'm not sure about meeting his parents. I mean, isn't that a big step?' So maybe it's me. I'm giving off don't-sleep-with-me vibes. I'm so scared of a real relationship that I'm subconsciously sabotaging it. Maybe I don't think I deserve someone who treats me so well. 'Do you think it's me?'

Chloe is staring at me. 'Hannah, listen to me. Too often we blame ourselves for our boyfriends' shortcomings. Trust me, it's not you, it's him.'

'Maybe you're just not that into him,' Stacy suggests.

'But why wouldn't I be? He's perfect.'

'On paper. But does he make you laugh? Not really. Is he interesting? Not really, by your own admission. Does he tear your clothes off and have wild, passionate monkey sex with you?'

Not ever. But I'm not willing to give up. What if there isn't another man out there who thinks I'm as fabulous?

Not even liquoring up before shopping or gossiping about my lack of sex life did much to improve Chloe's mood, so I really appreciate that she still offered to get us into the club tonight. Chalk one up for the British sense of obligation above all else; they spend so much time doing what they 'should do' that they might not even miss not doing what they want to do.

Stacy would like an aristo-rat to be her souvenir of London. So naturally we're going to stalk one tonight. I just hope the bar is air-conditioned. Summer in London is killing me. I don't do well in the heat. Or the cold. My ideal temperature runs between sixty-eight and seventy-two degrees Fahrenheit (with relative humidity less than 20 per cent, high barometric pressure and light winds, preferably from the north-east). It doesn't actually get that hot here, although whenever the temperature hits about seventy-five you'd think the ozone layer has burned off over the city. To be fair, the English aren't exactly equipped for the sun. I thought I was white until I saw these people. Some are translucent. Honest to god, you can practically see their organs. After the first sunny weekend, they acquire the patina of bacon after a few minutes in the pan. The city just isn't designed for hot weather. Air-conditioning is a real luxury (one that doesn't extend to the Tube). Apparently, despite the fact that it exists on the trains in New York, and Chicago, and Atlanta, and Washington, air-conditioning cannot be installed underground. The best the London Underground can do for us is to place helpful advisory notices in the stations that say things like 'It's hot. We know it's hot. We're sorry about that but we really can't be expected to control the weather. It's not in our union contracts, for one thing. So carry water with you in case you begin to dehydrate in our stinking metal tubes, and if you do feel faint, try not to fall down inside the carriage. Make your way to the platform and faint there. Eventually someone might come along to help, if they're not on a tea break.'

Well, they don't use those exact words, but that's the sentiment.

'Do I look okay?' Stacy wants to know. This is unprecedented. She never asks if she looks okay. London is really throwing her off her game.

'You look great. Those shoes are perfect.'

'Not too much?'

'Perfect. Ready?'

I didn't expect Boujis to be so small, or so shabby. Or in a basement. But I suppose after Hakkasan I shouldn't be surprised that Londoners revel in subterranean amusements.

'Is everyone blonde in this city?' Stacy is eyeing Chloe's tresses accusingly. To be fair, the entire bar *is* a sea of glossy blonde locks.

'Those of us who don't come from immigrants probably are,' Chloe shoots back at my brown-haired friend. Mee-ow.

Stacy puts a hand to her ear. 'I'm sorry, what did you say? I can't understand you.'

'I said – Excuse me, Hannah, I see a friend I want to say a quick hello to.'

'Sure thing, Chloe, see you in a minute.' There was no hint of British disdain for Americans when I met Chloe. Now, I have to admit it's there and being unleashed on Stacy in all its gory glory. I also have to confess that I can see her point of view. Stacy does seem louder than necessary, and her constant comparisons with home are getting monotonous. Plus she's being a real bitch.

'What a bitch.'

'Stace, cut her some slack. You haven't exactly been friendly.'

'Well, neither has she.'

This has the potential to degenerate into a hair-pulling fight. 'Just, for me, please try to be nice to her? I'll ask the same of her.'

'I really can't understand her. I wasn't just saying that.'

'Really?'

'Can you?'

'Yeah. Huh, I wonder if my ear is getting used to the accent.' I even understand Siobhan, though my flatmates are still linguistically baffling.

'So what, you think you're English now?'

'No, no. God, do you remember that stupid barmaid at the Pub, the fake Australian?'

'She's still there. And her accent is getting stronger, if you can believe it.'

'She probably topped it up watching Hugh Jackman in the outback.'

'Did I tell you I asked her about it once? She claimed some sort of Australian ancestry.'

'Right, like an accent is genetically programmed.'

'She's such a loser.'

'And who's she kidding with those boobs?' It's so nice to trash-talk with my best friend, knowing I can be as bitchy as I want and she won't judge me . . . So why am I judging her? Friends don't do that.

'Ohmygod, there's Harry! Look!'

She's right. He's just come out of that side room with a couple girls.

'I'm going to talk to him.'

'Stace, hold on. He's probably got bodyguards. You could get shot.' Admittedly there don't appear to be any goons packing heat nearby.

'Are you coming with me or not?'

'Of course.'

I can't believe she's really charging over to introduce herself to a royal. I suppose, as they say, in for a penny . . .

'Hi, 'scuse me.' She edges one of the girls out of the way. 'I'm Stacy. And you are?'

He's actually wavering. Brilliant!

'I'm Harry, how'dyodo?' He takes her offered hand.

'Would you like a drink?'

'Are you American?'

'Yep.'

'Thank you. I'm going to dance for a bit.'

'Okay.' She starts dancing. She's actually dancing with a guy who's third in line to the British throne . . .

Until a rather serious man taps her on the shoulder. Behind him stands the girl she hip-checked to get at the ginger prince. 'I'm sorry, but the prince is with his friends this evening. I'm sure you'd like to get back to yours.'

'Sure thing. Bye, Harry, nice to meet you.'

Who does these things? I love her. I truly do.

I think Chloe has ducked out in humiliation. At least she wasn't an obvious participant in the ambush, so they won't suspend her membership. My mother would be so ashamed, having spent the better part of my childhood fretting over invitations and reminding me to be a 'good guest'. She meant making my bed and saying please and thank you, but I'm sure that stretches to not harassing the other guests, particularly when they may wear a crown some day. I'll certainly call Chloe first thing tomorrow to apologize for pestering her monarch.

I can tell Stacy is glad that she's gone. It's safe to say these two aren't destined for friendship. But she's gone quiet again. She was uncharacteristically restrained all day too, not even drawn out to ridicule the women with white pants and terrible VPL[35] that have started to populate Oxford Street now that the sun is shining.

'Stace, what's wrong?'

'Nothing.'

'Are you sure? Do you miss Tye?'

'Wha–? No, no. I'm pretty much done with him. He's boring, Han. I just can't get around the fact that he's too *nice*. He'd do anything I asked him to. You can't respect that. It's never gonna be a real relationship, no matter how much he goes down on me.'

'No, I suppose not,' I say, thinking guiltily of Barry. 'You don't seem yourself though. Sure nothing's wrong?'

. . . 'Maybe I'm just getting sad.'

'How come?'

'Because I don't want to leave!'

I put my arm around her. 'Sweetheart, I don't want you to go either. But we still have a few days left. Tomorrow's Sunday, and it's supposed to be sunny, so we'll go drinking with the Aussies.'

'Do they always go together? Sunday, and sunny, and drinking?'

35. VPL = visible panty lines. Like nipples and dirty faces, obvious underwear brings shame upon our mothers.

'And Aussies. They seem to.'

'Sounds fun,' she says glumly.

'Come on, Stace – what is it really?'

'It's stupid.'

'What is?'

She slugs back her vodka and cranberry. 'I'm afraid we're going to drift apart.'

'What? Of course we aren't.'

'I think we have a little already.'

'Why do you say that?'

'Well,' she sniffs, 'suddenly you hate The Gap. You think American styles are "too conservative" . . . I'm not even sure what you think of me any more.'

I know I look guilty, having had unkind thoughts along the same lines. Still, you don't flush a lifetime of friendship down the toilet just because you realize your best friend isn't perfect. 'Aw, Stace – I hate The Gap *here*, because all they've done is change the dollar sign to a pound sign. I'm not stupid. I refuse to pay ninety dollars for a pair of chinos.'

'You insulted our style,' she says petulantly.

Honestly. 'I did not. I simply pointed out that when I got here I didn't fit in with London's styles. That's an observation, not an insult.'

She sighs. 'I know I'm being ridiculous. Really I do. I can hear myself. Never mind. I'm just being petty. I'm jealous, that's all, because you did it. Everybody talks about doing something huge, but you actually went out and did it. Meanwhile I'm stuck in Hartford, without you, living my same old life. I was never dissatisfied when you were there, but now . . . it's not the same. It's not as much fun and I feel like *I'm* stagnating. I've been wondering what the hell I'm doing with my life. Maybe it's contagious. And now you get to have all these new experiences . . . with new friends.'

I see what all this is about. 'Stace, you know that Chloe won't ever replace you, right?'

'I don't know. How do *you* know that? You guys are together all the time. What if you become best friends?'

'What? You can only have one best friend. And you're it, Stace, for ever. End of story.'

'Okay. I'm being overemotional. PMS. It just seems like you're having so much fun in London. I'm really jealous of your life. I want it too.'

Suddenly I'm so excited I can hardly breathe. 'Then why don't you move here!' How great would it be to have my very best friend in London? 'You could live with me till you found a place. Or we could move in together somewhere! I bet your company would even transfer you . . . Would you think about it?'

'Sure I'll think about it.' I can see that she's thinking already. 'Hey, do I get to meet Barry?'

'Let's just have a nice time together. Just the two of us, okay?'

'I'd like that.' She's grinning now. 'Though if you're going to meet his parents, I should get to know him, don't you think?'

'What are you, my father? Let's take one step at a time. Another drink?'

'Er, let's dance first.'

'Stacy, you may not talk to the prince again.'

'Oh fine. Double vodka and cranberry, then.'

The best way to prevent a hangover, my dad always said, is not to drink in the first place. Spoken like someone with willpower. I clearly didn't inherit my self-control from him.

''Nother Advil?' I offer to Stacy, who's rubbing her temples to clear her head on this, the morning after the night before.

'Can you overdose on Advil?'

'Not here. They only come in these little packs, not in bottles.' The time it would take to pop each pill out of its plastic-and-foil blister must, in itself, be a deterrent.

'Not even mini bottles for your purse?'

'I don't think so.' Stacy harbours a pharmacy in her handbag. As a result, she's usually accompanied by the sound of maracas, giving her walk a certain festive beat.

It's so nice to lounge here on the sofa, nursing our sore heads and rehashing every moment of last night. It's exactly what we always did back home. Except that one of us would have ventured out for bagels, and milk for our coffee (and probably coffee), instead of having stuffed ourselves at 3 a.m. on the kebabs that are now lodged in our colons. Having her here has really made me miss our old life together. I don't want her to go back now. I know I've been annoyed at times, but those are tiny mosquito bites in the scheme of things. Sure, if you focus on them, they'll drive you crazy, but I'll take a little itching any day to have the wonderful comfort of her friendship too. New friends are exciting, and fun, but old ones are where the real value lies.

'Hey, Stace, do you remember that girl-scout song we used to sing? "Make new friends, but keep the old . . ."'

'"One is silver and the other is gold."' She sings, equally off-key, with me. Exactly. We were thrown out of the scouts soon after learning that song, for teaching the troop to swear in Spanish. But we were thrown out together.

'I wish you could stay here. Will you really think about moving over?'

'I will, really,' she says. 'And I'd bring big bottles of Advil. I think we're going to need them!'

Partially recovered, partially believing in the veracity of the hair-of-the-dog theory, we're in the midst of the well-worn tradition known as the Sunday drinking session. 'Here you go, girls.' Adam hands us each a pint. Like the Church, it may have started with a couple of bored expats. But unlike the Church, it's wholeheartedly embraced by the British public. We're surrounded by men and women slurring in a variety of English accents.

'It looks like Amherst College,' Stacy observes. She means because the men are wearing loafers and at least three shirts each. 'I didn't realize they had preppy here too.'

'Aw, yeah, I was even preppy in Sydney,' Sarah says. I've loved my flatmates even more since Stacy arrived. They've welcomed her like one of their own. Plus they hate this pub, yet happily came along when I said I wanted to show it to her.

I can tell from Stacy's dumbfounded expression that the polo shirt's global appeal is something she's never considered before. 'We probably all wore the exact same clothes at opposite ends of the world.'

'And listened to the same music and watched the same movies and played the same games. Makes the world seem kinda small, doesn't it?'

'Yeah.' I can see Stacy knows exactly what I mean. That's the beauty of being with my best friend. We always get each other, and can count on the other, no matter what. Take this weekend for instance. She knew absolutely 100 per cent that I'd be right behind her when she approached the prince, ready to share a cell with her if necessary. Just like I know absolutely 100 per cent that she's not even going to flirt with Adam or Nathan. We never get off with a guy the other introduces us to (unless we're being introduced in a wing-man capacity). And through our long years together, Stacy has had more chances to go off with a man than a hooker at a Vegas convention, yet she's never taken the bait. To me, that's a critical characteristic in someone you have to rely on when drunk to get you home.

'Whaddya do there in Hartford, Stace?' Sarah wants to know.

'Oh, it's boring. I'm just an analyst for a bank.'

'Well, I guess it pays the bills. Cheers, I hope you'll come back to visit soon!'

I don't blame Sarah for not pursuing her line of questioning; Stacy's never been one to dwell on her career in polite conversation. This is pure modesty since I know for a fact that she's one of the super-analysts of her industry, a pure-hearted Svengali for the business world. And that's not just what her mother says; she's been on TV and everything. In fact, though she'd never tell anyone, Stacy is actually a genius. I mean an honest-to-god genius. We took IQ tests when we were kids, our parents having got caught up in their friends' I'd-send-my-child-to-regular-school-but-she's-just-too-*bright* boasting competition. While I was decidedly average, destined for neither rocket science nor the short bus, Stacy tested off the charts. Her mother even tried to send her to smart camp when we were eleven. Unfortunately, she didn't think through the conundrum of sending someone smart enough to figure a way out of anything to a place she wanted to get out of. Stacy was back to play in my front yard the next day and her mom put the whole summer camp idea behind her. I'm no psychologist but I suspect a link between my friend's underachieving track record and her mom's efforts to bask in some of the glow of her offspring's accomplishments. You can imagine her reaction when she found out Stacy applied to UConn instead of Harvard and Princeton. Families can sometimes be your worst nightmare when they're trying to be your biggest advocate.

21

I'm trapped in meet-the-family hell at least a half-hour walk from a Tube station, god knows in what direction . . . This is what I get for letting myself be lured to North London's suburbs. I've just answered Mrs Kaplan's first question. You'd think I've told her that I'm a table dancer for fun and profit.

'But you're not Jewish?'

'Mum, please.' Barry grasps my hand, looking like he regrets this invitation as much as I do.

'Well, anyway, welcome to our home, Hannah.'

'Thank you, Mrs Kaplan.'

'You're American?' Mr Kaplan has at least two inches of hair hanging out of his nose. Actually it balances him out – otherwise the stuff sprouting from his ears would look odd. I know that men are concerned about glimpsing their married future in their girlfriend's mother, but I wonder if they realize we make the same comparison with their fathers. They ought to think long and hard about that before introducing us to the family.

'Yes, I'm from Connecticut.'

'Good!' he proclaims, as if I've chosen the perfect state to be from. Maybe there's a Jewish connection to Connecticut that I don't know about.

In the corner, a dark-haired man is rubbing the pregnant belly of the woman next to him. 'This is my brother, Gabe, and sister-in-law, Eliza. This is Hannah.'

These don't strike me as air-kissing sort of people. 'So you're the brother that Barry beat up,' I say after shaking his rather damp hand.

'Huh?' He's a good-looking guy, better-looking than Barry. I feel a pang of guilt at the thought.

'When you were kids. Barry told me about the time he put your tooth through your lip.'

'What is this?' Mrs Kaplan is charging across the room. 'My Barry never hit anybody.'

'Barry never hit me.'

'Oh, ah, uh, sorry, I must have been thinking of someone else.' Poor Barry, he looks like I've just caught him in the bathroom with the Victoria's Secret catalogue. Why would he make something like that up? 'Anyway, when are you due?' I say to Eliza's belly. Jeez, I hope she's not just fat.

'October.'

'Excellent. Is it a boy or a girl?'

'We don't know.'

'That makes it tough to buy the right colour clothes, doesn't it? Nobody really looks good in yellow.' Hah, hah, hah. As I say this, my eyes are drawn to Mrs Kaplan's blouse. To be fair, she's proving my point.

'Ah, Hannah,' Barry says, kissing me on the forehead, 'Jews don't buy gifts for the baby before it's born. It's a silly superstition we have. I don't know why we still have it, really, since you're absolutely right, yellow's an awful colour.' Mrs Kaplan's flush is now nicely offsetting her blouse.

'Oh.' I'm making friends left and right. I may as well just pull some pork chops from my handbag and pass them around.

Barry notices that I'm quiet on the ride back because, let's face it, I rarely am. He has his hand on my leg. I wish he'd remove it. It's hot and his hand is sweating. 'What's wrong?'

'I didn't exactly fit in with your family.' The first half-hour was my least offensive performance of the afternoon. Barry made our excuses not long after I talked myself down a blind alley challenging whether wine could really be kosher. You'd think I'd goose-stepped through their living room.

'Oh, don't worry. They liked you.'

'No, they didn't.'

'No. They didn't. But that doesn't matter. I like you.'

How does he always know the right thing to say? 'So, was that a big thing?'

'What?'

'Me meeting your parents?'

. . . 'Yeah, it was.'

'And I failed.'

'No, Hannah, *they* failed. You're perfect. If they don't like you just because you're not Jewish, that's their problem . . .'

'I guess.'

'I've always done it their way, dating nice Jewish girls, and it's come to nothing –'

'I thought you said you've dated, er, out of the faith before?'

'I have. A few dates. But girlfriends have always been Jewish.'

'So I'm really the first.'

. . . 'Yes. I'm sorry, I should have told you.'

'A little warning would have been nice.'

'I know. I just, I guess I wanted to be sure . . . I've been stupid. I don't know what I was waiting for.'

'What do you mean?'

'Let's go to my place.'

Can he mean what I think he means?

He does! We're tearing each other's clothes off before he closes the front door. This is not the Barry I know. Maybe he's drunk on Israel's finest. Mazel tov! As he slides my dress over

264

my head, I remember I'm wearing slightly big pants. They're not terrible, but also not my first choice for seduction. Frankly, after so many non-starter dates, I've given up wearing spicy lingerie. Why suffer the wedgie only to go home alone? At least I shaved my legs yesterday.

He's whispering how beautiful I am, as if each body part exposed is a never-before-seen Rembrandt revealed. Flattery will get you everywhere, sir. Mmm. Remember when I said Barry was a slow kisser? While slightly boring on the lips, it's delightful on the body. He obviously paid attention in foreplay class. Why, Mr Kaplan, what a beautifully circumcised hunk of manhood! Chloe and Stacy had me worried that I'd either have to comfort Barry after a barely-there encounter or go to the hospital for stitches. Neither will be necessary. Like the third bowl of porridge in *Goldilocks and the Three Bears*, he's just right. And he's not lying on me either, as some rather more lazy men have done. It's hard to get into the moment with only a quarter of your lung capacity.

I'm definitely in the moment. I'd never have guessed some-one so conservative could be this *sexy*. He's a Dr Jekyll and erotic Mr Hyde. I like having sex with this man. Surely that, and friendship, are good bases for a relationship.

All of a sudden Barry yells, 'I love you!', grunts and collapses on top of me.

Oh dear. What does one say to a proclamation of love that's tangled up in orgasm? Perhaps he didn't mean to say it. Maybe he has sex-induced Tourette's. But what if he did mean it? Am I supposed to say it back? If I do, and he didn't mean it, then that puts him in an awkward position. If I don't, and he meant it, then he's going to feel bad.

The bigger question is: do I love Barry? The answer hits me square in the pit of my stomach. No, I don't. No matter how many perfect dates we have, despite his constant compliments and the sex, I don't love him. Despite his apparent perfection, he isn't the man for me. I should have paid more attention to the signs instead of trying to convince myself that he was Mr Right. You don't have to study for dates with Mr Right. I'm ashamed to admit it but I've started reading the newspaper. Not that reading is cause for embarrassment. The motive is. After our second date, I started stocking up on little anecdotes, just to keep our conversations moving along. It's been exhausting. As I lie here next to my perfect-man-on-paper, it occurs to me that one shouldn't have to cram for a date.

'Thank you, Barry.' I can't break up with him naked, obviously. This *is* a bit awkward. What's the appropriate time frame after having sex for dumping someone? I don't think Miss Manners has covered that but I'm sure it's more than seven minutes. All I can hope is that Barry's English code of silence keeps him from saying anything more about it.

'Thanks, Barry, for, er, a great, you know. But I have to go, I promised I'd call my parents at' – I check Piaget – 'six-thirty.'

'Do you want to call from here?'

'Uh, thanks, no . . . It's going to be a long call. It's my mom . . . *woman troubles*.' This deadly weapon against further male enquiry works as well on boyfriends as it does on bosses.

'I understand.'

'Okay, so, thanks. I'll, um, talk to you tomorrow.'

'Sure, okay.'

When he kisses me goodbye, he lingers a little, but doesn't say anything.

I do want to call my parents. Suddenly I miss them. There's a certain permanence to Mom and Dad, and even the things that drive me crazy are comforting in their predictability.

'How're you doing, kid?'

'Just great, Dad, thanks. How're you? Did you find a suit for Mrs Callahan's daughter's wedding?'

'I think so. You'll have to ask your mother.'

'Right. Any fun plans for the weekend?'

'I'm getting a new lawnmower.'

'That's super. A ride-on one?' My parents' yard is about a quarter-acre but all the neighbours have riders and I know my dad envies them.

'No, your mother says it's a silly extravagance.'

'Well, it is only a little yard.'

'You don't have to mow it every week.'

'That's true, but she let you get the snow blower last year.' Dad and I have very little to say that doesn't revolve around machines of one kind or another. My Nissan Sentra sometimes occupied us for up to ten minutes.

'Hi, honey.' It's Mom on the extension. 'When are you coming home?'

'Well, the fares are really expensive now. Maybe later in the year.'

'Your sister is trying to have a baby.'

'There's not much I can help with there, Mom.'

'I know. I'm just saying. How's Barry?'

I knew she'd ask. Like I said, sometimes predictability is a good thing.

'He's okay. I met his parents today.'

'Well! That sounds serious.' This doesn't make her happy. She'll never forgive him for being born 3,000 miles away from Connecticut.

'Yeah, maybe too serious. It seems a little early to be meeting parents, don't you think? It's only been a few weeks.'

'Well, if you really like him, then that shouldn't be a concern.'

'I'm pretty sure I don't like him the way he likes me.'

'Well then, honey, I think you should tell him that, don't you?' She can hardly keep the excitement out of her voice.

'I don't suppose there's any way I can just not call him again?'

'Have you had sexual relations with him?'

No daughter wants to hear those words from a parent. 'Once,' I say in a very small voice.

'Then I'm sorry, but you have to talk to him.'

'I know.'

It's no good hoping his feelings will simply wear off. Dragging things out is just going to make it harder. I have to be an adult. It's not fair to Barry either, letting things go on. Because I know deep down why I don't love him.

It's Sam. It's been Sam all along. I don't know a lot about a lot of things, but I know this. He may be seeing someone, and I really hardly know him, but I know exactly how I feel about him.

Okay, I'm going to do it. I'll dial the number. Maybe I should make a cup of peppermint tea first. My stomach is a little queasy.

'Hi, it's me.'

'I was hoping you'd call.' And there is hope in his voice. Sweet Barry.

'Well, I wanted to talk to you.'

'Look, if it's about what I said, please just forget it. I was caught up in the moment.'

'Then you didn't mean it?'

'Did you want me to mean it?'

I feel like such a bitch. 'No.'

'Then I didn't.'

'But you did.'

268

. . . 'Yeah.'

'Barry, I'm sorry, but I just don't feel the same way.'

'I know. But maybe you could eventually.'

'I don't think so.'

'That's not definite.'

I can tell by his tone that he's hoping again. 'I know I won't.'

'That's pretty definite, then.'

'I'm so sorry, I don't know what to say. You're, like, the perfect man, and I should be madly in love with you. You do and say all the right things. Really, Barry, you are perfect.'

'I'm just not perfect for you.'

'You know how you get that feeling sometimes, and it just hits you over the head?'

'Yeah, huh, actually I do.'

Ironically, so do I now. 'I didn't get that feeling.'

'Well, I guess it's better to know now.'

'Instead of waiting two years.'

He chuckles sadly. 'Yeah.'

'I'm sorry. Does it sound too clichéd to say that I really want to be your friend?'

'Not if you mean it.'

'I really do.'

'Okay.'

'Barry, you're being so great. It makes me . . . it makes me wish things were different.'

'Well, there's no accounting for love. It's either there or it's not.'

'You're going to make somebody very happy one day.'

'So everyone keeps telling me.'

'I guess I'll talk to you later.'

'Okay. Hey, Hannah? Thanks for being so honest. That takes guts.'

'No problem. Talk to you soon.'

I couldn't feel guiltier if I'd just clubbed a seal pup. It's a guilt compounded by the fact that I'm so relieved.

Barry hasn't called for two weeks. I'd be lying if I said I've thought about him constantly. He pops into my head at odd moments during the course of my day when something happens that I'd normally tell him about. But I forfeited the privilege of open communication when I broke up with him. Technically, I could call him. But that wouldn't be fair, knowing that he's probably hurting. I hate to cause him pain. And I hate that I'm feeling this guilty. At least when I get dumped I can take righteous comfort in being wronged. It takes the pressure off to know there's nothing I can do to change it. *Que sera, sera*, as Barry might even say. But here I *can* do something to take Barry's hurt away. I'm just choosing not to. Maybe I'm being harsh on myself, but technically it's true. I don't like having this power. If this is what it feels like to be the breaker-upper, thanks, I'll pass.

When he does finally call, I find my heart racing. 'Barry! How are you?'

'Still a little sad but don't worry, that's not why I'm calling. I was wondering if you, and maybe Chloe, were interested in a charity event tonight at Burberry. It's for Breast Cancer Research. Kate Moss is supposed to be there. I, uh, it's not a date or anything, of course, it's just that I found out about it through work and thought you might like to go. It's no big deal if not.'

He's forgiven me. No hard feelings. Isn't that what he's saying? This is an olive branch, a champagne-canapé-goody-bag-studded olive branch. Of course I'll accept it. But wait. I don't want to send him mixed signals. What if this isn't a peace offering, but an attempt to get back together? That'll make me a real bitch for leading him on. On the other hand, he did say he wanted to be friends, and this is well within the range of friendly activities. It's not like he's asked me to a candlelit dinner. And if Chloe is there, it definitely can't be construed as a date. 'Let me just check with Chloe. Can I call you right back?'

'Sure, I understand. Let me know.'

Chloe claims to have dinner plans. I know it's not just an excuse. She's not mad at me or anything. In fact, she was super-understanding about Stacy's assault on the royal family. I think she's come to expect a certain ballsiness from Americans, and she likes it. Just last week she had me return a dress (one of the few that she *hasn't* lost in her flat) to a store that claimed to have a 'no returns' policy. I was more than happy to bully my way into her refund. It's important to leverage our natural abilities in the name of friendship.

'But you have to come with me!'

'Why?'

'Because if you don't go, then I can't go, and I *really* want to go.'

'Well, I *really* want to snog Peter.'

'Who?'

'Peter. The guy I'm going out with tonight.'

'Come with us first, then go and meet Peter. Pleeeeease?' I don't know why she's making a big deal out of this Peter guy. She never seems to really like the men she dates, though she always has a string of them. She had a serious relationship all through college but she doesn't talk about it much. I gather that he ditched her for her room-mate. I think he broke her heart. It'd be such a shame if he scarred her for life, because she'll make an excellent girlfriend for the right guy. She's practically perfect, aside from her tendency to lock herself out of the house and lose her shoes.

'Fine. But you owe me one.'

Plus she's very loyal.

'Where are you?' It's Chloe, a couple hours later. I can hardly hear her over the din of the rush hour.

'Outside the Tube station.'

'Which exit?'

'Nike. Where are you?'

'Benetton. Walk over.' As I cross the street, my phone rings again.

'Hey, Barry.'

'How're you doing?'

'Good. Where are you?'

'Outside the station.'

'Which exit?'

'H&M.'

'I'm meeting Chloe at Benetton.'

'I'll walk over.' We're within fifty yards of each other but there are at least a thousand people, dozens of taxis and a wall of buses between us. If ever a city's residents needed mobile phones, London's do. You could be fifteen feet away from your friends and never find them in the crush of people. There's Barry now, loping across the intersection. From a purely platonic point of view, he looks good. He kisses me on the cheek. Does that feel weird? Other than the night we met, contact has always been lip to lip. Yes, definitely weird. A little nostalgia-inducing.

Two clipboard Nazis are stationed at Burberry's entrance. I loathe them on principle. In one disdainful look, they always dismiss me as a phoney. I should have known that Barry would make everything easy. He gives them our names. There's no disbelieving scan of the list or insistence that we're not on it. The girls smile as much as their Botox will allow and let us pass. He's Moses, parting the Rude Sea.

The whole room is pink (Breast Cancer Research's signature colour). A couple photographers are scrimmaging over the beautiful people. 'Drink?' Barry asks, gathering three champagne flutes from the waiter. 'So,' he says, 'I'm not sure what we're supposed to do now that we're here.'

'Eat and drink?' Chloe snatches a tiny hamburger from a passing tray and pops it in her mouth, bun and all. I truly love her steadfast determination to eat exactly what she wants, muffin be damned.

'And shop?' Barry suggests. 'I think the invitation said that some portion of the proceeds goes to the charity.'

'Oh, good.' Charity-schmarity. 'Is there a discount?' To tell the truth, I've never been a plaid[36] fan, even cut-rate plaid. You can only cover so many items in your signature cloth before crossing the borders of good taste.

Still, the food's good, though the waiters have the evasion skills of secret agents. In the middle of stalking those carrying goat's-cheese tartlets, I notice an intriguing scene playing out across the room. Barry and Chloe are engrossed in an animated discussion. I don't mean that Chloe is animated and Barry is listening. He's waving his arms and laughing. Remember when *I* first met him? He was so deadpan that I doubted his sense

36. Plaid, the US term for tartan, has a long and illustrious history in defining the very fabric (excuse the pun) of the Scottish clans. However brave, those fine burly men were not known for their fashion sense, and so, like helmets and chain mail, plaid is best left on the battlefields of history and off our catwalks.

of humour. He's a different person with Chloe. And she's acting like she thinks he's Billy Connolly. Am I jealous? Whether boyfriends or handbags, you know I covet things I don't have. Even when it was I who gave them away. Case in point: I always have pangs of doubt after donating clothes to the charity shop. But I'm not jealous. Not one iota, despite my good friend clearly telling me she thinks Barry's the catch of the day. Reel away, Cap'n Ahab. You won't be sorry.

'Hey, where'd you go?' Chloe notices me trying not to look like I'm skulking up on them.

'Oh, just looking around.' There's not one covetable item here. The whole collection is exceedingly monochrome and I'm no Safari Jane. Khaki might be chic on the runways but unless you're hiding from tigers, head-to-toe dung isn't going to work for most women.

Chloe glances at her watch. 'I'm sorry, Barry, I've got to go.'

'Hot date waiting?' he asks with a smirk. Flirty Barry.

'Oh no. Just a friend. By the way, here's my card. Give me a call, I'd love to talk to you more about opportunities.' They cheek-kiss, we cheek-kiss, and part.

'Barry, you and Chloe really seemed to hit it off.'

'Oh, well, yes.' He's blushing. 'Did I tell you I was thinking about moving jobs? She's going to put me in touch with her colleague who covers my space.'

'Well, I think that's great. And I think she's great. And obviously you're great. If you two happened to hit it off, that'd be . . . great.' Why do I feel the need to bless their union, like some stiletto-wearing Godfather?

22

'Now what are you trying to be?' This is how Felicity greets me at the Patels' fortieth wedding anniversary party. She's lucky I recognized that, as a white girl from Connecticut, I have throw cushions more Indian than me and therefore shouldn't try to pull off a sari. Instead, in a nod to the Patels' cultural heritage *and* to British restraint, I'm dazzling in Topshop's take on Asian hippy chic – pink paisley silk with gold and aqua. (No, not from the closet. That door is now closed to me for ever.) It floats around my knees when I walk, and I've got golden bracelets stacked halfway up my arm. They match my gold dancing shoes.

'Hello, Felicity.' Mwah, mwah. It's become easier with time to pretend we can stand each other. 'Do you want me to check on the drinks?' It's the only thing she trusts me to do these days. My hard-won triumph over her and Mark was short-lived. After recovering her composure, which took about four minutes, she assured me that while she couldn't fire me, she could make me wish she had. I have to give her credit. She was true to her word. I'm back to answering phones, making tea and surfing the Internet. I'm only here tonight because I threw a tantrum and threatened to expose her again. I did it partly just for spite. I don't want her relaxing now just because she's made partner. It's not mature, but given that my opportunities for advancement are non-existent, I'm getting job satisfaction where I can. And it's not all bad. She's been such a miserable cow that I no longer feel guilty about being a blackmailer. In a cosmic tit-for-tat, we're now officially even.

I have to admit that I'm impressed with her efforts tonight. I had my doubts about anyone's ability to convert the Patels' local civic hall into a tented mirage. Dark panelled walls and brown carpet will only accommodate so much whimsy. But the DJ is playing a mix of Bangla pop for the kids and sitar music for the oldies. She's had the walls covered in swathes of red cloth; gold candles are lit by the hundreds and even the bar has been transformed into an exotic tinker's wagon. The guests all seem to appreciate the effort and the Patels are acting like lovestruck kids, which is remarkable considering that they hadn't even laid eyes on each other before their wedding day forty years ago. What are the chances that soulmates are thrown together at random like that? About a zillion to one.

I'm not here tonight to see the Patels feed each other wedding cake. It's the catering company's last night working for us. Mark's sister-in-law finally decided that blood is thicker than money and pulled the plug. When Sam told me, and said he hoped I'd be here tonight, my heart soared. He wouldn't say that unless he had something to tell me. Despite Janey, despite everything, I can't help it. I have a terrible case of the Sams, and I fear I may be terminal.

I pour myself a glass of champagne. Why not? Since Black(mail) Monday, I've taken a *carpe diem* approach to work, even slipping out for a makeover last week. I feel a little guilty betraying my recently discovered work ethic like this. I really thought I was a changed woman, but let's face it, I'm not fooling anyone. Leopards and shirkers cannot change their spots. So, glass in hand, I surrender to my true nature and go to find Sam. He's stuffing brown goo into mushrooms.

'Need some help?'

'Nah, you'll get your dress dirty. Nice dress, by the way.'

'Thanks.' A blush creeps up my cheeks. 'So tonight's the last hurrah.'

'Hurrah.'

'Isn't Mark's sister-in-law cutting off her nose to spite her face?'

'Definitely, but vindictiveness is more important than revenue for her.'

'You can't live on vindictiveness.'

'Tell her that. Hey, did you ever resolve the funeral fiasco?'

I've purposely played down that night considering that I made a fool of myself, asking him out and then bursting into tears. To be honest, I've been avoiding him around the office. 'In a manner of speaking.' Do I really want to tell him that I've stooped to blackmail?

'You've kept your job, so you must have done something right.'

Oh, to hell with making him think I'm perfect. He's bound to find out eventually anyway. 'I don't know if you'd call it *right*, exactly.'

He stops mid-stuff, a curious smile crossing his face. 'What did you do?'

'I blackmailed them.' My stomach flip-flops while I'm saying this.

'About their affair?'

'Yeah. Stop grinning, Sam. I'm not proud of it.'

'Well, you should be! I think that's fucking brilliant.'

'It's immoral.'

'You can't apply morality to an immoral situation.'

'But two wrongs don't make a right.'

'Maybe not, but it makes you feel good, doesn't it?'

'Yeah, I admit it does a little.' I'm grinning. 'It hasn't done anything for my career though.'

'You don't really want to keep working for Mark, do you?' He takes a sip of my champagne, leaving a smeary fingerprint on the glass. 'Sorry . . . Given that it's our last night "to get down and party",' he says in his remarkably lifelike nerdy voice, 'we ought to go out with a bang, don't you think?'

'What do you plan to do, poison the guests or something?'

'I was thinking of drinks.'

'You're going to poison their drinks?'

'Drinks, Hannah. I was thinking of going for drinks.'

'Will others be coming?'

'Not unless you feel the need for back-up.'

Is it finally happening? 'As in a date?'

'If I say yes, will you say no?'

'No.'

'No, you won't come, or no you won't say no?'

'No, I –'

'Why is this getting more complicated than it needs to be? Let's start again. Hannah, do you want to have drinks with me tonight after the party?'

'Yes.' I'm so happy I could cry.

Sam has anticipated my dress's potential to end up over my head again. He hands me his courier bag. 'Here, put this over your shoulder. No, across. Yeah, like that. It might keep you from flashing oncoming motorists.'

'Are you sure you don't mind me wearing your handbag?'

'It's not a handbag.'

'Man purse?'

'I like to think of it as a backpack for the new millennium.'

'Whatever.' It takes a certain kind of (straight) man to unashamedly carry a pocketbook.[37]

'Here you go.' He hands me a glass of Sauvignon Blanc after saying hello to half the bar.

It drops to the floor and shatters. 'Shit!' The entire glass has just splashed up on to his pants.

'You're supposed to close your fist, you know, grasp the glass when I hand it to you,' he says, sadly surveying his soaking legs.

'I'm so sorry! I don't know what happened.' I do, actually. My hands are slick with sweat.

I'd love to spin a tale about how casual and cool I was on my first date with Sam. But everyone knows that's not something I'd ever be capable of. Not now that I feel this way about him. So, without apology or preamble, I'm pumping him for information with the single-mindedness of a CIA interrogator. By the time the lights come on and the bartender kicks us out, I know as much about Samuel Ulysses Parker as just about anyone except his parents. Aside from his middle name, I love everything.

'Why'd you grow up in Wyoming?' As a born-and-bred Northeasterner, I find this an odd place for people to settle voluntarily.

'I was born there.'

'Why?'

'Well, when two people love each other, they get urges . . .'

'Funny, Sam. I mean why were your parents there?'

'They're professors.'

'Ah, then academia runs in your family.'

37. American pocketbook = English handbag, but as Mr Shakespeare so aptly wrote, 'a rose by any other name would smell as sweet'. Especially if it's on sale and goes perfectly with that dress you just found.

'Like webbed toes,' he says.

'You have webbed toes?'

'I'm just saying.'

'So what exactly is in Wyoming?' I can't believe I've lived my entire life in the US and never, not once, thought about Wyoming. 'Is that where Wyatt Earp comes from?'

'Not sure.'

'The OK Corral? Do you have buffalo?'

'Me personally? No.'

'But there are buffalo?' I thought they were extinct. They definitely killed *tatonka* in *Dances with Wolves*.

'Millions. Tell you what. Let me save us some time, because otherwise I'm afraid this may take the next month. We have rodeos. We have wild horses. We have Shoshone and Arapaho Indians. We have cowboys and dude ranches. We also have Yellowstone National Park and Jackson Hole.'

Wow, in Connecticut we have sports-utility vehicles, gated communities and hedge-fund millionaires. I had no idea a guy could come from someplace exotic in the United States. 'Brothers? Sisters?'

'Two brothers. Older.'

'In Wyoming?'

'One's in Michigan, the other's in Tallahassee. They're professors.'

'You weren't kidding about it running in the family. Are you sure you don't have webbed toes?'

'Wanna check?'

'Isn't it a little soon to see each other's feet?'

'You're right. In feudal China, we'd have had to get married first.'

'Are you proposing?'

'Are you a Chinese woman from the seventeenth century?'

'I see your point.'

I think it's only fair that after I let him talk about himself all night he at least try to kiss me. I've been lingering here next to his Vespa for about a week.

'Hannah, I don't want to kiss you tonight.'

'Psh. As if I'd let you anyway.' My face is burning.

'Then stop puckering. I have . . . something to take care of first. We can't start that side of dating yet.'

'Janey?'

'Yes. Can I pick you up on Saturday morning?'

'Where are we going?'

'Wait and see. Be ready at nine-thirty.'

23

'Surprise!' sings Mom at eight-thirty on Saturday morning. I'll say. She and Dad are standing on my doorstep. 'Hannah, how many times have I told you to take your make-up off before you go to bed.'

Mom, I want to tell her, I didn't even take my clothes off. 'What are you doing here?'

'Well, you said you were too busy to come home, so we came to you.' My mother has a knack for making innocuous statements accusatory. How can the Fates do this to me? Sam is due in an hour. I can't radiate allure while chaperoned. It's probably too much to hope that they're only here for a day trip. 'How – how long are you staying?'

'Oh, just until Monday. Your father has to be back for his prostate exam.' Her pity-me face is legendary. Dad had a cancer scare a couple years ago but to listen to Mom you'd think the trauma was all hers. My poor father can't even get credit for a life-threatening disease.

'Well, uh, *where* are you staying?'

'Silly girl, of course we got a hotel room. You don't think we'd sleep on your floor, do you?'

My response is cut off by a half-naked man shuffling along our hallway. Living with Australians has had a few unexpected consequences. One is that I never know who's sleeping on my couch. 'Mornin',' he waves to Mom. She's trying not to stare at his erection, which is just about to poke through his boxers. Just great.

'So! What shall we do today?' Her tone assures me that she's not the least bit concerned about the poor company her daughter is keeping.

'It's eight-thirty in the morning.' I'd like to sleep for about four more hours.

'No, it's not.' She grabs Dad's wrist. 'It's . . . one-thirty.'

'Trust me, it's eight-thirty.'

'I already changed my watch, Barbara.'

She obviously believes this a lie. What's worse, Dad now looks doubtful about his own time-telling ability. 'How many hours difference is it?'

'Five.' We've had this conversation at least a dozen times.

'Ahead or behind?'

'Ahead.' Same as always.

'You're ahead? Or we're ahead?'

'Well, you're here. So we're both ahead . . . of the US . . . by five hours.'

'Are you sure? That doesn't sound right.'

As if the people looking after the clocks in Greenwich would change that sort of thing simply to vex my mother. 'I'm sure.' They don't look like they're going to go away. 'I guess we may as well go get something to eat. I just need to make a call first.'

'Sam? It's Hannah.' I hope my parents appreciate the sacrifice I'm making for them. Of course I won't tell them. All I need today are my mother's inappropriately personal questions coming from across the table. It's bad enough when they come from across the ocean.

'I'm on my way.'

'I'm sorry, I can't today. My parents just showed up.'

'Oh, well, don't worry, we'll do it –'

'Next Saturday.' I'm not leaving this to chance again. And

isn't it ironic that my mother, whose ideal view of the world has always involved sons-in-law, is thwarting my prospects like this? I know what you're thinking. Why don't I just make my excuses (lie), tell them to entertain themselves for the day and go out with Sam anyway? Because they've raised a good old-fashioned guilt-ridden daughter, one who has never been very good at confronting her parents. Given their jetlag and my hangover, today is not the day to turn over a new leaf.

'Well, sure, next Saturday. Enjoy your folks.'

As if there's any chance of that. My parents love the idea of Europe, as long as it's identical to home in all important ways. Now that my father realizes it's not the middle of the afternoon, he wants waffles. They're unconvinced by my explanation that the English haven't embraced the waffle tradition, unable to grasp the idea that everyone wouldn't want to eat fried batter with maple syrup for breakfast. 'What do they eat, then?' Dad wants to know.

'I don't know. Eggs.'

'Not pancakes?'

'I guess they eat pancakes. Look, I know a place where we can get pastries, croissants and things, and eggs, and probably an omelette.' Though I wouldn't bet on it. 'Let's just go there.'

'I don't understand,' he says miffily. 'We make the food *they* like.'

'No, we don't, Dad.'

'Tea, for instance.'

Boiling water. Big deal.

'And English muffins.'

'Those aren't really English. They don't exist here.'

'Don't be silly,' Mom says. 'Then why are they called English muffins?'

'That's right, honey. Mr Thomas brought the recipe from England.'

That's what the commercial says. Dad believes everything he sees on TV. That's why Mom no longer lets him use the credit card. Thanks to Suzanne Somers,[38] we both got Thigh-Masters one Christmas. I was disappointed but Mom hit the ceiling. You've never seen a woman give the cold shoulder like my mother.

'Fine, let's just go to your restaurant,' she pouts. 'We don't want to put you out.'

As if I've conspired with London's hospitality industry to keep waffles from my father.

'It's not putting me out, Mom. They don't eat waffles here!'

'Now don't get upset, dear. We're going to have a nice week-end together.' God forbid anything unsavoury like defending myself should cloud her vacation. 'Stand up straight. When you slouch, it makes you look podgy.'

I'd love to find dealing with my parents easy. It certainly isn't England's fault that it's not; they're this unreasonable at home too.

'Coffee, please,' says Mom to the waiter.

'Filter coffee?'

'What is he saying?'

'Cafetière?' the waiter tries.

'That's fine, thanks,' I tell him. 'It's okay, Mom, that's coffee

38. This actress shot to stardom on American TV in the early 1980s through the triumph of cleavage over character development, but her lasting fame came from her association with that loved/loathed piece of exercise equipment the ThighMaster. Correctly used, it probably results in coconut-cracking thighs, but improperly handled, it risks shooting from between the legs at velocity to maim any bystanders unfortunate enough to be in the same room.

like you like it.' Almost. I don't have the heart to tell her that her coffee is going to require some DIY.

There's a slight commotion when my father finds out that scrambling eggs is beyond the chef's abilities. 'They come fried, sir,' the waiter says again.

'They *come* raw in a shell,' he mutters. 'Why can't your cook scramble them?'

'I'll see if he'll do it.'

'What is this, Russia?'

'Dad, please. He said he'd check to see if the chef can do them.' When I cast a beseeching look to the waiter, hoping he has parents like mine, he smiles back. We understand each other.

Breakfast is served with almost no more trauma. Dad gets his scrambled eggs, most likely with a side of spit.

'What's this?' Mom's eyeing the cafetière like the waiter has set a monkey on the table.

'It's brewing the coffee.'

'What do you mean, it's brewing? It's a pot full of coffee grounds floating in water.'

Welcome to Europe.

Once caffeinated, I'm a little more ready to humour my parents. Not exactly enthusiastically, but at least I no longer want to poison them. 'What would you like to do while you're here?' I don't suppose I can convince them to go to Paris. I'll happily meet them at Heathrow on Monday to say goodbye. I'm ashamed to be ungrateful for their visit. I know they came to be with me. And that's very thoughtful. It just doesn't compensate for the grief I'm about to endure.

'Oh, it doesn't matter to us, we've been here before. Whatever you want to do is fine.'

I want to go back to bed. God, look at them. They're so

awake. 'What about a museum?' One of my main justifications for moving, besides having a non-refundable ticket, was the opportunity to immerse myself in London's cultural riches. I imagined myself as a highbrow junkie, one of those girls who debate the merits of the Korean film industry with trendy glasses perched intelligently on their noses. I had noble intentions, which have slipped with time. Movies now count as culture, especially if they're subtitled, or British (or star Rupert Everett). And new cuisines obviously count. And new bars, because they serve real ale . . .

'Oh. A museum?' Mom is hitching up her face with the it-pains-me-to-have-to-tell-you-this drawstring she keeps hidden behind her ears. 'Daddy and I were just in New York last weekend. We went to the Frick.'

Well, Fricken hell. 'It's a nice day. We could take a walk in the park, see the Princess Diana memorial.' Mom loved Princess Di.

'Well, your father's arthritis is acting up.'

My father has arthritis? Dad looks equally surprised to hear this. He'd never contradict her, of course. If she says he has arthritis, he has arthritis.

'Um, a movie?'

'We must have seen four on the plane. You know I don't sleep well these days.'

We could sit in my apartment and stare at each other until your taxi comes on Monday. How do you win with people like this? 'Dad, what would you like to do?'

He's shocked by the question, not having heard it in over twenty years. It'll take him a minute to formulate a response.

'Anyway, Mom, how's Deb?'

'Ugh, still not pregnant. You should talk to your sister more often.'

'That's not how you get pregnant.'

'Don't be smart.'

'Sorry.'

Dad suddenly sits bolt upright. 'Maybe we could go to Churchill's War Rooms?'

'That doesn't sound like much fun,' Mom says.

'That's what I want to do,' he retorts quietly, savouring the chance to exercise his free will, however short-lived it may prove to be.

Mom isn't giving up easily. 'How about some shopping?'

'You go shopping,' says Dad. 'I want to go to the War Rooms.'

This is unprecedented. Maybe a drop in cabin pressure has made him giddy. 'I'll go with you, Dad.'

'You two can't just go off and leave me.'

'Then come with us.'

'Oh, all right. But I don't see why we can't do something that everyone wants to do . . . won't insist . . . not interested in Churchill or his war . . . shopping . . . my vacation too . . . more fun . . . don't have to . . .'

Dad: 1, Mom: 0. It must be the lack of home field advantage.

'I have an idea, Mom. After the War Rooms, I'll take you for tea.' That'll appease her. I took her for her birthday to the St Regis in New York and you'd have thought I'd produced that grandbaby she so desperately craves.

'Can I have a nap instead?' Flushed with victory, he's making a land-grab, consolidating his position.

'Sure, Dad.'

. . . Of course there are no tables available at Browns when we get there. It's my fault, for forgetting that everything here, ev-ery-thing, must be pre-booked. The entire system is designed

288

to beat all spontaneity out of the population. I thought Siobhan was joking when she offered to book tickets for the first film we saw together.[39] Sure enough, it was sold out when we got there. I was shocked to learn that gyms encourage the same behaviour (though I know this only through hearsay, having no first-hand experience of the places myself). People actually set their alarms to make a reservation two weeks in advance for the aerobics classes in Central London. As if being forced to sweat in Lycra with twenty other hyperventilating women is something to get up early for.

'Are you sure about this place?' Mom looks suspicious. I admit it's a little heavy on the Formica and strip lighting.

'That's what the lady outside the Tube station said. You heard her.' Actually, what she said was: 'Just over the road, you'll get a loovely cuppa.' But she pointed so I knew where over the road was. 'Besides, it's either this or we go back to the apartment.' Increasingly, I feel like Mom and I have changed roles. When did that happen?

'Yuh?' Says the girl at my elbow, clearly delighted at the opportunity to take our order.

'Do you have a tea menu?'

'Wuh?'

'A tea menu? I'd like to have tea.'

'Anyfink else?'

'Um, maybe a scone with clotted cream?'

'No scones.'

They must be sold out. 'A plate of sandwiches?'

39. Americans will queue to buy their movie tickets (and popcorn), but booking ahead for something as democratic as a film flies in the face of our credo. It's not quite why we fought the War for Independence against the British, but if there'd been cinemas around at the time, it would have been towards the top of the grievances list.

'Wot kind?'

The English tea kind, with their crusts cut off. 'Just the usual kind.'

'Wot kind of *filling*?'

'Mom, are you okay with just tea?' We may have to cut our losses here. She nods, silently damning the waitress in the process. 'Never mind, just the tea, please.'

After popping her gum to thank us for our order, she meanders to the back.

She won't get my nomination for any customer service award. When Stacy and I had tea at Henri Bendel's,[40] with their gorgeous Art-Deco stripy teapots, the staff were frightfully formal, like Mary Poppins (with a Bronx accent). Those were nice days, whiling away the hours waiting in anticipation for the little cakes and –

'Anyfink else?'

'I think there's been a mistake. I wanted tea.'

'Yuh. Let me know if you need more wuh-uh.'

Where's the delicate teacup and saucer? The authentic silver strainer and tiny pitcher of fresh hot milk? The offer to 'Pour, madam?' This inelegant, tannin-stained ceramic mug, bowl of sugar packets and steaming metal pitcher can't be right.

'*This* is England's idea of tea?' cries my mother, suddenly seized by the spirit of Catherine the Great.

'Shh, Mom! Let's just make the best of it and get out of here.'

. . . I've just poured hot water into my mug. That's because the metal pitcher is full of it.

'Um, excuse me?'

40. The fabulous department store in New York that contains not one item for boys. It is truly a feminine paradise.

'Yuh?'

'I ordered tea.'

She's clearly tired of hearing me repeat myself. 'Yuh. Tea.' She digs a packet out of the sugar bowl. It's a Lipton tea bag. The kind with the little paper tab that my grandmother uses to squeeze every last drop of value from her morning brew. Perhaps I shouldn't be surprised, given the clientele in here, most of whom are flecked with odd bits of debris.

'Is that all, yeah?'

'Thanks' – for that wholly unsatisfying experience. 'Can we also have two coffees, please? To go?'

'Filter coffee?'

'Yes.'

'Takeaway?'

'Definitely.'

The café smelled like the inside of a deep-fat fryer. No doubt we'll waft Happy Meals with every step back to the apartment. I hope my dad, at least, enjoyed his nap.

24

Now that they're gone, I miss them, despite the fact that breakfast was among the least painful episodes of the weekend. I don't doubt that their motives were good, and no permanent damage was done, but god, they're difficult people to have in your family tree. So how can I now miss them? I suspect it may be Stockholm Syndrome.

And though they may have delayed my love life by a week, I forgive them, for at least Sam is here now. He must be excited too, or he wouldn't have been so annoyingly prompt. It's his own fault that he's now waiting in the living room, with the Aussies snoring softly on the sofas, while I start the lip-bleaching process all over again. The things we do for beauty.

'Ready,' I say, stepping into my sandals.

'I wouldn't wear that.'

'Of course not. You'd look stupid in a dress.'

'Jeans and sneakers will be better.'

'Why, where are we going?' I'm flashing back to the go-cart track.

'The New Forest. Have you been?'

'No.'

'Trust me, jeans and sneakers. And bring a jacket in case it rains.'

After tipping everything I own on to the bed, I finally find an outfit.

'Have you fallen asleep in there?' Sam calls.

'I'll be right out!'

'That's better,' he smiles when he sees me. 'You look pretty *and* functional.'

I'm not sure that's a compliment but Earnest Sewn, Adidas and Juicy Argyle do combine nicely.

Two hours later, we're on bicycles. Sam is squinting at a hand-drawn map. 'Ready? We can take this route and stop for lunch at the pub.' His helmet makes him look like Bob the Builder. I dread to think what I look like.

'Sure.'

'Are you okay?'

'Yeah. It's been a couple years since I was on a bike.' Give or take about twenty. It isn't that I don't know how to ride it. My dad taught me in our back yard after my fourth birthday. I loved my bike, with its pink banana seat, flowered basket and coloured streamers on the handlebars. I walked it all over my neighbourhood. I just never really got the hang of riding it.

'You're sure?'

'Uh, yeah.' Nobody says I *have* to change gears. Come on, Hannah, children who can't even cut their own meat can do this. 'Let's go.'

The bike-rental place is in the parking lot of the train station. It drops straight into a wooded trail that I have to admit is very pretty. The New Forest, Sam told me on the train ride down, isn't new. It's a 900-year-old royal hunting ground and there are thousands of wild ponies running around in it (which aren't meant to be hunted). Maybe it reminds Sam of home. It looks about as big as Wyoming. I'm glad he has a map, though he's almost out of sight round the bend. Cycling shouldn't involve this much pedalling but I'm not sure how to change gears. I try flipping one of the little levers on the handlebars. That's better. I'm speeding up. This is easy. I go round the bend after Sam, where the path dips downhill. Actually, it's really quite downhill. And sort of rocky. My tyres are bouncing left and right as they hit the sharp stones. My boobs are bouncing left and right as well. A sports bra, had I owned one, would not have gone unappreciated on this adventure. I might be going a little fast. But the path is getting steeper. There's an underpass at the bottom. It looks kind of low. Brakes. The things on the handlebars. I don't want to stop completely, so I squeeze just one.

The next sensation I have is of being launched through the air over my handlebars. I land hands first (followed shortly thereafter by knees) on the gravelly bank.

'Hannah!' Sam yells as he starts pedalling towards me. 'Are you all right?'

'I just hit the brake.'

'Which brake?'

'What do you mean, which brake? The brake on the bicycle!' Don't cry, don't cry.

'Are you bleeding?'

'I don't think so.' I roll up my jeans to check for permanent damage. Of course I'm bleeding. My knees have born the brunt of my clumsiness over the years. When I was in college, I tried rubbing fade cream on them to help with the scarring. That's not a beauty tip. It didn't work.

'Ouch, keep your jeans rolled up. That'll clot up in a minute. You were cookin' down that hill! I didn't think you were going to stop.'

'As you can see, I did.'

'Yeah. Nicely done. Next time you want to stop, you know, you don't have to throw yourself over the handlebars.'

Next time? He can't possibly think I'm getting back on this murderous contraption. 'Maybe we could walk. I think there's something wrong with my bike.' It did, after all, just toss me to the ground.

'If we walk, we'll miss lunch.'

'I don't mind.' Blood loss has taken the edge off my appetite.

He touches my arm. 'Hannah, you do know how to ride a bike, don't you?'

'Of course! I'm just rusty, that's all.'

He nods. 'And you're probably not used to mountain bikes. It takes a while to get the hang of them after a road bike. Here, let me show you. See here, it's got fifteen speeds. This side changes up one speed at a time and this one jumps up five speeds. Push the other way and you go down speeds. Left-hand brake is for front tyres, and right is for back. So don't just hit the left one or you'll launch yourself again. And that's about it. Okay?'

I love that he's pretending he doesn't know I can't ride a bike. 'Got it.'

'You go first. I'll follow.'

'Why, are you afraid I'm going to crash again?'

'No, I want to look at your ass.'

It takes us rather longer than expected to get to the pub. I suppose I could ride faster, but I've never been one for exercise. It's a guiding principle in my life to run only if chased. 'Cooked food is finished,' the waitress snaps when we look hopefully towards an empty table. Even at our snail's pace, I must have burned several thousand calories. She can't deny us food now. I gaze pleadingly into her spite-hardened face. She walks away.

Despite the surly service, I love the tradition of weekend lunches in pubs. It beats eating your own dried-out roast and overcooked veggies every Sunday. The only thing we can still order is a ploughman's lunch, which is okay by me since bread and cheese are two of my favourite food groups. But I'm not falling for that 'pickle' again. It must be the British equivalent of peanut butter, in the sense that most other cultures can't understand why we love peanut butter either.

In Sam, I've finally found a man who understands the power of the spoken word. I don't know why more guys don't realize that the way to our hearts isn't through our closets or jewellery boxes (though gifts are always appreciated) but through our ears. There's a reason the funny guy always gets the girl.

'Can I ask you a question?' he says over the top of his wine glass.

'Okay.' It's only fair, having quizzed him like the Gestapo.

'Do you like dogs?'

'That's your question?'

'It's a perfectly valid one.'

It would be if I were applying to be a vet. Where's he going with this? 'Why?'

'You don't want to answer the question?'

'You first. Do *you* like dogs?'

'I love them. You?'

'Yes.' As long as they don't slobber, shed or bark, stick their noses in my crotch or pull tampons out of the trash and deposit them on the sofa.

'On a scale of one to ten?' he presses.

'Two.'

'One being love?'

'Ten being love.'

'So you don't like them.'

'I like them a very little bit. Why, Sam? Are dogs important?'

'I'm assessing compatibility.'

'Then why not ask about something relevant in our lives, like . . . Thai food or something?'

'Do you like Thai food?'

'Yes.'

'On a –'

'Eight. What are you doing?'

'Thinking of the future.'

He's serious about me.

Sam's apartment isn't studenty at all. I don't know what I expected – perhaps a more intellectual version of *Animal House*.[41] He even has food in his fridge. In fact, it looks like he's stocked it in case of famine. 'Do you always have this much food?'

'Nope. I planned dinner, but I realized I didn't know if you were a vegetarian.'

'How did you know I'd come over?'

'Man's intuition.'

'It must come with the handbag.'

'You're not, are you? A vegetarian?'

'God, no.'

My phone rings. It's Stacy. Naturally she's up to speed on all recent developments. ''Scuse me just a sec.'

'TELL ME EVERYTHING! WHERE DID HE TAKE YOU? WAS IT ROMANTIC? DID YOU MAKE OUT? DETAILS, GIRL! DETAILS!'

'Hello, Stacy. I'm at Sam's. Can I call you back later?'

41. *The* definitive film on the life and times of an American college fraternity house, starring John Belushi, may he rest in peace. The film did more to immortalize the toga party than five centuries of Romans ever could.

'Ohmygod, you're at his *place*? What are you doing? Did I interrupt –' I press the off button.

'Sorry about that.'

'Stacy from Connecticut?'

'Uh-huh.'

'So' – he hands me a glass of red – 'she knows about me already? This must be serious.'

'Don't be so cocky. I *may* have mentioned you in passing.'

His smug look would be extremely annoying if it wasn't so cute. 'Face it, Hannah, you like me.'

'I – so what if I do?' There. I said it. My heart is thudding. This is uncharted territory for me, but suddenly it seems stupid to play coy games with somebody who already likes me. Maybe that was Barry's lasting gift to me. Thank you, Barry.

'So, I'm glad you finally admitted it. Now we're on an even playing field.' He takes the glass from my hand, puts his hands on either side of my face and kisses me. And if I was half in love with him before, the kiss seals it for me. He's the most sensual kisser I've ever had the pleasure of knowing. I could spend the next two hours doing this. Or I could if I wasn't getting so excited. His hands are playing in my hair. I can feel his leg against mine. Then the kitchen timer dings.

'I hope that doesn't mean we're done,' I murmur into his mouth.

'I hope not.' He reaches over and turns off the oven. He's right, it's getting hot in here. Oh, yes, good thinking. It's really too warm to be wearing that sweater. He's steering me towards the hallway. I doubt he's trying to give me a tour of the apartment.

''Scuse me. I have to, uh . . .' I nod towards the loo. I didn't plan for this. I've been riding a bike all day. I've sweated. I give my pits an exploratory sniff. I think I'm okay. Just to be sure I mummify my hand in toilet paper, wet it and scrub any place that might need freshening. There. Confidence restored. I pull my jeans back on and return to be ravaged.

He's standing in the hallway where I left him, looking a little out of sorts. 'Is something wrong?'

'Well, no, it's just that when you went into the bathroom, I didn't know what to do. Jumping on my bed seemed a little presumptuous, and going back into the kitchen would mean we had to start all over again. So here I am, uh, waiting to – carry on.'

He's too adorable for words. What kind of guy actually thinks about these things? He's like a girl with testicles. We're in his bedroom by the time I get his shirt off. He didn't mention he worked out, but six-packs like this don't sprout naturally from men's bodies. He's fascinated with my skin. He keeps stroking his fingers up and down my side. It tickles. Deliciously. A little tentatively he unbuttons my jeans. I do the same and we wriggle out of them at the same time. We don't stop kissing, lying there in our underwear. Then he starts to kiss all the way down my body. The song 'Going to the Chapel' suddenly pops into my head. Not now!

Sam slides down, down, down. And then he comes up, up, up, with a funny look on his face. He kisses me for a few more minutes, then says, 'Why don't you relax and I'll check on dinner.' He jumps up and goes into the kitchen.

Oh no! I smell. I've disgusted him. This is the most humiliating moment of my life, worse than the time my father found me naked on the bathroom floor where I'd knocked myself out when I was fourteen. Of course Sam's never going to want to have sex with me now. I smell like Potential and his chilli-beer festival Port-a-Potty. I need to call Stacy. Slinking to the hallway, I snatch my phone and race back to the bedroom before Sam can see me. 'Stace?' I whisper.

'Tell me everything!'

'It's awful! You won't believe it.'

'Are you okay? Why are you crying? Did he hurt you? I'll kill him!'

'He didn't do anything. We were fooling around, and everything was going so well – Stace, he's the best kisser I've ever met, but anyway, then he starts to, explore . . .'

'Explore how? Hannah, this sounds like a crisis. Now is not the time for euphemisms.'

'He goes down on me.'

'And?'

'He comes back up in, like, three seconds.'

'Ow, that's not good.'

'I know. Then he got up and started cooking dinner.'

'That's not another euphemism?'

'No, he's mashing potatoes as we speak.'

'When was the last time you waxed?' Only a best friend would ask this question.

'Last weekend. Things are pretty trim down there.'

'You don't think that freaked him out, do you? Wait, did you get a Brazilian?!' We've dared each other to do this for at least two years. It sounds good in theory until you realize you have to lie there with your legs wide open while some Eastern European pulls all the hair off your crotch by the roots. And I'm suspicious of guys who want their grown-up girlfriends to be bald as an eight-year-old.

'No, no Brazilian . . . I think I might smell.'

'Well, have a sniff.'

'What am I, a contortionist?' Honestly, sometimes I wonder why I ask for advice.

'Use your hand, you dope.'

So I do. Now I really want to die. My hand comes up covered in wet, white balls of goo. 'Oh no.' I start pulling on my jeans. There's no recovery from this humiliation.

'What is it?'

'The toilet paper.' This can't be happening.

'What?'

'When I cleaned up, I used wet toilet paper.'

'What – oh no. A dingleberry?'[42]

'Worse.'

'What's worse than a dingleberry during oral sex?'

'Clumps of gooey toilet paper that looks like a very bad infection.'

'That *is* worse. What are you gonna do?'

'I've gotta go.' The apartment is on the second floor. Maybe I can jump out the bedroom window without breaking a limb.

'Wait, aren't you going to talk to him about it?'

'Are you kidding? It's over.'

'I thought you were crazy about this guy.'

'I am.'

'Then talk to him.'

'I gotta go.' I hang up just as Sam pokes his head in the doorway. 'Ready for some dinner?'

---

42. This is one of those things, like colonic irrigation or a botched face lift, that we have a morbid fascination with but never want to experience personally. Suffice it to say that sometimes men aren't as robust in their toilet habits as they need to be and, due to the hairiness of most male posteriors, leave behind various bits that a good wipe with toilet paper should have taken care of. 'Dingleberries' are the result (a term that evokes a berry, dingling, and aptly describes what these foul hangers-on might look like). The condition is rare among women, but could theoretically happen.

'Uh, actually, thanks, but I've gotta go.' What with the years of therapy to book, the memory-erasing hypnosis . . .

'Don't you trust my cooking?'

'It's not that. I forgot. I have something to do. Listen, thanks for a great day. I'll talk to you later.' I grab my handbag and break for the door. I wish that, just once, I didn't burst into tears during a crisis.

'Hannah, wait. Don't leave like this.' His face is so earnest, it's making me cry harder. 'Listen, I'm sorry about my reaction before. If you're sick or something, I – it's okay. We'll deal with it.'

Suddenly the utter ridiculousness of the situation knocks the self-pity out of me. He thinks I have an incurable disease. He's mistaking toilet paper for syphilis. I start to laugh. Then I start to hiccup.

'Are you all right?' He's concerned the syphilis has infected my brain.

'It's toilet paper!'

'What?'

'Toilet paper. Little balls of toilet paper that got stuck when I cleaned myself up before we, we, you know.'

'Oh, thank god,' he says, as if he just realized he *didn't* lock his only set of keys in the car.

'But Sam, it doesn't matter. Today it's toilet paper. Tomorrow it'll be something else. I'm a mess. Not fit to date. Stuff like this happens to me all the time.'

'Like planning a death-theme party for a terminal cancer patient?'

'Uh-huh.'

'Or motoring through London with your skirt over your head? Or not knowing how to ride a bike?'

'Yeah, like that.' You don't know the half of it.

'Want a glass of wine?'

'Please.' Just pass the bottle.

He pours. We clink. 'I don't know how many more . . . fuck-ups . . . you have in store but Hannah, I like you. I'm not interested in you because you're perfect. I'm interested because you're you. Hey, hey, what's wrong?'

Crying, for me, has always been a little like washing my hair twice – I lather up much quicker after the first rinse. 'Nothing's wrong. I'm happy.' I'm aware that this may not be obvious from my sobs. I'm bawling because Sam is The One. Capital T, capital O. I want to tell him this instant. It's like knowing that someone won the lottery. You'd want them to know right away, right? Not that I'm comparing myself with a rollover jackpot. What am I saying? I'm not even thinking straight. It *must* be love. So it's true, then, being in love *is* like hitting the sweepstakes. It doesn't happen to everyone, and there's no way of saying who's going to win, but it changes your life when it does.

25

Sam is lingering by my desk, fidgeting as the legions of colleagues march by on their way home for the night. Finally, a break in the commuter parade.

'What's up?' I've been grinning semi-permanently since dinner at his place. Even Felicity's usual malice didn't dim my mood, though after a week, my facial muscles are feeling the strain.

'I'm asking you out. You like fancy shoes, right?'

'Naturally.'

'Thought so. Let's go, before the champagne's all gone.' He hands me an invitation.

Jimmy Choo preview event? Drinks? Nibbles? Twenty per cent off? 'Where'd you get this?' I don't mean to sound ungrateful, or quite this incredulous, but really. Sam has admitted that his most fashionable moment involved a pair of Chuck Taylor All-Star high-top sneakers at age eleven.

'Relax. It's not stolen. I pulled in a favour from a friend.' As he steers me towards the Tube, his hand now enveloping mine, I nearly have to stop for breath. To go from complete hopelessness to such dizzying heights is enough to make anybody lightheaded.

It's only the clipboard Nazis, in position at the door, that give me pause. Something tells me that Sam isn't going to get the same red-carpet treatment that Barry did. They see him. He squares up. 'Name?'

'Parker.' He doesn't look the least bit intimidated. I wish I had that confidence in the face of such condescension. Warily, they eye each other. Somewhere in the distance I hear the spaghetti-western music that often accompanies a shoot-out.

'I'm sorry, sir, you're not –'

'Right there, ma'am. Beneath your thumb.'

'Oh, did you say *Parker*?'

'Plus one.'

I'm his plus one!

'I don't know why you'd want to be around people like that,' he says, shifting from one foot to the other like a child in need of the facilities. I love him for taking me here, when he clearly feels so out of his element.

'I don't want to be around them. I just want them to let me come to these parties. Look at these!' Gingerly, I cradle a hot-pink patent peep-toe stiletto. I admit it, I've held babies with less care.

Stacy would go absolutely mental in the face of all this footwear stimulation . . . I've missed her so much since she left. I was a little surprised by the intensity of my emotions (since I went days at a time without even thinking about her once I settled into London); I assumed I'd cry heartfelt tears at the airport that dried into a few wistful memories. But I find myself thinking about her a lot and wishing she was here to share things with. Like this.

'I thought about giving you both tickets and letting you take Chloe.'

'Wish you had?'

'At the moment?' His teasing face is absolutely adorable. He looks like he's about to laugh, which of course breaks me up every time.

'Okay, we don't have to talk about shoes. Let's discuss what you're interested in, like economics or something.'

'Do you know much about economics?'

'Probably as much as you do about shoes . . . Are we really so incompatible?' I'm smiling, but . . . *Are* we really so incompatible? In fact, we don't have very much in common. He thinks fashion is silly and I don't understand what he's trying to be (a blah, blah, blah economist).

'Hannah, it doesn't matter that we have different interests. We like each other. That's what matters, right? We'll find things in common.'

'You think so?'

'Sure. Listen, I'll prove it. What kind of movies do you hate?'

'Hate? Or like?'

'Hate.'

'Movies about war.' I didn't sleep for a week after watching *Born on the Fourth of July*, and not just because Tom Cruise was ugly and bald.

'Hmm. What else?'

'Cop movies.' Or any of those 1970s flicks with the bad acting, bad clothes and porn-film soundtracks. You know the ones I mean, bom-ba-ba-bom-bom, bowww.

. . . 'One more?'

'Costume dramas.'

'Me too! See? We have that in common.' He looks pleased to have made his point so definitively.

I'm not sure we can base an entire relationship on a mutual disdain for bustles and butlers, but I feel a little better. At least, I feel better that this isn't an issue for him. Besides, our presence here proves that he'll be happy to indulge me even if whatever he's indulging isn't something that's personally interesting. And I'll do the same for him. That's what real relationships are all about. 'To us,' I say, raising a sparkling glass of not-very-good-but-free champagne.

'To us . . . And to my new job.'

'You found a job? Really? That's so great!' I don't care if I'm causing a stir in this temple to beauty and bunions. I'm going to kiss my boyfriend. My boyfriend. He really, truly is, isn't he?

'Really. Congratulate me. You're looking at the newest low man on the totem pole at the Center for Asian Policy Studies.'

This is wonderful almost beyond words. He must be so happy to have landed a job right out of school. As I've mentioned, I wasn't as lucky, so, by inverse extension, I can appreciate how worthy it must make him feel. And there can't be many jobs out there right now for, er, whatever it is that he's going to be. 'Sam, really, that's so great. You should be very proud of yourself. When do you start? And when are you quitting?'

. . . 'Not for a few weeks. And I did, today. I never have to face Felicity again. *That's* something to celebrate, eh?'

So we can goof off together every day until he joins the ranks of the working wounded. Now that my own job holds virtually no prospects for advancement, I feel no obligation to work a full eight-hour day. I can easily skip out to meet him. We could have long, boozy lunches, wander through the museums –

'I'm really excited. Hong Kong is one of my favourite cities.'

'You'll get to travel to Hong Kong?' Wow, vacations on other people's money. Where do I get one of those jobs?

. . . 'That's where the job is.'

This has to be a misunderstanding. Hong Kong was a colony. Please god, let there be a Hong Kong just outside London. 'You're taking a job in Asia?'

'Well, I took it, yes. Are you okay?'

'Er.' I'm shocked. My face speaks for me.

'Hey, don't worry. I don't leave for almost a month. We've still got time.'

Time for what, actually? He can't sweep me off my feet from a different time zone. And more importantly, how can I allow him to sweep me before he goes? I can't handle a long-distance romance. I'm obsessive enough about boyfriends who live in the same postcode. 'I don't think so, Sam.'

Now he looks shocked. 'Why not? I like you. I've liked you ever since you flashed me on my Vespa. I want to go out with you. What's wrong with that?'

'What are we supposed to do, go out for a month and say goodbye at the airport?'

'Well, no, not if we like each other.'

'What are you saying? You'd stay here?'

'Why do you have to think so much? Can't we just see what happens?'

Why do I have to think so much? He really doesn't know me at all. And what exactly is he proposing? I thought I had a future with him; he's telling me this is just a fling. 'When did you know about the job? When did you find out you had it?'

'A couple weeks ago.'

'Before or after you asked me out?' Please say after, please say after.

. . . 'Before.'

'And you asked me out, and you led me to believe' – tears are leaking now – 'you led me to believe that there was something here, that we maybe had a future, and we nearly slept together?!' People are staring at us. I don't care. 'Did you lie just so that I'd sleep with you?'

'I haven't lied!'

'Oh no? You knew you were moving when you asked me out two weeks ago.'

'That's not lying!'

'Then why didn't you tell me?'

'Because I didn't think of it.'

'Bullshit. It's because you knew I wouldn't sleep with you if I knew.'

'That's what you think of me?'

'What am I supposed to think?'

'How 'bout that I didn't tell you because I was afraid you wouldn't give me a chance, and I like you, and didn't want to lose that chance.'

Oh, again with the missed chance. That's what Mark said. Don't men have more than one excuse? Do they all default to flattery? It *is* flattering, assuming it's true . . . 'I can't do this. I can't. Goodbye, Sam.'

'Don't leave like this.'

It's too late.

26

Edinburgh may not spring to mind when thinking of exotic locales, but it's the best I can do on short notice. I had to get as far away from Sam as possible without leaving Britain, lest the immigration officials ask some rather uncomfortable questions upon my return. I toyed with Land's End, for its name has a certain air of hopelessness about it. It's the sort of place where women dying of consumption would go. Unfortunately for those of us without driving licences, they don't seem to go there by train. So I'm on the Caledonian Sleeper instead, which, as the name implies, is an overnight service and presumably passes through Caledonia. Though after my bus ride to the distinctly ungreen Camberwell Green, I'm not taking anything for granted. And this business with Sam has proven how foolish it is to make any presumptions at all. I didn't expect him to consult me in his career decisions, given that our official, i.e., kissing, relationship is a week old. But I hoped he'd at least consider staying in London. Surely someone who claims to have liked me for months, and to like me a lot, *and* now has the chance to be together, would at least think about it. Why did I hope that? Because I know I'd consider it for him.

I'm excited, at least about my physical progression, if in two minds about my emotional one. I've never ridden the rails before. Amtrak may connect major US cities, but our collective love of the automobile ensures that only foreign tourists recognize its full potential. As I remember, I did plan a trip around the country once, but chickened out when Stacy said she couldn't go. In any event, a route like the 'Heartland Flyer' may have a tantalizing ring to it, but in reality, it just carries passengers in airline-sized seats from Oklahoma City to Fort Worth.[43] Surely an overnight train has luxury written all over it. Imagine how the Orient Express or the E&O from Bangkok to Singapore must hark back to the glory days of travel, when the journey was as important as the destination. Why, women had entire wardrobes just for touring. In honour of those itinerant ghosts, I'm wearing my 1940s-style swing coat in a very wealthy shade of burgundy (in case anyone is in doubt about my suitability for such an extravagant train). I even have a jaunty make-up case, which the airport safety people cruelly rendered obsolete with their edict against reasonably sized toiletries. Using it on flights to carry my sad single Ziploc bag full of 100ml shampoos is just an insult to its craftsmanship.

It's possible that I've overpacked (again), but I'm going up north, where it's sure to be colder. And having never been to Edinburgh, I can't possibly choose just one pair of shoes. 'Excuse me.' There's a nice porter, no doubt here to take my bags. 'Is this the train to Edinburgh?'

'Edinburra.'

'What did I say?'

'Edinburg, ma'am.'

'Is this the train to Edin-burra?'

'Yes, ma'am.'

43. Oklahoma City is in, as the name implies, Oklahoma. This isn't as obvious as it sounds given that Kansas City is in Missouri. Anyway, lovely as I'm sure Oklahoma City is, its state's slogan, 'Oklahoma is OK', isn't exactly a resounding endorsement for visitors wishing to have more than a mediocre holiday. And Fort Worth's slogan, 'You get it when you get here', provides no assurances that visitors will like what they get if and when they do arrive.

It's purpler than I'd have thought, not quite the right shade to be regal, if that's what they were going for. My pointed nod to my luggage doesn't seem to be encouraging the porter to take my bags. Maybe he's waiting for a tip . . . no, I guess not, based on the fact that he's just walked away.

I've accidentally walked into a closet. No, wait, there's a bed. It is my room. Remember the torpedo launch tube I saw when searching for apartments? It appears I've rented one for the night. I poke my head out the door, where it is nearly decapitated by an employee passing through the metre-wide corridor. 'Sorry! Em, excuse me. Is this the *first-class* cabin?'

'Yes, ma'am.' My doubtful look encourages her to continue. 'Standard class is just through to the next carriage.'

'May I see a standard-class cabin?'

'Certainly. Right this way.'

'What, exactly, is the difference?'

'First class is private; you'll not have to worry about another passenger joining you.'

'And the cabin?'

'It's exactly the same. Except, see, the top bunk folds up.'

'I do see. Thank you.' Something tells me that Orient Express passengers don't sleep in bunk beds. I bet their decor doesn't bring to mind a bag of grape Fruit Sours either. On the plus side, a bottle of spring water is included on the shelf, which really compensates for spending £237 to sleep in a rolling dorm room. Or else the train wasn't cleaned properly.

It was probably too much to expect that this getaway (runaway) would distract me from my thoughts, but it was my first instinct after leaving Jimmy Choo. I toyed with the idea of going directly to the station to jump on the first train out, until I caught my reflection in a shop window and realized I was still wearing my work clothes. Being distraught is no excuse for looking so functional. I can be tragic *and* lovely . . . The same thing cannot be said of this lounge, where the designer's fondness for grape hues has again run rampant. This time, he decided to use it on the boxy leatherette sofas and metal-armed chairs, offset by the unusual application of mauve on walls and patterned carpet. At least they serve drinks through the night, should I wish to self-medicate, and I shouldn't really complain. After all, it's not often I can lay my head down in one city and awaken in another without a cricked neck and my seatmate's halitosis to detract from the experience.

I'm not going to drink. If I do, I'll end up blubbering into my wine glass at the injustice of the situation. Are the gods *trying* to give me a breakdown, bent on punishing me for my arrogance when Sam first asked me out? They've given me a taste only to snatch away the ice-cream cone. That's their MO. I've read *The Odyssey* (only as a school requirement, obviously). I should have paid more attention in class, because I can't remember how Odysseus escaped his fate. I guess it's not important, given that I'm not a mythical character in an ancient epic poem. I'm a real girl who has just been told the man she knows she's meant for is moving round the world, where she'll probably never see him again. This is so depressing.

We passengers awake to Edinburgh's bright sunshine, obscured only by the heavy clouds and pelting rain. Technically, this was a reawakening, since we were first roused around 6 a.m. when part of the train fell off. Don't check the papers; this wasn't a rail disaster. The carriages are meant to disconnect like this, sending passengers off on another track to Glasgow.

'Taxi. Hi, I'd like to go to the Radisson at 80 High Street, please.'

'Ye ken it isnae far frae here?'

'I'm sorry?'

'I cannae chairge ye, lass. Ye'll hae tae walk.'

'Okay.' He's not moving the car. 'The Ra-di-sson Hotel. Hotel.'

'Aye, I ken whit ye said … Two poonds sexty.' He's just driven around the corner. 'Dae ye hae anythin' smaller?' he says to my £20 note.

'No, sorry.' He was right, it isnae far at all. And it's right in the thick of things, which is important if I'm going to get Sam out of my head. I've never been good at quiet contemplation, preferring instead to jar loose any uncomfortable thoughts with vigorous stimulation. If Edinburgh's intriguing steep stairwells leading into the bowels of ancient buildings and grand castle brooding on the hill can't do that, then nowhere will.

'Guid morrnin'. Can ah help ye?'

'Checking in, please. Hannah Cumming.'

'Aye, rroom threee-sexty-fowar. Weelcome.'

The need for caffeine has overridden my fear of melting in the deluge outside. Edinburghers obviously don't share my concerns, for most of them are umbrella-less despite the downpour. The Scottish variety must be heartier than us delicate flowers in the south. It surely seems to be true of their breakfast. Eggs, sausage, bacon, tomato, mushrooms, black pudding and toast. The people of the British Isles do seem to embrace odd food combinations. Roast-beef-flavoured potato chips, for instance, or yeast extract on toast. In this case, though, I'm all for mixing breakfast with dessert. Pudding is such an under-rated treat. It was the highlight of my childhood lunchboxes, especially in butterscotch or vanilla. Everything looks delicious …

''Scuse me. What's this?' It looks like a hockey puck made of gristle.

'Black puddin'.'

'What's in it?'

'Bluid.'

Blue-id? 'Whose blood?'

'Peg's.'

I hope to god she just said pig's. 'Thanks, just the check.'

'I think that's yer phone.'

At least it's not Sam calling again. He's left at least a dozen messages. 'Hey, Sarah.'

''Annah, you okay?'

'Yeess, fine thanks.'

'Sam's called 'ere looking for you. We got worried. Are ya weeth Chloe?'

'No.'

'Ya sure scared the heel out of Sam. He thinks you've gone off the rails.'

Good.

. . . 'Do ya want me to come meet you? We'll grab a coffee?'

'I'm in Edinburgh.'

'Well, whaddya doing there?'

'I don't know. It was the first place I thought of.'

'You're by yourself?'

'Uh-huh.'

'That's not smaht. When're ya comin' back?'

'I don't know.' I really didn't think this through very well.

'Hang on . . . Immajizz the hotel?'

'Wha–?' Their accent just doesn't get easier. 'Uh, about a hundred pounds. Why?'

I hear muffled discussion. 'Sarah? Hello?'

'Right here, pumpkin. We'll be there this afternoon.'

'What?'

'We're coming up. Can't stay the noight but we can take the train back down. Keep your phone on, we'll call when we get there.'

'That's crazy, you shouldn't –'

'No ahgument, 'Annah, you need us. We'll be there. Hold tight, sweetie. We're comin'.'

'Haur, tak these.' The waitress has just handed me a fistful of napkins. Presumably to staunch the flow of tears, which is causing some alarm among the patrons. I have the greatest friends. How many people would drop everything to come to the aid of someone they've only known a few months? That's one nice side effect of the enforced cohabitation within London's rental market; people all over the city move in with complete strangers, taking their chances in the compatibility lottery and often finding good friends. I'm sure there's been the odd girl who discovers her flatmate watching his favourite TV programme in her underpants, but it generally seems to work out. Of course, with Australians, naked strangers on your sofa are a risk.

Despite the many attractions of Scotland's fine capital, the Ultimate Fighting Championship[44] continues to rage in my head. In one corner is my distrust of Sam now that he's lied about Hong Kong. In the other is my enduring hope that he's The One. They're formidable contenders, each with its own strengths and tactics. No matter how many rounds they've been through, they remain equally matched. How am I supposed to decide between my heart and my gut? I know what Stacy would say, which is why I haven't called her. My best friend can be uncompromising when it comes to what she thinks is in my

44. How is it ever a good idea to get into a ring with a steroid-crazed mutant determined to beat you to a pulp for viewer amusement?

best interest. She wouldn't accept any nuance here. And from an outsider's point of view, I can see her point. Sam knew he was moving to Hong Kong when he asked me out. He didn't tell me, and yes, it's possible that he withheld that information because he knew I wouldn't sleep with him otherwise. But isn't it also possible that he didn't tell me because he does wonder if I'm The One too? In which case, at least he's not a scheming bastard. He's a nice man who is soon to move 6,000 miles too far away to meet for dinner. What am I expecting will come from prolonging that final separation? I'm not expecting anything. Of course I'm hoping he'll change his mind, turn down the job and stay in London.

Even my usual meditation isn't calming me. I'm not sitting cross-legged on the sidewalk 'ohm'ing at passers-by. I'm in M&S. When I first moved to London I was unprepared for the depth of feeling that this store engenders in the British public (and I know a thing or two about passionate feelings for stores). Having been a British institution for a million years, like Rome, all roads lead to it when searching for a particular item. Saleswomen countrywide are trained to utter four little words when asked for anything that their store doesn't have: 'Try M&S.' According to English girls, it is *the* place to buy things like underpants. I'm not talking about sexy lingerie, for M&S is about as sexy as Sears. It's where you buy the stuff that's actually comfortable to wear, versus the stuff you put on for the sole purpose of (hopefully) taking it off in front of somebody later. However, it has a secret Aladdin's cave of treasures that I don't get access to. Chloe swears she buys half her great clothes there. Every time I go in, the only things I see are drawstring pants and maternity tops (I don't think they're meant to be maternity tops). Today's visit is no exception. How cruel. *Shoppus interruptus* when I most need the distraction.

Luckily, its Spanish cousin, Zara, is just up the street. If M&S is the homely, dependable relative, Zara is the one who sneaks out of the house to meet boys and smoke cigarettes. Her clothes are fun, and some are even on sale. Of course, these aren't the big discounts I came to expect all the time at home, for rather than having a year-round rack of sale items where the wounded and/or unflattering clothes are banished, Europeans only seem to have sales twice a year. As if a sale is a privilege, not a constitutional right. Naturally, this makes everyone somewhat desperate and, in my experience, it's never a good idea to agitate women seeking retail therapy. Even when the stores do mark their stock down, they start in increments that you need a calculator to notice. Despite these shortcomings, women in London speak about the sales like they anticipate Santa Claus to land on Oxford Street.

I've started to buy the hype, judging by the armloads of bags I'm a little surprised to be holding. I may have suffered a shopping black-out, only snatched from the brink by my bank, which just called to voice its suspicion about all the Edinburgh charges hitting my credit card. I find their concern touching and told them that I'm fine and having a great time. They suggested that, as I still have a slightly outstanding balance from last month, I might want to take in a sight or two that doesn't involve cash registers while I'm here.

True to her word, Sarah has rallied the flatmates. Chloe's here too, having called looking for me this morning. However, now that the war council is in place, I don't want to talk about Sam. I'm afraid I'll jinx it and he won't say he'll stay.

'It's Sam.' Chloe is peering at my phone.

'I don't want to speak to him.'

'Don't you want to tell him you're okay?'

'No.'

'Fine. I'll tell him, then. Hello, Sam? No, it's Chloe. Yes, she's fine; we're together. No, I don't think so. No. I don't know. I will. Okay, bye-bye.'

'What'd he say?'

'You didn't want to talk to him.'

'No, that's right, I didn't.' Is he reconsidering his move? 'I'm hungry. Can we eat?'

'Sure, I could eat too.' Sarah's got a weightlifter's appetite. 'What're you in the mood for?'

'I don't know. What do Scottish people eat?'

'Neeps and tatties and haggis,' she sings.

Oh my. 'What's haggis?'

'Aw, mate.' Adam looks unhappy to have to break this news to me. 'It's sheep's heart and liver boiled in –'

'And lungs,' prompts Chloe.

'And lungs, boiled in its stomach.'

Gaggis. 'I might be more in the mood for fish and chips.'

'One drink first.' Nathan is already halfway down the street, his finely honed radar for hand-pulled beer and easily pulled women leading the way. Edinburgh, being a college town, has an abundance of both. 'How 'bout this one?' I'm sure his choice has nothing to do with the nipply blondes smoking out front. It's not much to look at, but there's music thumping from a band somewhere in its bowels.

'Come on, 'Annah, you need a dance.' Adam grabs my hand and stalks off into the mosh pit. He has proven to be just as sweet as I thought he'd be when we first met, and just as unlucky in love as I feared. He's also got a thing for Sarah, but he seems to be realistic about his chance of success, so he doesn't let it get him down. He's singing like he's the lost Beatle, while Nathan head-bangs so impressively that I can almost imagine the kinky afro he had in high school. The lead singer doesn't look like he was out of diapers when the songs he's singing were recorded, but he's giving a credible tribute to Kurt Cobain, and the beer is flowing (mainly over me, but I don't mind). This is fun, and I'm again grateful to Sarah for dragging everybody up here, especially Chloe, who's being a real sport. She's dancing away next to me, with no hint of the discomfort she must feel at being so far out of her cultural milieu. I know her natural environment is the trendy cocktail bar, not this sticky-floored dive full of customers more likely to barf on, rather than covet, her shoes. I'm probably pretty drunk, but I'm feeling a little better. Beer does tend to put things into perspective. Of course he'll stay. He likes me, right? And he knows I like him. He also knows I'm upset about his leaving, and is concerned enough about that to call twenty times in twenty-four hours. And given that he found a job in Hong Kong, he's clearly very hireable; it'll be a cinch to find a job in London that'll be just as great. He must be realizing the same thing. All the signs point in the same direction. So of course he'll stay. Yes, I feel a little better. Maybe that's how Odysseus reversed his fate. He drank beer.

'Do you remember *The Odyssey*?' I say to Sarah when she hands me another pint.

'Vaguely. I wasn't much of a student.'

Like I said, it's really remarkable how randomly chosen flatmates can result in such a good match.

'I do.' Nathan was clearly the popular jock in school. I guess it was shallow of me to assume there's no brain beneath all that lovely brawn.

'What happened to Odysseus? How did he overcome the Fates?'

'Weel, pumpkin, he didn't. He wandered the world for, like, twenty yeahs trying to get back home.'

'Did he finally get there?'

'Yeah, but it was a hard road. He'd have been better off not pissing them off in the first place.'

I should have paid more attention in class.

27

I'm finally inside the magical clothes closet, with permission from Felicity.

And in yet another of the delightfully ironic twists that have marked my London adventure, it's completely empty. Not one shoe, no whisper of a scarf remains. It's just Siobhan and I (well, not at the moment; she's gone for coffees). And a floor full of drop cloths, paint tins and brushes. Sam's sudden resignation left a gaping peon-sized hole in the office. A hole that I've been pressed into service to fill (yes, I know, also ironic). So when Felicity, drunk with the power of newly minted partnership, decided that she could no longer stand to have bare plasterboard framing her lovelies, I was the obvious choice for renovator of the week. On the upside, it's taking up my weekend, so at least I'm distracted from my thoughts.

Painting is rather therapeutic. Once I got the hang of it and stopped splattering acrylic all over the floor, and myself, I found a rhythm. There's a certain beautiful symmetry to the strokes and a compulsiveness to cover every centimetre that's strangely calming. Plus with Radio One blaring, I'm free to dance around should a good song come on. Though I'll steer clear of that paint tray next time.

I've been forced to face an uncomfortable realization this last week. I'm not as happy in London as I'd assumed. It was easy, when I first got here, to gallop ahead into the adventure. All was exciting and new. Then Chloe and Siobhan and the flatmates provided the entertainment and ears to bend. I didn't even miss Stacy. Then, the prospect of a great new job, then Mark (then not Mark), Potential, Barry and, finally, Sam . . . My new life has swept me up in its current. I didn't stop to notice that, actually, it's falling a little short of my ideal.

I still have my friends here, of course, and I'm constantly grateful for them. But Stacy's visit shone a light into the shallows of new friendships. I have no doubt that those pools will fill with time, but it does take time, and shared experiences. There aren't any shortcuts, and they're never going to replace my best friend. Despite having all the others, I still miss her terribly.

I don't want to sound like I don't love London, because I do, or that I'm not still glad to live here, because I am. It's an exciting city, but it's also a decent and civilized city, where people take the time to enjoy the sun (when it shines) and the many small treasures that it has to offer. I think my angst might be a feeling that expats naturally face, once the newness of their move has worn off and they have to settle into living, just as they did at home. Is this what it's like to get married? Do spouses look at each other over the breakfast table one day and realize that, now that the wedding festivities are over and the honeymoon photos pasted into the album, their relationship is exactly as good, or bad, as it was before he popped the question?

Objectively speaking, I know my life here is pretty good. I may not have a career but at least I have a job. I may hate my boss but I like Siobhan. And Stacy might not be here but Chloe has turned out to be a very worthy friend. And my love life, well . . . I guess that remains to be seen.

'Here, take this.' Siobhan has a pastry bag in her teeth. 'They were out of bloody cup holders.' She fishes around in her utility pocket. 'Here's some sugar.'

It must be her size that makes her look chic even in painterly overalls, whereas I look like a failed gang member with this bandanna tied around my head. Only a supermodel, or Jack Sparrow, can pull that look off successfully. 'Thanks,' I say. 'Want to take a break?' I've been working nonstop for at least twenty-three minutes. That must contravene a law in somewhere like France.

'Of course. Here, I got us pain au chocolats.'

I've wholeheartedly embraced the Europeans' belief in chocolate as breakfast food. There aren't many places where you get the pleasure of starting *and* ending your day on a sugar buzz. 'Thanks. And thanks for helping me. I'd never get it done without you.' I'm choosing to ignore the fact that we're unlikely to get this amount of work done anyway. Better to shelter behind unbridled optimism with nearly the whole weekend in front of us. 'You can leave any time you want, by the way. Just because I have to stay tonight doesn't mean you do.'

'Nah, I don't mind. I don't have plans anyway. Did you have to cancel anything fun when Felicity told you to do this?'

I wish. 'No, no plans this weekend. I –' I haven't told her about Sam. I convinced myself it was because it's such a new relationship, but of course there's also the uncomfortable dating-the-office-boy issue. Though why that's been such a preoccupation, I'm no longer sure. It seems kind of silly now, doesn't it? 'I, er, could have had plans, I guess, but the guy I was seeing is, well, it's a little complicated. He's moving, you see, out of London in a few weeks and I think, why bother, when he's just going to leave.'

'But you like him?'

'Well, yeah.'

'Then what does it matter whether he's moving? Couldn't you still see him?'

Siobhan is sometimes too idealistic. In real life, these things don't work out. 'The problem is, I *really* like him. Really, really.'

She grins. 'You're in love.'

'Ugh, yes, and it's awful!'

'And you're afraid you'll get your heart broken?'

'Uh-huh.'

'But if you don't see him again, doesn't your heart break anyway?'

'But not as badly.'

'Hannah, you don't actually believe that there are degrees of "in love", do you? That, if you're in love, breaking up after a month is any better than breaking up after a year?'

'Yeah, I guess that's exactly what I'm saying.'

'Tell that to a newlywed at her husband's graveside. Do you think her pain is any less intense than an old woman's when her husband dies? I don't think it works like that. Heartbreak is heartbreak. Who is this guy anyway? How'd you meet him?'

'It's Sam.'

She stops chewing. 'Our Sam? From the office Sam?'

'Uh-huh.'

'Hannah, trust me. I've worked with Sam for years. He won't hurt you.'

I'd love to believe her. But what if she's wrong?

'Peace offering,' Sam says when I open the front door the next weekend. After a marathon session of phone calls with Stacy, who was surprisingly forgiving of Sam, I finally returned his messages. They were beginning to take on an air of desperation, which convinces me further that he's going to stay. He wants to start again, he said, pretend the last week never happened and see where we go from here. I still don't know whether to trust him not to drop another hand grenade on my fragile emotional state, and my gut is telling me this is a bad idea. But my heart took a flying leap from the top rope and beat it over the head with a chair, so it's keeping its opinions to itself for now.

I look at the ticket he's just handed me.

'Diamonds?' It's definitely a sign.

'I took a chance that it'd interest you. It's an exhibit. Have you been to the Natural History Museum?'

'Uh-uh. Can I –'

'No, you can't try them on.'

It never hurts to ask.

We're uncharacteristically quiet as we make our way to the Tube, but he grabbed my hand as soon as we set off and his smile is as open and goofy as always. That gives me hope, even if this silence feels a little awkward.

As I think about it, and since we're not speaking much, I have some time to think, this will actually be my second diamond-ogling experience here. The first was at the Tower, visiting the Crown Jewels. Personally, I don't understand why the Queen stores them there. I'd keep them in my bedroom to wear with my pyjamas whenever I needed a little pick-me-up. The Tower has to be one of the top ten attractions in London. What are the other nine? There's Buckingham Palace, for the Changing of the Guard. I didn't actually see that, being waylaid by the competing attractions in Harrods, but it's supposed to be worthwhile. Harrods, of course, is in the top ten, and I've been there often enough to be on a first-name basis with the doormen hired to keep out the backpackers. And the museums: British, V&A, Science, Natural History, National Gallery, Tate. Check,

check, not interested, going today, er, should probably see those others some time. And number ten, number ten? Oh, of course, Harvey Nichols! I've hit all the best highlights.

Wow, had I known how beautiful the Natural History Museum was, I'd have moved it up my must-see list. It could be a cathedral, or a great college, instead of the country's biggest museum dedicated to the natural world. Its carved flora and fauna snaking up the towering columns in the entrance hall, intricate brickwork and gilded ceiling mosaics are awe-inspiring, and we haven't even seen the dinosaur bones.

'Happy?' Sam asks after we're strip-searched at the entrance. I don't blame the guards. You can't be too careful when letting women into an exhibit full of diamonds.

'God, they don't even look real.'

'Look at all the women in here. You all look crazed.' I realize my mouth is hanging open unattractively. 'What is it about diamonds?'

Well, they *are* for ever. De Beers said so in the 40s, so it must be true. One clever little marketing campaign later and we, as a gender, are hooked. They could just as easily have addicted us to rubies or opals, or bananas, had it been Dole instead of De Beers that wanted to boost its sales. I know it's just slick advertising. Look at all the women who think their entire existence hinges on the size of the rock on their hand. I don't care. I bought the hype. I want the stones. I could tell him this, but I don't. Not surrounded by all these people. But what an opportunity. In a room full of diamonds, each one a little reminder of love's everlastingness. Besides, his choice of surroundings can't be coincidental. Surely he's planning to tell me he's staying. 'They're a symbol,' I murmur.

'A symbol of what, the man's monthly take-home salary?'

'Of commitment.' We're in front of a display with diamonds of about a hundred different colours. Why would anyone want a diamond that doesn't look like a diamond? Surely that's what semi-precious stones are for.

'Why can't the guy just say he's committed?'

'Some men aren't very good at that.'

'Maybe you've been dating the wrong men.'

Huh, that's ironic, considering the source. Exactly what is he committed to, beyond 'seeing what happens', the hypocrite. Don't say it, don't say it. This isn't the place. Definitely not the time. 'You haven't.' Well, what do you want? It's like he's asking for it.

'I haven't what?'

'Said anything.'

Sam stares at me for about a million years. How long does it actually take to make a diamond? Well, it feels like that long. Then he says, 'What do you want from me?' What do I want? I want him to stay, obviously. 'Haven't we had fun together?' he continues.

'Yes . . .' Where's he going with this?

'And we like each other, right?'

I nod.

'And we want to keep having fun together, don't we?'

'Absolutely.'

'Well, there you go, then,' he concludes.

'There I go, then, what?' This is like a nightmare I have sometimes, where everyone is talking to me but the words are all mixed up. They never understand why I don't know what they're talking about.

'Isn't that commitment?'

'To what, Sam? Having fun?'

'Well, yes. To having fun with each other.'

'That's not a commitment!' Has he never dated before?

'Why not? I'm committed to having fun with you in the future. You're the girl I want to, to have fun with.'

'How long into the future?'

'As long as we're having fun together.'

'But what's going to happen in the future?'

'I don't know. Do you know?'

'Yeah, I do actually.' To be clear, I'm not crying because I'm sad, I'm crying because I'm angry. 'In two weeks, you move to Hong Kong and we'll probably never see each other again.'

He puts his arm around me. 'You don't know we won't see each other. I still want to see you. Hey, stop crying.'

'I'm not crying!' I sniffle, but suddenly a small kernel of hope works itself free from this otherwise bewildering exchange. Could it be that we're simply talking at cross-purposes? He did just say I'm the girl he wants to be with. Perhaps, beneath the muddle, the message is exactly what I've wanted to hear. *Is* this his way of telling me we have a real future? Siobhan's words keep rattling around in my head. Sam won't hurt me. 'You do still want to see me?'

'Of course I do! And I've been thinking . . . Han, I'm not sure how a long-distance relationship would work. It's a long way away, and with the time zones . . . And I do really like you.'

This is it. He's going to tell me he's staying. He likes me too much (didn't he just say so?), so he's not going to Hong Kong.

'A job shouldn't tie you to a city, right?'

'Right. Absolutely not.'

'It's not like it'd be hard to get another one.'

'I'm sure it'd be easy.' I've got the prickly sweats.

329

'That's what I figured.'

And I'm a little giddy. 'I've been thinking the same thing actually.'

'You have? Of course you have. It's your future, after all. So whaddya think?'

It *is* my future. 'I think it's a great idea! Thank you, thank you, thank you!' The room is staring at us as I smother my boyfriend in kisses. They must think he's just proposed. 'Sam, I'm so happy.'

'You're being so awesome about this, Han.'

'Well, how could I not be? I can't believe you're staying.'

. . . 'I'm not staying.'

. . . 'You're not staying?'

'I thought *you* were moving to Hong Kong.' My expression asks the obvious question for me, prompting him to continue. 'You need to find a new job anyway, right? Why not in Hong Kong?'

'Then you're not staying in London, finding another job and staying here?'

'No. Why would you think I was?'

'Then what have we just been talking about?!'

'I was talking about you thinking about coming to Hong Kong.'

'I can't come to Hong Kong.' How can I have got this answer so wrong? I was 98 per cent sure that he was telling me he'd stay. On a game show, I wouldn't even have used a lifeline, or phoned a friend. It just goes to show how fortunes, and futures, get lost.

'Why not?'

'Because I hardly know you.' Where did *that* prudish line come from? A nineteenth-century drama?

'What does that have to do with anything? Hong Kong's a great city. And you've known me for as long as you've lived here.'

'But I don't *know* know you.'

'Do you mean secks-ually?' He smiles. It's a winning smile.

'Don't be an ass. Working together does not constitute a relationship.'

'Some people get married on less than that.'

'I'm not some people.'

'I just figured that since you moved here on a whim, you might want to do it again. Hong Kong's a great city . . . It was just an idea, forget –'

'I did not move here on a whim! I had very good reasons for moving.'

'Such as?'

'Look, I had my reasons.' I'm so lame.

'Are you in a witness-protection programme that I don't know about?'

He is *so* not funny. I can't just pick up and move round the world, away from everything I know, for him. This is totally different from him staying here for me. He already has friends in London, and business contacts and an apartment. Picking up my life to follow a man round the world? Imagine what Gloria Steinem would say about that. 'It's stifling in here. I need some air.'

'Do you want me to come?'

'No.'

'Come on, come on, come on . . .'

'Hi, this is Stacy. I'm doing something so fun that I can't answer the phone right now . . .'

331

'Shit.' *This* is why the President has that special red telephone. And he has only himself to blame for the Vice President getting the call when he doesn't answer.

'Hello?'

'Chloe? You won't believe what just happened.' My years of practice recounting conversations for Stacy has honed my testimony to star-witness accuracy. She gets the playback with nearly perfect recall.

'He's asked you to move to Hong Kong with him?'

'Well, not exactly with him. We didn't get into details.' He did ask though, right? I'm not imagining this.

'Still, that's so romantic!' This is a surprising reaction – Chloe's not a gusher. I count on her somewhat cynical level-headedness to counteract my tendency to blast ahead at a hundred miles an hour.

'It's not romantic, it's crazy.'

'What's the difference?'

'One gets you flowers, the other gets you committed. I can't just pick up and follow a guy to another city.'

'Would you do it if you loved him?'

'That's not the point.'

'But would you?'

Of course I would. I'd follow the man I love to Timbuktu. I recognize that that's not politically correct thinking, but I've always known that I'd give up an awful lot to be with my one true love. I've just always assumed that finding him would coincide geographically with the perfect job and a group of friends. Oprah wouldn't think that's too much to ask. 'I've gotta go. He'll think I've left.'

'Sure. Let me know what happens. And Hannah? Don't worry. You'll make the right decision.'

I'm glad someone believes that that's true. I've definitely

made some wrong ones in my life (usually involving men). I can't believe I'm even contemplating following a man I hardly know to Asia. It's insane, much more insane than moving to London on a drunken dare. So why am I thinking about it?

Because I'm in love. That's why I know I'm going to do it. I can't believe it, but I'm going to do it . . . we're going to live together in Hong Kong! Of course, we'll have to find an apartment that's convenient to his work. Maybe they have nice little brownstones, like in New York. I'll get to decorate the whole thing, since neither of us has any furniture. Not that I'd go crazy with his money or anything. In fact, I'll be the picture of budgeting efficiency. You must be able to get really cheap Chinese furniture out there. I saw some great lanterns in Harrods. They'll be a steal at the source. We'll be a minimalist couple. Maybe we'll even eat on the floor on little cushions and drink green tea. Wait, that might be Japan. Anyway, I'll have to find a job, but with Chloe's connections that shouldn't be too hard. I'd love to stay in party planning, but I'm not picky. If a great PR job comes along, I wouldn't say no. The important thing is to get on my feet as soon as possible after all the decorating is done . . .

He's waiting where I left him, with his back to me. 'Sam? Okay. You're right, I need a change anyway,' I say quietly.

'What are you saying? You're moving out? You're kidding. I didn't think you really would. I mean, that's fantastic! It's a great city, you'll love it . . . I keep saying that. But it is, the shopping alone . . .'

'I know!' Now I'm getting excited. Terrified, but excited. This is going to be so great.

'I'm sure you'll find a great job, make friends –'

'I can't wait!' What an adventure.

'I can help you find an apartment –'

'Obviously!' I'm not going to traipse all around Hong Kong on my own looking for our place.

'You might even be able to stay with me for a while till you do. I'd have to check with my flatmate but I'm sure he wouldn't mind.'

'I'm sorry?' Did he say for a while?

'Ah, well, you can bunk up at my place. Er, I assumed you'd need a place to stay till you found your own apartment. I'm sorry, is that insulting? I don't mean that you can't do it all on your own, um, I just thought . . . Never mind, that was stupid. After all, you're not moving there because of me.'

What just happened here? How did I go from living with Sam in our fantastic minimalist flat to moving there to fulfil some desire for personal growth? Does he really think I would move there if he wasn't there? Does he know nothing at all about me?

His look is so hopeful. 'So you're really going to move out?' So misinformed and hopeful.

This is something I could think about for months. I mean, it's a monumental step, a potentially life-changing decision. There must be at least a hundred pros and cons. It'd take days to weigh them all. And even then, there might not be a clear-cut answer. He hasn't actually asked me to move in with him. What if I'm just a nice accessory to his life there? Am I crazy to move with no firm commitment? On the other hand, if I don't go, I might never know if he's really The One. Everyone knows that long-distance romances don't work out. But what about the life I've made here for myself, and friends like Chloe and my flatmates? Granted, my friends can always visit, and the flatmates will move back to Australia eventually. And, really, as much as I love London, without a career, without Stacy and ultimately without Sam, how great is my life here anyway? It may become virtually perfect in Hong Kong. But it could also be a total disaster. It won't be easy, that's for sure. There's the job consideration (or lack thereof), finding a place to live, and my family to think about. It definitely deserves a lot of serious thought. Take my time. That's the adult thing to do. This isn't something that one decides on the spot.

'I guess I am. Yeah, I am.'

Well, I've never exactly been 'one', have I?

28

'You're really leaving? I'll miss you!'

Hush is becoming a favourite haunt, and while normally I'd be pleased to while away the afternoon here with Chloe, I know she's going to try talking me out of Hong Kong.

'I know, I'll miss you too. You can visit though. It'll be fun.'

'I'm just worried for you, that's all. You'll have no friends close by, and no job.' Chloe's always been career-minded, having recognized very early on the appeal of trouser suits and Mulberry tote bags made for laptops.

I admit that having to start a new career has been on my mind too, though I'd have to do that anyway, even if I stayed in London. Besides . . . 'I'll have Sam.'

'What about girlfriends? Who are you going to talk to about, you know, girl stuff?' She's acting like we regularly describe our period cramps over coffee. Besides, new friends, or at least acquaintances, are easy to make. I'm away from Stacy anyway in London; if I move to Hong Kong, it won't be any worse. I'll still be away from her.

'I can make friends.'

'I know you will. Does he plan to marry you?'

'What are you, my legal guardian?'

'Well, has he made any commitment at all?'

I know I can sometimes get ahead of myself, but this doesn't feel like one of those times. It may only have been three weeks since Sam and I first kissed, and I know that love at first sight often goes terribly wrong. But I know I'm in love. I don't need more at this point. But that doesn't answer Chloe's rather annoyingly specific question. 'He likes me a lot.' No, that doesn't answer it either. We might have to agree to disagree on this.

'I'm sorry, petal, I don't mean to give you the third degree. I actually asked you here because I have an ulterior motive.'

I knew it.

'I wanted to talk to you about Barry.'

I didn't know that. 'Barry?'

'Yeah.' She puts her hands up. 'I completely understand if you think it's weird, or feel uncomfortable or anything, but I wanted to see if you would . . . if it's okay with you if, I, we went out.'

'You didn't get me here to talk me out of going to Hong Kong?'

'God, no! But you should really think it through. As long as you can get everything sorted out, I think you should go.'

'Then I think you should date Barry!' After all, one magnanimous gesture deserves another.

'Really?'

'Absolutely. I suspected he liked you when you met at the Burberry thing, you know.'

'Mmm, he did call me later that week to take me for a coffee. He didn't talk much about a job change.'

'That's great. Have you been out on a real date?'

'Not yet, but I'll put the signals out.'

'Do you want me to talk to him, to tell him it's okay?'

'Jesus, Hannah, will you please stop coming over all Oprah Winfrey? I've told you, we don't do things like that. He'll eventually get the hint and ask me out.'

I suppose it's best for Barry to stick with his own kind after all. Much as we want to understand each other, it's still sometimes a very long stretch across the cultural divide. Occasionally we grasp hands over the chasm, but just as often we have to settle for a friendly smile and a wave as we wonder at our differences.

Stacy's answering-machine message is even more demanding than usual.

'Stace, it's me, what's up?'

'I'm coming to London!'

'Really, when?' No wonder she's so excited. She must have found an amazingly low fare. Somehow she always gets the best of everything, at half-price.

'I haven't worked out all the details yet but sometime in the next few months.'

'Er, that's great! But book your flight soon. These cheap fares sell out fast. Except on Air India!'

'Can't, till I know when I'm coming. Besides, I'll be flying business class!'

'Did you get an inheritance that I don't know about?' Not that she needs one. Despite her penchant for Prada, Stacy is a saver at heart.

'What? The company will pay.'

'Which company?'

'My company, stupid. Did I wake you from a nap or something?'

'No, no. I'm just confused. Why would they pay for you?'

'Well, they can't expect me to move to a new country on my own dime! . . . What's the matter? You don't sound very excited.'

'*You're moving here?!*'

'Yes, Han, that's what I just said. I've been thinking constantly about my visit and it dawned on me that you're the most important relationship I have in the world. I miss you! I mean, we've been best friends our whole lives, we're like sisters. There's no especially compelling reason to keep me here. And you've had such an excellent time in London, and everything's worked out for you and I'm jealous. I want to have a fabulous life too. Besides, it's time for a change anyway, so I asked my boss if she'd consider moving me to London for a year . . . you're not planning on staying more than a year, are you?'

I'm not planning on staying more than a month. 'Uh, no.'

'Great, because my boss agreed to transfer me out there for a year! It turns out they want to get more of us doing stints abroad. I think I can get them to pay for my apartment and everything. I'm going to be an expat! How 'bout that?'

'Wow, that's incredible.' I did mention that Stacy is prone to rash decisions, right? And that she reinvents herself annually? I mean, normally it's a matter of hair colour or embracing the rock-chick look . . .

'I know! Can you believe it?'

'Hardly.'

Suddenly I've got what might be the best idea of my entire life. Maybe if she's willing to move to London . . . 'Uh, Stace, how do you feel about Hong Kong?'

'As a concept?'

'As a place to live.'

'It's supposed to have good shopping . . . Why?'

'Well, Sam . . .'

'OH MY GOD, ARE YOU TELLING ME YOU'RE MOVING TO HONG KONG?!?'

'YES, I JUST TOLD SAM, I KNOW, IT'S SO EXCIT-ING!' I scream back at her. Somewhere in Mongolia, dogs are howling again. 'Listen, I think it's *so* great that you're moving

339

here, and if this is really where you want to live, then I think you should still come.'

'Are you kidding? I'm totally moving because you're there.'

'Then would you –'

'Move to Hong Kong instead?'

'Yeah.' All of a sudden the idea of moving halfway round the world to be with Sam doesn't seem so crazy. I mean, moving there on my own could be interpreted as stalking, if you take an unsympathetic outsider's view. But going with my best friend, who already has a job, and an apartment, well, that practically makes the fact that Sam is there irrelevant. Who knows, I might have moved there anyway, even if I'd never met him. As I wait for Stacy's answer, I realize I'm going to burst into tears if she says no. I'm too close to the perfect solution to have it snatched back now.

Finally she says, 'Why not? I'll ask my boss. We have offices there, don't we? Of course we do, we're like the biggest bank in the world. I'm sure she'll let me go. Yes, I'll go. Definitely, yes, let's move to Hong Kong!'

'I can't believe we're going to do this,' I say.

'I know. Have you told your parents yet?'

Not exactly. There are a million details to take care of before I go: my job to quit (I can't wait to see the look on Felicity's face), all those museums to see, friends to say goodbye to . . . and my parents. I don't suppose I could send a postcard from the airport?

Dear Mom and Dad, I've decided to follow my heart to Hong Kong. His name is Sam, by the way. Don't worry, he's American, and Stacy's coming with me so I won't be alone. I know it's far away and I don't have a job and

Sam hasn't exactly asked me to marry him, but this is really what I want and I just know everything's going to work out perfectly. Thanks for understanding. Love, Hannah.

PS. Mom, the time difference is twelve hours from Connecticut, which should be a lot easier to remember.

*

How do you say goodbye to a city? Is a clean break best, not looking back or allowing second guesses to cloud your future? Or does London deserve a respectful goodbye, a revisiting of favourite haunts in tribute to all it's given me?

I'm paying tribute to all that London has given me. At Harrods, of course. It's still the most sumptuously tacky public interior in London, possibly in the world. I've just paid homage at the temple.

'Your card, madam,' nods the temple priestess.

'Cheers,' I tell her, grasping the green bag greedily to me.

Wandering along the bustle of the Brompton Road, at first the pavement seems less crowded. It takes several minutes to realize why. I'm not knocking foreheads with anyone. Like synchronized dancers, we each move gracefully, and naturally, to our left. I'm finally on-side. When I pass the little ice-cream counter across the street, I hear a strong American accent saying, 'But I don't have anything smaller!' A young woman is grasping an ice-cream cone and trying to pay the angry man with a £50 note.

'I can't make change,' he says again.

'First the cab, and now you. Why would the cash machine give it to me if I can't spend it anywhere?!' she laments to no one in particular. God, I remember what that's like.

'Here,' I say to the man, approaching with my purse, 'how much is it?'

'Three-fifty,' he says, quite unhappy to have his game of torture-the-tourist thwarted.

'What are you doing?' The woman is grasping her rucksack to her body as if I'm about to steal it.

'Nobody'll take your note. You have to change it in a bank to spend it. I'm happy to buy your ice cream.'

'Gosh, thanks, that's so nice! I'm Aleck.'

'Hannah.' I lean in as I take her hand, giving her a quick cheek kiss.

'You sounded American,' she says, surprised no doubt to be kissed by a complete stranger.

'I am, but I live in London now.'

'Wow, that must be amazing. I'm visiting for the first time but I'm already in love. I'd love to live here some day.'

'I know what you mean. Enjoy your stay.'

It's official. I've marinated in London's cultural juices long enough to have acquired its flavour.

ex·pat·ri·ate

1: (*noun*) A very lucky person living in a foreign land.
2: (*verb*) To choose to experience all the highs and lows of the world outside one's native country.

Definitely a noun with verb tendencies.

He just wanted a decent book to read ...

Not too much to ask, is it? It was in 1935 when Allen Lane, Managing Director of Bodley Head Publishers, stood on a platform at Exeter railway station looking for something good to read on his journey back to London. His choice was limited to popular magazines and poor-quality paperbacks – the same choice faced every day by the vast majority of readers, few of whom could afford hardbacks. Lane's disappointment and subsequent anger at the range of books generally available led him to found a company – and change the world.

'We believed in the existence in this country of a vast reading public for intelligent books at a low price, and staked everything on it'
Sir Allen Lane, 1902–1970, founder of Penguin Books

The quality paperback had arrived – and not just in bookshops. Lane was adamant that his Penguins should appear in chain stores and tobacconists, and should cost no more than a packet of cigarettes.

Reading habits (and cigarette prices) have changed since 1935, but Penguin still believes in publishing the best books for everybody to enjoy. We still believe that good design costs no more than bad design, and we still believe that quality books published passionately and responsibly make the world a better place.

So wherever you see the little bird – whether it's on a piece of prize-winning literary fiction or a celebrity autobiography, political tour de force or historical masterpiece, a serial-killer thriller, reference book, world classic or a piece of pure escapism – you can bet that it represents the very best that the genre has to offer.

Whatever you like to read – trust Penguin.